GODS ^{AND} HEROES

RISE OF FIRE

I0592613

GODS AND HEROES: RISE OF FIRE

ISBN: 978-0-6484294-1-8

Brendan is not currently represented by any publishers or literary agents. He can be contacted at: enquiries@brendanwrightauthor.com

Connect with Brendan:
Instagram: @brendanwrightauthor
Facebook: /brendanwrightauthor
Website: brendanwrightauthor.com

Cover art by Rebecacovers via Fiverr
Map illustrated by Renflowergrapx via Fiverr

This book is dedicated to my best friend and my brother, Damien. Without your friendship, your advice, and your unfailing support, I would not be where I am now and this book would never have been written. I will never forget the day you finished reading my first draft, and you told me I'd written something worth publishing. No other compliment has ever brought me such joy, and I hope you know how much that meant to me.

No matter what happens, as long as you love my books, I know I've made it as an author.

Acknowledgements:

All of my love and thanks go to my mother, Christine. You encouraged and fed my love of reading and writing from a very young age, and I cannot thank you enough for that. You instilled in me a belief that I can achieve anything I set my mind to; and with your love, support, and positivity, I have. Thank you. I also want to thank anyone who read drafts of this book, and provided feedback to me. A huge thank you goes to my sister-in-law, Emily, for catching more inconsistencies than I thought would be present in the first drafts, for helping immensely with formatting, and for being so passionate about the story. I also want to thank my friend and fellow author Jack Heath for inspiring me and being a shining example of success as a Canberran author. You paved the way, and I'm not sure I would have tried at all if you hadn't tried and succeeded before me. And lastly I want to thank everyone who buys and/or reads this book. It's insane to think that I've written something that might be sold and bought in an actual book store by a stranger. So if you're one of those strangers… Thank you so, so much.

ERMOOR

ERMOOR

SHANAKEN

SARNIA

AZAR

OMATUS

CARMERTH

TARSIUM

N

PANDEIA

Prologue

A seemingly endless desert stretches to the horizon and beyond. Dark grey sand is punctuated by dark stone and occasionally by small, barely living trees. The deserts of Omas resemble a dead, ash-filled wasteland. Even the scarce trees grow in hues of bright red and orange, swaying in the slight breeze, giving the appearance of fires burning. In the dark of night, the effect is even more brutal; deep shadows crowd every tree and boulder and the usually bright trees are dulled to a grey to match the sand. A massive volcano rises from the exact centre of the desert. The top of the volcano is flat, and as wide as a small city. Out of view of the small camp fires crowding the Thearan army's camp-site on the volcano's plateau, a bonfire burns in the night. A massive cloaked figure watches the fire, tending to it until it becomes a massive, roiling inferno. He takes a dagger to his wrist, holding a cup underneath to catch the blood. Once the cup is filled, he throws it into the fire and whispers an ancient, forgotten spell.

As his wound bleeds, the fire changes from pale orange to a deep, bright red. A whistling sound emanates from the centre, and a deep rumbling follows soon after. The rumbling grows in volume until the figure flinches in pain, and then it suddenly stops. Burning logs move and shift, and a small, slim, fragile looking creature emerges from the bonfire, crawling out from under the wood. It steps onto the sand gingerly. Its body is made from pieces of still burning wood, its face a jagged stump with two furrowed whorls for eyes, glowing red hot from deep within. Its limbs are spindly, and the fire burning at them makes them look as though they might collapse at any moment. The creature turns back towards the fire and reaches in, grasping a flickering tongue of flame and pulling, sweeping a cloak made of pure orange fire onto its shoulders.

"My Lord," The man kneels, bowing his head.

"*Rise, servant*," replies the fire-cloaked creature in a jagged whisper. "*We haven't much time.*"

The huge man rises and looks down, directly into the eyes of a Fire God.

"I have a deal to make with you."

"*I know. I accept.*"

The man hesitates.

"Just like that?"

"*Yes.*" The fire god sounds amused, though its whisper is fading.

"I see. Thank you, my lord. What do you ask in return?"

"*You know the price, mortal. You know what it will cost you and your warriors. The only question is whether you are willing to pay.*"

The man stands, still and silent for several moments. Then, he gives a slight nod, and in a low voice, responds:

"Yes, my lord."

The plains of Omas stood silently in the starlight, grey sand sweeping through a mostly dark camp-site. There were one or two fires amongst the dozens of tents. A woman's piercing scream shattered the silence, and the warriors guarding the outer perimeter of the camp whipped their heads around in the direction of the noise. One of them barked an order to another and two warriors ran off. They slowed as they reached the large tent the screaming emanated from. It was the healer's tent. The two warriors looked at each other uncomfortably. The healer was a mysterious and frightening woman. Her strange ways had grown even stranger in the last few moons, her medicines more effective and her spells more powerful. She had started chanting in the early hours of each day about Fire rising from the Shadows, only getting louder any time one of the tribe told her to stop. Screaming started again from the tent, and the warriors glanced at each other, deciding in unison they would leave this business with the healer. They both turned and headed back to their post.

Footsteps faded outside the tent. The Thearan healer paid them no mind. A young woman screamed in agony and writhed on hide blankets on the tent floor. She was giving birth. The child, if it survived, would be one of a very few pure-blood Thearans left in their tribe. Hours passed in the large tent. The air was stiflingly hot; a fire had to be lit inside so the healer could see what she was doing. She whispered to the young Thearan woman, trying to quiet her down. The pain must have been unbearable; the healer had never given birth herself, but she could imagine. Still more hours passed, until finally, the healer caught a glimpse of the child's head. Brilliant white hair and dark brown skin emerged, more and more, until the child was finally born. The mother let out a ragged sigh of relief and exhaustion, and looked upon her baby for the first time. Tears spilled slowly down her cheeks, and the healer noticed the strength still left in the young woman's eyes; her love for the child was instant, fierce, and immeasurably stronger than the ordeal she'd just been through.

Sunlight finally broke over the horizon, and a gust of wind blew the tent flaps open, spilling dawn's light throughout the tent. It blew through the large tent, forming a tiny tornado as it rustled hides and knocked some of the healer's tools off a small table. The fire roared in response to the wind and flared bright as the sun. Watching the miniature storm inside the tent, the new mother smiled and looked at her baby. The healer handed the child over, and whispered in a dry rasp, "she's a girl. What will you name her?"

The young woman's smile grew deeper. "Aella." In ancient Thearan, it meant Whirlwind. The healer smiled too.

Atillus

Atillus Argyris hated his family. His father Thorinos was perpetually angry that the crown didn't belong to him. His younger brother Alliphis was as furious as Thorinos, and resentful of Atillus for being first-born. The youngest of the three siblings, Anamas, never spoke a single word to anyone. And his mother, Eirene, spent all her time trying to sooth her husband and second son. Atillus was routinely ignored. He wasn't old enough to know what life was like as a Prince; his father's father, Agimos Argyris, was overthrown by the Megalos family before he was born. Yet the event had overtaken his life all the same. Thorinos' bitterness ran deep, and on the rare occasions he did speak to his oldest son, there was always anger in his voice.

Ten years of constant fury at the Megalos family had seeped into Atillus' mind, and he couldn't help but feel it too; his family deserved the crown, and he'd be next in line right now if things were as they should be.

So he took to hiding from them all. Atillus, just like his mother and youngest brother, was an avid reader. And just like Anamas, he much preferred the company of books to people. He read all the time, spending most of his days in the Omati Library. Before long, he tired of the limited selection and constant presence of strangers. Even silence felt heavy in the crowded rooms, as if the people reading around him were staring at him.

He took to exploring the city itself, sticking to smaller streets and alleys at first to avoid the crowds. The Noble houses were located in the same district as the palace, and separated from the commoners by the largest river in

Pandeia, the Alpheus. He stayed on the Noble side, as there were far less people. Thorinos owned quite a few stores in the shopping district on the Noble side of the city, and Atillus learned a lot by simply watching them for a while each day. He never spoke to the shopkeeps, but he saw everything they did from the roof of a nearby building.

He saw them set aside a small amount of coin from each sale in a secret drawer. They gave discounts to certain shoppers who looked wealthy enough to buy the entire inventory. When his father walked down the street, they hid their misdeeds. Their backs straightened, they shooed away the shoppers who received discounts, and they made sure the secret drawer was closed and hidden.

Atillus watched his father converse with the shopkeeps one by one, checking their ledgers and inventory. When he left each store, Atillus saw the faces of the shopkeeps change from respectful humility to open hostility. They stared at him the way Thorinos himself stared at the King. Smiling, Atillus climbed off the roof and returned to his chambers. He wasn't the only one who despised Thorinos Argyris.

Atillus was only ten years old, but already much smarter than most. He knew his father was plotting to take the crown back, and he knew if that happened he would be next in line to rule Omatus.

Thorinos was a bad father and would make an even worse King. He thought whatever damage was done under Thorinos' short rule would be worth it for what he could accomplish as King He loved the city. Not for what it was, but for what he knew he could turn it into; A paradise. The envy of all of Pandeia. He just needed to make sure Thorinos was successful in his schemes, but didn't drag the city down into the dirt before Atillus was old enough to rule. King Megalos built a name for himself as an effective but brutal leader; loved by the other Nobles and hated by the commoners. Thorinos spent the last twelve years helping the commoners and spreading vicious rumours about the Megalos family through the lower Noble families.

It was a good long term strategy, but after twelve years Thorinos was still no closer to the crown. Atillus didn't mind. The longer his father took to become King, the shorter his reign would be before Atillus took his rightful place. Besides, despite the time it took, Thorinos was building a solid foundation on which the Argyris family could rule.

Atillus returned to the Omati library one day to read about the history of the Royal Families. Most of the books he found were as he expected; list upon list of names and dates, with a short passage describing the King or Queen's rule. One book gave him pause. It was titled *The Royal Palace of Omatus; a detailed history of the largest palace in Pandeia.* He read the entire tome that day, enthralled by the information. It was written hundreds of years ago and likely quite out of date, but the author didn't hold back any details. It described hidden passages and rooms, and contained a map of all the slave's corridors that ran through the entire palace. There was a private library, with more collected knowledge than anywhere else in Pandeia. His breath caught in his throat. It would be perfect for him; silent, endless books to choose from, and best of all, empty.

Getting into the library was far easier than he expected. Maps of the slave's corridors and entrances laid his path plain before him. He stole a plain white slave's chiton from the quarters in his own family's palace. Wearing it, he became invisible. He was tall for his age, and among adults he fit in perfectly. As he approached the palace, he focused on balancing the confidence of familiarity with the humble submission of slaves. He kept his head lowered, and avoided going too close to other people, but moved with purpose. Nobody questioned him, or even gave him a second glance. Almost an hour later, he snuck through a small secret entrance into the Royal Library.

It was cavernous, stretching out in endless aisles of ancient knowledge. Empty. Silent. Atillus smiled and stepped into the giant space, breathing in the smell of old dry paper. Finally, he found a place that felt like home.

He'd read many books on politics and just as many on war. The more he read the more he realised they were one and the same. He was searching for another such book now, trying to find something new and interesting to learn before the feast. A regular occurrence in Omatus, feasts were thrown seemingly every other night. It made no matter to Atillus, who much preferred the company of books to people and who didn't enjoy food half so much as most of the other Omati Noblemen.

Atillus turned into another aisle in the maze of the library, and paused. After six months of exploring, he'd never been this deep in the massive room before. He walked a little further on and noticed a closed door at the end of one of the aisles. It was the only door other than the main entrance and the secret tunnel he used. It looked solid, most likely reinforced with metal or Omasi stone behind the old-looking wood Atillus could see. It was relatively small, only just big enough for the average person to enter, where the main doors were giant arched stone doors that looked like they would be deafening if opened. It was once locked, but the lock either rusted away or broke long ago. *Odd,* he thought, *this door does not appear on the maps I saw.* He pushed against it, gently at first, and then harder when it wouldn't budge.

Finally, the door creaked slowly open, the sound painfully loud after the library's pressing silence. Atillus winced through the sound until the door was open wide enough for him to enter.

A long, narrow corridor followed from the doorway, pitch black and as silent as a grave. Most of the castle was built from Omasi stone, which was a pure black and could be polished to a mirror sheen. It was beautiful and almost as strong as steel, but it made for dark housing, and there were no torches lit in the corridor. There weren't even sconces adorning the walls; this place was *supposed* to be black. Atillus couldn't help himself. He needed to learn what this place was. Keeping his left hand to the wall beside him, he ventured into the corridor.

It was cold, and there seemed to be an immense pressure squeezing him, as if the castle itself was trying to squash him for trespassing. He kept walking, slowly and carefully. Even going as slowly as he was, it didn't take him long to reach the end of the corridor. His left hand bumped into stone, and he stopped abruptly, trying to see with his hands. The corridor couldn't possibly be this short. From the door it looked as though it went for miles. Though the more Atillus thought about it, the more he realised he hadn't actually seen much of the corridor; it fell to darkness quickly, and it gave the impression of incredible depth. He shook his head, marvelling at this place. His hands continued exploring the end of the corridor, but there was only smooth stone. He breathed a sigh of annoyance, but the heavy silence somehow wasn't broken. He blinked, though it was pointless as he just shifted from pitch black to pitch black. Surely he'd made a sound. He wanted to shout, just to hear something. But suddenly the thought of breaking the silence made him uneasy. He turned instead, painfully aware of not being able to hear his own footsteps, and looked for the doorway through which he came.

It was there, sure enough, and from this side it looked much closer than he remembered. The light streaming through from the library was almost blinding, but when he turned again he still couldn't see the walls around him. Atillus couldn't make sense of it. The corridor was unlike anything he'd ever read about. He walked back towards the library, quickly this time. The heavy door started moving, closing, slowly but too fast for him to reach in time. Despite the awful noise it made earlier, it was completely and utterly silent as it swung. Just as he reached the end of the corridor, the door slammed shut without a sound, wrapping Atillus in complete darkness. He reached out, touching only smooth stone. He screamed at the top of his lungs. He heard only silence.

Zanela

Zanela sprinted along a thick tree branch, careful to avoid the stones whistling through the air in her path. She wasn't sure how to properly dodge them. They moved far too quickly for her to even see them clearly, let alone react in time. The fact she hadn't been hit so far was pure luck. Dakesh shouted encouraging compliments from a neighbouring branch. He threw the stones hard, but probably not as hard as he could.

She ducked and weaved as much as she could, though the movements were random. She was perhaps three quarters of the way along the branch when a stone hit her ankle a fraction of a second before it landed. It twisted her ankle just as she stepped on it, and she dropped forwards, smashed her shoulder on the branch and plummeted down into the forest. She didn't have time to scream as she was yanked out of her fall by the safety net hanging below the branch.

She lay in the safety of the net, calming herself, when there was a sudden jerk and thumping sound, and she was almost tossed over the side. Dakesh appeared beside her, grinning.

"You did pretty well. Next time maybe try not to get hit by the stones."

There was no concern on his face. She punched him in the shoulder as hard as she could, and he watched without dodging. He didn't even flinch; she might as well have laid her hand on him gently. She rained punches on him, snarling and trying not to laugh as he tried to pretend she wasn't hitting him.

"So would you like to keep-" she slapped his face - "trying the exercise, or would-" she punched his stomach – "oof, you like to rest for-" she hit him in the face again, this time with a fist – "a little while?"

She couldn't help herself; his deadpan expression as he tried to ignore her punches was too much. She burst out laughing. He laughed too, and they climbed out of the net together. She tripped, grabbed his arm for support, and dragged him back onto the net with her. They both scrambled at the same time to get up, tripping over each other and only succeeding in becoming more tangled. They both laughed even harder. Zanela was still giggling as they climbed the tree trunk and stepped onto the wide black platform.

"I think some rest is a good idea," she said through giggles, "I've had enough *training* for the day."

She was limping, and she knew her ankle wouldn't take any more. Dakesh was training her to take the *Shenzai*, the warrior's tests next year. At fourteen, she was still a *Kuulshen*; a young one. A warrior-to-be. Their parents trained her too, but they were far less fun. It was fairly common for training sessions with them to end in tears. She knew they were helping her become strong, but it didn't help her enjoy the training at all.

Besides, she was far less passionate about becoming a great warrior than Dakesh seemed to be. Her favourite thing was simply wandering the forest. The beauty of the trees and the animals never failed to astonish her. Being surrounded by so much life and energy made her feel... right. Home. Comfortable. She couldn't find a better word, but those were close.

She had no interest in fighting. She understood the need to be properly trained, and understood the importance of the three tenets and the oath. The one part of the Shenza warrior culture she did enjoy was the *Zuunshai*. The blade dance soothed her and made her feel more deeply connected to the forest. But Dakesh made training fun. He still pushed her hard, but he could always make her laugh, even when she twisted her ankle.

They walked back to the city, over metre-wide branches and black metal pathways suspended between the trees. Dakesh walked slowly beside her, never losing patience despite her limp. They didn't talk, but it was a comfortable silence. When they reached the city, they split up. Dakesh headed towards the living quarters. Zanela made her way to the kitchens.

The kitchens were her favourite place in the city itself. Tall, wide windows let the smoke and steam out and afforded an amazing view of the canopy. Set into the floor of the kitchens, huge tubs of salt water clung to the tree trunk. Hundreds of fish swam in the tubs, alive and fresh and ready to be cooked. Growing from trenches lining the windows and walls were dozens of different herbs and even more types of vegetables.

In the centre of the room, two massive benches each held an oven with a metal cooking plate on top. They contained ancient magic which Zanela would never understand; a simple gesture from one of the cooks and they grew hot enough to cook in minutes with no fire. Nashan, one of the cooks she liked, was already working at one of the ovens. She sat at one of the low tables close to the ovens. The heat was intense, but worth it for Nashan's company. He was always friendly to her.

Several cooked fish were already sitting on the side of the cooking plate. They smelled delicious, and Nashan gestured to them when he saw her staring.

"Eat, Zanela! You just get back from training with your brother?"

She nodded, taking a huge bite from one of the fish. She stood, snatched a sprig of her favourite herb from the window, and sprinkled it onto the meat. Nashan laughed and shook his head.

"I should get you in here as a cook," he grumbled, "since you clearly know better than I do."

She didn't bother answering. She was halfway through the fish. Nashan always said things like that when she added flavours of her own to his cooking. But she knew he was joking. She pretended to have trouble chewing on the soft white meat.

"Yeah I do. I wouldn't have overcooked it so badly!"

She closed her eyes and screwed her face up into feigned disgust. A live fish smacked her in the face, spraying her with water. She gasped and opened her eyes, trying to catch the fish and instead falling onto her back. It snapped in random movements on the floor, gills pumping wildly. She struggled to get hold of it while Nashan laughed, and finally succeeded in dumping it back into one of the salt water tubs.

She slumped back down at the table. Nashan howled with laughter. She was a sight to behold; covered in seawater, her black hair tangled and bits of cooked fish and chopped herbs sticking to her tunic. Her ankle ached from struggling to catch the fish, and the water left her cold despite the heat of the ovens. Nashan finally stopped laughing as he noticed Zanela hadn't joined in. He raised his hands as if in surrender.

"Okay, sorry little one. Maybe throwing a fish was a bit too much."

She sighed theatrically, and stared at him with the angriest expression she could summon. Nashan burst into laughter again, shaking his head. Zanela shouted in wordless exasperation and left the kitchens. Nashan's laughter followed her out into the afternoon. As soon as she was out of the room, she started laughing.

Zanela climbed up the swirling metal frame which clung to the giant tree trunk as fast as she could. This time, stones were pelting the wood and metal of the tree, clanging and thudding in her ears. One of them hit her thigh hard enough to bruise. She grunted but kept climbing. Today she trained with her father. He didn't hold back; the stones rained down on her like hail in a thunderstorm. Her lungs burned, her hands cramped. She felt every spot her father hit her.

She jumped onto a nearby branch, only just making the landing as a small stone hit her hand. It cut the skin at her knuckles but she kept climbing. She glanced around for somewhere else to move, ducking under a stone aimed at her face. A branch jutted from the trunk about seven feet above where she stood, on a slight angle. She took a few quick steps backwards, out to where the branch she stood on became less sturdy. She crouched low as more stones flew, then bolted at the tree trunk. She had one chance; her father didn't allow safety nets when they trained.

She leaped, planted her right foot on the trunk, and pushed off with all her strength. She reached, missed, and for a moment of terror she started falling. A small branch, barely more than a twig, hung from the bottom of the branch she aimed for. She snatched it, halted her fall, and swung her other hand up to get a grip on the branch proper. Just as her hand clamped down on a thick knot, the twig snapped. She almost fell but managed to keep her grip, the cut on her knuckle throbbing as her fingers turned white from the pressure.

Digging her other hand into the branch higher up, she swung herself over to the top and lay where she landed. She was temporarily out of her father's sight, and took the opportunity to rest. Her heart pounded. Her lungs roared. She closed her eyes and slowed her breathing. Soft padding sounds rose from the forest floor; her father was climbing the tree. He was almost silent, but moved too fast to cloak all sound. She whispered a curse to herself and rolled to her feet.

The faint sounds of her father climbing reached her ears from seemingly every direction. She had no idea where to go. This was a new test; she was determined to pass. He was tricking her, masking his location and giving her false bait. He was a *Kaizeluun*. This sort of thing came easy to him. She stopped for a precious few seconds, thinking. The sounds grew louder, but she focused on shutting them out. He was below her, and climbing. Her normal response should be to climb to avoid him. But she watched him climb and fight and move every day; the giant trees of Shanaken were no obstacle to the *Kaizeluun*. If he wanted to be where she was, he could do it in seconds. Even if he wanted to be above her -

She dropped to the branch, grabbed for the knot she used before, and rolled off without checking her grip. A thud reverberated through her hand as her father landed on the branch from above. She hung from the knot in the branch, still swinging from her roll. She kicked her feet and used the momentum to swing into a jump off the branch. The fall angled her towards the tree trunk, but there were no branches she could reach. She collided with the trunk, sliding down its rough surface and scrabbling for purchase.

Finally, the twisting black metal grips appeared, and her fall was stopped as she grabbed them with both hands. The sudden stop jarred her shoulders, and she almost lost grip. She pulled herself into a stable position, her feet resting on the metal frame. Glancing up, she couldn't see her father anywhere.

She moved as quickly as she could, climbing down to the forest floor. She heard nothing behind her as she was yanked off the tree. There was nothing physically pulling her, and as she fell, sheer terror seized her. The forest floor smashed into her, the air knocked out of her lungs. Bright black spots erupted in her vision, and pain flared through her entire body. Groaning, she tried to roll onto all fours. She barely raised herself an inch off the ground before collapsing again.

A hand like the jaws of a Zuzuk clamped around her neck and lifted her from the ground. The grip didn't choke her, but it wasn't gentle, either. Her father's deep red eyes

16

filled her vision. There was no anger, but plenty of disappointment.

"You need to feel the forest around you. Listen to it. I wasn't hiding at all, the trees were screaming with my every step."

She didn't have the strength to struggle, or to argue with him. He stared, close enough that their noses almost touched. Then, growing tired of the lesson, he dropped her back to the ground.

"You and Dakesh are the same," he said distantly, "such disappointments. If only I fathered a child like the girl Dakesh is smitten by. She is a true warrior."

He walked away without another word. Zanela lay on the forest floor, aching and dizzy, until she felt strong enough to stand again. The sun was set by then. She made her way home in the darkness.

Aella

Aella twirled around her mother, a wooden sword in each hand, blocking every strike she threw at her. She was ten years old, and took to combat training like an Omasi Fire-Hawk takes to flying. She was already better than her parents, though they'd never admit it. They danced in the desert, wooden blades clacking, until both were out of breath and sweating profusely. Aella's mother motioned for her to stop, and her uncanny sense of discipline stopped her instantly. They stood in the grey sand together for a moment, regaining their breath. Aella's mother, Helene, smiled at her.

"I have something for you, little warrior", she said.

Aella's eyes shone. "Is it a real sword?" She asked.

Helene laughed, walking over to a leather bag she carried with them when they left camp for training.

"Actually, no," she laughed, and Aella's face fell.

Helene turned and knelt at the bag for a moment, rummaging for something. She stood again, turning and smiling broadly.

"It's *two* swords!"

Aella squealed and ran to her mother, dropping her wooden swords and reaching for the real ones. Her mother held them back, eyes wide to get her attention.

"These are very dangerous, Aella," she said gravely.

"I know how to use a sword, mother!" Aella replied. Helene shook her head and knelt down so she could talk to her daughter closely.

"These are no ordinary swords. They are very rare, and they contain Fire Magic within them," she said as she

18

unsheathed the short swords, turning them in the sunlight so Aella could see.

"The magic was dormant until shortly before you were born. Before that, they'd just been regular swords passed down in our family. Something happened to awaken Fire Magic in the world once again."

Aella noticed the way they hummed slightly, as though they couldn't restrain the magic they held. Her eyes as wide as they could get, she watched as her mother focused on the blades. They grew bright and the humming grew louder, then they suddenly burst into flame. Aella's mother stepped back a few paces from her. The flames spread quickly, flowing down the hilts, onto Helene's hands, down her arms and over the rest of her body.

Aella gasped, but her mother seemed fine. She laughed at the shock on her daughter's face, and went into a series of swordfighting moves so fast that Aella could barely keep track. She twisted this way and that, twirling and leaping, slicing the air with fire. The whistling of the blades and the roar of the fire mixed together to make a beautiful music. Aella was completely lost to the magic. She'd never seen anything as amazing as what her mother was showing her now. This was beyond her skill level; even Aella could tell she was performing techniques faster than she was physically able to. Faster than *anyone* was physically able to.

Helene stopped moving after a few moments, and the flame went out with a whooshing sound. Aella watched as her mother's head drooped and her hands fell, grip loose with the swords pointing towards the ground. She rushed to her mother and took the swords out of her hands. Helene sat heavily, almost falling to the sand, and looked at Aella with a tired smile.

"They can make you invincible for a short time. You'll be stronger, faster, and you'll burn anything you touch." She was watching her closely, Aella realised. This was an adult discussion, and her mother was trusting her to handle it. She tried not to get too excited, tried to be calm and adult-like as she went on about the swords.

"They don't work for long. It's a miracle they work at all, in truth. The magic put in them when they were forged must have been unbelievably powerful. So you can't rely on this to win a fight, but if you time it right, it could be the difference between life and death."

Her mother looked at her, searching her eyes. She must have seen something great, because she smiled gently then. Her gaze wandered down to the blades in her daughter's hands, and she frowned. Before Aella could ask her what was wrong, she shook her head slightly and kept talking:

"You can activate the magic whenever you want, but you need to be careful. No one outside of this family knows about these swords, and your father and I want to keep them secret. That's not the only reason you need to be careful, though. Using this magic will take most of your energy, and if you don't stop in time the magic could even kill you. You should only use it when there's no other choice. But you should practice every now and then, when you're sure you're alone."

Helene was still breathing heavily, and Aella was a little frightened at how much energy the swords took from her. She looked at them, humming slightly in her hands, and realised they fit her hands perfectly. They were balanced and weighted as if for a child, but still heavy enough to wield with force. She took a few practice swings, and marvelled at how perfect they were. Even without using the magic within them, she would be able to fight well with these swords.

"Thank you, mother," she whispered. She never took her eyes off the swords.

Aella sprinted past tents with a bundle of leather in her small arms, breathless and excited. She received odd and curious looks from all the warriors who knew her; she was always very quiet and composed. It was unusual for a ten year old to be so withdrawn, especially in Thearan culture, but for Aella, it was the opposite. At the moment she was far too excited to be calmly walking through the camp as she normally would. She had to show her best friend, Athanasius, her new gift. She rushed toward his tent, and all but dived through the entrance when she arrived, cannoning into him with more force than she meant to.

Athan let out an annoyed "oof!" and shoved her off him.

"What are you doing, you idiot?" He said, frowning. He didn't have much of a sense of humour. Neither did Aella, but she was in a good mood.

"I have something to show you!" She all but squealed it, still out of breath. That got Athan's attention, and he glanced at the package Aella was holding. She placed it gently on the floor of the tent, and unwrapped it as quickly as she could while being careful. When the Fire Blades were revealed, Athan's face lit up, his eyes so wide they seemed to take up half his face.

Aella picked the blades up and showed them to Athan the way her mother showed her before, turning them slowly so the sunlight streaming in from the open top of the tent danced on the metal. Even when the magic wasn't active, the blades looked like they were made of pure fire when touched by sunlight.

Athan barely moved, eyes wide and unblinking, mouth hanging open. Aella laughed, and that broke the spell; Athan blinked and laughed too.

"They look like magic," Athan whispered. "Where did you get them?"

"My parents," Aella replied. "And they *are* magic."

Athan narrowed his eyes at her, half frowning and half smirking.

"No they're not!"

"They are, I swear!"

Athan shook his head, and they both laughed. He didn't believe her then, no matter how much she argued; But she knew she would show him eventually.

"Besides," Athan said, "you'll need to practice before you can use them. Let's spar!"

They left his tent, and Aella left her swords in the leather wrap on the floor. Athan grabbed two wooden training swords on his way out; every child in their tribe owned training swords, even those lucky enough to have real swords. They ran out together to a spot a little away from the camp, but still within earshot; at their age, if their parents called for them, they had to return quickly. They faced each other, and as always, Athan wanted to make a game of it. He always pretended they were heroes from Ancient Theara, the warriors their parents talked about around camp fires before bed.

"I will be Aniketos, slayer of Oromus!" he said seriously. Although older and taller than Aella, she found it so cute when he tried to be intimidating.

"I will be Roxane, the most powerful fire mage in history!" She replied, pretending to throw a fireball at him. He jumped to the side, watching the pretend fireball as it passed him by. They fought, but as always with Athan, it was for fun and not improvement. She didn't mind.

Atillus

Hours passed in complete darkness. And worse, complete silence. Were it not for the sensation of touch reminding him he was buried in stone, he would have thought he'd died. Atillus sat on the cold floor, trying to be calm. He didn't understand what was happening, and that scared him more than what he was experiencing; He hadn't come across anything he couldn't understand until now.

He tried to distract himself by reciting books he'd read, recalling the pages and the words in as much detail as he could. He got through three entire volumes on the tactics of battle before he couldn't concentrate any more. His head pulsed with the silence; he heard the blood rushing through his veins, and his lungs fill with air and empty again. He knew it was driving him insane, but there was nothing he could do about it. He had no idea how much time passed, but it felt like an eternity.

Suddenly light spilled over him, and although nothing ever looked so beautiful, the brightness forced his eyes shut. The door was open. After Atillus stood, he stopped cold; the door that opened was on the other side of the corridor. It didn't lead back to the library. Even as he feared for what might be beyond, he knew he needed to leave the corridor. Nothing could be worse than the living death of being buried alive with only the sense of touch to keep him grounded in reality.

Atillus stepped through the doorway into a small room. It was mostly bare, and though it looked incredibly old, it was clean. The only furniture was a small table and chair against the far wall, a small bookcase, and an ancient looking wooden chest banded with some type of thick metal. The bookcase contained a small handful of old books and scrolls of parchment, and there was an open book on the small table. Other than that the room was empty. There were no other doors, and Atillus suddenly realised that there was no fireplace, nor any torches. Not even a window. There was just light. It filled the room with the warmth of natural light, with no visible source.

Atillus approached the open book on the small reading table. He felt warmth coming from the book itself, and he started to make sense of what he was experiencing. He'd read about magic, though he saw no proof of its existence. But he realised that the pitch black, silent corridor and this warm, mysterious light could be some sort of ancient magic spell. There were so few books in this small hidden room, and he endured hours of looming insanity just to get to them. The few references to real magic he came across in the library all mentioned ancient spellbooks which instilled a mortal being with the power to wield magic. He knew then, before he even reached the open book, it was some powerful artefact of ancient times; when magic was as much a presence in Pandeia as the sand in the Omasi deserts.

Other than the warmth, and its obvious age, there was nothing special about the book. It was bound in ancient black scales that he recognised as the hide of an Omasi Sand Panther, which wasn't uncommon for older books written in Omas and Theara. Unlike countries such as Tarsium and Shanaken, the animals living in Theara and Omas were almost exclusively covered in armoured scales, and anything that would otherwise be built out of leather had to be built using scales.

Atillus gently touched the open book. Although he was prepared for some new mysterious catastrophe, the pages reacted to his touch the same as any other book might. He breathed a sigh of relief and turned a page or two. Every page featured at least one crudely drawn picture of fire or flames, and the words seemed to be explaining how to

24

harness one's energy to create and manipulate fire. Atillus closed the book. When he saw the cover his breath caught in his throat:

A Complete Encyclopeadia
of the Arcane Arts
Volume Three:
Fire Magic

He looked at the bookshelf next to the table. None of the books in it were volume one or two from this Arcane Encyclopeadia. Disappointed, Atillus went to the bookshelf anyway, checking each book and scroll. There were some ancient maps and books on ancient mythical creatures either fictional or extinct. A few of the scrolls just contained huge, nonsensical symbols scrawled all over them in what appeared to be old, dried blood. Atillus collected all of the books and scrolls, and piled them onto the small reading table. He didn't know if he'd ever get out of this mysterious little room, but he was determined to learn all he could from the books it contained, especially if it was actually possible to learn to harness and use magic.

Plenty of tales about the Thearan nomads and their ability to wield Fire Magic were scattered throughout the Royal Library, but there was no definitive proof he could find. He dismissed the stories as boastful myths spread by the Thearans to increase their reputation as dangerous warriors and mercenaries. But the more he read of this mysterious new book, the more he was convinced magic could be wielded by mortals.

Atillus read for hours, absorbing everything as he always did. He poured over the information on Fire Magic again and again, intending to remember every word. When he read it three times through, he moved to the centre of the room and sat cross-legged on the floor, assuming a meditative stance for concentration as the book suggested. He sat perfectly still, willing some force of the world, some mysterious magic, to live again. He pictured flames,

25

roaring and rumbling, burning an entire village down in his mind's eye. He imagined his body was heating up, growing warmer and warmer until he himself burst into flame. But nothing worked. No matter what he tried, Fire Magic was simply out of his reach. He stood stiffly; he'd been sitting motionless for what must have been half a day. He read through the rest of the books, if only to distract himself from the disappointment of the Fire Magic volume.

After a little while, he tried to use Fire Magic again. When he failed, he stood and paced the small room, furious at the ancient tome for falsely promising such power. He was furious at himself as well. Even at ten years of age he knew he was likely the most intelligent person in Omatus; if anyone could teach themselves to use magic, it should be him.

After an eternity pacing the small room, Atillus was lost his patience. He went back to the door he'd come through and tried to open it. A sharp panic twisted his gut as he realised the door wouldn't budge. He shook his head, refusing to believe he was trapped. The door was the twin of the one on the other side, connecting the corridor to the library. Atillus stared hard at the old, solid wood, and blinked. Right in the centre of the circular handle, there was a tiny rune carved into the wood. An unsettling feeling of familiarity took hold of him suddenly, and he shivered. Although he was sure this was the first time he'd ever seen the symbol, he couldn't help but feel like it meant something to him. He paced again, accepting that the door was out of his power for the moment. He sat in the small reading chair, thinking on the carved rune in the door handle. He glanced over the room, furious at everything and nothing. He'd read every book the mysterious room contained, and explored every inch of it. Casting his gaze restlessly around the room, he suddenly stopped. The room still had one mystery left.

Atillus knelt in front of the ancient wood and metal chest. Slowly, he placed his hand on the curved top. He felt it humming with energy, and wondered what else he would find in this mysterious place. There was a strange silence about the chest, despite the humming. Not the dead, maddening silence of the corridor; a tenuous, anticipatory silence, like the heartbeat between a flash of lightning and the clap and boom of thunder. He found himself holding his breath accidentally, and shuddered as his lungs filled again. The chest was locked, but the padlock didn't appear to be made from the same metal as the black steel bands set in the ancient wood. It was rusted, and though thick, there was very little actual metal left.

Atillus grabbed one of the huge tomes from the reading table and carried it over. He lifted it above the padlock, and slammed the heavy book into it as hard as he could. The lock didn't budge. He tried again, and again, and on the fourth try he felt the padlock loosen. On the fifth, he heard and felt a sudden snap followed by a heavy thud on the stone floor. The ring of the padlock was still resting in the brackets of the chest, the rest of the lock lying on the floor. He smiled and pulled the broken ring out of the chest.

The lid was heavy, almost unbelievably heavy, but he eventually pushed it far enough to stay open on its own. He was sweating and breathing heavily by then, his pale brown hair sticking to his bronze skin. Despite his exhaustion, he needed to see what was in the chest; so instead of listening to his aching muscles, he knelt again and peered inside.

At first what he saw made no sense. He blinked and wiped the sweaty hair from his eyes, certain it was a trick of the eye. But after his eyes cleared, he realised what he saw was real.

The chest was completely lined with the same black metal as the bands on the outside; the wood was just a covering. Laying in the centre of the chest was a massive

27

burnt book. It was charred to a deep, shiny black so dark that it was barely visible against the metal it lay on. Warmth emanated from it. As he stood above it, the warmth slowly grew to heat, then to a fierce burn that pulsed from the open chest, making his eyes water and his skin feel scorched.

Suddenly, thin lines opened like scars in the centre of the book's cover, dragging from point to point, as if an animal was tearing its claws through the paper. Pure, blinding light shone through the cuts, and through his half blind, watery eyes, Atillus saw something which stopped his heart: The rune from the door handle. Only this time when he saw it, he was certain he *had* seen it before finding this cursed room. He had a vivid memory of seeing this exact book, in fact. His clear memory of the book warred in his mind with the absolute certainty that he'd never seen it before today. While half of him was sure he'd read the book and knew it well, the other half desperately needed to find out what was contained within. His mind whirled and fought, and for a moment he was sure he would vomit. The heat from the book pounded his sore head, dizzying him and scattering his already conflicted thoughts.

There was nothing else he could have done. Even as he scolded himself for recklessness, he reached into the chest. The second his fingers touched the book, an explosion of flame roared to life from the cover. The heat was immeasurable, and although only the tips of two of his fingers touched it, he didn't think he'd ever been in as much pain as he was in that moment. Some part of him needed the book open, so through the pain, Atillus flipped the cover.

Once the book opened, the fire calmed, settling into a flickering glow. Atillus leaned closer, sucking his burnt fingers, and read the title on the first page:

Sithares: God of Fire

This book was the first and only compelling evidence Atillus ever came across for the existence of a God. He started reading, mesmerised by the idea of a real live God. The pages on the inside of the book were hot, but not hot enough to burn him. He shook his head in amazement as he kept reading:

Sithares is, like all Gods, a being made of pure energy given consciousness. Its power mirrors that of its energy source, and its weaknesses also. Sithares gains strength from destruction; from the burning of objects, buildings and (perhaps most of all) of people. Like all Gods, it also gains strength from the prayers of those who follow it. It can share a measure of its power with its followers, giving them the ability to create and control fire, though this is a gift reserved for only the most devout as doing so takes power directly from Sithares itself.

He stopped at that. Sithares wasn't worshipped anywhere any more that he was aware of. There were possibly Thearan tribes in the Omasi deserts who still worshipped the Fire God, but he hadn't read anything about active worship in his life. The only previous references Atillus saw of Sithares were brief mentions in mythical stories and legends; nowhere near enough to inspire belief. But this book was something else.

Atillus leafed through the pages, knowing he would eventually read it all, until he came upon what he was looking for: A prayer to Sithares. He hoped one would be written somewhere in the book, and it made sense, but his breath still caught in his throat when he saw the words:

O great God of Fire
I, your lowly servant, pledge to you my life and soul
I give to you all that I have, and pray that you see fit to bestow upon me but one small gift
I beg of you, Sithares, God of Fire, grant me the power of Fire Magic, that I might greater serve you

I swear on my life and soul, with the fire you give me I will burn so bright that Shadow itself will be torn from the world

Atillus read the passage several times, committing every word to memory. He sat again as before, in the centre of the room, cross legged and still. He closed his eyes, focused intently on the image of burning flames. He recited the prayer out loud, trying to sound confident and older than his ten years.

The very instant he finished, the images he pictured became chaotic reality. He heard the flames, felt them licking his skin, saw the red glow behind his eyelids. He felt fire inside his body, heat swelling until he felt he would explode. He opened his eyes and couldn't see the room; the flames were real. His heart skipped as the entire room became enveloped in raging fire. He looked down and saw his own body burning. He screamed, flailing and swiping his hands over his body, desperately trying to put out the flames. It was no use. After the panic died down, he realised there was no pain. He felt the heat, and though intense, it wasn't hurting him. His skin wasn't burnt, and he could still breath with no problems. If anything he felt more alive than ever before.

Just as his heart began to slow back down to a normal beat, he heard the whispered voice of the God of Fire.

Aella

Shouts drifted over the camp. Aella walked between tents and dormant camp fires, on her way to practice with her two short swords, when the shouting stopped her. A crowd formed a loose circle around something, cheering and booing; and in Thearan tribes that only meant one thing: a fight to the death. Aella ran towards the crowd.

A stranger stood in the clearing left by the crowd, Pure-blood Thearan, just like her. He was huge, possibly even seven foot tall. Heavily muscled. Even his stance screamed lethal. He stood across from one of the Thearans in her tribe, Platon, who was almost as tall as the stranger and even bigger across the chest. At a glance, Aella knew exactly what was happening. Whenever a stranger wanted to join a Thearan tribe, they had to prove their skills. Some tribes were more forgiving, but the tribe Aella grew up in demanded death as the price for entry. The same price had to be paid for leadership; the current leader of any given tribe only gave up their position of power to the Thearan who killed them in one-on-one combat.

The stranger held a cheap-looking grey steel sword; not Thearan steel. Wrapped around his torso was a much more elegant and expensive looking weapon, something Aella had never seen: It was a long, heavy chain ending in a brutally sharp Thearan spearhead on one end and a heavy spiked metal ball on the other. The spearhead rested in a sheath on the stranger's back, and the spiked ball hung secure at his waist. This weapon, unlike the cheap sword he held, was definitely forged from Thearan steel. The chain remained untouched, however, and the stranger seemed content with the dull grey sword in his hand. Platon was unimpressed with the newcomer, and announced his feelings to the crowd, to deafening cheers from his fellow warriors.

The newcomer seemed completely unconcerned by the tribe's apparent contempt for him, and stood calmly staring down his opponent. Platon finally grew sick of taunting and approached the Omati warrior confidently.

"What is your name, stranger?" he asked without breaking stride, "I would know so I may whisper it to the fire when I burn your corpse in the desert." Platon stabbed at the stranger's throat without waiting for an answer, and the crowd screamed and cheered.

The unknown warrior slipped underneath Platon's blade with no effort and swept his empty hand, balled into a fist, viciously into Platon's side. He sidestepped and stood as Platon grunted and fell to his knees in the grey sand.

"Kerberos." He said. His voice held absolutely no emotion. Platon rose faced his opponent, ready to fight again, but Aella had seen all she needed to; Kerberos would win this fight. The thought made her uncomfortable. The newcomer was a beast of a man, a deadly, brutal warrior, but that wasn't the reason. A foreboding, malicious energy seemed to emanate from him in waves. The word that kept flashing in Aella's mind was *powerful.* But it felt like a purely antagonistic kind of powerful, and Aella realised she was truly scared of him. And Platon, despite looking like a hulking monster, had always been friendly to Aella. She didn't want to see him die just to be replaced by this dangerous newcomer.

They were fighting properly now, blades singing and sand flying up in clouds as they stepped and twirled around each other. Even at eleven years of age, it was clear to Aella, if no one else, that Kerberos was merely playing with Platon. She watched him as her mother taught her to watch all warriors whenever she had the chance to witness them fight; analysing, memorising, watching for patterns and habits. Watching for weaknesses. Kerberos was a brilliant fighter. He'd assessed Platon the same way Aella was weighing him up now; but he'd done it at a glance, before they even started the fight. Despite his size, he was blindingly fast. Aella couldn't follow some of his strikes, and she knew she was incredibly fast too, even at her age.

After a few moments of Kerberos' toying, during which Aella was dismayed to see Platon becoming arrogantly sure of victory, the Thearan warrior finally dropped his act. He disarmed Platon and swept his cheap steel blade through his throat, so deep he almost beheaded the man entirely. The crowd cheered, but now for Kerberos, chanting his name and stomping their feet. There was no place for sentimentality in the desert; only strength.

It seemed like Kerberos was now one of them. Aella slipped away from the crowd, dark thoughts clouding her young mind.

A month after Kerberos joined their tribe, a massive group of Thearan warriors appeared in the distance. It was the largest tribe she'd ever seen; a full army. Thousands. Her tribe of perhaps three hundred was absolutely dwarfed by them. Her heart hammered, and every member of her tribe was out of their tents and staring along with her. There were two possible outcomes Aella could see: outright battle, or a merging of tribes. Either way, there would be death. Even the most tame merging of tribes demanded that the leaders battle to the death, with the winner taking control of the new tribe. The more likely scenario, however, was that one leader was trying to take control of a different tribe by force, which meant the entire tribes battled instead of just their leaders.

Over thousands of years, Thearan tribes segmented until there were none larger than Aella's, around three hundred warriors. The sight of such a massive army was terrifying. Whoever their leader was, they'd successfully taken control of many tribes. She hoped desperately that her leader, a woman named Iliana, would agree to a one-on-one battle instead of committing their whole tribe to battle. It would be suicide for them to fight such an army.

A handful of warriors from the massive tribe approached them, and Iliana strode forward to meet them with a similar number of her own warriors. They met within the camp itself, and Aella was close enough to overhear them.

"Greetings," one of the strangers said, "are you the leader of this tribe?" Iliana nodded and introduced herself.

"What is your purpose here?" she asked them.

"We are gathering the largest army Theara has ever seen, to serve Sithares and spread the Fire of God throughout all of Pandeia!" The warrior's voice rose as he spoke, and by the last word he was almost screaming. The wild-eyed fanaticism in the young warrior's face brought a fresh new wave of terror to Aella's heart. If the entire army was this devout, there would be no reasoning with them. She'd heard a few old legends about Sithares, none of which were comforting now that she was facing an army who fought in the Fire God's name.

"You would have us join you?" Iliana said. Aella's stomach lurched. Iliana had an unmistakably rebellious tone in her voice.

"Yes," replied the warrior, "Our leader will take your tribe, or we will destroy it. The choice is yours." Iliana was silent for a moment that seemed to stretch into an eternity. Finally she hung her head.

"I will fight this leader of yours. Where are they?"

"Here!" A voice boomed from a few metres behind Aella. She jumped, her heart throbbing painfully. She turned to see the owner of the voice was Kerberos.

He walked past her towards Iliana. He stopped in front of her, and members of her tribe encircled them to form the ring of combat.

"Draw your sword," he said, emotionless. "Your time has come to burn."

Zanela

Peace without weakness;
Strength without aggression;
Growth without forgetting;
I pledge my soul to the Shenza forever.

The three tenets and the oath of the Shenza. Every one of the peaceful warriors of the Shanaken forests lived by those words. Zanela recited them every day when she performed her *Zuunshai*. She wasn't allowed a sword yet, so she performed the blade dance without a blade as all *Kuulshen* did. That would change soon, if she was successful.

The *Shenzai* were designed around the three tenets. The first test addressed the first tenet; Peace without weakness. Despite being lethal warriors, the Shenza were a peaceful people. They didn't kill except for food and self protection. But their peaceful lifestyle didn't indicate weakness. Hunting, fishing, and the strength and agility required to climb and jump between trees every day kept the Shenza strong and fit. They never sought out battle; but were always ready to fight. And they tempered their peaceful nature with an unseen strength that baffled outsiders.

The first test required the *Kuulshen* to fight against an armed opponent without a blade of their own. They must end the fight without drawing blood. Zanela passed, fighting against a fellow *Kuulshen* named Shaiden. She dodged and weaved until Shaiden grew frustrated and lost control. Then she simply waited for him to make a mistake. She didn't have to wait long. He was the same age

35

as her, and patience wasn't his strength. He stopped searching her movements, instead swinging the training blade wildly in front of him. She dove to the side, rolled to a crouch behind him and swept his feet off the ground.

He dropped the sword as he fell, and she jumped on him. They grappled, grunting and rolling around on the wide platform until Zanela finally gained the upper hand, securing his neck in a tight hold between her legs. She held his arm in her hands, twisted up in a painful lock, and demanded he yield. He smacked the platform with his hand, and she let him go.

The second tenet, strength without aggression, was about self discipline and control. The Shenza believed strength and power were worthless if they weren't under control. Unprovoked aggression, and violence outside of training and self-protection, were among the worst crimes in Shenza society. According to the *Duulshen*, aggression was the sign of a weak soul.

The second test required the *Kuulshen* take as much pain as they could before yielding. They were whipped and beaten mercilessly until they gave up. They were not bound or restrained in any way; they had to stand still on their own. A sand timer measured the minimum time the *Kuulshen* was required to withstand the pain; there was no maximum time, and greater scores were awarded to those who endured the longest. Greater scores were also awarded to the *Kuulshen* who made no sound. Zanela was silent the entire time, watching the timer with her fists clenched.

She stood naked in the centre of a wide platform, high in the canopy. The only people on the platform were her father, two *Duulshen* to judge, and the Shenza tasked with administering the test. Dakesh was elsewhere, called away to prepare for his Shadow Trials. She was happy for him of course, but she desperately wished for his reassuring presence now. She lasted through the minimum time, forcing herself into silence. When the timer ran out, she squeezed her eyes shut and lowered her head, bearing

36

through the pain for as long as she could stand. Every second felt like an hour. The Shenza behind her lashed her back and legs, threw rocks, and shouted taunts at her constantly. The pain she expected; the teasing she hadn't. It was almost as hard to bear as the physical pain. Just as she felt she could take no more, she opened her eyes, ready to yield. She opened her mouth, about to scream for the pain to stop, when she locked eyes with her father. He watched dispassionately, staring at her as though assessing the work of a blacksmith or cook.

She maintained eye contact with him, reciting the tenets in her head. She focused on nothing else; the bored, red eyes of her father, and the sacred words of her people. Tears streamed down her face as the pain continued, but she repeated the words to herself over again. *Peace without weakness strength without aggression growth without forgetting peace without weakness strength without aggression growth without forgetting.* The words became a blur of thought as her body screamed. Her father dissolved into a meaningless shape against the bright blue of the sky as pain finally overcame her; the world faded into shadows and the last thing she felt as her consciousness slipped away was relief.

When she woke, her beaten, naked body was covered by a blanket. She stared up at the *Duulshen*, who informed her that she passed the test. Her father was already gone.

The third tenet, growth without forgetting, revolved around the Shenza belief in the circle of life. Growth and self-improvement were the purpose of Shenza life, and they believed that stillness bred weakness. The forest was always in motion; so the Shenza were also. At the same time, they believed that the past was useful and should never be forgotten. The third tenet reminded the Shenza to strive for greatness and keep moving forward, but to remember the lessons of the past.

The third test was by far the most difficult. *Kuulshen* were required to climb a special tree, the *Zailak*, as fast as they could. The climbing frame on the *Zailak* was altered, making it different to the frames on other trees in several ways. The limbs of the frame were further apart and didn't curl around the trunk evenly, meaning the climber must pay careful attention to where they were going. Hidden all through the tree bark and the climbing frame were various traps and trick handholds. A fair way up the trunk was a painted target. Touching the target meant the traps would deactivate, and the test was passed.

As the *Kuulshen* climbed, the trap would glow a second before it was sprung, giving them a chance to avoid it. Once they passed the trap, it would be sprung again at their feet, forcing them to either remember the placement and type of trap, or fall and fail the test. When the climb began, traps were sprung almost constantly. The *Kuulshen* needed to keep an eye on the traps they were reaching for while simultaneously keeping track of the traps at their feet. Zanela was terrified. Each test was reset for each *Kuulshen* who attempted it; no *Kuulshen* were permitted to watch another's attempt. Other than the horrifying description Dakesh recounted after passing his test, Zanela had no idea what to expect until she started climbing.

One thing was very clear: *Zailak* was designed to be dangerous, and could definitely kill the *Kuulshen* who wasn't careful. She stared at the tree as intently as possible before starting her climb, trying to locate any traps. Nothing was out of place. Nowhere that she could see looked even remotely like a trap. Her body still ached from the beatings she received the day before; *Kuulshen* were only given a day's rest between each test. Several wounds on her back and legs still bled openly, and her head pulsed painfully with each heartbeat. The *Duulshen* tipped the sand timer, and she raced forward.

As soon as her hands and feet were on the tree, three glowing circles appeared in different places just above her head. A second later, a spike shot out from the closest one, missing her head by barely an inch as she pulled herself up. The second trap was off to her side and she didn't see what it was. The third trap triggered; just as she got a hand hold right next to it, the glowing section of the climbing frame simply disappeared. A fourth and fifth glowing circle appeared above her as she kept climbing.

She narrowly avoided the spike at her feet as another jutted from the tree above her shoulder. One of the glowing circles did nothing once the glow faded; she avoided the spot completely. She had no desire to see what might happen if she touched it. Traps appeared endlessly as she climbed. Time was lost on her; there was no way of knowing how much time was left to reach the target. All she could do was climb.

Smoke and steam filled the dark room, filling Zanela's lungs and eyes. Sweat poured from her. The clanging of metal on metal rang through the room as heavy hammers smashed down on massive anvils. She was in the *Shenzashed*, the warrior's forge, along with a small group of other successful *Kuulshen*. The warriors were supervised by a few experienced blacksmiths, and a group of young Shenza children who were being taught how to work a forge.

All Shenza learned blacksmithing. It was one of many skills considered necessary for a warrior to possess. Zanela didn't enjoy being in the forge, but she'd made swords before. She knew enough to forge her own. Loud hissing screamed from the forge next to her as a warrior cooled their sword in a bucket of water. She felt the steam add to the room's heat. Zanela hated heat. She needed the cool breezes in the forest canopy; the crisp winds off the ocean in a fishing boat. She needed the blast of cold as she dove into one of the perfectly clear rivers in the mountains.

But the *Shenzashed* was the furthest from nice cool breezes and beautifully cold rivers as it was possible to get. The Shenza forging their blades were all naked from the waist up, and covered in a thick sheen of sweat. Everyone else in the room wore their usual tunics. Zanela didn't envy them.

Her blade was coming along nicely. Despite the awful heat and thick smoke, watching it take shape as she folded the metal onto itself and beat it flat again was incredibly satisfying. She was also fascinated by the forges; it was another piece of ancient Shenza magic she didn't understand. The stone structures were filled with a type of sand which could withstand temperatures hot enough to melt steel. Shenza blacksmiths stood nearby, touching a particular stone in different places to achieve different temperatures. The sand changed temperature instantly, and metal could be pushed into it and pulled out seconds later, glowing red and ready to be worked. As much as she hated being in the room, it was a great process to watch.

All swords in Shanaken were made from black Shenza steel and made in the same style. The only visual difference between a standard Shenza blade and a *Kaizuun* were the intricate runes carved into the metal and hilt. Even the training blades forged by *Kuulshen* learning the craft looked the same; except they were dulled so they couldn't cut.

Shenzuun, the standard Shenza swords, took months to create and finish. Zanela was almost finished the forging process, but after the blade was forged it needed to be sharpened, polished, and fitted with a hilt. Every stage of the process was sacred to the Shenza, and care had to be taken throughout to avoid ruining the blade. Shenza steel was incredibly lightweight, but still one of the strongest materials in all of Pandeia. Shenza swords were coveted by every other country, but no *Shenzuun* were ever sold or given to outsiders in Shanaken's history. Zanela was proud beyond words to be forging her own. Once she was finished, she would be *Daishen;* a true warrior.

Atillus

What is this?

Atillus gasped, blinking, and looked wildly around the room. The voice was weak, barely a whisper, but sounded close.

You, child!

He turned his head in every direction, heart hammering as he feared the worst from this new intruder.

I am no intruder, mortal! I am Sithares, God of Fire!

Atillus stopped dead, mouth open. His heart was still beating fast and loud. He closed his eyes tightly, trying to calm down. He was either going insane, or speaking with a God. After what he'd been through, he was entirely unsure which was the truth. But he knew either way that panicking wouldn't help him. His heart slowed, and he focused on what was in the room, what he knew to be real.

You're not insane, child. You do well to calm yourself and think. You will go far, and achieve much, I am certain of it. And with my help you will be unstoppable.

"Why would you help me?" Atillus' voice sounded weak and small in the tiny room; almost as weak as the whispering voice of the God.

41

You helped me first, mortal. You freed me from the Shadows beyond this world. I have been greatly weakened, but if you will serve me, you can restore my power. The more power I gain, the more power I will gift to you.

Atillus nodded his head. He read as much in the fire bound book. He thought about all he could do with Fire Magic, how he could destroy the Megalos family and restore the crown to the Argyris family. He could rule himself, and with the power of fire at his disposal no one would be able to stop him. He longed for the crown; not for the power it would afford him, but because he knew he could rule fairly and well, and certainly better than any other member of his own family or the rival noble families of Omatus.

No.

Atillus almost didn't hear it, the voice was so quiet.

You cannot take the city yet. You must bide your time. You are intelligent, and strong for your age; but you are still a child. You must make yourself truly unstoppable before you can rule Omatus properly. You will have the city, I promise you that, as a reward for freeing me. But first, you must serve me.

Atillus thought about what Sithares was saying. It made sense, he knew it. He wouldn't be able to take the city as he was now; he would surely be killed. Besides, his performance as the idiot child whom everyone ignored had worked too well. He was barely an afterthought to the people of Omatus. He needed true power to take the crown for himself, power which he didn't have. For the moment. So, slowly, he knelt and bowed his head.

"I will serve you, Sithares."

Good. Now go, back to the castle. Act as if nothing is different. No one can know I have awoken. I have much planning to do.

Atillus rose, flooded with renewed ambition and purpose. He walked to the door, and found that it opened willingly for him. Fear seized him at the threshold to the silent corridor he'd come through. He wasn't sure if he could stand another eternity in silence.

I'm different now, he thought, *the shadows in there cannot touch me if I'm made of fire.*

It was an odd thought, but somehow it gave him the courage to walk into the black silence once more.

The door shut behind him, silent. He didn't turn back. He kept walking, slowly, with his hand to the wall as he had before. But this time, after a few steps, he focused on the fire burning inside him. He pictured it like a beast, alive and hungry and ready to feast. He unleashed its power, and the corridor suddenly appeared before him. The sound of roaring flames rose like music in his ears. He screamed then, half laughing and half straining to burn as brightly as he could. He kept walking, and the blank stone wall where there should have been a door cracked and thundered. It opened before him, as if it was afraid of his power. He laughed again, and as he stepped through the doorway he let the fire go. The boom of the door exploding and the whoosh of flame disappearing happened simultaneously, merging and destroying the serene silence of the library.

Atillus was free. *And so is Sithares,* he thought. *Should I be afraid?* But he knew no matter what destruction the Fire God wrought on Pandeia, he would be protected. *As long as it leaves me enough of a world to rule, it can burn as much as it likes.* He smiled and walked towards his secret tunnel, the one that led to the corridors near the Royal Bedrooms. He wasn't sure how long he'd been gone for, and he was starved and exhausted. But he was excited.

I need to rest a while, he mused to himself, *but then I will train harder than any living soul has ever trained.*

His smile grew even wider.

Omatus will be mine.

Atillus ducked, but not fast enough. The wooden practice sword smacked him in the side of the head, hard, and he fell roughly to the ground. His vision swam, and he tried standing but fell again. His trainer, an Omati mercenary called Amphidas, smiled and lowered the point of his wooden sword.

"A man your size should be fast," he said. "You'll grow a lot more once you're a man proper, and most people think big means slow. If you get fast, you'll take your enemies down before they know what's happened."

Atillus nodded. He didn't speak much while training. He took a little time to wait for his vision to stop spinning, and stood again. Amphidas had been training him for a few months, ever since he opened the book on Sithares. Of course, he didn't mention the Fire God to anyone, and Amphidas never asked why he wanted to fight so badly. He was the perfect teacher; willing to impart all of his considerable knowledge of combat to an eager student without any qualms about teaching a child to kill, and without prying into Atillus' personal life. The lessons were going very well. He'd already learned a lot and was getting the impression that Amphidas hadn't expected such a fast learner; he reacted to every move Atillus picked up with raised brows and emphatic nods. They trained for hours every day. Atillus went to bed bruised and beaten every night. His parents didn't notice. Neither did his brothers. A small part of him was annoyed that his family thought so little of him, but the isolation suited his plans perfectly.

He gained size fast; he grew taller, of course, but also gained a lot of muscle due to his training. He was careful to wear loose clothing to cover his toughening body. His appetite went up by an incredible amount, and he started gorging himself at the Argyris family feasts; one more thing his oblivious family failed to notice. They were each wrapped up in their own stories, he thought, yet even so they made the time to acknowledge each other. All but him. Atillus was always the odd one out, not just in his family; in all of Omatus. But lately it felt as though he was being actively ignored, as though he'd done something awful. He decided to leave it be; if his family wanted to stay out of his way, he was more than happy to let them. For now.

Amphidas launched a new attack, the wooden sword dipping and weaving around Atillus, striking him wherever it could. He saw an opening and thrust his own practice sword through Amphidas' too-wide swing, jabbing him in the left shoulder. The blow forced his opponent back and sideways, and Atillus used the chance to swing down into Amphidas' neck. If they'd been using real weapons, the strike would have killed his opponent almost instantly. But then again, if they'd been using real swords, Atillus would have died well before he had the chance to land that blow.

Amphidas drove an open hand into Atillus' wrist so suddenly that before he felt the attack, his sword was in his teacher's hand. He dropped both swords to the ground and rubbed his neck where Atillus hit him.

"Well done," he laughed, "that really hurt!"

Atillus nodded silently again. He was pleased with his own improvement, but he never let victory turn him proud. He read that overestimating oneself was a quick way to die in battle.

"You're a very serious child, Atillus. Most children are running around chasing animals and laughing at your age."

"I know." Atillus spoke quietly. "But what would that achieve? I much prefer spending my time learning something useful."

Amphidas shook his head and laughed. "I can't argue with your logic. But I think we're done for the day. And other than sparring, I'm not sure how much more I can teach you before you know more than I do!" He laughed again. Atillus frowned.

"I need to know more," he said, "I am not finished learning." Amphidas gave his standard response of raising his brow and nodding enthusiastically.

"I know some people who'd be able to help. I'll need to find them first, but I'm sure they'll agree to train you... for the right price."

Atillus nodded dismissively. "You know my family; price is not an issue. Find them, and I'll pay you for the service."

Amphidas smiled. He always smiled when the prospect of money showed itself. He was ambitious, hard working and highly skilled. Atillus thought Amphidas was perhaps quite wealthy himself; he was willing to do anything for gold, and he'd been hired by the Argyris family for many other jobs before this; it was how Atillus knew of him in the first place.

"I'll find them as fast as I can, master Atillus. You'll be the most dangerous man in Pandeia in no time."

Atillus stood in the centre of the tiny hidden room in the back of the Library of Omatus, flames coursing over his body. He chose this room to practise wielding Fire Magic, as it seemed to be unburnable. Even the ancient books were never harmed by fire. He improved his ability to summon flames at a moment's notice, wrapping himself almost instantly in a cloak of powerful flame. It was difficult to maintain for any length of time, but his stamina was improving. He found that while covered in fire, he was stronger, faster and far more lethal. It was intoxicating.

He experimented with other ways of using Fire Magic, and tried to use everything he learned from the ancient Thearan Encyclopaedia. He spent any time when he wasn't training in combat down in this room, practising Magic.

He found he could create specific shapes out of fire if he focused for long enough, though it was excruciatingly difficult. He started with a simple globe, small enough to rest in his palm. From there he created a rough, barely distinguishable Fire-Hawk. It melted into nothing but flame after a few seconds of perching in his hands. A few weeks later, he got it to spread its wings before it burst into shapeless fire again, but its shape was much more defined.

After some experimentation he could increase the temperature of objects around him. He brought large books in from the proper library and lay them on the floor, resting his hands on them and feeling them heat up under his fingers. He burned a lot of books accidentally, but they were all books he'd already read. No one else in the city would care, or even notice.

He practised a lot in the months Amphidas was away, travelling to find him suitable teachers. He knew Amphidas would return; he was being paid far too much to find a better offer elsewhere. And as eager as Atillus was to continue learning to fight, there were other skills to practice. It wasn't just fire magic, either. He studied politics and warfare avidly. And history, and the Gods of old Pandeia. He practised any skill that might help him become powerful and deadly. He even found a book on the methods of non-magical sorcery used by the Royal entertainers hired to astonish guests at his family's feasts. The tricks were simple, but he'd seen them performed and knew they were convincing; and he was sure that sort of skill would prove useful.

By the time Amphidas returned, he could create a convincing Fire-Hawk which flew straight and fast as an arrow at a target he drew on the wall. It exploded on impact, and he was sure it would have caused a lot of damage if his practice room wasn't immune to fire. He was yet to figure out how to make it change direction, but he made a huge amount of progress all the same. He also practiced with keeping the cloak of fire burning; it was exhausting and he always needed rest immediately after, but he could keep the flames burning for much longer now. His power grew every day.

Aella

A year passed since their tribe was merged with Kerberos', and other than the huge number of warriors in their camp, surprisingly little was different. The only other change was the mandatory worship of Sithares. They prayed each day, and listened to Kerberos as he taught the tribe more about the God of Fire. They were taught a prayer shortly after they joined his tribe. The second she finished reciting it along with all the others of her old tribe, she felt a rush and a flare of energy, and she burst into flame. From that moment on she felt an even greater connection to the Fire Blades her mother gave her; and an even greater need to keep them secret. If Kerberos found out she was wielding ancient magic swords, he would kill her and take them for himself, she was certain of it. She'd wrapped the hilts in old lion hide so they looked like more standard swords; and although the magic in them made them perpetually sharp, she made a point of running a whetstone over them by campfires so others would see. It had been her idea, and her mother beamed at her cunning.

The hide wrap was ugly and made her hands ache a little. She wished she didn't have to conceal the swords; the way the hilts felt in her hands without the old wraps was amazing. But she made do, and she could still fight with the hilts covered.

Her and Athan were sparring. Lately they actually sparred instead of playing around as they did only a year ago; although Athan still announced which hero he would be at the beginning of the match, and stared at her until she told him she was Roxane. It still made her giggle.

She ducked underneath Athan's sword easily, though she made sure to keep a frown on her face and pretend it was difficult. He was sweating and breathing heavily, trying desperately to land a blow. They sparred all the time, as they spent all their time together anyway and Aella had no one else of a similar age who would train with her. Athan was three years her senior, but even at fifteen he was no match for her. Truth be told, she would have much preferred to spar with the adults of their tribe, but her mother told her that her skill should be hidden as much as possible from them.

"If your talent was known to all, it would only invite constant challenge," her mother said, "and that could only end one of two ways: You'll either kill everyone who challenges you, and eventually become the leader of our tribe. Or you'll be killed. And at your age, both of those are as bad as the other."

So she sparred with her parents in secret, and she sparred with her best friend Athanasius, pretending she was evenly matched to him. She only used one sword against him, although she could use two swords at the same time just as well. It was just another one of her secret talents, and she was getting used to keeping secrets. It upset her to keep things from Athan, but she knew that he wouldn't understand. He was already too quick to judge himself harshly, and if he found out that she could beat him without trying, she didn't think he'd cope.

Aella aimed a lunge at Athan's shoulder, but slowed herself down and aimed for the shoulder most protected; all he had to do was twist slightly and sweep his blade to the side and he could block her attack. He tried to dodge instead, mimicking her duck underneath his earlier blow, but he wasn't quite fast enough to get out of the way. She raised the tip of her sword as quickly as she could, and instead of stabbing him full in the shoulder, she sliced the edge of his arm in a shallow cut. He gasped as his arm opened, and stepped away from her. She lowered her sword and stood, waiting for him, her concern for him stopping her natural instinct to push the attack in her opponent's moment of weakness. Athan looked at her, and for a moment he looked angry, and almost suspicious. But then he suddenly laughed and shook his head.

"I get the feeling you're a much better fighter than I am, *Roxane*," he laughed; but there was a hint of that suspicion still lingering in his eyes as he said it. She smiled back, hoping that she didn't look too guilty.

"There's one way to test that, *Bion*," she replied, trying to make it sound light hearted. Today he was the leader of the first tribe to leave Theara and wander into the desert; Bion the Nomad. She, of course, was Roxane; she never chose any other hero in the years they'd been playing this game.

He laughed again, and raised his sword to her. They fought for a while longer, Aella trying harder to let him win. By the end of their sparring, they were both sweating and exhausted, and he landed a few cuts on her arms and legs to match the cuts she'd given him. He looked satisfied, and Aella was happy that she'd convinced him they were evenly matched.

They wandered back to camp; most warriors sparred within the proximity of the camp and usually even around the campfire or near their own tents. But Aella and Athan both preferred to be away from the other Thearans most of the time, and sparring alone allowed them to talk freely and enjoy each other's company without fear of interruption. Athanasius went back to his tent, and Aella went to her own. Helene, her mother, was sitting inside the tent as she entered; as she wasn't yet a woman grown, her tent was always set up right next to her parent's and they commonly shared the space between them. She sat next to her mother and they embraced warmly.

"Are you well, little warrior?" her mother asked. "You have far more cuts than usual!"

Aella giggled "Of course, mother," she said, "I was just trying to hide my talent like you taught me." Her mother

51

gave her a sad smile at that. She put her hand on Aella's cheek and sighed gently.

"Let us pray, then," she said. They knelt next to each other and recited a prayer taught by Kerberos. It was more like meditation than praying to Aella, and as she focused her mind on the image of cleansing fire, it was not God she felt connected to, but magic itself. As always happened with the prayer, her cuts and bruises blazed with sudden pain and discomfort. It grew in intensity until it was all she could feel, and then suddenly disappeared. Once it was gone it was as though it never happened.

The prayer could be used to heal almost any wound, and could even replace a full night's sleep to make the warrior feel refreshed and rested. Aella mastered it quickly, as she did most things. She sighed as the healing finished, and opened her eyes to see her mother giving her a sad smile again.

"You're so talented, Aella. It's such a shame you must hide it." Aella didn't know how to react. Her mother looked close to tears and was speaking so softly that even in the silence of their tent, she needed to lean closer to hear.

"You are the most powerful Fire Mage your father and I have ever seen," she said, and her eyes took on a fierce pride that cut through the sadness. "And still so young! Your potential power could even outshine the legends of Old Theara; Remember the heroes I've told you about?"

Aella nodded enthusiastically. She loved the stories her mother told; the heroes were almost always women, and it made her happy to imagine herself as the hero of a new story. Most of the legends the warriors told each other around camp fires were about men, but Aella didn't care about those. Her heroes were the ones who made her feel like she could be a hero too.

There was Hypatia, the first Queen of ancient Theara, who had her husband executed for trying to undermine her and take over the throne. She ruled all her life, and was well loved by the people of Theara. She was a great warrior too, and was always at the head of her army, leading the charge herself against the Omati and ancient Ermoori and any other opponents brave enough to face the Thearans in battle.

There was Xanthe, daughter of Zoe and Bion, the leaders of the first tribe of Thearans to venture out into the desert. Xanthe was the first to be touched by Sithares. It was said that before Sithares blessed her, she was pale and had darker hair and pale brown or yellow eyes, same as most of the ancient Thearans. But afterwards, her skin darkened, her hair grew pure white and her eyes bright gold. She was outcast as an abomination for years due to her drastic change in appearance. But she wandered the desert completely alone and once she returned to her tribe, she showed them the powers Sithares granted her, and they worshipped the Fire God. The entire tribe were similarly blessed with Fire Magic, and were all made to look like Xanthe too. After that they embraced their new look and called themselves pure-blood Thearans. Aella's parents had told her several times that their family line traced directly back to Xanthe. When they first told her, she got so excited she raced around the entire tribe, telling every warrior who would listen.

Then there was her personal favourite, Roxane. Roxane was the most powerful Fire Mage in history. Legend said she could summon a live Phenix at will, and destroy hundreds of warriors in seconds with massive waves of unquenchable flame. When the settled Thearans of Omatus decided to destroy the nomadic tribes, it was Roxane who single-handedly walked out to meet their army on the battlefield. Against thousands, she left but one survivor; to rush back to Omatus and tell them of the power of the pure blood Thearans. Ever since, the Omati feared and avoided the Thearan tribes, even going so far as to stop calling themselves the 'Thearans of Omatus'; they became simply the Omati. It was one of the greatest Thearan victories in history.

Aella loved that story; her mother always told it with such passion. It was Roxane's bravery that inspired Aella to train as hard as she did. She couldn't imagine being brave enough to face an entire army on her own, but despite that she still wanted to change the world like Roxane did.

Her mother was giving her an amused look, and Aella giggled as she realised she'd been staring blankly at her face for several minutes, caught up in the fantasy of her heroes. Helene laughed too, and pushed Aella over playfully. Her mother's smile faded, though only slightly, and she pulled her daughter gently back to a seated position on the tent floor. She pulled her into a hug and held her there, burying her face in Aella's hair.

"You will be so powerful, little one," she said softly, "but please be careful." Aella tried to nod, lost for words, but only ended up rocking both of them slightly back and forth. Helene held her even tighter then, and Aella suddenly felt panic spread through her. She realised her parents were genuinely terrified that something awful would happen to her. She knew there were risks, otherwise they wouldn't have said anything in the first place, but in the urgency of her mother's embrace, the danger suddenly felt very real. Her eyes stung with tears and she felt her breath become ragged. Her mother pulled back a little and saw her crying.

"What if-" She sniffled and wiped her nose, "- What if I'm not brave enough?" Helene looked honestly baffled for a moment, and then stifled a sudden laugh. Aella was furious. Her mother was the one who'd made her cry, and now she was laughing at her tears! Her mother noticed her outrage and stopped laughing; her brow creased with concern instead.

"What makes you say that, little warrior?" she asked, the humour gone from her voice now.

"I don't think I can be as brave as Roxane from the stories. What if I'm too much of a coward to face a whole army like she did?" Helene took Aella's face in both of her

54

hands, staring into her eyes with an intensity that almost scared her.

"*My daughter*? A coward?" She laughed again, but this time Aella could tell it was pretend. A timid smile broke through her tears.

"My brilliant, talented daughter is no coward," she said, eyes set on her own. After a pause, she said: "There is no shame in being cautious, Aella. And there is no shame in hiding your power from those who would do you harm for it. That doesn't make you a coward. All the bravest Thearan heroes knew that sometimes fighting would achieve nothing. They knew sometimes even they would lose and that it was more important to live to fight another day. They knew sometimes they must run instead of fight."

Aella nodded, her tears drying. She stared at her mother as they held each other. Although Aella already surpassed her on the battlefield, she realised suddenly that her biggest hero was Helene of Theara.

Zanela

The new blade gleamed in the sunlight. Zanela held it in one hand, feeling its perfect weight and balance. She slowly moved through the *Zuunshai*, finally performing the dance with an actual blade. The movements were different, and she had to re-learn them. Balanced on the balls of her feet, she twisted, swinging the sword through a slow horizontal arc in front of her. She brought it up, swung it down, then twisted again, crouched low and swung the blade up behind her.

It was a dangerous dance for beginners, and after weeks of sharpening and polishing, her new sword was razor sharp. Lightly touching the edge with a finger could cut deep. So she moved as slowly as she could, keeping her body and blade under total control. She practised for hours every day.

Dakesh returned from his shadow trials shortly after Zanela finished forging her *Shenzuun*. He failed. He was distraught and furious. Even worse than failing the shadow trials was the fact that he was sent to the city's border to act as *Lakshele*, a tree guard. Such were unfit for any other role, sent to watch the forest to learn patience and peace. Dakesh possessed neither. She visited him as much as she could, almost every day, and they talked while he stood his post.

He was bitter now. Not much Zanela said could cheer him up. They talked of her *Shenzai*, and the forging of the *Shenzuun* afterwards. He let out a reluctant chuckle when she told him how long she held on in the second test.

"You remained silent until you passed out?" he sounded proud, and Zanela nodded, beaming.

"And you stared father right in the face as they beat you?" Another nod, and he finally laughed with real humour.

"I bet he loved that!"

Zanela shrugged. "As much as he loves anything else."

He looked as though he was about to respond, then closed his mouth and gave a short nod.

"I haven't spoken to them yet, you know," he finally said. "Mother and father. I'm sure they know by now I was refused, but I haven't the heart to tell them myself. I suppose that makes me a coward."

Zanela was shocked. Dakesh, coward? He fought the Ermoori when he was barely eighteen. He survived for two years on the battlefront in one of the most brutal battles in Shenza history. Zanela remembered hearing news of carnage and death every day. Every time a scout ran into the city from the battle, her heart pounded and ached. For two years she was constantly terrified for her brother, and it wasn't until she saw him again two years after the invasion that she finally believed he was going to survive.

She remembered the sheer terror she'd felt, never knowing when Dakesh might have been struck down by the enemy. That much fear, and she was never even close to the battle itself; and yet Dakesh never hesitated when he was called on to fight for Shanaken.

"A coward? How could you even say that?"

He shook his head, his eyes distant.

"There are different kinds of bravery, sister. I can run into battle, even when I'm terrified. But some things I cannot face. Sometimes I think I deserve to keep this post forever."

The city's border was the quietest place in all of Shanaken, except for a fishing boat out on a calm ocean.

The sounds of the forest were present, of course, but other than that there was only silence and the rippling green of the treetops. Zanela enjoyed being there with her brother, despite his grouchiness. They sparred, played games, and talked about everything. Dakesh recounted his time on the battlefront to her, telling tales of Ermoori weaponry which she found hard to believe.

No one visited the outposts of the *Lakshele* but to bring news and supplies once a day. It was a lonely existence, and Zanela pitied Dakesh. He was posted there, alone but for her - and the once-a-day supplies drop off - for three years. He became steadily more distant and angry as the time wore on. She did her best to keep his spirits up, but her visits felt like a chore after a while, and she saw him less and less.

She wanted to see him every day, but she missed the man he was before the shadow trials; the man he'd become was a quiet, faded echo of Dakesh who made her feel empty and scared. And so it was that on the day Ermoor invaded once again, Zanela was sitting in the kitchens laughing with Nashan instead of with her brother, and he was called away to war.

Deep, booming horns rang out through the canopy, instantly alerting the Shenza to invasion. Zanela and Nashan stopped laughing. They glanced at each other. Ermoor last invaded Shanaken eight years ago, when Zanela was only ten. She was far too young for battle then, but the stories she heard about the Ermoori were terrifying; impenetrable boats with gigantic cannons lining the shore and spewing thousands of heavily armoured soldiers onto the soft white sand.

Their armour was strong but allowed them to move as fast as the Shenza, and their weapons could be held in one hand but had the power to tear people into pieces in an instant. They wore helmets which covered their faces, and spoke in an ugly, alien language. They were ruthless, using explosives and cannons to massacre thousands instead of facing their enemy head on. Explosions ripped through

58

their own soldiers, yet still they fired on the beach, killing indiscriminately.

Another deep horn blast filled the kitchens, and Zanela jumped out of her seat, running for the outpost where Dakesh was stationed. She had to at least say goodbye.

"Zanela, wait!" Nashan cried as she ran. She ignored him.

She ran as fast as she could, but by the time she reached Dakesh's outpost, he was gone. Another Shenza man stood in his place.

"Where is he?"

The *Lakshele* shrugged and waved vaguely towards the northern shore. Towards the Ermoori. Without saying anything further, she ran north. She had to see him one more time. He needed to know she loved him. He needed to know he was more than just some useless *Lakshele* to her; he was her hero.

She ran, jumping between trees and searching the forest ahead of her desperately. She saw no one, and eventually slowed down. Finally, she stopped altogether; she stood at the northern outpost of the city. Even her desperation to see Dakesh one more time couldn't drive her any closer to the northern shore. Heart hammering, she sat heavily on a thick branch, staring aimlessly into the forest. Dakesh was gone. All she could do now was hope he survived a second battle against the armour and technology of the Ermoori.

Zanela flew through the *Zuunshai*, never hesitating, never slowing. It was half a year since the second invasion, and reports were coming in every day of new levels of destruction and death. *Just like last time,* she though as she swept her blade through the air. She kept expecting to hear that the Shenza were defeated, that the Ermoori breached the forest and were on their way.

She trained hard every day now; it was all she had left. Her parents were just as cold and unimpressed as always.

59

Nashan was sent to the battlefront a few months after Dakesh, as part of the second wave defence. Her friends were caught up in the excitement of war, telling each other the rumours they'd heard about the Ermoori and the Shenza heroes defending their great country. Most of them didn't have older siblings fighting the invaders and were too young to remember the fear they felt as their parents left the city to fight. Zanela remembered all too well.

It made her sick. They talked and giggled as though the war was just some story, as though none of them were in any danger. She breathed with her movements, reciting the three tenets and letting her anger go. She was growing, into a better person and a better warrior. She felt it, and she let that knowledge fill her with certainty and peace as she finished the *Zuunshai*.

Since she withdrew from her friends after growing tired of the way they talked about the war, her days were free to roam the forest. She couldn't help dwelling on Dakesh. The fear he wouldn't survive a second invasion was inescapable. Training provided a great distraction. She spent most of her day pushing herself as hard as her body would allow, drowning her fears in sweat and blood. In an effort to honour Nashan and distract herself further, she also took to spending hours in the kitchens learning to cook. The new cook, Zailek, was polite but quiet. She only spoke when Zanela pushed her, or to teach her something new about cooking.

She spent one day a month climbing the *Zailak*, the testing tree. The traps were different every single time, and it pushed her beyond her limits. More often than not, she ended up crashing to the ground, covered in cuts and bruises. But she felt herself slowly improving. Fear drove her to train as hard as she could; not just fear for her brother, but fear for herself if the defence of the northern shore failed and the Ermoori breached the forest. She woke in the darkness most nights, terrified and breathing hard. The image of faceless, metal-clad soldiers swarming over the city wouldn't leave her mind, even in sleep.

So she trained, knowing full well she was part of the last line of defence against the enemy. And then the news came. Not that Ermoor succeeded in breaching the forest or even that the Shenza were victorious; no, the war was still raging. The news that Dakesh had stolen a *Kaizuun* and fled the battle.

Screams and shouts flooded the forest as the courier delivered his news. Almost every person in the city demanded his blood. Her own parents were quick to disown and condemn him. When their hateful eyes turned in her direction, she ran.

Dakesh

It was a beautiful day. Sunlight poured onto the white sand of the beach, a slight breeze taking the worst of the heat. The forest beyond the shore was layered with deep, vibrant greens, the trees swaying slightly. The ocean was calm. Dakesh looked at the sand, beautiful and pure but for his friend's blood pumping onto the soft earth. Explosions assaulted his ears, and all around him the chaos of battle raged while he looked into Kailen's hollow eyes. Numb, Dakesh spotted Kailen's Shadow Blade, newly forged and all but unused. It was close to Kailen's body, and would soon be swallowed up by the pool of blood spreading around him.

What a waste, Dakesh thought, staring at the black-bladed sword. He came so close to earning the right to forge his own, and he had never longed for anything so much in his life.

You deserve it.

The whisper was weak, but still cut through the sounds of the battlefield. It came from someone else, *somewhere* else. But it was right. *I do. I should have forged my own,* he thought.

Dakesh remembered his Shadow Trials a few years past. A series of brutal tests, all designed to push his people, the Shenza, beyond their limits. Only the absolute best made it through to become *Kaizeluun*, Shadow Magicians. He trained for years to reach his peak. He and Kailen, childhood friends since before either could remember, trained together every day when they were children. Dakesh won every sparring match. He learned techniques from their masters before other students. Dakesh was faster, stronger, better. Their other childhood friend, Elana, agreed. Elana was older than Dakesh and Kailen, and surpassed them both in skill, but trained with them anyway. Dakesh remembered the surge of pride and excitement he felt when Elana pointed out his obvious superiority in battle. Kailen's eyes had dropped slightly. At age fifteen, Dakesh passed the *Shenzai*, the warrior's tests. He savoured a congratulatory hug from Elana. Kailen passed too, but only barely. Dakesh felt a vicious stab of victory over Kailen that day. Such petty satisfaction was below a *Daishen,* the elite warriors of the Shenza, but he couldn't help being proud.

Two years later, Elana passed her Shadow Trials, and became a Shadow Magician; *Kaizeluun*. She showed them her newly forged Shadow Blade in the training yard, and they gawked like children. She leapt straight over their heads, and sent three magic throwing blades spinning from her hands where there were none only a second before. All three blades hit three different practice targets right in the centre, before disappearing in a puff of black smoke. She told them it would not be long before they were *Kaizeluun* too, and all three of them could train together with magic. She said if the Ermoori ever showed up again, they wouldn't stand a chance.

One year after, the Ermoori invaded the north shore of Shanaken. Dakesh, Elana, and Kailen were sent to fight together. The battle was long and brutal, raging for almost two years before the Ermoori were repelled. Dakesh caught glimpses of Elana fighting through the enemy ranks during the battle. She looked like a demon wreathed in shadow, slicing through armour and weaponry like it was nothing to her. Kailen struggled to keep up, almost getting cut down several times, but Elana always seemed to know when he needed her. Dakesh held his own, killing almost as many Ermoori as Elana. The three of them were bonded by battle from then on, closer than ever before.

On their way back to the Moving City, Elana complemented Dakesh on his fighting. He glanced at Kailen, who looked proud despite getting no attention from Elana. Dakesh felt powerful then, he remembered. He'd fought almost as well as Elana herself, without magic and with years less experience. He knew he would get his *Kaizuun* when his time came for the Shadow Trials, and he'd even imagined Kailen being rejected. He felt a pang of regret at imagining such things, but at the time he was too caught up in his own advancement to care. As soon as he returned from battle, Dakesh trained again. At the age of twenty three, he undertook his Shadow Trials.

He was refused. He argued with the elders, the *Duulshen,* for hours. They wouldn't permit him to go through the trials again, and grew sick of his arguing. They called him petulant and ungrateful, and sent him to act as *Lakshele*, a treeguard; nothing but a watcher at the city's border. Something a child could do. He was stuck at his post on the city's edge for three years, miserable and alone but for his sister's visits.

Until the alarms sounded, signalling that the Ermoori invaders had landed on the northern shore again. The *Duulshen* were eager to send him off, and though being sent to battle was an honour for the Shenza, he couldn't help but think they secretly hoped he would be slain. He left anyway, determined to prove he deserved a second chance in the Shadow Trials. A replacement *Lakshele* appeared within seconds of the alarm sounding, along with one of the *Duulshen*, who ordered him to the battlefront.

He not only survived, but killed many Ermoori, surprising even himself with his ferocity. And then Kailen appeared with his tattoos, black sleeveless tunic and *Kaizuun*, grinning and boasting. For half a year he fought beside Dakesh, his overconfident attitude getting worse and worse. Finally, when Dakesh began to hate his best friend, he finally leapt into battle without even paying attention.

Kailen was ripped almost in half by one of the magic, exploding stones the Ermoori launched at their enemies through brutally powerful cannons. Now he lay on the sand, a wrecked corpse staining the beach with his blood.

He was deemed worthy of that blade by the Duulshen, *and look at him now. If only they could see him. If only they could see me, and all I've accomplished since they sent me here.*

Dakesh watched as Kailen's blood seeped closer and closer to the brand new blade. A wild anxiety seized him, and he suddenly couldn't stand the thought of the blade being tainted by the blood of its wielder.

He could not handle its power, that whispered voice raged. *But* you *can. Take it for yourself!*

Dakesh blinked hard. As quiet as the voice was, it had a hypnotic power to it. He shook his head, trying to think his own thoughts; but it was no good. It made too much sense for him to take the sword. After all, he proved himself in battle where Kailen failed. He worked tirelessly to be the best warrior he could be, and received nothing in return.

This is your reward.

Dakesh's eyes grew wide as he heard the voice again.

This blade will make you even stronger. Faster. It will give you powers unknown to normal warriors. You will be the best fighter in all of Pandeia.

He felt an almost physical pull from the jet black blade in front of him. He thought he heard it humming, but he wasn't positive. Suddenly everything around him fell away, the sounds of the still raging battle nothing but a distant echo; there was just the shining black sword in the sand.

And the blood creeping toward it. Dakesh pictured himself wielding the sword, and all he could achieve with it. He couldn't remember why he shouldn't have it, though it vaguely occurred to him that something about it was wrong.

Why would it be wrong? This blade was made for you. It's owner forged it and brought it here, to lay at your feet.

Dakesh exhaled and briefly closed his eyes. He knew the voice was right. And the blade was humming after all. It was calling to him. He knelt in the sand. The power of the *Kaizuun* was visceral this close. Dakesh felt the skin on his arm prickling as he reached for it. As soon as he touched the sword, a cold wave of exhilaration swept through his body from the hand holding it right through to his feet. The battle around him suddenly came into sharp focus, his senses almost overwhelmed. He saw the Ermoori battleships resting at the shoreline, cannons firing into the battle. He heard the shouts of warriors both near and far, the song of Shenza blades slicing through Ermoori soldiers. He could smell the stinging aroma of the Ermoori cannons as they exploded and the salty sweet smell of the ocean. He watched one of his fellow Shenza warriors as she danced through her opponent's reach. He knew exactly where her blade was heading just before it slid through an Ermoori warrior's neck. He saw her muscles tense slightly as she leapt over him to meet another enemy. Dakesh felt the rush of magic launch from her and saw her tattoos burn with energy as she swung her arm in a vertical arc towards an Ermoori 10 metres to her left. He knew before it happened that the enemy would be struck in the face, chest and groin by three jet black throwing blades.

He stared back at the shining black sword in his hand with renewed awe.

It was slim, perfectly straight and with a wickedly sharp edge. The entire sword was covered in barely visible Shenza runes, even burned onto the wrapped hilt. The guard was a small circle perpendicular to the blade, and the hilt was long enough for two hands, though the blade wasn't more than a metre long. It was lightweight, as all Shenza steel was, and perfectly balanced. It felt perfect in his hands, and he knew it belonged to him now.

Others will not want you to have it.

Dakesh remembered why; A *Kaizuun*, a shadow blade, was linked forever to the warrior who forged it. It was why the *Kaizeluun* were required to forge their own blades when they passed their trials. Because of that sacred bond between warrior and sword, it was forbidden in Shenza culture to take another's blade.

There is no other course. To keep the blade, you must flee this land. Go west, to the great desert of Omas, where you will be free to pursue greatness.

An Ermoori soldier, covered in armour and brandishing a hand-held cannon, appeared to Dakesh's left. He saw the cannon rise and point at his chest a second before it happened, and ducked to the soldier's right side. Less than a second later, the Ermoori hand cannon exploded next to Dakesh's head, but he was outside the soldier's reach. His blade swept up, so fast it was barely visible, and sliced clean through his opponent's arm at the elbow, armour and all. The dismembered arm and weapon hit the sand with a thud.

Dakesh's opponent turned towards him and pointed his now missing arm at Dakesh's face. He blinked and looked down, and it was only then he realised what Dakesh had done. His look of disbelieving horror filled Dakesh with a savage satisfaction as he swept his new blade through the man's face. It barely slowed as it cut through the soldier's skull and helmet, and as his enemy fell, Dakesh saw there was no blood on the blade itself.

Go now, while the battle is raging. No one will notice in this chaos.

Dakesh ran, cutting down Ermoori soldiers whenever they crossed his path, and crashed through the edge of the forest past the beach. Once hidden from the battle, he started heading west.

Atillus

Amphidas found three warriors to train Atillus. He introduced them one by one; Karak, a Tarsi assassin skilled in stealth; Shaila, a native of Shanaken who called herself a Shadow Walker; and the Thearan, Amares, known among the desert tribes as a fierce and fearsome opponent. All were unique and interesting to Atillus, but it was Amares who stole his attention immediately; the tall, well-muscled man was striking in a way he'd never experienced before. Amares had smooth dark skin, pure white hair and vibrant golden eyes. He wore very little above the waist, which showed off his impressive figure. At his waist was a skirt of black Lionscale with silver Thearan Steel plates sewn into it for protection against even the most dangerous weaponry. Over his left shoulder he wore a layered pauldron made of the same scale and metal plates. Several pouches were attached to the pauldron's strap which wrapped diagonally over his chest and under his right arm. Thearan Steel gauntlets covered his forearms, and simple leather boots his feet. He moved very little. When he did move, it was slow and deliberate, almost hypnotic. His golden eyes seemed to glow in the sunlight, and an intense intelligence lay behind them. When introduced, he stared directly into Atillus' eyes and slowly nodded. Atillus could think of no words to greet the man. He found his reaction to the Thearan deeply unsettling; normally his dumbfounded silence was an act.

Karak, the Tarsi, would have been the most notable member of Amphidas' recruits were it not for Amares' stunning beauty. Atillus had never seen a native of Tarsium in person. Karak was incredibly short, only standing waist height to Amares. He had mottled grey skin, huge silver eyes with vertical slits for pupils and disproportionately large hands with long, thin fingers. He wore a thick, heavy looking grey cloak with a massive hood. The cloak seemed to be far too large for the tiny man; it was folded in on itself numerous times and secured with several ribbon ties in various places. Underneath, his black tunic and trousers were impeccably clean and perfectly fitted to his small frame. His face, mostly due to his massive eyes, had a child-like look of innocence about it, and he blinked a lot as he looked around the sun-lit private courtyard where their training would take place. He had absolutely no hair, which made his almost comically innocent looking face resemble a newborn baby.

Shaila, the Shadow Walker, was dangerous looking, though in a different way than Amares, whose brute strength was immediately apparent by the rippling muscles on his mostly unarmoured torso. Shaila's intimidating nature emanated instead from her eyes and stance. Her eyes were a deep, unsettling shade of red. She stood as if she was ready to pounce at any second, tense yet somehow relaxed at the same time, her hand never far from her sword. She was tall, though not as tall as Amares. Her skin was pale, and she had long, pitch black hair. She wore a simple layered fabric tunic of dark grey and black, with a dark blue sash around her waist. She had an unnerving way of almost never blinking.

Atillus learned everything he could from all of them. He trained for hours every day, building the basics at first, then getting more and more advanced with each of his teachers. He quickly found that although the Shenza martial art called *Zuunshai* was beautiful and elegant, he much preferred the Thearan style, Pyrokratos. It was brutal and efficient, and he knew that once he was a man grown his size and strength would be better suited to the brute power of Pyrokratos. He also preferred spending time with Amares. The man was stunning, not just physically

70

beautiful but an unbelievably talented fighter. Atillus wasn't entirely sure if his preference for the Thearan fighting style was purely a result of his infatuation, but he thought not. The movements felt more natural to him than those of *Zuunshai*, and he was learning Thearan techniques much faster. Amares almost never talked, but his Golden eyes were oddly expressive and his body conveyed his meaning almost effortlessly. Atillus learned a lot from the Thearan warrior.

The Tarsi, surprisingly, didn't have a fighting style at all, but their methods were amazing and useful to learn.

The Tarsi were masters of stealth. Not the simple, silent stealth of the Shadow Walkers from Shanaken, but a complex and mysterious method of becoming unseen that fascinated Atillus immensely. Karak, without speaking, turned from Atillus at the beginning of his first lesson and walked to the far side of the courtyard. He moved to a corner and started walking along the wall, behind the giant pillars set evenly along the walkway. He passed behind the first, and a completely different figure emerged from the other side. Twice as tall, and much wider, the figure turned to look at Atillus. Under the heavy cowl shone the golden eyes and chiselled jaw of Amares. He walked past the second pillar and this time Shaila emerged wearing the cloak. From the third pillar, it was Atillus himself who turned to look at him. He couldn't help but shudder as gooseflesh crawled up his arms and neck. The last pillar revealed something else entirely. As the figure emerged, Atillus assumed it would be Amphidas under the cowl, but this time when it looked at him, the hood contained nothing at all. The heavy cloak suddenly deflated, falling to the ground. A hand as strong as a vice clamped Atillus' arm.

He tried to swivel, ready to fight, but the grip was so strong it was all he could do to strain his neck to see behind him. Karak's massive, gentle eyes were staring up at him, passively watching as his grip loosened. Atillus couldn't believe his eyes.

"How did you get this side of the courtyard so fast?" He asked. The words seemed to tumble out of his mouth unbidden. Karak looked at him, blinking.

"I wasn't fast," he said. His voice was raspy but deep. "You were merely looking elsewhere, so I walked behind you." He gave the tiniest hint of a smile, his small mouth curling upwards slightly.

"I was *not* looking elsewhere, I watched you the entire time!"

Karak barked a short laugh that sounded like the croak of a toad. "You watched my cloak, child. Your mind told you I was in it, and even when your eyes told you otherwise, you chose to believe you were watching me."

Atillus narrowed his eyes, trying to puzzle out how something like that could work. He walked over to the cloak, crumpled on the floor, and picked it up. There was nothing odd about it, other than its size compared Karak. He walked back to Karak with the cloak. Handing it back to its owner, he shook his head in puzzlement. He gave another croak of laughter, a small but genuine smile curling his thin lips up.

"The Tarsi have been using magic for thousands of years, even after Fire Magic died out and Shadow Magic grew weaker. Ours is a magic of subtlety and patience, not like the brute destruction of Fire Magic or the energetic intensity of Shadow Magic. We use it to protect ourselves and our way of life, not to conquer or destroy. If you are to learn what I can teach you, no one can know of this magic. It is the most guarded secret of our people."

Karak's constant blinking was almost enough to distract Atillus from his words, but he knew when to pay attention and the significance of the Tarsi's words wasn't lost on him.

"Of course. Just as no one can know of the training I am undertaking. We both agree to stay silent on the matter," he replied. Karak nodded his agreement. "But, if I may ask, why teach me at all, if this secret is so precious to your people?"

Karak's small smile disappeared. His blinking stopped, the sudden shift incredibly unnerving. His massive eyes seemed to see all of Atillus, and all the way through him. He felt exposed in a way he never had before. The Tarsi remained silent for a long time. Finally, he spoke:

"My reasons are my own, child. I am here to teach you magic, not discuss my life. Suffice it to say I need the money you offered enough to warrant disclosing some knowledge of Tarsi magic. But know that if you break our agreement and tell anyone any Tarsi secrets, you won't live more than a day beyond the moment you betray me."

Atillus believed every word. In any case, he had no interest in sharing the knowledge he would gain from the Tarsi.

"You have my word, Karak, no one else will learn what you teach me here." Each teacher he trained with sent the other teachers away for his lessons; every day he spent a few hours with one at a time. It meant keeping his training secret was actually quite easy.

Karak seemed satisfied with Atillus' word. He gave a short nod and suddenly returned to his constant blinking and subtle smiles. He launched into the theory of Tarsi magic with such fervor that Atillus barely kept up. He realised how much there was to learn. The mysteries of Tarsium were a whole world unto themselves, something completely different to the skills he was learning from the other teachers, and even different to the Fire Magic he was teaching himself. He wasn't sure he could wield this power as well as he could pick up most other skills and abilities, but if he could learn even a fraction of what Karak was teaching...

He smiled to himself; He was standing at a precipice, overlooking a whole new world, and he knew that world would belong to him.

Dakesh

Mottled sunlight pierced the dark green air of the forest. The sounds of insects, birds and predators mingled to create the ambient and peaceful sound Dakesh grew up hearing. He travelled along the forest floor, quickly and quietly; the forests of Shanaken were brutal and deadly, even to the Shenza. They were home to countless predators, large and small, and a massive range of venomous insects and plants. But it was more than that; the forest exuded a dangerous magic of its own, almost as if it were conscious. Many Shenza disappeared in the forests, never seen again.

Dakesh kept the Shadow Blade in his hand as he ran. Its magic increased his senses and awareness to an incredible degree; he could somehow see predators a hundred metres away, through the massive tree trunks. Their silhouette glowed clearly, regardless of the distance. He saw birds and insects too, their auras smaller but just as bright. A vibrantly red glow snaked out at his ankle as he ran. He recognised it as a Viper Vine, a type of carnivorous plant which detected movement and snatched small animals from the forest floor, curling its thick vines around the unfortunate prey's body and crushing it into a pulp to digest. People were far too large for them to actually consume; but they could easily destroy a limb or two beyond repair in a matter of seconds once they had a grip. He leapt over it without breaking stride.

His thoughts raced as fast as he did, clashing and speeding through his mind as he tried to focus on the dangers of the forest. He stole a Shadow Blade; as soon as the *Duulshen* discovered his treachery, he'd be marked as an outsider forever. He'd be shunned and hated by his own people.

You were already shunned. They dishonoured you by refusing to name you Kaizeluun. *They do not respect your strength.*

The words, still whispered, seemed to pierce through his scattered thoughts like shafts of sunlight through the dark forest air.

That title was earned, and they took it from you. So you took the blade from them. A fair trade.

He nodded grimly and ducked under a tree branch at the last second. Finally, he saw one of the climbing structures the Shenza placed around giant trees to help them move faster into the canopy, and out of danger. They were swirling metal ladders that snaked around the trunks of the trees, forged from magic so no heat was necessary and the trees weren't damaged. The Shenza only placed their structures around fully grown trees so as not to restrict their growth.

He leapt onto it at full speed, running a few steps up the trunk and climbing with his left hand while he sheathed the blade with his right. Immediately, his strength and energy disappeared, and the forest was suddenly much quieter. The countless bright auras surrounding him vanished, and the climb up the tree trunk became arduous. Finally, he reached the canopy, and stopped for a rest; the trees of Shanaken were not only as wide as buildings, but taller than any building in Pandeia.

The Shenza, over thousands of years, constructed endless walkways and passages between the great trees of the forest. It was possible to travel from the southern edge to the northern edge of Shanaken without touching the ground. Not only could they travel through the trees without being seen by predators on the forest floor, but they actually lived up there, within flowing metal structures built around the trees in the canopy itself.

The Shenza didn't live in one city. Among the great trees, scattered over their mysterious country, were five concentrated hubs where the Shenza settled for a little while at a time; places which contained everything they needed as a society. The hubs were collectively called *Kashainuukza;* the Moving City. Rumours of the Moving City were whispered through all of Pandeia; but all that was truly known outside of Shanaken was the name, and the Shenza earned a notorious and mysterious reputation as a result.

Dakesh stood and started running again, trying to get as far as he could as quickly as possible. The battle at the beach was chaotic, but he couldn't rule out the possibility that someone saw him take Kailen's blade. He needed to get as far from Shanaken as he could.

The forest became a different place for Dakesh after he fled the battle. Once so peaceful and familiar, it now felt dangerous. He felt the way an outsider must feel when venturing into the forest for the first time; Alone and vulnerable. The only time he felt better was while holding the *Kaizuun*. He couldn't hold it constantly. He had to sheath the blade to sleep and eat. Sleeping was difficult during his journey. The sounds of the forest at night were now hostile and terrifying. The first night, he barely slept at all. In his mind's eye, he kept seeing a figure appear from the darkness, wreathed in shadows, wielding a *Kaizuun*.

Opening his eyes didn't help; the shadowy figure appeared in the empty blackness between tree branches. He couldn't quite convince himself he was seeing things. When the sun rose he sat up, exhausted and miserable. The forest was a little less terrifying now he could see everything. But he knew his visions weren't based on paranoia alone. The *Duulshen* would send someone after him as soon as they discovered his treachery.

He thought about his family. His parents would be furious with him. The shame he would bring to them weighed heavily. He thought about Zanela, his sister. She was far younger than him, and looked up to him the way he looked up to Elana. She would have to survive without him from now on. Even worse, she would be taught to hate him for his betrayal. For a moment, he entertained the thought she might leave Shanaken in search of him. They would reunite and live as outsiders together, protecting the people of Pandeia by hiring out their services as guards and mercenaries.

It was stupid, just a foolish fantasy, but it helped to imagine even one person might not hate him. He unsheathed the *Kaizuun* and read the ancient words engraved in the blade.

Deshuul nalduul ladza; Deshan, nalduul ladshuul;
Nuu'ishuul, nalduul naldi. Nakel lek nashuul kad ka Shenza duul.

The three tenets and the oath of the Shenza. The words every warrior of the forests lived by once they became *Daishen:*

Peace without weakness; Strength without aggression;
Growth without forgetting. I pledge my soul to the Shenza forever.

Tears sprang into his eyes. The hypocrisy of holding the *Kaizuun* while fleeing Shanaken as a criminal tore through him to his core. He almost turned back. If he returned to the *Duulshen* before they realised his intention, he could tell them he was bringing Kailen's blade to its rightful place.

No. That will achieve nothing. They already know. Returning now would only assure your death.

He sighed. Of course they would already know. The *Duulshen* knew everything that happened in their forests. The only way he could survive was to be faster than whomever they sent after him. If he reached Tarsium before he was caught, he could disappear into the teeming crowds and be lost to the elders forever.

But the words on the black blade pulsed and throbbed in his mind as he held the sword. Even if he got away, he would live the rest of his life a cowardly traitor. Even if he became as powerful as he dreamed, was it worth the crime he'd committed?

Reach into the blade. Feel its power.

He did; the *Kaizuun* reacted to his will. Energy flowed into him. He felt as though he'd slept the entire night. Alert, and ready for the journey ahead. He felt more certain about his decision. He could leave the Shenza, start again. Their hate wouldn't effect him if he never saw them again. The power flowing through his body wiped misery away like a river swept away a fallen leaf.

That is a fraction of the power to be found in the deserts of Omas. The blades of the Shenza are nothing compared to the magic of the Thearans. You will see.

Reassured, he ran west again. The *Kaizuun* propelled his spirit and his muscles, and he sprinted through the forest until the sun sank low on the horizon. A pang of uncertainty remained in his mind; the image of his little sister's face, crying and reaching for him. He tried to outrun it, pushing harder and harder until the forest became a blur around him. That night, sleep eluded him once again.

Dakesh reached the west coast of Shanaken three days after running from the battle against the Ermoori. The journey would normally have taken him a week, but with the *Kaizuun* in hand he ran much faster and for longer. There were no ports this far north that offered transport, only small fishing villages with their own piers for bringing in fresh hauls. He approached one of them, hoping the fishers wouldn't notice the *Kaizuun* sheathed at his hip; he put the Shadow Blade in his own sheath, and slipped his old sword into his belt on the opposite side when he took Kailen's.

The hilt of the Shadow Blade was marked with runes, and was far nicer than his old sword; but the sheath helped to make it less obvious. He still looked odd with two swords on his belt, and felt even more odd than he looked. One of the fishers noticed him, and waved. He returned the greeting, and walked up to her.

"Greetings, friend," Dakesh said.

"Greetings, brother. What brings a *Kaizeluun* to our humble village?"

Dakesh's heart sank. Of course the blade would be noticed; even among the Shenza, the *Kaizuun* were rare and revered. The fisher watched him. He wore a standard *Daishen* tunic; mottled grey, brown and green with a solid brown sash over his waist. He wasn't dressed in the sleeveless black tunic of the *Kaizeluun*, and didn't have the tattoos. He had two options, as far as he could determine: try to lie and bluff his way onto a fishing boat, and sail to Tarsium; or kill the fishers and take a boat by force. All Shenza were trained as warriors, and even fishers carried their swords on them wherever they went; but he had a Shadow Blade now. Even without the tattoos of the *Kaizeluun* granting him magic and mastery over the *Kaizuun*, he could still use its magic to a lesser degree. Even without training, the blade made him stronger and faster than any other Shenza.

He took a deep breath, and stared back at the fisher with as much confidence as he could muster.

"I'm being sent on a mission to Tarsium. No one must know I am *Kaizeluun*. No one must know I was here. I need one of your boats; a transport is too dangerous."

The fisher's face went pale. Her eyes were wide. *She believes me!* He thought, trying to hide his excitement.

"Of course, anything for the *Kaizeluun*."

Aella

Aella twirled around a training spear, ducked under a blunted short sword and leapt, still twirling, over a second spear. She parried, dodged and countered endlessly. The four young Thearans sparring against her were starting to lose their temper. She was fifteen, and far more confident about showing her abilities. She'd also grown into her body, and her muscles were far stronger; she was a far better fighter now, and she was already one of the best in the tribe.

She used both of her short swords openly now, and didn't hide her speed or skill. Athan didn't take the change well. They'd drifted apart over the last year or so, and they very rarely sparred together now. The four young warriors she was training with were relatively new friends, and two of them only joined their tribe about half a year before. One of those, a boy of fourteen named Erasmus, showed an interest in her immediately; she returned it. They talked every day and she enjoyed his company far more than she would have predicted. His combat skills were severely lacking, however; sparring against the four of them felt more to her like sparring against two or three. She barely needed to use both of her swords.

Though quiet, Aella was a little more social than Athanasius, and while he withdrew from the whole tribe, she started to gain more friends. She attracted the attention of many of the adults in the tribe as well; now that she wasn't hiding her combat skills, the older warriors noticed what she could do. She was still closely guarding her two magic swords, however. Her mother was wise to advise her to keep the Fire Blades hidden. Although Kerberos had been their leader for four years, she still didn't trust him or the zealots who followed him. Athan was spending most of his time with the Warleader, and though they no longer spoke as often, she was worried for him.

She saw Athanasius training one-on-one with Kerberos most days. His skills in combat were improving drastically. She also noticed that Kerberos watched her sparring on several occasions and seemed to give her a particularly intense stare whenever she was training. She was fine with the attention, as long as no one but her, Athan and her parents knew about the Fire Blades. She hoped Athan wasn't getting close enough to Kerberos to tell him about them.

They did seem to be getting very close, however. She began to notice they weren't just sparring together; Athan spent every meal at Kerberos' campfire, and plenty of time in Kerberos' tent alone with the terrifying tribe leader. Aella hoped he knew what he was doing. Kerberos was perhaps the most dangerous person in Pandeia. If they were lovers, as she suspected they must be, Athan shouldn't be in any danger; but with someone as mysterious and brutal as Kerberos, there was no way to be certain.

Her mind had wandered too far, and one of the wooden spears slammed into her chest. She was knocked to her feet, dazed and fighting to inhale. Natasa, the warrior who landed the blow, dropped her spear and rushed to Aella's side.

"Aella, are you hurt?" she asked, sounding terrified. "I didn't expect you to miss that thrust! I was just trying to distract you so Timothea could land a killing stroke!"

Aella finally managed to breathe again. She coughed, and then laughed. "I am fine, Natasa. My mind wandered, that's all. You put a lot of strength into that thrust; I would have expected a feint to be a little gentler!" The girls laughed, and Erasmus smiled distantly too. He might have guessed her mind was on Athan; he was jealous of the close friendship she shared with him, and his jealousy didn't let up even after her and Athan started drifting apart. He seemed to have trouble accepting that their friendship was purely platonic. She quickly grew sick of the argument. It was one of the reasons she no longer went out of her way to speak with Athan; Erasmus grew bitter every time she spoke with him. Athan seemed jealous too, and his withdrawing hurt her far more than Erasmus' petty arguments.

She stood and gingerly touched a hand to her chest, testing for breaks or cuts. It hurt, and she would have an impressive bruise, but other than that it was fine. She stretched, wincing as the muscles in her chest screamed. She could continue to fight through the pain if she wanted to, but decided to rest for the remainder of the day instead. The five warriors wandered to a campfire near their tents and sat down together.

The campfires were more than just places to eat since Kerberos took control. They were almost sacred now; used as shrines to Sithares, places to pray and burn offerings to their Fire God. They no longer required wood to burn, either; every Thearan had the ability to conjure a handful of fire which could burn for at least an hour. Several warriors would gather and set their fires together to build a larger campfire. The combined magic helped them burn longer, and they would tend to it as needed, each throwing another handful of fire onto the blaze occasionally.

Since their magic was awoken, campfires were a far more common sight. Wood was scarce in the Omasi desert, and although they always found enough to burn for cooking, they could now set campfires as freely and easily as they wanted. Aella gathered a ball of fire in her palm as she sat with the others. She held her cupped hand above the campfire and tipped it in a pouring motion, letting the magic fire spill slowly like water. It was a difficult trick, and Erasmus always laughed and shook his head when she performed it in front of him. This time, however, he was staring vacantly into the fire as Aella's magic slowly trickled away.

A few more years passed. Athan and Aella were almost completely estranged. Her and Erasmus became lovers, and his passion for her outweighed the sense of loss she felt for Athan's friendship. He also didn't mind that she was obviously far superior to him in combat, which meant she could spar against him and several other warriors and he never got upset or angry when she won. They hunted together every day, shared the same tent, and spent most of their time together. He was kind and loving, and Aella was happy. Occasionally, though, she thought about Athan and how close they used to be. She missed him dearly, and it frustrated her that he couldn't get past his own jealousy and pride and remain her friend. And it frustrated her more that even if Athan had been able to move past his problems, Erasmus was too jealous to allow them to be friends. It was the one thing about Erasmus she didn't love. She found it difficult to get too mad at him about it now though. If Athan had actually wanted to stay friends with her, she would have fought Erasmus tooth and nail to keep his friendship; but since he withdrew, Erasmus' jealousy was just another excuse to leave Athan to his own devices. Besides, he seemed to be quite happy with Kerberos.

Oblivious to her thoughts, Erasmus beamed like a child as they sat by the fire, eating dried greysnake meat. Their sparring match was intense that day, and Erasmus actually managed to hit Aella under the ribs with the flat of his sword, and again on her thigh. Of course it was while she was fending off four other warriors, and she still won the match, but looking at his face anyone would think he'd bested her single-handedly. She laughed, and at the sound his grin widened even more. She laughed harder and he joined in.

"You know that still doesn't count as you beating me, right?" she laughed.

"What about now?" he countered, launching himself at her. They tumbled to the ground, rolling until Erasmus was on top of her. He pinned her wrists to the ground, and although she could easily have overpowered him, she enjoyed letting him hold her down. It felt nice to give up her strength to someone she trusted. He kissed her suddenly, and her whole body tingled. She let out a quiet moan, and he kept kissing her. She felt him grow hard against her, and her body responded with the tingling, tense feeling of anticipation she'd become used to around him. She wanted him all the time, so much that he occasionally had trouble keeping up with her. There was no such trouble now, however; she felt him, large and pulsing, grinding slowly against her. She moaned again. He rose to his knees suddenly, pulling her hide pants up to her knees and his own down to the ground.

She saw his hard member briefly and it brought a flush of fresh lust to her; she was dripping wet and breathing heavily. He entered her gently and she gasped. He was always gentle at first, which she loved about him, but he was large and no matter how gentle he was, it always made her gasp. He slid deeper slowly, staring into her eyes until he was completely inside of her. He pulled back and she whimpered as he pushed slowly forward again. He held the back of her head with one hand and cradled her breast with the other, gently squeezing as his thrusts gradually picked up speed. Her gasps grew loud, turning into moans.

They kissed, and Aella's lips felt like lightning. She pushed her fingers into his hair and held on. Their faces were close, their breath mingling. Even his breath on her face and neck felt like the dancing sparks above a fire. They were breathing in unison now, and the camp-site around them disappeared until nothing existed but the two of them and the place where they became one. Aella felt the fire within her building, being stoked by their passion; every thrust feeding the flames. The thrusts became harder

85

and faster, filling her completely and building the fire up until she could no longer contain it; as she climaxed, she lost control of the magic within her, and the two lovers burst into flame as Erasmus continued thrusting even harder.

She screamed his name, her entire body burning. Waves of pleasure as intense as the fire itself overcame her, and she lost herself to it. Erasmus wasn't slowing down, and she stared into his eyes in shock as another climax swept through her body. She heard the rushing sound of fire over their ragged breathing, and heard it boom with each climax. He started moaning, and she felt him swell inside her, becoming even harder. She screamed again, and her body shuddered uncontrollably.

They climaxed together then, and after the fire went out they lay next to their tent until their heartbeats returned to a steady rhythm. She held Erasmus close, and whispered in his ear.

"I love you." He kissed her and said it back. Finally, they stood and retired to the tent to sleep.

The next day, when they sparred, Erasmus didn't land any hits on her. He wasn't disappointed at all. That night they made love under the stars again.

Thorinos

Thorinos Argyris was the wealthiest man in Omatus. Many said he was also the most powerful man in the city, despite not sitting on the throne. For all that, he sat halfway down the massive table in the Argyris Feast Hall, seething and feeling far from powerful. One of his offspring was missing, and the youngest was hiding behind a thick book, ignoring the food and the company. His second son, Alliphis, sat to his right, observing all the etiquette and charm his father taught him. It wasn't hard to see why Alliphis was the favourite son. He looked the most like his father, was ambitious, strong, and talented when it came to winning friends and allies. Anamas, Thorinos' youngest, was the complete opposite. He looked so much like his mother people often mistook him for a girl. He was small and weak, with no social skills to speak of. He spent all of his time reading silently. Thorinos had no idea how to fix him, deciding instead to spend his time and energy on Alliphis. His favourite son was going to turn into a great man, and would sit the Omati throne after him once Thorinos took it back from the Megalos family. He would make sure of it.

And then there was Atillus. Thorinos had no idea how to fix his oldest son either. Atillus took after Thorinos in all but intelligence and ambition. He was big for his age, and would have been strong too if he bothered learning combat like Alliphis. He had the Kingly, authoritative looking facial structure Thorinos and Alliphis possessed. He also occasionally displayed hints of intelligence, but he was so vague and absent-minded that any intelligence he may have was wasted. And the most frustrating thing about Atillus was his constant disappearances, especially during events such as feasts and carnivals. At fifteen, Thorinos thought his oldest son would attend feasts if only for the many high-born girls. He started disappearing around five or six years ago, if Thorinos remembered correctly, and he still didn't know where the boy was going. Truth be told, he didn't much care as long as he didn't damage the Argyris family name.

Shaking his head, Thorinos returned his focus to the feast. His beautiful wife, Eirene, was sitting to his left, and asked him to pass her a side dish of marinated olives.

"Of course," he smiled and handed her the food along with a quick kiss on her cheek. She looked at him in that piercing, knowing way she had and put her hand on his forearm.

"What's wrong, my love?" She asked. He sighed. She always knew.

"Atillus," he said, tension tightening his voice. "Why must he be so difficult?" Eirene smiled sadly, gently squeezing his forearm. She hesitated, obviously mulling over a response. It was something he admired in his wife; she was incredibly diplomatic, and could calm even the wildest arguments with the perfect choice of words.

"He isn't being difficult, Thorinos," she said evenly, "he's just being himself. He's still young, and finding his path." Thorinos shook his head again.

"Alliphis is younger, and already all but equipped to sit the throne, Eirene!"

"Yes, and that's Alliphis' path. Not everyone is meant to rule, my love. If that were so, how would everyone else be ruled? You should feel lucky that our three sons aren't fighting each other for the right to rule; the Megalos family's sons are constantly fighting. I'm grateful every day that our children didn't turn out that way."

"But that's the problem exactly, Eirene; Atillus is not a ruler. But he's the oldest son, and when I get the throne back, he'll be the next King. I'm trying to restore our

88

family's name to its former glory. How can I do that if my useless son is wearing the crown?"

"So spend some time with him, Thorinos. Teach him. Help him. You're his father, only you can turn him into the man you want him to be."

Thorinos frowned and grunted in begrudging agreement. Her argument made sense; but Atillus simply didn't have what it took to be a King. His anger far from quelled, Thorinos tried to think of a solution that didn't involve Atillus taking the throne. At that moment, the doors to the feast hall opened and Atillus walked in quietly, with a large Thearan warrior striding confidently next to him. Thorinos' frown grew even deeper; He'd seen this mysterious golden-eyed warrior occasionally over the last few years, mostly wandering alone through the grand markets of Omatus on days when Thorinos was supervising the stores he owned. He had no idea what the Thearan was doing in the Argyris family feast hall, least of all with his oldest son.

They sat next to each other at the huge table without so much as a glance towards Thorinos. The feasts hosted by noble families in Omatus were notoriously exclusive and strictly invite-only; Thorinos certainly didn't recall inviting this strange, silent warrior. Thearans were savages who lived out in the desert and dressed in animal skins. This warrior didn't belong in the Argyris family hall. Thearans had no use other than warfare and violence. Thorinos hired them as mercenaries and guards, but otherwise had no respect for their kind and no wish to be associated with them.

He stood, and was pleased by the speed with which the large room turned quiet. His arms addressed the room at large, but his eyes never left Atillus'.

"I'm glad you could join us, Atillus," he boomed, keeping a mocking ring in his voice, "and with cheerful company besides!"

The crowd was quick to laugh, but where their fast silence at his standing satisfied him, their eager laughter served only to grate on his nerves. He would have much preferred to resolve this privately, but Atillus publicly insulted his father by bringing an uninvited guest; It needed to be paid for publicly. Atillus glanced at his golden-eyed friend, and the Thearan warrior returned the look with what appeared to be reassurance. Thorinos saw their hands touch in an unmistakeably loving way, and his stomach churned. Atillus faced his father, staring directly into his eyes. For the first time, Thorinos saw a glimpse of something in those eyes, something which scared him. He saw power, intelligence, and scariest of all, he saw confidence. It was a half-step down from outright defiance. Recovering from the brief moment of inexplicable fear he felt, Thorinos' emotions turned once more to anger. He addressed Atillus again.

"But, as cheerful as he seems-" there was a brief but annoying spatter of laughter again, which Thorinos continued talking over, "-I don't believe your... friend... was invited."

The laughter died as quickly as it started. The feast hall was stunningly quiet now. Not even the soft sound of chewing rose from the captivated audience. He stared at Atillus, and his son stared back, taunting him. Then, disconcertingly, Atillus smiled and that damned newfound confidence grew, lighting his face up and making him seem much older than his fifteen years.

"But he *was* invited, father. I invited him. There is plenty of room, and plenty of food. Or would you not extend your hospitality to those who give their friendship to your own son?"

Atillus and his Thearan friend touched hands once more, not even trying to hide it. Something snapped in Thorinos.

"*Is* it friendship he gives you, boy?" he sneered, "Or does he offer more than that behind closed doors?"

That wiped the confidence off his arrogant son's face. A few gasps punctuated the silence engulfing the hall. Thorinos found the satisfaction of landing a strike against

Atillus' honour didn't quite outweigh the fury he felt, nor his disgust at seeing their hands touch. His son's reaction was more than enough to prove the two were lovers, and the public manner in which they were revealed meant it would be talked about through all of Omatus. Thorinos would be a joke to the other noble families; Atillus single-handedly crushed his father's reputation in a matter of minutes. Instead of appearing regretful, or beaten, or ashamed, or any of the other reactions Thorinos might have expected, Atillus looked furious.

"He gives me happiness, father. Something you've never bothered to offer."

Thorinos shook with rage. Atillus looked equally livid, and they stood staring at each other for what must have been at least a full minute. He shook his head slightly, and let out a soft, ragged breath which he hoped no one close enough to hear mistook for weakness.

"Let him give you happiness then; but I won't tolerate this filth in my hall. You've sullied the Argyris name. Get out."

He gestured dismissively toward the main doors, turning his back on Atillus and looking instead towards the armed guards flanking the walls. In the Argyris feast hall, the only weapons allowed to be carried were held by the guards and by the head of the family, Thorinos himself. It made easy work of removing unwanted and unruly guests.

"Guards, escort them out."

A group of about a dozen guards drew their swords and strode to where Atillus was seated. Atillus and his feral lover were standing by the time the guards arrived, and let themselves be led towards the doors. A few metres from the entrance, Thorinos raised his voice and addressed Atillus again:

"I hoped you might eventually grow into a real man, Atillus. I can see now how wrong I was. I see I don't have three sons after all. You've chosen to live instead as my daughter; and with a boy-loving Thearan savage as your lover!"

91

Thorinos kept his tone as light as possible, and the crowd laughed heartily in response.

"I should be glad. I never wanted you as my son. I never wanted to give you the crown."

The Thearan warrior started towards Thorinos' seat, and several of the guards moved immediately to block his way. After that, everything seemed to happen at once.

Atillus stepped forward and called out, "Amares, no!", and was restrained by two of the guards.

One of the guards shouted at Amares to halt. Several of the other guards raised their swords in a ready stance. Amares took another two steps before one of the guards thrust their sword at his chest. He swatted the blade away almost lazily with one hand, and swept his other in a deadly, blindingly fast arc at the guard's throat. He tore out a handful of flesh like it was nothing, and the man died clutching his gaping throat and gurgling while Amares moved on. The next two guards attacked at the same time, and the Thearan ducked and swerved with liquid grace, avoiding both blades easily. One of the guards recovered quickly and attacked a second time with a thrust towards Amares' neck. Amares twisted around the attack and grabbed the guard's wrist, pulling him close. Using the guard's own momentum, he smashed his fist into the man's face and pulled his arm hard at the same time, and a loud cracking sound exploded from the Guard's neck. As he fell, Amares snatched the sword from his lifeless fingers.

The third guard attacked again, but Amares was armed now and parried the guard's thrust before sweeping his blade clean through the soldier's neck in one blow. Before his severed head hit the ground, Amares sliced the throat of another Omati soldier and took another step towards Thorinos.

Guests were screaming and scrambling away from the deadly Thearan warrior, but Thorinos was fiercely proud to see his guards were still pressing the attack. Two of them circled around their opponent and another three faced him head on, spaced out and ready. Amares seemed to know who would move before the attacks came, and danced around and between the five blades surrounding him effortlessly. His own blade danced too, ringing as it clashed with his opponent's swords.

One guard fell with his throat cut, and another toppled and screamed as his leg was hacked off at the knee. Amares grunted as one of the guards finally landed a blow, slicing through his left bicep and upper back, and a few seconds later another guard thrust his sword into the Thearan's right side, under the ribcage. Amares let out a rage-filled, animalistic growl and spun on his heel towards the guard who landed the blow, slashing savagely through the man's head. It made a sickening wet crunch sound that carried clearly across the hall, twisting Thorinos' stomach.

One of the guards now behind Amares swung low, slicing deeply into the warrior's calf, and had the foresight to jump backwards to avoid a retaliatory strike from Amares. The guard next to him wasn't so lucky. His stomach opened in a disturbingly deep cut, spilling his insides onto the smooth stone floor. His screaming continued for far too long, piercing the entire hall. Several of the guests started vomiting and a few fainted, crashing listlessly to the floor.

The first soldier's luck ran out. Amares singled him out, and relentlessly pursued him, ignoring the other guards in his fury. He slashed chaotically at the man, completely missing once and hitting his opponent's blade twice before it shattered into several pieces. He kept slashing, and the next few blows hit flesh. He cut through the guard's wrist, hacked into his shoulder, his other arm, his neck and finally brought the sword down through the soldier's face. He slashed at the man a few more times even as he fell, and while he was still attacking the dead man, two of the surviving guards thrust their blades into Amares' back, piercing deep. He turned and swept his sword in a deadly arc, catching one of the soldier's in a shallow cut to his face, and missing the second entirely. The first guard screamed and dropped his sword, bringing his hands to his

93

face and dropping to his knees. The second guard stepped closer to Amares and stabbed him in the gut.

Amares grunted, dropped his sword, and grabbed the guard's head. Before he could wrestle out of the big man's grip, Amares hooked his fingers in the guard's mouth and wrenched his lower jaw completely off his face. The guard tried to scream but instead made a high pitched gurgling sound and sprayed blood all over Amares' face. As Amares collapsed to his knees, his head lowering, the dead guard fell to the floor.

Thorinos drew his sword and rushed to the fallen Thearan. Out of the corner of his eye, he saw Atillus struggling with the guards. The guards looked like they were actually having trouble keeping him in check; his son was large for his age, but Thorinos knew he'd never had any combat training, and through his fury he felt a moment of doubt. *The guards shouldn't be struggling so much with a mere child,* he thought. Then he saw something which almost stopped his rush towards Amares. The Thearan warrior glanced at Atillus with visible effort, and shook his head weakly. Atillus reacted immediately, calming down and allowing the guards control over him again, though he was weeping and begging for mercy for the feral warrior. It only served to feed Thorinos' rage.

"You will never be head of this family, boy. No matter what happens, when our family regains the crown again, you will never be King. You don't deserve the Argyris name, and you will never be a real man in my eyes."

He gestured with the blade of his sword at Amares, and his voice filled with venom.

"This is what filth like him deserve, Atillus," he snarled at his son, "if you show your face in this hall again, I promise you will meet the same fate."

Without hesitating, he swept his sword up and down in one graceful move, sheering clean through Amares' neck.

94

Aella

They travelled far more often now. As nomads, Thearans spent a fair amount of time marching through the desert, and their camps were built to be quickly and easily taken down. But before Kerberos became their leader, travel was slow and Aella's tribe spent days or even weeks in the same place, training, hunting and talking. Now, however, they walked almost every day, and only set up camp to sleep and eat. Omas was a gigantic country, the vast majority of it merciless desert, so even at this pace they would take a long time to get anywhere worth going.

They headed south, for Tarsius, to trade and replenish supplies. Aella hated Tarsius; it was far too busy. Thousands of people packed into a tiny trading settlement, talking and shouting and shoving. Just the thought of it made her shudder. Most of the time she stayed in the camp while the others ventured in to trade for what they needed; Thearan tribes set up camp outside the walls of Tarsius while smaller groups travelled into the settlement itself. Quite often, there would be more than one tribe camped outside, and fights often broke out. But within the walls of Tarsius, there were no fights. Even rival tribe leaders could sit shoulder to shoulder at a tavern and share a meal without shedding blood. Now, of course, Kerberos' tribe had grown far too large to invite challenge, and even if there were other tribes camped outside the settlement walls, they would keep their distance from the camp-site of the Son of Sithares.

Several of Kerberos' most devout followers referred to him by that name, and it still made her uncomfortable. He was incredibly powerful with Fire Magic, there was no doubt; but the son of a God? She thought he either invented the name himself or his fanatics started it, and he encouraged them. Either way, it struck her as self-aggrandising and boastful, and a man such as Kerberos shouldn't have needed to rely on a title to show his power.

She was walking with her mother in companionable silence. They didn't spend quite as much time with each other now as they used to, though they still saw each other most days. Helene was as quiet as she was, and Aella found comfort in their shared silences. They still talked about battle, and Fire Magic, and the heroes of Old Theara; but for now, she was happy not talking. The walk was too hard for talking, anyway. The grey sand this far out in the desert was soft and smooth, and the dunes caved under their feet like water. Climbing a dune took a huge amount of strength and stamina, and they were endless.

Aella's mind turned to their destination once again. Tarsius was on the other side of the country, and on the other side of the Omasi Mountains. The mountains ran from the north east all the way to the south west, cutting through the desert like a jagged saw blade. Puncturing the very centre of the mountain range and sitting squarely in the centre of Omas itself was the gigantic volcano, Sitharkos; known by the Thearans as the Heart of Sithares. They would most likely not be passing nearby the volcano, but they would have to cross the mountains to get to Tarsius.

Although it was difficult, Aella enjoyed travelling over the mountains a great deal. There was more life, for one thing. Trees and animals were far more common on the slopes of the mountains, and even fresh water. Aella loved climbing, and loved the view of Omas from up high. From the top of the southern slopes, the massive walls and the royal palace of Omatus were visible on the horizon.

Some tribes actually lived permanently in the mountain ranges, staying out of the desert in caves and small clearings. They were fierce fighters and were very protective of their territory, which was odd for the nomadic Thearans. She couldn't imagine living in one place for that long. They also had to share their territory with a species of particularly vicious cat called the Omasi Sand Panther. Sand Panthers, despite their name, lived almost exclusively in rocky territory, and were especially common throughout the Omasi Mountains. They were notorious killers, known for killing for sport as well as food. Aella had several terrifying memories of her old tribe fending off Sand Panther attacks while travelling the mountains. Sand panthers always killed at least a handful of Thearans before either being killed themselves or disappearing into the mountains like silky black shadows.

She wasn't particularly worried about Sand Panthers any more, however; not only was their tribe thousands strong and still slowly growing, they wielded Fire Magic. The panthers hated fire. She was mostly looking forward to climbing again, and maybe spending some more time with her mother in the mountains as they did when she was little. They used to climb to the highest point they could reach and sit for hours, talking and pointing out distant landmarks. It was on one of these mountain peaks that Helene first told her the story of Roxane, the Fire Mage who destroyed the entire army of Omatus. They sat facing Omatus, and her mother pointed at the city and the desert as she told the story, describing the movements of the ancient warriors. Aella was spellbound, picturing the battle vividly as her mother gestured and spoke.

The journey from where they were now to Tarsius would take months, and though the tribe was moving at a brutal pace, she desperately hoped she would have time to stop in the mountains, even briefly. Somehow, she doubted her hopes would change anything.

Two weeks later, they reached the foot of the first mountain. They camped for a night before starting the climb. Aella set her tent up next to her mother, and they built a campfire together.

"How long has it been since we last climbed the mountains?" her mother asked. She glanced up; Helene looked pensive, and a little sad. She cast her mind back, and nodded when she found the memory.

"Before Kerberos. More than ten years." Most tribes visited Tarsius at least once a year, especially the smaller ones. Aella's tribe used to as well, before they joined the massive tribe belonging to the 'Son of Sithares'. Now, however, they were large enough that they could raid the settled cities of Omas without fear of defeat. They'd been raiding the cities on the western coast for the last thirteen years, travelling up and down consistently from one city to the next. The desert on that side of the country stretched all the way to the ocean; it didn't become greener as Omatus and Tarsius did to the south, so their journey was just as difficult as travelling through the middle of the desert.

"I would very much like to climb with you again, little warrior," Helene said quietly, "and look out over Omas." Aella nodded, taking her mother's hand in her own.

"I would like that too." Helene smiled, and they talked for a while about climbing. Her mother's smile always made her happy. They talked until the sun started reaching the horizon, then hunted together. This close to the mountains, there was far more food; they killed three Diamondbacks and two Omasi Huntsmans. The spiders were less common in the mountains than on the south east coast, and slightly smaller than the coastal variety, but there were enough of them to hunt.

Aella took the lead; Helene was nowhere near as stealthy as she was. Her mother was a great shot with a bow, however, and once Aella spotted their prey, her mother shot it from at least thirty metres behind her. They arrived back at their campfire shortly after the sun set and invited Natasa, Timothea, and Erasmus to share their hunt. The five of them ate and spoke amiably until all the food was gone, and Aella went to sleep happy, full and glad that her mother felt the same.

They reached the opposite side of the mountains three weeks later; and just as she hoped, Aella and Helene had time enough to climb to a high peak overlooking the south of Omas. The climb itself felt alien to her, but she dismissed it as a consequence of time; she hadn't done this in more than a decade. But as soon as they reached a wide shelf of stone, flat except for a large boulder on the outer edge, she suddenly remembered being here as though it were only the day before. They sat on the flat stone for a few moments, regaining their breath. Then Helene stood and moved to the edge, leaping lightly up onto the boulder and sitting right on the precipice. Aella joined her, and once again she stared out at the enormous desert with her mother, feeling that same sense of wonder. The wind whistled around them, but at this height there was no stinging sand blown with it, and the breeze was refreshing on her sweating skin.

They sat for almost half an hour in comfortable silence. Finally, Helene spoke.

"You've been sparring with more people lately," she said. She said it conversationally, but there was an unmistakable edge of concern in her voice.

"Yes," she replied, "but I never use the Fire Magic in the blades. Not in front of anyone."

Helene nodded. "But you're no longer hiding your skills in combat?"

"No."

"You're older now, Aella. But you're still vulnerable, especially with-" She cut herself off, and even at the top of the mountain with no one but the two of them, she glanced around before continuing. "-with Kerberos in charge."

"I know that, mother. And he has noticed me sparring. But if I don't challenge him, why would he attack me? As

99

one of his tribe, he would just see me as another warrior fighting for him."

"But if he thinks you're strong enough to challenge him, he might want to kill you before you do."

Aella stopped, thinking about it. The intense stare he gave her every time he watched her fight supported Helene's theory. It was a menacing stare; there was nothing benevolent in Kerberos' eyes. She shook her head, angry at herself. She'd already become arrogant of her abilities, and ignored her mother's wise advice.

"It's too late now," she said, more harshly than she meant to, "He's seen what I can do. If he wants to kill me, he will. But he doesn't know the limits of my power yet."

"You don't either, yet," Helene said quietly, "don't overestimate yourself, Aella. That will get you killed, especially against a warrior such as Kerberos."

Aella stared at the desert spreading out below them. Helene taught her to think tactically and to fight with her mind just as much as her body. They spent less time together lately, and Helene's lessons were apparently wearing off. She couldn't believe she could be so stupid; she turned herself into a target for Kerberos and his most avid followers. She knew she was talented, and there was a massive well of magic within herself, regardless of Helene's warnings of overestimation. But even so, she may not win a direct fight against Kerberos; especially if his fanatics attacked too.

She watched him training whenever she could. It was almost always with Athanasius. Even considering Athan's drastic improvement, Kerberos moved easily and almost thoughtlessly, as if they were performing a dance practised hundreds of times. She was still a far better warrior than Athan, but seeing how Kerberos moved unnerved her. The prospect of fighting him wasn't an appealing one; not only was he inhumanly talented, he was also utterly brutal and merciless. He wouldn't hesitate to make an example of her in some gruesome way; *Here is what happens when I am challenged.*

Even at a young age, she'd never feared a fellow Thearan. She never doubted she would win a fight against any of them, if she needed to. But Kerberos instilled a cold flush of doubt in her mind since the moment she first saw him fight, and the feeling never went away.

She wished she could train against someone as talented as Kerberos. Someone she could trust. She wanted to be able to unleash her full power in battle, just to see what her limit was. The power she felt, especially while wielding her Fire Blades, was unbelievable. Her mother had no idea; not because she was hiding it, but because she didn't know how to describe it.

"I will be careful, mother," she said. The conversation turned to Tarsius; it was further north than Omatus, and they saw it slightly clearer than the massive city to the south.

"It always looks so peaceful from up here," Aella said. Helene smiled. "You really don't like Tarsius, do you?"

When she shook her head emphatically, Helene laughed into the wind the way she used to. She liked Tarsius, and was more often than not one of the warriors who went in to trade, while Aella and her father trained and hunted.

"I don't know how you can stand to be there long enough to trade and buy supplies. It stinks, it's crowded, and Tarsi food is disgusting!"

"Every city stinks, Aella. And every city is crowded. Our way of life suits you, which makes you lucky. But for most, cities are a beacon of civilisation; a place to connect with others, to trade and share and experience all of Pandeia in one place. So the stink and the crowds are worth it to people who want that experience." She stared at the small, distant settlement as she spoke. A mischievous smile tugged at her lips.

"You are right, though; Tarsi food is disgusting."

They both laughed, and Aella forgot all about Kerberos in that moment.

Atillus

Atillus screamed and thrashed against the guards holding him. They both fell to the floor like toys, not expecting Atillus' sudden burst of strength. He stood for a moment, staring at his father with unmasked hatred. It took every bit of willpower he possessed not to burn every living person in that hall to ashes. Breathing deeply and unevenly, he tried to get his emotions under control before the fire burning in his soul was unleashed upon his father. He saw an unfamiliar expression on Thorinos' face as they stared at each other. It looked to him almost like regret.

He couldn't take any more. He walked as quickly as he could from the great hall.

Watching that fight was the most difficult experience of Atillus' life. He argued with Amares before the feast about what might happen if they showed up together. Amares was stubbornly confident, and over-simplified things the way warriors often did. Atillus knew better, and tried to convince the beautiful Thearan man it would end in trouble, even if swords weren't drawn. He said he didn't show up to most feasts, and no one would notice if they weren't there. It was true, and Amares knew it; they never went to feasts together, and Atillus only showed up to a half dozen in as many years.

But for some unknown reason he refused to divulge, Amares suddenly decided the Argyris family feast was of huge importance. Atillus stormed down the great black stone stairs that lead from the Argyris family palace down to the street in the Noble district of Omatus. He was furious and distraught. As well as losing the person he loved, his father all but disowned him in front of all of the guests at the feast. He mocked Atillus for his love. He proved Atillus could never live up to his expectations or even be considered his son. His chance at the crown was completely lost.

He was breathing heavy before he even reached the street, though out of emotion rather than exertion. When he stepped onto the stone paved street, he stopped and looked around himself, fuming and conflicted, not knowing where to go and not knowing how to process his feelings. Dimly, through his rage and grief, he realised he left the palace without taking any belongings with him. Atillus set off along the street. His legs were shaking and there were tears in his eyes. He felt pain in his hands and realized he was clenching them into fists so tightly his nails were cutting his palms. He walked blindly for what felt like a long time without looking where he was going. The image of his father beheading Amares wouldn't leave him, instead playing itself over and over again vividly in his mind's eye. Closing his eyes didn't help. He walked faster, hoping but not really believing he may be able to outrun the horrible events of the feast. After a while walking at speed, he reached one of the many small entrances to the kitchens and slave's quarters of the Royal Palace and slipped inside without thinking. He wasn't fully aware of wanting to come here, but it made sense. There were slaves rushing around at a more commonly used entrance further down, and the bustling sounds of preparation for a feast greeted him. The Megalos family must be feasting also. This day meant nothing to Atillus, but it wouldn't have surprised him to learn it was some important anniversary. Regardless, the noble families of Omatus were constantly hosting feasts. He wasn't very worried by the slaves or general business of the palace; this particular doorway was rarely used, and the slaves apparently had more than enough on their minds. It was through this doorway that he first reached the Royal

Library at ten years of age. He still used it even now, to get into the small room with the odd light and magic tomes.

He knew the way through the cramped corridors without even looking, and was inside the library within moments. Despite its labyrinthine size and layout, Atillus learned how to navigate the library well over the years. The door into the pitch black and horribly silent space of corridor leading to the small room was broken when he first emerged, and he didn't wanted it resealed; going through that hell once was more than he could bear. So in the years since first discovering the room, he cleared away the remnants of broken door and stone, and simply dragged a small bookcase in front of the doorway. He needn't have bothered; even he'd taken a long time to find the door, and he was quite sure he was the only person to explore the library in a long time. But it was in his nature to be cautious and cover his tracks, and so he did.

He pushed the small bookcase out of the way and slid it carefully back in place behind him; he fashioned a couple of handholds on the back of the thing to be able to move it from within the corridor. He entered the small room and sat at the reading desk. He sighed heavily, put his head in his hands, and wept.

A short time later, Atillus knelt at the ornate chest at the far end of the room and picked up the book bound in fire. He'd read it many times, but it was somehow a slightly different book each time. Some stories contained within never changed, and the introductory chapter was always the same, but other than that the book rewrote itself between each reading.

After the first time he touched it, he was never harmed by its perpetually burning cover. In fact, he was completely invulnerable to heat and fire of any kind now. He tested himself many times, and remained unburned. Holding the book now gave him strength and peace, and he knelt in front of the chest for a few moments, simply holding the book in his hands. The peace he gained from Sithares' book was short-lived, however. His father's words

104

echoed in his head: *You will never be a real man. You will never be head of this family. You will never be King.* It made Atillus unspeakably furious; Thorinos had no idea what his disowned son was capable of.

So show him, then.

Atillus hadn't heard Sithares talk in a long time. As relief and a fierce kind of exultation pulsed through him, he realised he desperately missed the voice of the God.

"How would I show him? He won't allow me near him after today."

Do what he cannot. Spread the fire and destroy those who must be destroyed.

Atillus suddenly understood. If he pulled it off, his father might even forgive him and accept him back again. He put the book back down in the ornate chest and stood. *I'm already inside the Royal Palace,* he thought with a savage grin. *Time to show my father what kind of man I really am.*

He waited until he was sure it was the dead of night. As a child, Atillus explored the Royal Palace extensively, without ever being noticed. He was seen a few times, but since he first entered through the slave's quarters, he stole a slave's chiton and kept his head down. Whenever he was noticed, he acted subservient and scurried in a different direction. Over the years, he learned to navigate the palace just as expertly as he could the Royal Library, or even his own home. Wearing a slave's chiton once again, he walked quickly but quietly to the Royal Quarters. The corridors were deserted. He turned the last corner onto the walkway leading straight to the King's chamber. There were two heavily armed and armoured guards posted outside the door. They were alert and perfectly still, standing with the discipline of well trained soldiers.

Atillus didn't slow down. He saw the guards posture change slightly as they noticed his presence; their grips tighten on the hilts of their swords, their feet shuffle a little wider into a combat stance. He cursed inwardly. These men couldn't be taken lightly and, nor bribed. But there were ways to out-think an enemy, no matter the situation. Karak taught him that.

He slowed his walk and whispered when he was still a few steps away from them. They both leaned forwards and turned their heads slightly, as he knew they would. He stepped in between them and leaned forward as well, and they moved even closer. They were wearing heavy belts which held a sword on the left side and a dagger on the right. Atillus slid both daggers from their sheaths and buried them in their owner's throats before the two realised he'd moved. He grabbed them both and held them tightly to himself while they convulsed, trying to minimise the noise. He could do nothing about the choking, gurgling sounds they made, and it sounded loud in his ears, but the door to the bedroom was thick and he was sure that no sound would carry through.

When he was sure they were dead, he carefully laid them on the floor. He eased the huge door to the King's chambers open as slowly and quietly as he could, slipping inside as soon as he could fit. He left the door ajar and crept into the room. The King and Queen were still asleep. Atillus breathed a sigh of relief. He moved closer to them, as silently as possible.

The King muttered something and rolled over. Atillus moved to within a few feet of the sleeping couple and stood over them for a few moments, picturing himself laying in the Royal bed. His father's words once again echoed in his mind and his fury grew. His heart started beating faster and his hands tightened into fists. A violent red glow started to light up the room. It grew brighter and Atillus felt fire rising in his body. The glow approached

106

the strength of the morning Sun. Heat came off him in waves. Atillus let it build until he held enough power to incinerate the two sleeping people in front of him.

Finally, the King and Queen woke, confused by the heat and light. The King stared at Atillus for a moment, too bewildered to be scared yet. Atillus pulled his lips back from his teeth in a savage grimace, and screamed "This is from the Argyris family!"

King Andron Megalos started saying something in reply, but Atillus had already unleashed a massive burst of intense flame right at the bed, engulfing the King and Queen. A deep, rumbling boom battered the walls, the glass windows shattered, and the two burning Royals screamed. Atillus was sure he made enough noise to wake at least a few people. While the King and Queen burned, screaming, he took a scrap of paper from a pocket within his chiton and dropped it on the floor. Then he ran out of the room.

He walked quickly, head down, past a few half-awake slaves and a pair of fully alert guards as they rushed to investigate the disturbance. Other than that, the corridors were still deserted and he was able to slip into the slave's quarters and down the narrow walkways to the library. Once back in the secret room he sat in the reading chair, satisfied. He smiled as he thought about what Thorinos' reaction would be. He'd walked into the Royal Palace alone, unarmed and unarmoured, and assassinated his father's biggest enemy single-handedly. And all after his father disowned him and told him he wasn't a real man.

Well, he thought, *we'll see how much of a man Thorinos thinks I am now.*

Akakios

Akakios, Royal Guard of Omatus, rushed through the corridors of the palace. Eugeneia, a fellow guard, kept pace beside him. They turned the last corner and saw the thick wooden door to King Andron's bedroom standing open. The guards posted for night duty were slain, laying in a huge pool of blood. Akakios felt his heart thump painfully in his chest. They kept running, unsheathing their swords as they arrived at the entrance. Eugeneia got to the door a step in front of him and slipped inside, her mouth forming a grim straight line as she stared at her fallen comrades. He followed immediately after, saw the bed, and uttered a wordless cry. Eugeneia was already searching the room for intruders. Akakios stood staring at the scorched bed, his sword all but forgotten in his limp hand. He lowered his eyes, his mind racing. The King and Queen were dead. King Andron wasn't particularly well loved, and Akakios himself didn't cared for him one way or the other, but he failed in his duty as a Royal Guard. There would be consequences. He saw something on the floor and frowned, distracted. He bent to pick it up, realised he was still holding his sword, sheathed it and bent again. It was a piece of paper with small, neat writing printed in the centre. It read:

The throne belongs to the Argyris family. Vacate the palace and rescind your claim.
This is your only warning.

Akakios felt his whole body grow suddenly cold. He wasn't a guard when the Argyris family reigned, but he knew as well as anyone how bitter the fight between families was. A fragile peace had held since the Megalos family took over, but if the fight was starting up again...

Like most of the Royal Guards, Akakios was a mercenary. He had no particular loyalty to any family in Omatus. He took pride in his competence, and when the money was good he was willing to risk his life to protect his charge. But the Megalos family only barely paid enough for soldiers like Akakios to show up. If an all-out war started between noble families once again, he had no interest in fighting for his now deceased King. He knew quite a number of his fellow guards would feel the same. He showed the note to Eugeneia, and after reading it she stared for a moment before looking at him with an expression that matched his thoughts.

"The Argyris family... such a blatant act of treason would mean they could never legitimately take the throne back."

Akakios nodded. It was the only reason the war between families stopped in the first place.

The Argyris family ruled for a thousand years, and over that time the people grew to hate them. When they were overthrown, it was with the support of all the other noble families in Omatus. Since then the throne of Omatus was won and kept based on votes from the nobles and more powerful merchants. The Megalos family were well loved, and Andron ruled for decades with no problems. The throne wasn't openly contested, although nasty rumours were spreading about Andron and his family and were gaining traction among the slaves, guards and lower merchants. The noble families weren't aware of such rumours, but if all of the rest of Omatus was aware of them, it was only a matter of time before they were heard by the powerful. And then the noble families might decide the Megalos heirs shouldn't be inheriting the throne after all.

Akakios doubted the Argyris family would ever be supported again, but it couldn't hurt their chances at the crown if the most powerful family in Omatus was stripped of their title. Even if the Argyris family didn't take over, this surely meant the bad blood between families would rise to the surface once more. For people in Akakios' line of work, this was almost certainly a death sentence. If he didn't die in an outright fight against the guards of a rival family, he could be killed by an assassin as the two guards outside the Kings chambers were. Or, if the rumours were true about the temper of Andron's eldest son, he could be executed by his new King for any number of reasons. Or he could even be killed by a civilian if the Megalos family gave reason for unrest among the masses.

Akakios knew being a royal guard meant facing danger, but if he wanted to be involved in an all-out war he would have hired himself out to some army, or joined a Thearan tribe. He wasn't a coward, but he was also not willing to die for a petty squabble between spoiled noble families. He would need to report the King and Queen's death of course, but after that he would disappear. He shared another look with his partner, and knew she was thinking the same thing.

Omatus was about to become a war zone.

Dakesh

Tarsium was mesmerising. He'd heard of the other countries of Pandeia, but he'd never travelled as he was too intent on training to spend any time away from Shanaken. He arrived in Azar a handful of days ago, and was still amazed by everything he saw. Azar was the largest district in Tarsium, he learned, and it was far larger than any of the five hubs of the *Kashainuukza*; probably even larger than all of them combined. It was beautiful, and busy, and alive in a way he wasn't used to. There were no giant trees, although every now and then he saw a building made using Shenza steel twisted into organic shapes the way the cities were built in Shanaken. They looked jarring to him, almost naked; they weren't built into the limbs and trunks of enormous trees like they were supposed to be. But as out of place as they looked to Dakesh, they still seemed to fit with the other buildings in the streets of Azar.

Tarsium was a hub for all of Pandeia, and had been for thousands of years. The architecture of every country and culture was present on every street in the three districts of Tarsium. Right next to the Shenza steel building, Dakesh saw a sturdy hut made from thick wooden planks, and next to that he saw a massive tent made from silver scaled animal pelts. In the distance he saw a mountainous hulk of a building which seemed to be made from pure marble, looming above the entire district.

And then there were the people themselves. The Tarsi were incredibly odd-looking and mysterious. The most noticeable thing, though far from the most shocking, was their height; they were about half the height of a normal person. Their skin was a mottled grey, their heads completely devoid of hair, apparently regardless of age. They had massive silver eyes with vertical slits for pupils, and shockingly large hands with long, dexterous fingers. Dakesh also saw Thearans and Omati wandering the Tarsi streets. He couldn't help but gawk at every person he saw. Thearans and Omati looked much the same, but Omati people seemed to be the paler versions of their more wild countrymen. Thearans had very dark skin, with vibrant gold eyes and pure white hair; Omati people had a more bronzed skin colour, pale brown eyes and blonde hair. He felt like he stood out, with his long black hair, pale skin, and violet eyes. He made a conscious effort to avoid other Shenza, and to keep clear of any Shenza buildings he encountered. He chose an old wooden inn a street away from the closest Shenza house, and traded his old steel sword for a fortnight's stay. He also knew he needed to get rid of his clothing; it clearly marked him as *Daishen*, elite warrior among the Shenza. He liked what the Thearans wore, and found a Thearan tent stall to trade his layered mottled tunic for an animal hide vest and a desert-worthy travel cloak.

The journey was tiresome so far, as Dakesh hadn't granted himself any time to rest until he'd completely left Shanaken. He ran for three days after fleeing the battle, and passage across the narrow strip of ocean between Shanaken and Tarsium proved to be exhausting. Shenza didn't carry much into battle, and didn't believe in ownership so much, so they only carried coin on them for trading with other cultures who were much more focused on money and belongings. It was Dakesh's second day in Tarsium and he'd already almost completely run out of coin. He had a few items he supposed he could trade if it came to that, such as his small collection of potions made by the Shenza healers, and his fishing gear which could pack into a small pouch on his belt. He had a small supply of dried Neluud meat on him too, and heard it was fairly valuable in other countries, but he needed that for himself.

He wasn't sure how much longer he'd be able to afford food.

His room at the inn was larger than he expected. There was even enough room to perform his *Zuunshai*, the blade dance. He was glad to be able to do it away from the many strange faces on the Tarsi streets. He needed to dance every night to keep his skills as sharp as his new blade, so if he was forced to, he knew he would have danced on the street rather than not dance at all. He wouldn't have enjoyed it at all though, he knew. Every warrior in Shanaken performed the *Zuunshai* every day. Not only was it a practice of deadly and efficient combat moves, it was essential to keeping the body strong and the mind in tune with the body.

After his *Zuunshai*, he wandered the streets to experience Tarsium. He became more comfortable being outside the longer he stayed, although the voice in the back of his mind was constantly urging him to keep moving. It was only a matter of time before the *Duulshen* sent someone after him.

Once his money ran out, he took up work as an assistant blacksmith. He spent a lot of time learning the craft in Shanaken, as with all Shenza, and forged his old blade himself like all warriors should. The Shenza were revered for their smithing, and it was easy to get the work; all he needed to do was find a nearby forge. They paid well and he enjoyed the work. He managed not only to survive, but to build up a pouch full of Tarsi coin, which could be used across all of Pandeia.

As much as he enjoyed his time in Tarsium, Dakesh knew he had to move on as soon as possible. After two moons waxed and waned he decided his time had come. He informed the blacksmith, and turned down several offers for a rise in pay, each far more than the last, before the man understood that Dakesh's decision was made. He paid the last of what he owed to the inn keep, took one more meal in their main room, and left.

From Tarsium, Dakesh travelled next to Tarsius, which was a port and small extension of Tarsium on the shore of Omas. Omas was the largest land mass in Pandeia that Dakesh was aware of, although it was mostly an unforgiving and inhospitable desert. It was as far from Shanaken as Dakesh could go. He felt the weight of his distance from home as he stepped off the massive barge which carried him here. The barges that travelled between the three countries of Shanaken, Tarsium and Omas all looked exactly the same, and Dakesh was shocked and even a little upset to see they were made from the wood of *Laknuudza*, the enormous trees in his home country. He couldn't remember ever hearing about the *Laknuudza* being felled, and had never seen the wood other than as part of a whole living tree before. He wanted to ask the elders about it, but that was no longer an option for him.

All Dakesh ever knew about Omas was that it was one giant desert shared between two people: the Thearans, who were nomads who actually lived out in the desert itself and never settled down anywhere; and the Omati, who lived in a gigantic city on the south east coast of the country called Omatus, as well as smaller cities scattered around the country. That was where Dakesh was heading, although he thought the nomadic lifestyle of the Thearans would be easy for him to get used to. The Shenza travelled a lot too, although they lived in one of the five hubs for months at a time before moving on. The only thing he may not get used to was the complete lack of trees. Dakesh had never seen a desert before. He knew they were nothing but sand, for untold kilometres in every direction. He wasn't sure how he'd feel about that until he saw it, but the thought of it terrified him a little bit.

Tarsius felt very similar to Tarsium in a lot of ways, but it was a tiny settlement as opposed to an entire country with three massive districts. There were a lot more Thearans and Omati on this side of the ocean though, and

114

on his way out Dakesh saw Thearan tents crowding around the mini-city for what seemed like forever, stretching into the distant horizon. Thearans swarmed everywhere, talking and fighting and trading. He was captivated by their culture; they seemed to genuinely love fighting and combat, and gave in to any emotion they felt, positive or negative. The weapons they wielded were beautiful and varied widely from spears to short swords to longbows made of what looked like black bone. Passion and energy poured from these people, and he turned off the road towards the tents to see more. The group he was travelling with didn't even slow, but he'd made no friends and didn't much care for their company besides. He wandered out into the camps, and soon realised there were actually many different tribes, each with their own leader and hierarchy. They were unapologetically violent with each other away from the city, but as soon as they crossed the border between the camp-sites and Tarsius, they were as friendly to their enemies as to their own tribes.

Dakesh attracted odd stares from the Thearan warriors. He realised he'd wandered so far he almost couldn't see Tarsius any more.

"*Gyol!*" One of the Thearans yelled at Dakesh. He turned and stared at the man. He was about the same height as Dakesh, but with much more muscle on his heavy frame. His eyes were a pale, dull brown, the same as his hair. His bronze skin was covered in scars, and his clothing was the same scaled animal hide as Dakesh's vest. The warrior spoke again.

"*Barl sonn teid fer gyol?*" The man asked. Dakesh knew just enough Omman, the language spoken by both Thearans and Omati, to know the warrior was asking him something about a tribe.

"I'm sorry, I don't know!" Dakesh replied, suddenly feeling acutely aware of his pale skin and black hair amongst this sea of pale haired warriors. But he saw another Shenza in Thearan's clothing. And he realised the man he was speaking to was Omati, not Thearan. He took

115

another look around the gathered crowd, and realised the tribes were far more diverse than they first seemed. The scarred Omati was talking again, and Dakesh swivelled to face him. He was screaming into the crowd behind him in what seemed to be a very negative tone, but shortly after a black haired, pale skinned Shenza man was standing before Dakesh.

"*Zalshan, nalek kesha danuud'de?*" The warrior said. The shock of hearing his own language spoken in this alien place was so great that at first the words didn't mean anything to him. Then the meaning sank in; *"Hello brother, I trust this day you're found well?"* Dakesh smiled at his fellow Shenza; suddenly the distance and the months fell from him and he almost saw the vibrant green of the Shanaken forests.

"I'm very well, thank you. I didn't think I'd see another Shenza so far from home!"

The warrior laughed and replied: "This is as close to Shanaken as I've been in a decade. What brings you here, if it's so far for you to travel?"

"I'd rather not discuss details if you don't mind, brother."

The man paused, his eyes finally glancing at the *Kaizuun* hilt in Dakesh's belt. His eyes swept quickly over Dakesh's bare arms and face, where the tattoos of the *Kaizeluun* should have been. His mouth set in a straight line. He nodded almost imperceptibly.

"Very well. Let's get back to Aniketos then," and the Shenza swept his hand back towards the scarred man who'd first spoken to Dakesh.

Aniketos spoke, and the Shenza, whose name was Dakai, translated. Aniketos was asking Dakesh which tribe he was going to join, which up until that moment hadn't entered Dakesh's mind. He answered that he wasn't sure, and asked if there was a good way to choose. That was met with raucous laughter from all the watching tribes. Dakesh, completely out of his depth, laughed along with the warriors.

116

"You pick the tribe for your own reasons, but you must remember, tribes live and die together. The tribe you pick will be your family." Dakai gave him a measured look. "Are you here to join a tribe? You seem to know very little about the tradition."

Dakesh wasn't about to lie to these vicious warriors, so he said "honestly, brother, I didn't even know it could be done. It's not why I was here. I'm here to start a new life. But I like what I've seen of the Thearan lifestyle, and if a tribe will have me, I'd gladly join." Dakai translated and cheers went up among the crowd. It seemed odd to Dakesh, as moments before he was convinced he was unanimously disliked by these strangers.

"Very well brother!" Dakai smiled and nodded. "Stay with these camps a while, Thearans settle at Tarsius for longer than anywhere else. It's one of the only places we can pick up supplies and where all warriors are the same, so there's no fighting."

Dakesh frowned. "If you don't want to fight each other, why is peace so difficult outside of Tarsius?"

"You obviously don't know our culture very well, or the reputation of the Tarsi!" Dakai laughed, and when he translated what Dakesh said, many others in the crowd laughed too. Dakesh knew little about the Tarsi, but having never travelled, his knowledge was based purely on rumour and hearsay. What he'd heard is that the Tarsi were mysterious and not to be trifled with. He'd heard that the only law they enforced in their cities was "no violence". Other than that, anything was legal in Tarsium and its smaller counterpart Tarsius. Anything and everything could be bought, sold or traded, and the Tarsi didn't care what happened in their lands as long as no one was hurt or killed.

He also heard those who broke that law disappeared soon after, and were never found again. He wasn't sure how much of it was true.

"The thing about Thearans is we *do* want to fight each other. We revel in violence. Fighting and killing are what

117

we do, and what we've always done. Occasionally, peace is necessary; we need to repair and replace our weapons, resupply food and clothing, and trade for anything else we may need. We enjoy coming here to trade, rest and prepare for the next fight. But if we stay too long, peace makes us weak; and Thearans despise weakness. So we don't stay long, and when we are away from Tarsius, we fight each other. We only maintain peace in Tarsius because the Tarsi are powerful sorcerers, and they don't allow fighting. We enjoy peace in small doses, but we *want* to fight. We need to. The purpose of every Thearan's life is to be the best warrior in all of Pandeia."

Dakesh was captivated. All he wanted was to be the best warrior he could be, and that was all the Thearans lived for.

The Shenza were holding you back. You belong here, where your talent and ambition will be rewarded.

That voice pierced Dakesh's mind again, and again, he knew it spoke the truth. So he decided. "What must I do, to join a tribe?"

"You must fight one of its members," grinned Dakai, "to the death."

Thorinos

Thorinos was visiting a few of the markets he owned with Alliphis when news of the King and Queen's death reached him. It was early on the morning after their assassination. Barely a few moments after finding out that the King and Queen were dead, a company of Royal Guards marched into the street, surrounding Thorinos and his son. One of the guards stepped forward to address him.

"Thorinos Argyris," he proclaimed in a voice loud enough to carry across the street, "you are charged with plotting the assassination of King Andron Megalos and his wife the Queen." Thorinos couldn't keep the shock from his face. Almost the entire street stopped and were watching, transfixed.

"Plotting... how dare you! I was only just told of their murder, of course I didn't plot it!" He gestured around him, his shock giving way quickly to outrage.

"Would I be walking around the market district with no guards if I'd just killed the King?" The guard hesitated, noticing that the crowd were listening to Thorinos.

"I'm sorry my lord, I'm under orders." The guard seemed to remember he was surrounded by his heavily armed fellow guards and his confidence returned. "Whether you are guilty or not is no concern of mine. Either way, I'm to escort you to the royal palace. Alliphis as well."

Thorinos was beyond words. He shook with rage and disbelief. Even after he proved his innocence, the accusation and arrest would mar his reputation significantly. He decided for now to let himself be led to the palace; there was no other choice. The damage had already been done. He exchanged a glance with his son and nodded. Alliphis followed him and they fell in with the company of guards, heading for the royal palace.

Atillus

Atillus stood in the crowd, completely unnoticed in the massive courtyard of the Royal Palace, watching his father and brother judged for his own crime. He was still wearing a slave's chiton, and not a single person so much as glanced at him. Thorinos and Alliphis were shackled and kneeling on the raised platform in front of the murmuring crowd. He felt a sweet but cutting swell of satisfaction at the sight of his father in chains.

"Thorinos Argyris!" a Royal Guard barked, "Alliphis Argyris!" The guard paused until the murmuring of the crowd died down to silence. "You are hereby charged with the assassination of King Andron Megalos, and his wife, Queen Korinna. This note was left in the Royal Chambers, clearly stating the involvement of the Argyris family."

Atillus stared intently at his father's face, watching the barely controlled rage and helplessness bubbling under the surface. It took constant conscious effort for him not to grin from ear to ear. His father and brother would either be executed or imprisoned and he would be able to convince his mother to take him back in the Argyris palace, where he would eventually win the trust of the household as the new head of the family. He would use all he learned in his years of researching politics and warfare, and win the trust of the other Noble Families; then he would win the throne. He could see it all in his mind's eye, and although he knew there were many variables and obstacles, he thought there was a chance he could achieve his goals. He would need to be careful and bide his time. And he knew his father and brother would have some words to say at this trial; they were innocent, after all, and they knew it. Atillus was anticipating the heightened emotions of the guards and public, along with the severity of the crime, would ensure that Thorinos and Alliphis' words were all but ignored.

"How do you plead?" The guard screamed to be heard above the low din of the crowd's judgement. Atillus noticed with growing excitement the tone of the crowd, the anger painted on every face, and the almost dismissive way the guard addressed the prisoners. Thorinos' head rose, scanning the crowd, and for a brief moment Atillus was sure those eyes met his. But there was no recognition or surge of fury, and Thorinos looked around for a few seconds more before raising his eyes above the crowd entirely.

"I am innocent!" he shouted, and there was an immediate swell of cries and booing from the crowd. He shouted something else at the top of his lungs, but the crowd utterly drowned him out. Atillus' joy soared. At that moment, victory felt as certain as the ground upon which he stood. The guard shouted an order, realised he couldn't be heard, and instead drew his sword and swept it horizontally at the faces of those in the crowd. Most of them took his meaning, and the noise slowly died down to its former murmuring.

"It was not me!" Thorinos screamed. "It was my son!" Alliphis' eyes went wide with shock and outrage, and he turned to stare at Thorinos, but Thorinos was addressing the crowd and the guard standing over them.

"I swear it, I am innocent! I swear to all the Gods in the heavens, I swear on the grave of my father! My son did this!" The crowd looked as though they were starting to listen. Perhaps they thought as Alliphis did; that Thorinos was placing all the blame on the man shackled next to him to save himself. Atillus knew better, and waited for what he knew his father would say next.

"It was Atillus Argyris!" The guard made another threatening gesture at the crowd to silence the explosion of shouting that followed. Atillus' heart hammered in his

122

chest. He expected this much; there was no way to avoid his name being mentioned during the trial. But although Atillus was prepared for it, he had no way of predicting the crowd's reaction, let alone the final verdict, with any certainty.

"Have you any proof?" The guard asked him. Thorinos frowned and thought.

"He has no proof!" someone shouted from the crowd, and a few seconds later another person added their voice: "He's guilty!"

"Silence!" The guard screamed at them. "The next person who speaks will join these prisoners and meet the same fate they do!" The threat worked wonders, and the crowd fell into an uneasy silence. Thorinos was still thinking hard. Suddenly his eyes lit up, and Atillus found himself anxious.

"The note!" Thorinos blurted, "The note that was left behind! Check the handwriting! There must be notes written by Atillus somewhere in my palace!"

Atillus almost laughed out loud. It was too perfect. He considered that when he wrote the note, of course. He forged Thorinos' handwriting almost perfectly; it wouldn't match his own. Although the sheer tone of desperate certainty and hopeful victory in his father's voice seemed to be winning over some of the crowd. Now instead of judgement, the tone of the murmuring seemed to be doubt and even a little sympathy.

The guard ignored the murmuring and regarded Thorinos directly. "Even if the note was written by Atillus, and you didn't commit the murder yourself... How can the Royal Guard be sure you weren't the one who ordered your son to murder the King and Queen?"

The crowd's volume grew a little and Atillus had to fight even harder not to smile. This was exactly the question he hoped the guard would ask. Now even if there was some shred of proof against him, and even if he was caught and brought to trial, he could simply play stupid and claim that his father ordered him to assassinate the

King and Queen and that he had no other choice; The idea was already planted in the minds of the people, and hearing it come from Atillus would just confirm what everyone was already sure of: Thorinos was guilty. Atillus didn't plan on being caught in the first place of course, but his back-up plan was set and ready if the worst came to pass.

Thorinos fought to remain calm, and lost. His face grew red and his breathing erratic. Atillus saw defeat in the man's eyes; he knew he was going to be either executed or imprisoned. This was a pivotal moment, and no matter how excited Atillus was he was fighting just as hard as his father to remain calm. When men were cornered, with no hope of escape, they fought their hardest. Atillus was prepared for anything his father could say.

"Put a price on Atillus' capture." Thorinos said, with far more confidence than he had any right to, "I will personally pay the reward to whomever captures my son. He has sullied the Argyris name. I disowned him and exiled him from the Argyris Palace last night, in front of hundreds of guests... witnesses! You will see! When he is captured, I will force him to admit his guilt in front of all of Omatus-" Thorinos paused and actually smiled. It looked vicious and animalistic.

"... and I will behead him myself."

Atillus rifled through his bedroom chamber as quickly as he could, taking anything of use or value, and stuffing it into the largest carry pack he could find. He left the courtyard before the trial concluded, as early as he dared without drawing attention to himself, moving slowly and humbly avoiding others in the crowd. As soon as it was safe to do so, he broke into a sprint towards the Argyris family palace. He knew the palace even better than he knew the royal library and all the tunnels leading into it; getting to his room undetected was easy.

Thorinos and Alliphis were both charged on suspicion of conspiracy to commit treason, and sentenced to jail until Atillus could be caught. He heard that much before he left, and the part of him not focused on escape and survival was absolutely thrilled. Once his belongings were packed, he left the way he came in, a window in the corridor just outside his chambers. He ran on the roof, keeping low, to the other side of the palace. A series of balconies at different heights allowed him to descend to the ground. This side of the palace faced the city wall, although most of the balconies were high enough to see over it. The lowest was twelve feet off the ground, but there were smaller windows and decorative ledges which made easy handholds. He ran to one of the smaller entrances into the city, one of the supplier entrances that the cooks and slaves used to bring food from the farms straight to the Noble family's households. They were guarded, obviously, but much less heavily than the main entrances, and Atillus predicted that the trial would have brought most of the Royal Guards to the Royal Palace and away from their standard duties.

Two guards stood at the small open doorway. Above the entrance, a huge slab of stone loomed, held in place by several massive metal chains attached to a lever in the lookout station directly above. Atillus knew an identical slab on the entrance's other side waited to be used in the rare instance of an attempted attack. The lookout was outward facing, however, and by the time the guard on the wall saw Atillus escaping, the stone slabs would do nothing to stop him. But Atillus planned on getting out without being noticed in the first place. And he'd learned how to hide in plain sight.

Artemisia

Artemisia saw a slave walking towards her carrying a large carry pack. Slaves coming in and out of the exit she guarded was normal, and seeing handcarts or carry packs was very common, as this was a supplier entrance. She would still need to search the pack and question the slave of course; she'd been placed on high alert since the assassination of the King and Queen the day before. They were on particular lookout for Atillus Argyris, and told he would try to escape the city if he hadn't already. Drawings of the Argyris' oldest son were handed to every guard station, already memorised by most of the guards, Artemisia included.

The slave who approached them looked nothing like Atillus Argyris of course, but Artemisia was a dutiful soldier and stared intently at his face to be sure. After reassuring herself that the slave leaving the city wasn't the now infamous Nobleman, she had no reason to hold him up beyond the standard search. She halted him while her fellow guard, Seleukos, took the carry pack and rifled through it. The slave kept his eyes downcast, but didn't fidget.

Seleukos frowned and looked up at Artemisia. She returned his look with raised eyebrows. He looked again into the bag and then at the slave.

"Why are you carrying this?" he asked. The slave replied without raising his eyes, keeping his voice low and respectful.

"These are some of the belongings of the criminal, Atillus Argyris." At the sound of the name, both guards snapped to attention, staring hard at the slave. He kept talking, oblivious.

"I belong to the Royal Family and I'm to take these before one of them Argyris' can get them. I don't know why. I'm to take them out of the city and meet with one of my masters outside the walls. That's all I know, I swear."

Artemisia glanced at her fellow guard, hesitated, then nodded. It was no business of hers if the Royal Family wanted to deprive the Argyris family of their son's belongings. And even if the slave was lying and stealing the bag for himself, there was no way Atillus was already outside of the city walls; the only reason the slave would be doing this was to try to escape slavery and buy his own freedom. But Royal slaves were branded, and he would be found and executed before long. Slaves made attempts like this occasionally, and Artemisia had seen them caught and executed by the guards who patrolled the farms outside Omatus every time. Dealing with rogue slaves was one of the main duties of the guards who patrolled outside the city, and she didn't want to go out of her way to deal with a possibly recalcitrant slave with a much more important duty to perform. Besides, if the slave was telling the truth, which was much more likely, then the consequences of stopping the slave from carrying out his orders would be severe.

"You may go, but be careful outside the city, slave," she warned, "the guards who patrol the farms are not kind to wandering slaves."

The slave nodded quickly, and took the carry pack when Seleukos offered it back. He scurried out the narrow entrance and into the desert. Artemisia ignored him the moment he left her sight and turned back to her watch. Seleukos glanced sideways at her.

"With all this treason and treachery, we're likely to have a new Royal Family in power soon. Care to place a wager?" Artemisia heard the smirk in his voice before she turned and saw it painted on his face.

"With all this insubordinate talk, you're likely to have a few bruises on that face of yours soon, especially if a superior officer overhears you. Care to show some discipline?"

Dakesh

Dakesh stayed outside of Tarsius far longer than he had in Tarsium. He wandered from camp to camp, from tribe to tribe, and stayed with each one a week or so before moving on. He learned a lot, and after a few weeks even spoke basic Omman. He was still confused about what exactly differentiated the tribes; they all devoted their time to combat, they all spoke the same language with all the same traditions and culture. They even laughed at the same jokes. Dakesh came to realise that what Dakai said to him was far more true than he would have believed; the Thearans fought simply for the sake of fighting. Even though they all shared the same country and the same culture, they killed each other constantly and mercilessly. Dakesh couldn't quite get his head around the concept of fighting and murdering those who shared the exact same values as himself, but at the same time, the Thearans made the idea seem so casual and matter-of-fact that he couldn't help but accept their way of life.

The tribes varied in size, from a handful of warriors to over a hundred. Dakesh enjoyed his time with each one, but when he came across Kerberos' tribe, he knew he'd found his new home. Kerberos was a giant of a man, pure blooded Thearan, with a bald head and a full beard of bright white hair. His gold eyes shone with intelligence and controlled rage. He gave off the aura of a crouching Zuzuk ready to pounce. The Zuzuk was a huge land-dwelling predator in Shanaken. They had rough, mottled green fur and pure black eyes, with massive black claws and two rows of jagged black teeth. Despite their size, they were dazzlingly fast, and surprisingly intelligent. As Dakesh looked at Kerberos, he felt more and more as though he were staring down a Zuzuk in the forest. It was unnerving, but also hypnotic. There was a deep, unshakeable power to Kerberos, and it was no wonder his tribe was the largest in Omas; they numbered in the thousands, and their camp-site was staggering.

He stayed with them for a week, but was certain he would join their tribe within the first day. There was a different atmosphere in their camp, a far stronger sense of unity and family than any other tribe. He went hunting with a couple of them, a young man called Erasmus and a younger woman called Aella. Erasmus was friendlier and talked a lot more, but Aella was clearly the better hunter. She moved silently, even when she wasn't trying to hide. Her movements were always measured and smooth, never hurried, and she only spoke when she felt it necessary. She was a pure blooded Thearan just like Kerberos, her smooth dark skin punctuated by stunning golden eyes and vivid white hair. Erasmus was Omati, and the difference, though subtle when spoken, was shocking to see when they stood next to each other. Erasmus' hair was a pale, flat brown, the same as his eyes. His skin was a pale brown too, though nowhere near so pale as Dakesh's own. His build was slight, where Aella had a true warrior's muscle. Erasmus carried a sword of Thearan Steel and a longbow. Aella carried a longbow too, and wielded two short swords with diamond-shaped blades. She also carried a few throwing blades, which seemed to be rare among Thearans. She sharpened and cleaned all of her weapons every day, and she also spent time after every hunt alone, practising in a similar manner to the *Zuunshai* Dakesh performed every day. She preferred privacy when practising though, and Dakesh only saw a glimpse of it before Erasmus pulled him away saying Aella would be furious to catch him watching.

They went hunting most days, which Aella said was much easier this close to the shore. She said there was much more game here as there were trees and grass, but Dakesh was shocked by how little hunting there was. He despaired at the thought of even less once the tribe started moving into the desert again. Still, hunting was exciting with the Thearans. Aella almost became invisible she was so stealthy, and Erasmus obviously hunted with her enough to know he'd be more help hanging back. They didn't need to talk at all to know where they both needed to go, and they seemed to already have a plan each time they hunted without Dakesh hearing a word between them. He stuck with Erasmus for a while, then when Aella realised he could be stealthy too, she started bringing him along with her.

The first time they went hunting, Dakesh hoped for something similar to the Kenad; a fat, flightless bird hunted and even bred by the Shenza for food. It was incredibly tasty, and a staple of the Shenza diet. What he found instead what so repulsive that at first he thought the Thearans were testing him or making fun of him to see how he'd react. Aella stalked silently through the trees, Dakesh beside her. She put her hand up suddenly to stop him, and once he'd stopped she slowed and stopped a few feet in front of him, facing a nearby tree. She turned to him and motioned towards the tree, and then put a finger to her lips, raising her eyebrows to ask if he understood. Dakesh nodded, and kept quiet. Aella turned and silently nocked an arrow to her black longbow, kneeling and aiming at the tree in one smooth motion. She loosed after a few seconds, and Dakesh was impressed by how silent the bow was as the arrow streaked towards its prey. A dull wet thumping sound echoed through the trees, and an animal Dakesh didn't recognise fell out from the leaves, Aella's arrow jutting from its body. Dakesh started towards it, but Aella held up her hand again. She nocked and loosed three more times, each time killing another of the same animal. Finally, she stood and motioned for Dakesh to follow her. As they got closer, Dakesh realised to his disgust that the animals were actually giant grey spiders, about the same

131

size as a Kenad; their bodies were almost two feet long and about a foot thick. Their bodies were covered in a fine, mottled grey fur and their shiny black fangs were at least an inch long. Dakesh actually took a step back when he recognised what they were. He'd never seen a spider that big before. The forests of Shanaken were home to all sorts of spiders of course, but none of them got any bigger than the size of a man's hand. Then he realised that she'd killed four of them, and he had an awful feeling it wasn't for sport.

"Please tell me I'm not supposed to eat these," he said to Aella as she knelt by them and started pulling her arrows from their corpses.

"What else would we do with them?" she laughed. They bundled the spiders up in a rope and headed back to camp.

When they arrived, she cut off the abdomen of each one and threw it aside, stuck a metal rod through the corpses and set them up over a cookfire covered in oil and a few spices. When Dakesh looked at her in confusion, she explained that the abdomen, although the largest part, was also the worst part to eat as it contained the animal's guts, excrement and eggs. She said nothing of the many eyes that she'd left on the roasting animal, nor the uncomfortably large fangs. When the spiders were cooked, Aella offered one to him, and he accepted half-heartedly. He watched Aella and a few fellow warriors eat before starting on his own meal; he wasn't sure whether to cut through the skin to eat the flesh beneath, or take off the legs and face, or eat it some other way. It turned out to be far simpler than that; the Thearans just bit off chunks of meat regardless of what body part it was. Dakesh, fearing the worst, followed suit.

The legs were crunchy, with a fairly pleasant taste, though he suspected that was mostly just the oil and spices. When he bit into the body itself though, he was surprised at how much he liked it. The flesh was white, soft and tender, and tasted like a mix between Kenad meat

132

and Luduk, the large fish commonly eaten by Shenza. The spices used by the Thearans were delicious, and helped a great deal. Dakesh still completely avoided the face area, as it unnerved him, but he found after eating the rest that he was very happy with the meal. He went hunting with the Thearans every day after that, and very quickly settled into their way of life.

Eventually, the Thearans decided to pack up and keep moving into the desert. Dakesh made his mind up long before that he'd stay with them, but now he was forced into officially joining the tribe, which unfortunately meant challenging a fellow warrior to single combat. He spoke about it at length with Erasmus; Aella sat quietly with them, joining in the conversation only when she had something she thought worth saying.

"To the death of course," explained Erasmus, the day the tribe meant to leave. "Thearans are willing to accept anyone into their tribes, but you must prove firstly that you're a capable warrior, and secondly that you're willing to kill whoever stands in your way. You can issue the challenge to one you choose, or if someone doesn't like you or doesn't agree that you belong, they may challenge you." Dakesh wasn't challenged, thankfully, so he challenged a young warrior named Andreas. He'd been hunting with the warrior once or twice, and they'd never really gotten along. He felt awful about having to pick someone to kill, but he desperately wanted to be a part of the tribe, and he would have done anything to get away from the *Duulshen,* the elders of Shanaken, and disappear from their reach. By now, he was sure someone had been sent to kill or capture him, as they wouldn't take the dishonour of a stolen blade lightly. So, he challenged Andreas to combat, and later that day, they stood facing each other in a ring in the sand cleared of obstacles and surrounded by watching Thearans.

Dakesh drew his blade and waited for Andreas to move. He could feel his opponent's strength and energy; from the moment he drew his sword he sensed these things as clearly as he saw the sand, heard the slight breeze, and felt the sunlight on his skin. The magic of the sword still awed him, even as he was getting used to its power. He sensed the energy of every Thearan warrior nearby, and although individually he knew his power was greater than most of them, the sheer magic surrounding him was intense. It felt like standing in the centre of a ring of bonfires, waves of heat washing over him unceasingly. Even through the wall of energy, he felt a mountainous inferno of untapped magic to his left; if the rest felt like bonfires, this felt like the sun itself. Glancing quickly towards the source, trying to keep Andreas in his sight, he recognised the warrior straight away. He expected Kerberos, of course; but in the centre of that raging inferno of pure magic stood Aella, watching him intently. She was alert, but in a thoughtful way; ready to study the fight. She was unaware of the aura coming off her. He sought out Kerberos, curious, and saw the intense aura emanating from the leader. Though smaller than Aella's, it was more solid and seemed to run deeper. Dakesh blinked and turned back to Andreas, focusing on the fight once more.

His opponent wielded a Thearan spear, one of the most common weapons for Thearan warriors. Each warrior cut their spear to a length that suited their fighting style, some using short handles and wielding them like swords, and some using full spear-length shafts of wood. Andreas was one of the latter, his spear taller than he was. He stood with the butt of his spear resting on the ground next to his foot, eyes narrowed at Dakesh. The spearhead, made from Thearan steel, was about two feet long and diamond-shaped, with edges that looked razor sharp. Finally he swept the weapon into a fighting stance, and started moving slowly towards his opponent. Dakesh waited a little longer, then suddenly charged at Andreas.

He leapt at the last second, just as Andreas' spear lunged at his stomach. It passed through where he'd been with almost no time to spare, so fast he couldn't even consciously follow. He let the blade's magic guide his way, straining to focus on his new senses instead of trying to think. He flipped in the air, landed in a crouch behind Andreas, swinging his sword in a horizontal arc just as his feet hit the ground. The point of his blade just touched Andreas' calves, slicing the animal hide boots he was wearing and a tiny bit of his flesh. The spear appeared suddenly to Dakesh's right, heading straight for his face. He'd seen it before it happened though, and was already out of the way by the time it hissed past him.

Andreas looked furious, and a little confused. Facing each other now, they fought proper, and Dakesh had a hard time getting past the spear now Andreas was used to his speed. Constant thrusts and horizontal strikes bombarded Dakesh, and although he could parry them easily enough with the foresight granted him by his magic blade, he didn't have the time to return blows. Still, they were both breathing hard by now, and Dakesh could see Andreas starting to lose energy, but he'd never felt better. He was sweating, but the sword gave him more energy the more he fought. He also saw the toll his shallow cut was taking on Andreas' footwork; Andreas was taking small, almost ginger steps and avoided even that when he could. They kept fighting, Dakesh blocking and dodging furiously while Andreas attacked constantly. A forward lunge of the spear was swept aside by Dakesh's blade, but Andreas only used the momentum of the block, moving with Dakesh and twisting, swinging the butt of the spear at Dakesh's face. Dakesh ducked, but Andreas kept turning and this time the spearhead swung at Dakesh's belly. Dakesh leapt backwards, but the spear tore through his vest and ripped into skin beneath. Pain lanced through him, but he somehow knew without looking that it was a shallow cut. It wouldn't stop him from winning.

A surge of energy suddenly hit him. He twisted his head to the side as the spear streaked towards his face again. The lunge would have smashed straight through his nose had he remained where he was. His left hand darted up and snatched the shaft of the spear just below the blade, his own blade sweeping straight through the wood. The black blade sliced through Andreas' spear with almost no effort. Andreas looked at the end of the wooden shaft he was holding in utter disbelief. Dakesh drew his left hand back and before Andreas realised what was happening, threw the spearhead with all his strength. The spearhead moved so fast it couldn't even be seen; it punched straight through Andreas' head and kept going, impaling itself in a second warrior's chest with such force that she flew off her feet several metres before the point of the spearhead buried itself into the ground, pinning the unfortunate warrior to the dirt.

Andreas was still standing, the ragged remains of his head spurting blood. The broken spear shaft fell to the ground as his hands opened and closed a few times, grasping at nothing, before his corpse crashed to the ground. Dakesh was speechless, and numbly realised he wasn't even out of breath. He sheathed his sword. Wild screams erupted from all around him, and Thearans rushed at him from every direction. He felt a moment of panic before he remembered that Thearans loved combat and destruction. What he'd done apparently greatly impressed them. He had to admit, he was impressed himself. He'd never seen anything like it, and in that moment he felt incredibly powerful. He was a Thearan warrior now. He embraced his new tribe, cheered with them, and spent the rest of the night celebrating. The next day, they packed up and headed out into the desert.

Aella

Tarsius stood before them, the noise and smoke and smell making Aella's head ache even from a distance. It was an ugly, hunching beast of a city; buildings thrown together seemingly at random, every size and style pressed together violently. People from every country pushed and shoved each other, and shouting in every language was perpetually competing to drown the other out. Even outside its walls, Aella felt suffocated. She headed back to camp.

They stayed at Tarsius for far longer than Aella expected; Kerberos insisted on almost constant travel since taking over their tribe, but now he seemed content to settle down for a while. They took on new warriors, both from the many tribes camping near theirs and from Tarsius itself. Fights broke out almost constantly, though the warriors from her tribe won most of them. None of the other tribes worshipped Sithares, and the Fire Magic wielded by Kerberos' army was a keen advantage in one-on-one combat.

She never entered the city itself. Erasmus, Natasa, and Timothea all visited fairly often, and her mother went almost every day. Aella spent her time training, sparring against anyone willing, and hunting. She also travelled into the trees along the coast whenever she could, finding somewhere private to practice using the Fire Magic within her two ancient swords. She was powerful even without the Fire Blades, and unleashing that power made her feel free and light hearted; but since she never had much of a chance to practice, she wasn't as in control of the magic as she wanted to be.

After about a month, A potential new tribe member named Dakesh came hunting with her and Erasmus. He was Shenza, and although their tribe contained quite a few of the pale-skinned, black-haired warriors, he was striking. There was something different about him.

He was a far better hunter than Erasmus. While Erasmus usually hung back to let her make the kills, she realised Dakesh would actually be quite useful. The first time they hunted together, she killed four large Omasi Huntsmen, and when Dakesh realised what they were his face turned as grey as the mottled fur of the giant spiders.

"Please tell me I'm not supposed to eat these," he said to Aella as she knelt by them and started pulling her arrows from their corpses.

"What else would we do with them?" she laughed. She bundled the spiders up in her rope, and they headed back to camp. As she prepared their kills to eat, she had to explain to Dakesh that their abdomens weren't edible. He seemed to be of the opinion that no part of them was edible. After they cooked, he was hesitant to try eating the spiders, and sat staring at the large fangs as her and Erasmus started eating. He still looked sick as he tentatively tried the first bite. Exactly as she predicted, his expression changed almost immediately to pleasant surprise, and after the second bite it changed just as suddenly to outright pleasure. Her and Erasmus exchanged a glance, smirking and trying not to laugh. Every warrior who tried spider meat for the first time had the exact same reaction. It never failed to entertain the Thearans. Though Erasmus joined the tribe relatively recently, he grew up as a slave in the farmlands outside Omatus, where the huntsmans were most common. Like every other slave, he was only given a single meal per day by his Omati masters, so he took to eating the spiders for survival.

They went hunting together every day after that, and Dakesh became a closer friend to her than Natasa and

138

Timothea. A few weeks later, the tribe finally started packing to leave. Dakesh was talking with another Shenza named Dakai. She couldn't follow, as they were speaking in their native language; but shortly after the conversation, Dakesh challenged a young Thearan named Andreas to one-on-one combat. She was glad; he was pledging himself to their tribe.

The circle was formed around the two warriors, and Dakesh drew his blade. He took a moment to breathe; perhaps nervous, perhaps weighing Andreas. He turned suddenly and stared straight at Aella. For a single second, he looked at her the same way Kerberos' fanatics looked at their leader; pure, unmasked awe. She masked her feelings, simply staring back at him as though she hadn't noticed his odd expression. Then it was gone, and after a brief look at Kerberos, he blinked and turned back to Andreas.

The fight was short, but intense. Dakesh moved much faster than she first judged. He moved in a smooth, natural way, almost as if he knew where to move to avoid Andreas' attacks. Usually she was an accurate judge of combat abilities, but with Dakesh she was totally wrong. He was incredible.

He landed a shallow cut to Andreas' calves, and slipped past a sudden and vicious lunge at his face which even Aella might not have dodged. Andreas stepped up his efforts, laying on a constant stream of attacks. Dakesh dodged or blocked them all, but didn't seem able to counter. Andreas' calves were obviously suffering, however, and he was starting to slow down. Dakesh was apparently losing no energy at all. Quite the opposite; incredibly, he was speeding up.

Andreas suddenly landed a blow, slicing Dakesh's stomach. Dakesh didn't slow down. Andreas aimed a thrust at his head, and when he twisted aside to dodge it, his hand snatched the spear behind the blade. His own blade swept down through the wood as though it was fabric and without hesitating, he brought the spearhead back and threw it inhumanly quickly. Even staring intently at the battle, Aella only saw a slight blur as the spearhead flew. Barely a split second later, Andreas' entire head disappeared, and Timothea, who was watching from behind him, flew several metres backwards. It took a few moments for Aella to realise the spearhead killed her. Dakesh threw it so hard and fast it passed right through Andreas' head, impaled Timothea's chest, carried her several metres, and forcefully pinned her corpse to the ground.

Aella gasped as she watched Timothea die. Andreas was an expected casualty, but Timothea was simply watching the fight. Dakesh was equally as shocked by her death, judging by his expression. It was hard to be mad at him; he clearly didn't murder her on purpose. And besides, this meant he was a proper member of their tribe now. Although she mourned Timothea, Aella celebrated with the rest of the tribe that night.

Zanela

The forest chattered and whispered around Zanela as she sat alone in the canopy outside the city. A slight breeze rustled the leaves, turning her entire world into a vast, rippling green ocean. *Kuulshen* were all taught a healthy fear of the forest as they grew up, and even as a *Daishen* she wasn't immune to that lifelong fear. But the forest felt far safer to her now than the city.

Dakesh couldn't betray the Shenza, she knew it. He was angry at the *Duulshen* for refusing to name him *Kaizeluun*, but he would never steal the blade of another warrior. But w*hat if it's true?* There was nowhere for him to go but west, to Tarsium. The *Duulshen* said it was a haven for people who wanted to remain unfound; a place where lost souls went when they had no more growing to do.

She desperately hoped he knew better than to settle in such a terrible place. The soul couldn't grow in a city that squatted on the stony ground like the carcass of some dead beast. Far too many people packed into buildings made of stone and animal hide, never training and never wandering through the vibrant life of the forest. Slowly dying as their souls grew stagnant and the circle of life overtook them. She couldn't imagine anything worse. The thought of Dakesh's soul decaying as he hid from the *Duulshen* for the rest of his life in Tarsium brought stinging tears to her eyes.

But there was nothing she could do. Either the news was false and Dakesh was still fighting, or he was already fleeing Shanaken. The battle still raged on the northern shore; even if she could get to a safe position and watch from a distance, she would never find Dakesh amongst the chaos. And if the report was correct and he was on his way to Tarsium, there was no way she could catch up to him now.

Zanela breathed slow and deep, closed her eyes and hugged her knees against her chest. She breathed in the forest, listened to its song. She recited the three tenets to herself. They always gave her strength. *What's the worst case scenario?* She forced herself to focus on it. One of the only pieces of advice her father gave her when she was training for the warrior's tests was "Expect the worst, and come prepared.". She found it oddly helpful.

Dakesh either killed in battle or being marked an outsider for the rest of his life; those were the worst case scenarios. If he was named outsider, he would never be allowed in Shanaken again. He would be treated as a stranger by those he loved. But he would also be hunted for his crime. Taking the *Kaizuun* from another warrior was akin to taking their very soul. The Shenza didn't have much in the way of possessions. Everything contained within the Moving City was common property, belonging to all of the Shenza equally. They shared houses, food, and use of all other buildings and resources. The money gained from selling fish and other produce was returned to the *Duulshen* and distributed to any who needed it.

The only things an individual Shenza owned were their sword and the clothing they wore, and both were hand made by the warrior themselves. So taking one of the only two possessions a Shenza owned, one which took months of careful hard work to perfect, was one of the worst things one warrior could do to another. When the stolen blade was one imbued with magic and earned through the brutal Shadow Trials, the crime became even worse.

Zanela prepared herself by imagining Dakesh was already dead. She pictured it; his corpse laying on the forest floor somewhere, torn apart by a Zuzuk or sliced open by the blade of whomever was sent to hunt him down. The image burned in her mind and heart, but she

142

forced herself to see it clearly, and to accept it. If she moved through the pain now, it couldn't hurt her when it happened later on. She mourned Dakesh. She was alone now. Alone in the forests of Shanaken. *Expect the worst, and come prepared.*

Sunset turned the greens of the forest to gold, glittering in the breeze as quiet settled over Shanaken. Zanela perched at the very top of an ancient tree, staring out over the forest. Almost a year had passed since Dakesh disappeared. Almost a year of living alone in the forest. At night she slept in a small hollow she found near the top of a tree high up in the canopy. During the day she hunted and foraged for food. Every day she practised the *Zuunshai* and recited the three tenets.

A peaceful life. She grew used to the solitude. The forest always made her feel alive and connected to life. Best of all, she was free of her parent's judgement. She knew if she were to return to the city, she would most likely suffer the same fate as Dakesh when he was finally hunted down. The *Duulshen* would definitely view her as guilty. Who wouldn't? She ran out of the city the moment her brother was revealed as a traitor.

There was no way to find him, and nothing to go back to. She loved the forest, but knowing there was no choice in her being there made it a little less beautiful. She was attacked occasionally by predators, and was now learning their movements and habits. Zuzuk, the largest predators in Shanaken, slept most of the day away. They rose in the twilight before sundown, and used the low angle of the sun to their advantage, letting the light blind their prey.

For all their size, they moved as silently as a light forest breeze, and mottled green fur helped them blend perfectly into the trees around them. As massive as they were, they were sleek and agile. Their pitch black eyes burned with intelligence, and two rows of jagged black teeth

143

punctuated every low growl. Their claws were massive and razor sharp, able to slice through almost anything except Shenza steel.

She barely survived the first attack. No sound gave the animal away as it crept towards her. Its mottled fur moved with the rustling leaves in the soft breeze. She stared right at it without realising, until it pounced. If she was facing any other direction, she would have died almost instantly. Without thinking, she leapt sideways off the branch, falling until her shoulder smashed into a second branch and she grabbed desperately with her other hand.

Stopping her fall, she swept a leg up over the branch and caught her breath as silently as she could. Again, she heard nothing above her. The forest held its breath. Slowly, she slid her blade from its sheath. The silence was terrifying; not even the ever-present chirping of insects pierced it. In that quiet moment, she knew she was going to die. Even seasoned *Kaizeluun* didn't always survive against the mighty Zuzuk.

In ancient stories, the best fighters of the Shenza, precursors to the *Kaizeluun*, were blessed by Amalus and turned into Zuzuk to better protect the forests. They were bonded with Shadow Magic and shaped into invincible monsters. The rest of the Shenza were shown how to wield the magic in human form, and their combined power built the great *Kashainuukza*. After the city was built, the Shenza kept to the city and the forest canopy while the Zuzuk protected the forest floor.

It was said that over time, the Zuzuk forgot they were once Shenza; living in the forest without family and friends forced them to shed their human thoughts and feelings. Now, they roamed the trees, intent only on killing anything that didn't belong in their territory.

Zanela held her breath, listening for any hint of sound. Her heart beat so loudly she was sure the beast would hear it. She slowly rose into a crouch, ready to fight or dive again. Her sword was a comfort in her hand, light but dangerous. Her hand fit the grip perfectly, and it never slipped once it was unsheathed. She settled on the branch, as still as the tree itself.

Rustling leaves brought her attention to the left, above her. Barely a second later, a thick branch creaked softly behind her and she swept her blade around with all her strength just in time. The Zuzuk landed on the branch where she stood just as her *Shenzuun* swung through the air at its throat. She hit it at an angle, cutting its neck but not deep enough. The force of the beast's landing shoved her violently, but her blade was lodged in its neck. They struggled, the Zuzuk trying to bite her face and neck and Zanela trying to rip her sword out of its thick skin. It was massive, and made almost entirely of muscle. Every movement could have killed her. Every second being caught with it on the branch was another chance to be torn to pieces. It growled and shook its head as she held on to her sword desperately with both hands. Finally, it pulled backwards and snapped forward again, and her blade slipped free. She managed to keep it in her grip as she fell.

An enraged roar battered her ears as she smashed into another branch, flailing and slipping again. Her legs caught in a tangle of vines hanging off a lower branch, and she hung upside down, swinging and trying to catch her breath. Cracking sounds floated down to her; the massive beast jumped from branch to branch without trying to remain silent. Her heart resumed its normal pace as she realised the sounds were fading.

She grabbed the branch above her and cut the vines holding her to it. Her feet swung down and she sheathed her blade and climbed back up to the top of the tree. After she got over the terror of nearly being ripped to pieces by a massive, vicious predator, she moved to a quieter part of the forest. It was there she found the hollow in the top of the tree where she made her home. By the time she found it, the sun was gone. Darkness wrapped the forest in shadow and fear, and she cried herself into an uneasy sleep.

Dakesh

The Omati desert was bleak, harrowing, and brutal. The sand was grey, the rocks black, there were no signs of living animals and the few trees they happened across grew with bright orange and yellow leaves; Giving the disquieting impression of an endless field of ash and fire. It felt as far from Shanaken as it was possible to get, both literally and figuratively. Sand dunes rose and fell, the wind threw stinging grey sand into Dakesh's eyes and face; he'd never felt so vulnerable in his life. He realised how much he'd come to rely on the safety and reliability of the gargantuan trees the Shenza lived in. But he looked around him; his fellow Thearans were hard and unforgiving, and as vicious as the desert itself. Even as he suffered, he looked forward to the strength he knew the desert would forge in him.

He learned the Thearans weren't just great hunters, they were expert foragers and survivalists, able to locate and dig up food and water in the unlikeliest of places. Aella showed him what looked like a black rock half buried in the sand, but which turned out to be a kind of hard plant with roots that buried deep underneath the desert. He was shown how to harvest water from them, and that the flesh underneath the shell-like skin was not only edible, but blessedly juicy and refreshing. It tasted mostly like dirt, but the water contained in it more than made up for lack of flavour. He was shown how to tell when a ridge of sand was actually a greysnake lurking just under the desert surface, and how to kill them. They were also edible, but the fangs were to be very carefully avoided. He was taught

146

about Diamondback Lizards, which mostly lurked around trees and rocks, and were non-venomous, harmless but for a particularly vicious bite. Diamondback Lizards were edible too. Dakesh learned that almost everything but the sand and rocks themselves were edible if you knew how to prepare and cook it, and where to find it. The Thearans never ate anything without cooking it first, as they didn't trust anything that couldn't be cleansed by fire. The one exception was the rock-like plants, and only because they were consumed for their water content, and were counted by the Thearans as a drink instead of a food.

Dakesh grew used to carrying everything he needed on his own back; as nomads, Thearans needed to be able to pack up and move quickly, and they had no mounts to carry their tents or weapons. So everything a warrior needed, they were expected to carry themselves. Each warrior generally carried a small tent and bedroll, a supply of dried meats and spices, their weapons, and whatever money they owned.

Dakesh was told that unlike the rest of the Thearan tribes, Kerberos' followers worshipped the God of Fire, Sithares. It was explained to him that through prayer and proper worship of Sithares, a Thearan warrior could gain the power of Fire Magic; the ability to create and manipulate fire, among other things. Kerberos taught the prayer to all new tribe members in a group once he was convinced they deserved the power. Dakesh's eyes lit up when he learned of Fire Magic, and he felt a ravenous hunger for power.

You will gain this power. You are chosen.

Dakesh was used to the voice now, accustomed to its reassuring whispers. But the tribe had been travelling through the desert for what felt like weeks, and he was taught no prayers. So that night he prayed on his own, though he'd never done it before.

"Sithares, God of fire, I am your humble servant," he began, "heed my words and grant me the power of Fire."

What will you give me in return?

Dakesh's eyes opened. This was the same voice which spoke to him since the day he took Kailen's *Kaizuun. So,* he thought, *this is the voice of Sithares. This entire time, a God has been speaking directly to me.* He wasn't sure if he was surprised or not, but it felt right to him regardless. He was led here by Sithares, the God of Fire, and it was clear Sithares favoured him in some way. He knew he was willing to do anything to become the best warrior in all of Pandeia, and now an actual God was willing to provide him with the means to achieve it.

"Anything."

Very well. When you wake next, the fire will be burning in your soul. In return, you must devote yourself to me completely. You must do as I command. I need my servants fanning the flames of my power, and you will find that the more power I gain, the more power I grant to my chosen.

"How do I give you more power?"

You already know. The Thearan lifestyle was created by me, you've heard them talk about battle and killing. You must give me death, destruction, and fire. Burn your enemies and destroy their homes and families. Help the fire spread across all of Pandeia.

Dakesh thought about fire magic. Thearans could do some incredible things. Most of them were quite weak, just able to conjure a small flame to start a fire or to raise their body temperature slightly on the colder desert nights. But the more powerful ones, the most avid followers of Sithares, could create fireballs with enough explosive power to kill a handful of people at the same time, and shoot powerful streams of flame from their hands for a few seconds. They were completely immune to being burnt by fire, and Dakesh had even heard of more impressive fire magic, things the ancient Thearans could do back when Sithares was feared by all. Fire magic had undoubtedly dwindled since the ancient Thearans, but Dakesh still saw the opportunity to gain power and strength, and if he really devoted himself to Sithares' power rising, he could potentially become as powerful as the legends he'd heard. He knew what his answer would be before he even thought about it, and he knew that Sithares knew as well. The thought of all that power belonging to him was too much to ignore.

"As you wish, Sithares. I'm yours."

Vivid dreams of fire and battle chased Dakesh into the morning light. He woke with a start, sweating and overheated. He felt new energy inside himself, radiating from his chest. Sithares fulfilled his wish. He held his hand up, cupped as though holding a bowl. He focused intently on the centre of his palm. A dim light began to emanate. He focused harder, picturing a flame, willing heat and light to appear in his hand. He felt the heat grow. A tiny spark fizzed where his eyes were staring, then the light faded.

It was a good start, but Dakesh longed for the power of the ancient Thearans. He wouldn't stop until he had it. He felt the heat and magic within himself; he knew with practice he could be powerful.

He practised almost constantly, as much as he trained for combat. He found himself making friends with the other Thearans who could wield fire magic, and they trained together. It was dangerous training. Thearans didn't hold back, and it was normal and even fairly common for warriors to die in sparring sessions. Dakesh was pushed to his limits, which he found exhilarating. He improved phenomenally over the next few weeks and months, and eventually caught Kerberos' notice.

"Shenza!" Kerberos called over the clangour of sparring one day. The warriors stopped immediately. Not normally the kind to instantly follow any order, Thearans were fiery in nature as well as in battle. But Kerberos commanded, and others listened; it was the way of things. He emanated power and control. Dakesh turned to him, sheathing his black sword and nodding a slight bow towards Kerberos.

Kerberos smiled. "You fight well. No need to put away your blade. I will spar with you."

Dakesh was speechless for a moment. Kerberos was a near legendary figure among the Thearans; undefeated in every battle he'd fought. He was massive, with muscles as hard as steel and a torso that reminded Dakesh eerily of the gargantuan trees in Shanaken. For all his size, he was unbelievably fast and agile, and his mind was as sharp as his weapons. His calculating gaze held Dakesh captive for a moment before he finally regained control, and nodded to show his agreement.

"Of course, Kerberos. As you command."

The Thearans didn't appoint titles to their tribe leaders. They didn't believe power could be held with a name alone. Instead, power was gained through strength and skill. Most of the tribe addressed him as "my lord", but he didn't seem to expect it, or even want the title. In most tribes, the Thearan leader changed hands as often as the wind blew, but as far as Dakesh heard, Kerberos had been in control for more than a decade.

Kerberos stood still as a statue, relaxed but alert. He held a spear as tall as he was, seven foot at least, in his right hand. It rested perfectly parallel with the ground. His preferred weapon was a long chain with a Thearan spearhead at one end and a heavy spiked metal ball at the other. It wrapped around his body in neat loops with the spiked ball resting secure at his waist and the spearhead in a sheath on his back.

150

Dakesh faced him, his *Kaizuun* poised in a downward angle. He felt its energy pulsing through him, and embraced it as much as he could. He knew this would take all his skill, and he knew he could easily die by Kerberos' hand; but at the same time he'd never been more excited for a fight. This would be a true test of his abilities, and if he held his own he could gain Kerberos' respect.

A crowd of fellow warriors gathered, forming a circle around them. Kerberos' spear started moving slowly, twirling around his body in smooth, controlled arcs. His eyes never wavered, locked with Dakesh's in a fierce glare as unnerving and hypnotic as the spinning spear in his hands. Suddenly the spear disappeared, and Dakesh saw nothing but a razor sharp blade knifing through the air towards his face. He ducked just as Kerberos threw the real spear, hearing it slice the air just above his head. He was getting used to the split second of warning the Shadow Blade granted him. By the time Dakesh rose from dodging the spear, Kerberos' chain was half-way unwrapped from his body, swinging around and around him, gaining speed. He looked as though he was dancing, going through a series of complex but elegant and controlled movements that allowed him to unwind the chain quickly and efficiently.

The spearhead flew in a circle around Kerberos. Within seconds it unwound enough to reach Dakesh. It sang through the air, whistling in front of his face then at stomach level a second later. Kerberos was metres away, and already leading a barrage of attacks difficult to avoid or block. The spearhead swiped at his throat, his feet, then his chest. Every swing of the chain was expertly placed. Every one would have been Dakesh's death if they connected, but he swayed away from each one, seeing where they would hit before they did. Blocking was useless; the chain was Thearan steel the same as the blade itself, heavy and strong.

Suddenly the blade and chain disappeared. Almost instantly the spiked metal ball shot straight from Kerberos,

151

cannoning into Dakesh's chest. He was smashed off his feet, the air forced from his lungs, and he landed heavily in the sand. Excited cheers swept through the watching Thearans. It happened so fast he thought the ball that hit him was another premonition.

Kerberos watched him intently, neither smug nor concerned; just watching, weighing. Dakesh slowly pushed himself to his feet, panting and hunched over. Kerberos nodded.

"No one has lasted as long for quite a while," he said. Dakesh couldn't tell if he was annoyed, or proud, or upset. He didn't think it was any of those. He sighed heavily.

"We don't have to stop now."

Kerberos laughed. In the same instant the spearhead shot from nowhere, streaking for Dakesh's heart. He ducked and swept his *Kaizuun* up horizontally at the same time, bracing the bladed end with his left hand. The heavy spearhead glanced off of Dakesh's sword with such force that it pushed him backwards in the sand a foot or so, jolting his entire body and sending sparks from the blades of their weapons. Kerberos swung it back around and launched it again, but this time Dakesh jumped over it. The spiked ball appeared, flying towards his chest again, but Dakesh twisted away in mid-air, one of the spikes tearing through the front of his vest and breaking skin.

Dakesh landed knowing he needed to immediately roll to avoid a downward slash of the spearhead followed by another jump to dodge a low swipe from the spike ball. Desperate, he threw everything he had into focusing on his empty left hand, picturing a bright burning fireball. Without waiting, he made a throwing motion at Kerberos while still mid jump, landed and rolled, bringing his sword up ready for another attack.

The crowd went silent. Dakesh realised he wasn't being attacked. He stared at where Kerberos had been, but instead saw him a few metres away from there on the ground, his chain strewn around him in the sand. Kerberos stood at the same time as Dakesh, a painful-looking scorch mark on his chest. Other than the burn, he didn't look harmed, and thankfully didn't look too angry either. They stood staring at each other, both wounded.

Kerberos' mouth twitched in a slight smile, and he nodded to Dakesh.

"Well done, Thearan!" he said, and the Thearans cheered.

"Very impressive. But be clear, you still would not have won were this a fight to the death."

The crowd jeered and laughed at Dakesh, but he didn't feel ashamed in the slightest. He smiled at Kerberos and nodded another bow at the Thearan leader. The fight went better than he thought it would, considering he thought there was a good chance he wouldn't survive at all. And he thought he'd seen the faintest glimmer of respect in Kerberos' eyes.

Atillus

Omatus was a giant city, split in half by the largest river in Omas, the Alpheus, and joined by a massive bridge. Each half of the city was a vast circle surrounded by an impenetrable stone wall. One side was home to all the citizens and merchants, and contained stores, inns, and other buildings. On the other side of the river sat the Royal Palace and the luxuriously huge palaces of the other noble families, along with a shopping district that made the stores on the commoners side look like dilapidated hovels.

The Royal Palace was positioned in the centre of the noble side of the city, with its own stone wall forming a concentric circle parallel to the main city wall. The giant bridge that connected both sides of the city extended all the way to the Royal Palace's main entrance, where there was a courtyard for public announcements, trials and other such gatherings.

Atillus exited through one of the smaller entrances on the opposite side to the bridge. There were plenty of farms in the area along the river, as the land was fairly fertile, but he wasn't interested in the farms and hopefully wouldn't encounter any of the patrolling guards mentioned by the soldier who'd let him out of the city. Once he was out of eyesight of the entrance, he let go of the small Tarsi spell he'd been holding in place to change his face. The magic of the Tarsi was fascinating, and incredibly difficult to use; but he picked up a few things from his teacher and was able to put together a small handful of spells when the need arose.

He ventured away from Omatus, heading East towards where the river opened into the ocean. There were many small trading boats and fishing boats that strayed into the massive river, heading to and from Tarsium or the North-eastern coast of Omas; Atillus knew he'd find one he could board to get north quickly. He managed to fit quite a bit of gold in his carry pack, so travel would be fairly easy in the short term. And once he got where he wanted to go, gold would be far less important to him.

After several hours of walking, Atillus spotted a small village on the edge of the water. It looked like a brief stopping point for small ships; there were two small piers, one building that seemed to be a general store, and perhaps the smallest inn Atillus had ever seen. There were a handful of temporary trading stalls as well. He could see that both docks were in use at the moment, a small fishing skiff tied to one and a medium sized barge at the other.

As he approached the tiny settlement, he constructed the Tarsi spell he used before, but this time altered the face to that of an old man. He used his right forefinger to draw ancient Tarsi symbols on the palm of his left hand, fingers splayed wide and straight as arrows. Each symbol, after being drawn, left its shape on his palm, pale and raised like an old scar. When the word was spelled out, the symbols merged together and peeled off his skin. In his hands it grew and shifted into the shape of a disembodied face. Without a skull to give it shape and muscles to move it, it looked pathetic and empty; almost comical in its lack of realism. But Atillus knew once the spell anchored to his face, it was utterly believable.

He pressed it against his face and felt it set itself into his skin. It was an odd feeling; one he didn't think he'd ever be able to accurately describe to someone who'd never felt it themselves.

The fishing skiff was no help to him; it was only good for a tiny crew and wouldn't take passengers besides. But the barge looked as though ferrying travellers was a large part of its purpose. Atillus wandered over to the Shenza woman standing at the boarding ramp. She glanced intently at him for the barest of moments, and he could see her studying his body, his movements and his face for signs of threat. He expected this; the Shenza were intelligent and pragmatic warriors, and never underestimated potential opponents. His spell was incredibly effective, however, and he was hunching his back and shoulders and affecting a slight limp. Only a Tarsi specifically looking for active spells would be able to tell something was amiss, and Atillus was yet to spot any Tarsi people. His first destination was Tarsium however, and so he was going to need to remove his spell before it was spotted there.

"Greetings, elder. Where are you travelling?" The Shenza woman asked. Although she dismissed him as no threat, she maintained respect for him.

"Greetings, *Daishen*. I am making for Tarsium. Is there a place for me on your barge?"

The woman smiled, though it looked slightly sad to Atillus. "I'm no *Daishen*, though I thank you for the compliment. I'm more of a *Zuudshen*, if truth be told." She laughed lightly, but there was sadness behind that too.

Ah, thought Atillus, *Zuudshen – an outsider. Either exiled or left of her own accord.* He nodded slightly, but kept his face blank in that vaguely uncomprehending way he'd done his whole life. *Play stupid, and you will slip beneath your opponent's notice.* He didn't expect to fight this warrior, but he needed to be prepared for battle wherever he went from now on. She noticed he apparently didn't understand the term she used, but let it go.

"We are heading for Tarsium, but we still need to make a trip down the Alpheus to trade with the farmers. You are welcome to board with us now of course, though we will be stopping here again before heading to Tarsium if you'd prefer to stay here."

Atillus thought the risk of heading back down the river, even with his disguise, was far too great. He could only hold the magic in place for a certain amount of time before the spell started disintegrating, and continually renewing the spell would cost him far too much magic. Besides, if they were travelling all the way back along the Alpheus, the trip would be at least a week each way; the river was massive, and they would be stopping to trade. The Shenza woman took his silence as genuine uncertainty, and leaned in to whisper to him.

"To be honest, it would be cheaper and far more restful for you to stay here a while anyway."

He smiled in what he hoped was a grateful expression, nodding. "I believe I will stay here, then. Thank you for your honesty." She nodded back and gave him a gentle, and surprisingly beautiful, smile; there was no sadness hidden there this time.

He didn't end up staying at the tiny inn for two weeks after all; three days after he arrived, a new ship docked to pick up passengers on its way to Tarsium. Atillus was a little regretful he wouldn't get to travel with the Shenza warrior he spoke to; she seemed an honourable person and he would have liked to spend more time with her. But there was no room for sentimentality and no time to make friends; he needed to keep moving at every opportunity.

Atillus spent most of the three days holed up in the tiny room at the inn, mostly so he wouldn't need to keep the disguise in place. But he also found the privacy peaceful; the innkeepers were respectful of their guests and he wasn't bothered, except when invited to meals.

The first time they had knocked on his door, he scrambled to his feet and grabbed his travel cloak, throwing it over his head, his heart hammering wildly in his chest. There was no time to cast the Tarsi disguise spell. But the older man left the door closed and said in a raised but gentle voice "Meals are being served in the main room if you're hungry!" and moved on to the next door.

He had breathed a ragged sigh of relief, realised he'd drawn two of the symbols onto his left palm out of pure instinct, and finished the spell. With the disguise in place, Atillus went down the narrow, groaning stairs and into the cramped main room. The meal was good; fresh fish brought in from the many fishing boats that docked in the small village, and soft brown bread baked at the inn itself. He ate as much as he could, savouring the fresh food, knowing he would be surviving on salted and dried foods while he travelled. After his meal, he set out to briefly explore the tiny market stalls lined up along the docks. He was always looking for potentially useful items and opportunities.

He found a bag of Tarsi oranges and a hunting knife of black Shenza steel; he thought it too risky to carry weapons in the pack he brought from Omatus, as he knew the guards would search him. The gold he was able to wrap in his bedroll, but almost everything else he packed was clothing, dried and salted food, and camping supplies. The top layer, which the guards obviously saw first, was a rich looking tunic and some meaningless gold and silver trinkets that decorated Atillus' quarters. He never cared for them, not even for their value, but they helped sell his story to the guards on his exit from the city, and since they hadn't taken the valuable things as a bribe, he could sell them. This tiny place was no proper market, however; he would need to wait until Tarsium to sell his wares.

Near the end of the first day, a large group of Omati Royal Soldiers marched into the tiny village. Atillus was carrying his purchases back to the inn when he saw them. It took almost all of his considerable willpower not to react more strongly than a normal old man might. The soldiers split up and started questioning every person they came into contact with. One made eye contact with Atillus and headed straight for him. Atillus gave a nervous smile, trying to keep up his innocent old man act. The soldier gave a half-hearted smile back. There was no sympathy in that smile, but there was also no suspicion.

158

"Greetings, old man," the soldier said with authority, though amiably enough, "we are here looking for a criminal at large, a very dangerous man named Atillus Argyris." The man held up a piece of parchment with Atillus' face sketched onto it in charcoal. The likeness was unsettling, and staring into his own face left Atillus suddenly feeling exposed under the false skin he was wearing. But he cleared his throat weakly and smiled nervously again, looking the soldier directly in the eyes.

"I'm terribly sorry, son, I've not seen this man around these parts. Tell me though: is this the Atillus Argyris of the Noble Argyris family? Is he really a criminal?" With his arms underneath a large bag of oranges, he was able to hold the hunting knife unseen by the soldier, and if it was necessary he could draw it and drop the heavy bag within seconds.

"Yes, the very same," replied the soldier, "and yes, he is a very dangerous criminal. He assassinated King Megalos and the Queen."

Atillus feigned a look of shock and outrage. "The King and Queen are dead?"

The soldier nodded solemnly and put a heavily armoured hand on Atillus' shoulder. He hesitated a little, staring into Atillus' eyes for a few seconds longer than Atillus thought was necessary. He tried the nervous smile again, and kept talking. People didn't like constant talkers. Atillus certainly didn't.

"They have a few sons, don't they? Was it two or three? Do you think the next eldest will get the crown? I heard the sons fight a lot. I hope they don't fight over the crown. Maybe we could have joint Kings, eh? Wouldn't that be something to see? Two or three Kings at the same time, all brothers! Your job would be much harder I'd imagine, what if two Kings gave you two different orders? Who would you obey?"

Halfway through his rambling, the soldier started looking uncomfortable. By the last few words, he was clearly ready to move on to a less annoying civilian.

Atillus gave a quacking, creaking old man laugh and shook his head as though he just said the funniest thing he'd ever heard, while the soldier thanked him for his assistance and walked quickly away. Atillus turned and made his way as quickly as he could to the inn.

Now, Atillus sat in a small cabin below decks in the ship on his way to Tarsium. He knew his father and the royal family would be sending soldiers after him, and he knew at least a few of them would be smart enough to head to Tarsium. It was the centre of Pandeia, both geographically and culturally. A massive melting pot of every culture of Pandeia, it was also the preferred destination of almost every criminal and outcast. There was a strict no violence policy and the laws of the other countries held no sway over the mysterious Tarsi. Anyone who broke their rule somehow disappeared within 24 hours, never seen again; and although Atillus learned many Tarsi secrets, he still had no clue as to how it was possible. What he did know was he needed to get to Tarsium to be safe. The Journey would take at least a week, but he was on a ship and moving, and as far as he knew there were no Royal Soldiers following him. So far, everything was going according to plan.

Aella

They travelled through the desert, heading north once again. It was getting close to summer, and the entire tribe knew what that meant; they were travelling to Sitharkos, the Heart of Sithares. Sitharkos was the gigantic volcano in the centre of Omas, and every year since Kerberos took control, at the height of summer, the tribe travelled to the volcano and celebrated the fires awakening within its depths. They climbed to the top, lit bonfires of their own and camped on a huge plateau near the vent. They looked for shapes in the giant plumes of smoke that rushed from the volcano, and took part in challenges and sparring matches. Aella loved being at Sitharkos, and loved the festival. When the volcano was active, being close to it made her feel as though her very soul was burning with limitless magic. The power it gave her was utterly intoxicating. She felt connected to every other member of the tribe too; the Heart of Sithares joined them all in Fire Magic, even the warriors with little or no real power.

The already hot-blooded Thearans let their passions go wild during this festival of fire, and many newborn Thearan warriors were brought into the world nine months after the festival each year. Aella couldn't help but think of Erasmus. She didn't want children of her own, at least not yet; he did. Her own mother gave birth to her at seventeen years of age, which was not uncommon for Thearans, but Aella wasn't comfortable with the idea of childbirth even at twenty-five years of age. It was a difficult conversation to have with someone who wanted children as badly as Erasmus did. She knew he would be a great father, and she thought she might be a good mother too, but she couldn't bring herself to bear children. Even worse, she couldn't properly explain why. Erasmus, as usual, was very understanding. He was frustrated, but he respected her choices and usually never pushed the idea on her.

She wandered from her mother and caught up with Erasmus and Dakesh, who were walking with a small group of warriors. She laid a hand on Erasmus' arm when she fell in step beside him, and he smiled as he turned to her. Dakesh grunted at her in greeting; he was still not quite used to the constant travel, or the desert, and was breathing hard.

The journey took at least a month; heading into the centre of the desert was far harder than travelling around the coast where Tarsius was located. They slowed their progress, though Dakesh still seemed to struggle. She supposed Shanaken was far easier to travel through. Her and Erasmus taught Dakesh all about survival in the desert. They taught him about Petrafyte, the plants that looked like rocks but had a soft juicy flesh which contained plenty of water. It tasted like dirt but was clean and refreshing. They taught him about the various species of lizards, snakes and spiders and how to prepare them for eating.

They sparred together every day. Dakesh was a great fighter, and Aella enjoyed sparring with him more than anyone else in the tribe. One day, as she approached him to ask for another sparring match, she noticed him sitting by a campfire and practising Fire Magic. She paused.

Kerberos hadn't yet led the new tribe members in his group prayer; she thought perhaps he was waiting for the Fire Festival. So how could Dakesh awaken the magic in himself? She sat next to him. He let the fireball in his hand go out, and smiled at her excitedly.

"I'm getting better! The first night I could only conjure sparks, and that was only a week ago!"

"How can you use Fire Magic?" She asked, trying to sound nonchalant.

162

"I prayed to Sithares," he said. He said it in a thoughtless, matter-of-fact way, like he was telling her the desert was dry. He focused on his hand again, and after a few seconds another fireball appeared. Aella decided one of the other warriors must have taught him the prayer, and she didn't pursue it any further. Dakesh was always pushing himself to be faster, stronger, and better, so it made sense that he would ask about Fire Magic before Kerberos taught him.

A little while later, Aella was resting after a particularly brutal sparring match and eating at a campfire when Kerberos shouted over the camp-site. Many Thearans were training, and although the sounds of fighting were everywhere, Kerberos' voice thundered over the top of it all. Every warrior stopped instantly.

"Shenza!"

She looked up at the sudden shout and saw Dakesh sheath his sword and bow to their leader. They exchanged a few words she couldn't hear from her distance and then a crowd gathered quickly, cutting off her line of sight. They formed a circle around Dakesh and Kerberos; they were going to fight.

Dakesh lasted longer than most against the giant tribe leader. He spent most of the battle trying desperately to dodge Kerberos' lightning fast attacks. The moment that shocked her was when Dakesh, while in mid air leaping away from Kerberos' lethal chain, threw an incredibly powerful fireball at Kerberos. It hit him squarely in the chest and he was flung to the ground. Every warrior gathered to watch went completely silent.

Kerberos stood. He looked uninjured, and somehow he looked amused.

"Well done, Thearan!" he said. The crowd cheered.

"Very impressive. But be clear, you still would not have won were this a fight to the death."

The crowd jeered and laughed at Dakesh, but he didn't seem to mind at all. He bowed to Kerberos, and the crowd dispersed.

Dakesh became accustomed to travelling through the desert, and the journey to Sitharkos was far more pleasant for Aella now that she didn't have to teach him everything about survival. They reached the giant volcano after a month or so, and Aella could feel its energy well before they reached it. It was already heightening her power and her senses, making her feel like her power was limitless. When they were close enough, she couldn't contain her excitement any longer, and ran to the sheer wall-like base.

"We're here!" She laughed, placing her hand on the endless wall of black rock. Dakesh gave her an odd look, and she explained.

"This place is where fire magic is strongest. It feels like home."

Dakesh glanced up at the towering rock and back down at Aella. Erasmus walked over to them at the base of the mountain.

"We are camping here tonight," he reported, "and we'll be climbing to the top with the first light."

Dakesh look up once again.

"We're going all the way to the top?"

"We do every year at the height of the Summer season, when the sun sits directly above the mountain and the fires within it start to stir."

Dakesh gaped at the mountain. "It's a *volcano?* And we're climbing to the top?"

Aella and Erasmus laughed together, shaking their heads at Dakesh. He truly was from an entirely different world. She thought in that moment that were she to travel to Shanaken, she would look as much a fool as Dakesh did to them. Erasmus and Dakesh continued talking while Aella's mind wandered. Her hand was still placed against the smooth black rock of Sithares' Heart, and as she always did when she was this close, she felt as though the magic inside her was an extension of the volcano's unimaginable destructive power. As though they were one and the same. Ever since she'd been given the ancient Fire Blades by her mother, she felt like she was born to wield fire magic.

Camping next to the volcano, Aella slept restlessly. She desperately wanted to be on the plateau, setting great bonfires and competing against her fellow warriors. She usually held back during the competitions, either losing on purpose or just barely winning, and she only ever used one sword.

Mindful of her mother's warnings, she knew she would need to control her power once again. But there was something calling her this time, something demanding that she shine as brightly as the sun for all the Thearans to see. It felt to her like an inexorable pull, like being stuck ankle deep in a shifting sand dune as it pulled her down to a deep, dangerous desert pit. It ate at her mind, telling her that Kerberos could be beaten, that she deserved to lead the tribe, that she was the most powerful being in all of Pandeia.

Sick of laying still, she left her tent. She moved gently, but quickly. Erasmus kept sleeping. She walked up to the giant wall and walked next to it, away from the camp, with her hand trailing its smooth, powerful warmth. She always felt much more energetic this close to Sitharkos, but this time it was more than just energy. It felt different to her; ominous. She felt like something huge was on the horizon, hidden for now by the massive volcano.

She closed her eyes. She could feel something within the rock. The pull she was feeling... It almost sounded like a voice. It was quiet, whispering and raspy; but at the same time deep and unimaginably powerful. Her eyes flew open. She gasped, taking her hand off the wall, suddenly afraid for the sun to rise. She couldn't make out any words, but it was definitely a voice. Breathing heavy now, she turned and ran back to camp.

She was still sitting in front of the fire when Erasmus emerged from their tent just before dawn. She hadn't bothered trying to get back to sleep. He sat next to her and put his arm around her in silence. They stared at the fire together. Eventually, she shifted uncomfortably and turned to him.

"Something is going to happen soon, Erasmus," she said, "Something bad."

He looked into her eyes, frowning. "How do you know?"

"I -" she paused, suddenly afraid that he would think she was either trying to trick him or crazy. "I heard something. I touched Sitharkos last night, and it felt... different. Something is coming for us. Something dangerous."

Erasmus looked troubled. She couldn't tell if he believed her, or if he thought she was mad. He gently put his hand in hers, and kissed her.

"Unless Sithares itself attacks us, I think we will be fine," he said softly, "we are thousands strong, and Kerberos is the strongest leader in Thearan history."

He smirked. "And you are the most powerful warrior ever to live. I truly don't believe we're in any danger, my love."

She smiled, and returned another kiss when he gave it. But she wasn't so sure any of them were safe.

Dakesh

After what seemed like months of travel, they reached the base of the largest mountain Dakesh had ever seen. The Thearans called it the Heart of Sithares. It seemed to almost touch the sun itself, filling their vision completely when they stood next to it. Aella was happier than Dakesh had ever seen her.

"We're here!" She laughed, placing her hand on the endless wall of black rock. At Dakesh's look, she explained.

"This place is where fire magic is strongest. It feels like home."

Dakesh glanced up at the towering rock and back down at Aella. It did seem to have a strange energy to it. Erasmus walked over to them at the base of the mountain and told them they would be camping the night and climbing to the top at first light. Dakesh again turned his head to the top of the mountain.

He couldn't see a way to climb up the sheer face, and when he asked Erasmus if they were really climbing it, his response left Dakesh even more bewildered than before; Sitharkos was a volcano, and the tribe was going to camp at the top, while it was active. Dakesh gaped at them. Aella and Erasmus laughed together, shaking their heads at him as though he was crazy.

"We're Thearans, Dakesh," said Erasmus, "We need not fear the flames of Sithares. Here is where we are most powerful, where Sithares' power lies. We celebrate the Fire Festival here once a year, and the fire within the mountain

167

has never killed one of us. It's the fighting you have to worry about."

Dakesh made the connection himself. "There are competitions in the Festival." He said it as a statement; he already knew it was true.

"Yes," Erasmus said, "violent and brutal, to properly honour Sithares. There is a lot of open space at the top of the mountain, and we set up bonfires and fighting pits away from the volcano itself. We stay up there for two full weeks, and on the last day the sun aligns with the volcano and we pray to Sithares. Up until that last day, every day is spent fighting and burning fires."

He'd grown used to the Thearan lifestyle now, mostly, so it didn't surprise him. He nodded and they set to work putting up camp for the night, still talking about the Festival.

"We haven't always been so devout," Erasmus was saying, "and we only started celebrating the Fire Festival once Kerberos became our leader."

Dakesh frowned. "So the tribe didn't worship Sithares at all before then?"

"Most Thearans don't worship much anymore. Religion became less and less a part of Thearan culture. The ancient stories tell of direct contact between Sithares and its followers, but something like that hasn't happened for thousands of years, if it ever happened at all. Kerberos claims to have spoken to Sithares, but I've never seen it. We're a practical people, and if we can't see something, it might as well not exist. But Kerberos has a strong faith, and his power is undeniable. At first we prayed with him because he is a great leader, but after a while, we noticed our own power increase too. Even if it isn't Sithares, praying and following Kerberos seems to be strengthening our tribe."

They don't even think Sithares is real! Dakesh couldn't believe it. *I've spoken to it myself!*

But I don't speak to them.

168

Dakesh jumped, startled. He hadn't heard Sithares' voice in months, not since the night he was given the power of Fire Magic. *Sithares only speaks to me,* he wondered.

You and a select few others. You are chosen.

He grinned. Erasmus frowned at his expression, confused, and he realised he hadn't responded.

"Sithares is real," he said, his smile vanishing. "I have heard its voice, just has Kerberos has."

Erasmus looked at him for a moment, still frowning. "I don't doubt you, brother," he said quietly.

Atillus

Three days into the journey, Atillus firmly decided travel by boat wasn't for him. While uneventful, the days at sea were absolutely awful. His fellow passengers were just as interested in being alone as he was, thankfully. Cold meals were taken individually to each cabin and it seemed only a handful of the crew maintained any interest in talking and drinking together; although this they did with great enthusiasm. Atillus managed to keep his disguise in place whenever he needed to, and though it was exhausting, he found the constant practice was actually improving his ability to hold the spell for longer.

The other passengers on board were almost exclusively Omati; and by the look of them, most seemed to be escaped slaves. There was a Thearan warrior, whose dark skin and bright hair and eyes brought a sudden and cutting ache to Atillus' heart. Amares' death was still a fresh wound. One of the passengers was a Tarsi; Atillus had to study the small being's face intently to be sure it wasn't Karak, his mentor. He avoided the Tarsi for the rest of the journey.

Other than meals brought to his door, and a few too many offers to join the crew mates for drinks, Atillus spent all of his time alone; either violently ill or desperately trying not to be violently ill. The journey lasted 6 days.

Tarsium was a revelation for Atillus. He'd read about it, of course, but seeing it in person was something else entirely. The port where they landed was fairly unimpressive, but Atillus admired it for its stark and simple layout. It was a small port, barely even a village, on the southwest coast of the country. The buildings were all Tarsi architecture, and the entire port was built with function in mind, at the expense of aesthetics. Docking, unloading, and herding passengers off the ship was all done incredibly efficiently by a team of Omati workers led by a small group of Tarsi, and Atillus was relieved by the careless anonymity with which he was treated. He made sure to keep his body language in line with his old man disguise, however; he remained uncomfortably aware that Tarsi could spot their own magic if they were looking for it.

He made his way into the small port settlement, found a transport, and requested passage to Carmerth. Carmerth was the trading district of Tarsium, where everything was for sale or trade. Most visitors headed straight for Azar, the largest district and home to the largest concentration of inns, taverns and residences in all of Pandeia. It was easy for outlaws and wanted beings to get lost in Azar, and while that certainly appealed to him, it was surely the first place people would start looking for him. Instead, he needed a place to obtain supplies and get rid of the valuable belongings taken from Omatus. The journey to Carmerth didn't take as long as he expected. The transport he took, some sort of large cart, wasn't tied to steeds as he originally assumed. Rather, it moved completely on its own, being driven by magic unfamiliar to Atillus. It was far more efficient than a steed-drawn carriage might have been, and glided along the smooth paved road with no apparent effort other than a low humming sound.

The landscape of Tarsium was beautiful, and a far cry from the dry, brutal deserts of Omas. It wasn't until seeing the low, rolling hills covered in lush green grass and vibrant trees of the Tarsi countryside that Atillus realised even the most fertile areas of the Omati farms were dry and unforgiving. He'd never seen as much green in his life, and the peaceful sounds of birdsong and insect calls almost lulled him to sleep without needing to pretend. They passed a few small rivers, and again he was struck by the beauty of the place. A few hours later he was entering Carmerth. He may have been able to maintain his disguise the entire trip, but instead he raised his hood to cover his face and feigned sleep. There were two travellers in the cart with him, with space for a fourth. They didn't bother him, merely conversed in low voices with each other for most of the journey. Once the gates of Carmerth were visible in the distance and the driver of the cart announced they'd be arriving soon, Atillus quickly drew the disguise spell runes onto his palm again without moving the rest of his body. Pretending to wake up, he feigned rubbing his face and eyes as he attached the disguise onto his face.

Carmerth was an incredible city. It was considered the hub of trading for all of Pandeia, and evidence of this was visible even seconds after arriving. Every other building was designed in a different architectural style and with building materials from every country. There were temporary stalls, permanent buildings, and street vendors lining every road. No building was like any other, and none fit the building next to it, but somehow this made for a mosaic that looked natural. Atillus was particularly taken with Shenza buildings. Black metal twisted and shaped into organic looking branches wrapped around deep brown wooden huts with circular windows and doors. He knew in Shanaken the buildings were constructed high up in the gigantic trees native to the country, and the wood of the trees was used without chopping it or damaging it in any way. He was sure Shenza architecture would look far more beautiful in the trees of Shanaken, but these ground based buildings still impressed him a great deal. He headed for a Shenza inn, and was slightly disappointed to find it staffed by a Tarsi and several Omati workers. He paid for a week, took the sleek black metal key to his room, and went out to find a place to sell his belongings.

On the third day in Carmerth, Atillus was found. A Shenza assassin snuck into his room in the middle of the night. She was utterly silent, and Atillus survived only because he was already awake. He was staring out the window at the stars, his eyes almost closed, when the assassin appeared from nowhere. Barely controlling his instinct to attack, he instead waited for her to enter the room properly. She slid down onto the floor with a liquid grace that spoke of lethal talent, and even straining to hear her didn't help Atillus pick up any sound of her movement.

Under his thin blanket, Atillus' hand grew hot as he readied a small fireball. He stopped just short of actual flame though, as it would glow through the sheet and give away his awareness of the assassin. But in this state, the fireball could be generated within a second or two. He waited for her. She remained crouched on the floor just inside the window, staring at him. Her head cocked to the side slightly, and Atillus realised she was listening for his breathing.

Her face suddenly snapped back to face him, and her hand flew forwards in a silent flash. Atillus moved as soon as she did, and whatever she threw thudded into the wooden bed frame where his head had been a bare second before. As he rose, Atillus drew and launched the fireball at the woman's chest. She dived low, rolling and throwing two more projectiles as she came out of the roll. The fireball glanced off the bottom of the metal window frame and streaked out into the night sky. Atillus ducked underneath the two throwing knives, feeling one nick his shoulder and hearing the sharp thudding sound as it hit the wall behind him.

Not seeing any larger weapons sheathed, Atillus decided to take the fight to his assassin. He excelled with almost every style of combat, and although unarmed close quarters fighting was not a style he particularly enjoyed, he could use it just as well as any other. He made as if to

173

run to his bed, and then quickly changed direction and launched himself at his attacker. She picked up his feint and instead of diving away, she leapt to meet him. Atillus felt a begrudging respect for the assassin; her adaptability and quick appraisal of combat situations was very rare. He got one hand around her throat and used the other to quickly sweep her body for weapons. A sheath in the small of her back held a long, thin dagger, and she quickly tried to stop his hand from taking it. Her other hand was mercilessly jabbing his kidney, over and over, and he started grunting in pain at each hit.

He slid her dagger from its sheath and buried it in her stomach. She gave a small gasp, but kept hitting him, and now used her second hand to hit him as well. She jabbed his neck, face, stomach and groin. He kept his grip on her throat and bore through the pain. She was nowhere near as strong as him and her strength was quickly failing. He thrust the dagger into her again and again, between her ribs and into her lungs, into her armpit and then once more into her stomach.

She stopped hitting him, and her breath was now almost gone. He held her up, her feet dangling above the floor. She went totally limp, and he felt how light she was. An odd sadness came over him then, and he put her down gently, looking at her face properly for the first time. She was so young. He sighed, staring at her slight form as she lay dead. He stood like that for a few moments, grieving for both a talented warrior and a young life.

He was unsure why it hit him so hard; in life or death situations, remorse shouldn't have been a factor. Or so he had believed. There was something about this young woman, however. Although he knew she came to kill him, she seemed... gentle. She didn't have a cruel face and although she was obviously adept at killing, it seemed purely business to Atillus. He couldn't properly articulate why that saddened him as it did, but he somehow knew if the assassin was personally furious at him, he wouldn't have felt bad for killing them. He sighed again, packed his things, and left the inn as silently as he could.

He sold all of his belongings in the three days before the attempt on his life, and had a new stash of gold as well as a proper sword and Thearan travelling clothes. He left for Azar that night, walking instead of relying on travel by cart. He had no idea how long the assassin was tracking him for, and thought it would be safer if he travelled on his own.

The countryside was even more beautiful when travelling through it on foot. Even though he knew he was being hunted and may be attacked again at any time, the journey through Tarsium left Atillus feeling at peace. He camped each night, hunted and ate by streams and beautiful old trees. He walked as far and as fast as he could each day, stopping only to eat and make waste. He'd read a lot about Tarsium, and remembered all of it. He knew the flora and fauna, what could be eaten and what would harm him. He'd also seen a map a long time ago, and although much could have changed since the map was drawn, the three major districts would be in the same place. He could picture the map in his mind with perfect clarity, as he could with everything he read. Starting from Carmerth, he was certain he could make his way to Azar.

There were small, sleepy villages scattered around the countryside. Atillus avoided them, but strayed close enough that he could admire the peaceful atmosphere. He wandered for over a month in the direction of Azar, and despite having much to brood on and darken his mind with, the days of walking were some of the best of his life. He hadn't felt so at peace since his training started in Omatus.

Eventually, he came upon Azar. There was a truly uncountable number of people living in Azar, and almost immediately Atillus felt himself get lost among the vast crowds. He thought it next to impossible for an assassin to find him here, and cursed himself for heading to Carmerth first.

He walked for hours, and still wasn't even close to the centre of the massive city. He walked randomly, making turns onto roads without thinking and without planning. He stopped for some food at a stall made of hides, where an elderly Shenza man sold fish roasted in large yellow leaves. Eventually, he came across an Omati inn he liked the look of. He paid for a week again, sure this time no one could have found him.

He ended up staying in Azar for a month, changing inn every week. On the third week, he left the inn without a disguise on. He shaved his head, and was pleased to see how much of a difference it made to his appearance. When no one recognised him and another week went by, he stopped using the disguise altogether. He left Azar after that, and travelled to another port on the Western coast. He intended to go back to Omas, but he wasn't going back to Omatus. That would come much later.

Zanela

Zuzuk mostly stayed near the forest floor. Zanela had no idea where they slept, or if they even slept at all. Like her ancestors and the modern Shenza, she kept to the canopy. She only ventured down to hunt and to drink. She survived a few Zuzuk attacks, but each time it seemed to be pure luck. Each day, she grew more fearful her luck would run out.

She considered trying to leave Shanaken, But the idea was as brief as it was ridiculous. She belonged here, even if the Shenza wouldn't have her. The forest was her home. Without knowing exactly why, she travelled every month or so, heading slowly towards the centre of the forest. *Dulkuud*. The Eternal Mountain. It towered above even the tallest of the gigantic trees of the forest. Home to Amalus, the God of Life, it was sacred to the Shenza. It was said to be the resting place of all Shenza who lived and died honourably, and the birthplace of *Kaizel*; Shadow Magic.

She wondered now if it was possible to see the spirits of the dead if she climbed to the top. If it was possible to see Amalus itself. The stories made no distinction between the physical mountain and the mountain of the afterlife; they were the same thing. An odd cold feeling crept over her skin as she stared at the giant mountain. Could a mortal person really just walk into the afterlife? What if the stories were false and there was nothing at the top but grass and rocks?

What if the stories aren't *false?* Somehow, the thought left her terrified. What would happen if Amalus greeted her at the top of the mountain? What if she survived the climb and Dakesh's spirit was already waiting for her? Suddenly the climb was all she could think about. She needed to know if the Shenza afterlife was real. She needed to know what really lay at the top of *Dulkuud*. Even if she didn't survive the journey, so what? No one would miss her. She wasn't welcome in the city. Dakesh was gone.

Packing her things wasn't necessary. Her clothing and her sword were her only belongings. A small amount of fruit huddled in a large leaf in the hollow where she slept; she took that too, but she would forage as she went. As dangerous as it was, the forest provided no shortage of food for those who knew where to look.

Climbing and jumping between trees was second nature to Zanela, even without the climbing frames of the Shenza for help. Still, travel was slow. Foraging could take a while; the steps she took to avoid detection by any potential predators in the area made everything take far longer than it should have.

Zuzuk weren't the only threats, either. Almost every form of life in the forest was a weapon honed by Amalus to protect Shanaken. The *Duulshen* said Amalus started small, when the trees of Shanaken were still young; first making plants which could trap and devour threats to the forest. Ancient Ermoori travelled to the newborn forest, coveting its beauty and wanting to make it their home. But they cut through the small vines and young trees and started building homes of stone and metal over the soft grass.

As the trees grew taller, their protectors grew larger: after vines and carnivorous plants came venomous spiders and snakes. The Ermoori developed medicines and traps to protect against Amalus' new creations. Then as the trees reached new heights, the Lakshaidan were created to swing through the canopies and watch over the forest from above. The Lakshaidan were the same body shape as the Ermoori, but covered in mottled green fur with toes as long and dexterous as their fingers. They were stronger and faster than the invaders, and knew how to use simple tools and weapons.

When the Ermoori started out-thinking the Lakshaidan, Amalus created the Shenza. The Best of these warriors were turned into Zuzuk, and after the Zuzuk were created Amalus was done. The Ermoori were defeated and banished, and Amalus retired to the peak of *Dulkuud* to rest.

Carnivorous trapping vines, venomous snakes, spiders and the Lakshaidan were still plentiful in Shanaken. Zanela took her time travelling through the forest. The canopy was mostly safe. Lakshaidan were peaceful unless attacked, but were fiercely territorial. She avoided them as much as possible, travelling in wide circles around the massive trees they gathered in.

This far from the city, the forest was thick and wild. No Shenza magic touched this place. This was pure life, intense and chaotic. Despite the constant sense of danger, Zanela loved it. Out here she felt free and wild. The feeling grew stronger the closer she came to *Dulkuud*. By the time she reached the mountain's base, the forest was so thick she could almost walk through the canopy from tree to tree without climbing or jumping.

Dulkuud itself was gigantic. When she reached the foot of the mountain and stared up at it, it was as though nothing else existed. Even the massive trees of Shanaken looked insignificant compared to the towering mountain. The trees growing on the mountain itself were far smaller than those of the forest, but they were plenty big enough to climb. Without a look back, Zanela climbed.

How long has it been? Weeks? Months? Surely no longer. Zanela sat on the branch of a tree, looking out over the forest of Shanaken from impossibly high up the Eternal Mountain. Shanaken was a sea of mottled green, so far below her it was almost featureless. Beyond the forests,

179

just visible on the horizon, was the bright blue of the ocean.

Dulkuud brimmed with life, yet felt oddly quiet. Beings of every type moved constantly on the ground, in the air, and through the trees. The water of the rivers was so clear the riverbeds would have been easily visible were it not for endless schools of fish swarming downstream. Creatures she never knew existed crawled, leapt and flew all around her.

A powerful sense of calm enveloped the entire mountain. On the first day of her climb, she had come across a Zuzuk as it prowled around the trunk of a tree and saw her. Its eyes regarded her with an intense stare and it stepped closer to her. Even on all fours, it was as tall as she was. They stood eye-to-eye for a moment; a young Shenza woman and the ultimate predator. Still, the calm of the mountain dissolved any fear she may have felt. Staring into the predator's eyes, she saw its intelligence, its curiosity. It was almost like looking into the eyes of a fellow Shenza. The ancient myth was suddenly all too real in her mind.

"I wonder what your name was before you became... this." She laid her hand on its cheek gently. It looked down, thinking, and then back up at her and shook its head. The meaning was painfully clear; the beast didn't remember. Her heart broke for it.

"I'm sorry," she whispered. She stepped away, heading again for the top of the mountain. The Zuzuk let out a low growl. Stopping, she frowned and looked back at the massive animal. It sat on its hind legs and lowered its head to the ground, looking up at her. A deep loneliness emanated from its eyes. She walked back to where it sat and lowered herself to the ground next to it. Something about the creature's presence was comforting. They slept next to each other on the forest floor that night.

Zanela woke with the sunrise, curled up on the forest floor. The Zuzuk lay still next to her, wide awake; waiting for her. She stood and stretched the stiffness out of her body, looking up towards the mountaintop.

"Are you travelling with me?" She asked the beast. Its head nodded up and down. They set off together, across the forest floor. There was no danger here; no need to stick to the canopy. She couldn't think of anything more to say to the animal, and it couldn't talk at all, so they walked in a comfortable silence.

The Zuzuk moved with grace and absolute confidence through the forest, and Zanela followed close behind. Now that she didn't have to avoid danger or spend too long foraging for food and shelter, the journey was far easier. The Zuzuk occasionally stopped to tap the ground with its massive paw, staring at her intently until she nodded. *Stay here*. Then it disappeared in a blur of movement. Within an hour, it returned with one of its giant paws full of fruit, vegetables and fish.

She could do it herself, and the Zuzuk knew it, but the beast still took care of her as they journeyed up the mountain. Eventually, they came upon a thick fog which obscured everything. The entire forest disappeared underneath a cold blanket of white. She called out to the Zuzuk ahead of her, losing sight of it. She felt a small stab of fear for the first time since beginning the climb. Nothing happened. She felt life teeming through the forest around her, but saw absolutely nothing. A bird or possibly some giant insect swooped past her ear, close enough to feel its scratchy wing. She ducked and closed her eyes.

A friend of her parents, a warrior named Kalesh, was blinded by an Ermoori weapon during the last invasion when she was a child. He could walk slowly along the platforms of the city, but needed constant assistance and care. Now, huddled in an endless field of impenetrable fog, Zanela felt overwhelming sorrow for Kalesh. He lived this terror every day, every moment.

More creatures zipped past her, finding their way effortlessly through the fog. Every chatter, every wing flap, every sudden squawk grated on her resolve. She flinched at every sound. A giant creature stomped on the ground right next to her and she screamed. A wet, cold nose gently nudged her face. After a few moments of paralysing fear she realised it was the Zuzuk travelling with her. Letting out a ragged sigh, she threw her arms around the beast and held it until her heart slowed again.

When they set out again, Zanela kept a hand on the Zuzuk's back. It walked slowly for her, and they continued like that through the fog. Hours later, the Zuzuk disappeared to find more food for them, and she was again left alone in total blindness. She closed her eyes and sat on the ground with her hand resting on the hilt of her blade, willing her heartbeat to remain steady. When the Zuzuk appeared again, her eyes flew open and she embraced it a second time.

They continued through the fog, and after another half day's walk the forest gradually reappeared before her eyes. Behind her, the path now looked like the shoreline of an opaque white ocean. Treetops emerged from the fog like mountains on a distant island. Together, they moved further away from the fog. When they were far enough from it that she could relax again, she climbed a tall tree while the Zuzuk waited on the ground.

Not fog, she marvelled, *clouds! We've climbed so high we're standing above the clouds!* Stretching out in every direction, the billowing clouds looked utterly different from anything she'd ever seen before. The sun shone down on them, turning them a pure, bright white. They somehow looked rough and soft at the same time. Her breath caught in her throat as she saw a gap open up. A slight stretch of sand and trees appeared, and a deep blue streak of ocean. It was unbelievably tiny. From above the clouds, trees that had dwarfed her became smaller than her little finger. She turned, craned her neck and glanced up the mountain, the way they were heading. Even this high, above the clouds, they were still far from the top of the mountain.

Aella

As soon as the sun rose, the tribe packed up and started the long journey up the volcano. It took more than a month to reach the plateau where the festival was held. Aella couldn't shake the feeling of unease and impending doom as they trudged up the side of the gigantic mountain. As she walked, she heard the odd whispering constantly. It never grew in volume, but it was always present, gnawing at the edges of her mind the way sand and wind slowly grind ancient stone buildings down to nothing. She could barely focus, and it was all she could do to keep putting one foot in front of the other. She tried joining the conversation of the warriors around her, but eventually the wordless whispers drowned them out.

Summer began, and the higher they travelled, the hotter it became. Every year before this one, Aella was filled with energy and magic during the journey up the volcano. Now she fought to avoid collapsing, and desperately hoped she wasn't going insane.

Erasmus noticed her change in demeanour. He knew she was a quiet person, and didn't push her to talk. Instead he walked beside her, always there and ready to support her if she needed it. She loved him deeply in that moment, and somehow, like a sudden cool breeze in the middle of the desert, the whispers stopped. Her sudden smile almost made Erasmus trip on the rock-strewn path, and her smile turned into a laugh. He smiled in return, and she loved him even more. She kissed him, and suddenly the mountain path didn't seem so ominous to her.

Over the long journey, Aella felt faint whispers every now and then, but Erasmus kept her sane with his silent, comforting presence. When they finally set up camp on the plateau, she was feeling almost herself again. When they lit bonfires and starting chanting and dancing around the fire, her doubts fled. She was filled with energy again; she thought it must have been the fires.

This was one of her favourite parts of the festival: The welcoming. They lit the bonfires, prayed to Sithares and offered tributes by burning them. They sang and danced, beating small but surprisingly loud drums, stomping their feet and chanting. Nothing made her feel closer to her tribe than this, and even Kerberos' fanatics were relaxed and smiling during the welcoming ceremony.

There were never any fights on the day the tribe arrived at Sitharkos; not even sparring. They spent their time setting up camp, celebrating the beginning of the festival, and talking amongst themselves.

She didn't realise it until she woke the next day, but from the moment the festival started, she completely stopped hearing the maddening, not-quite-there whispers in her head.

The plateau was absolutely massive, fitting every member of Kerberos' tribe with enough space left for bonfires, fighting rings, and an area set aside for non-competitive sparring. The volcano's peak rose from one side of the plateau, only about twenty metres in height. There was already smoke drifting from it on the second day of the festival. When the sun rose that morning, the fighting started.

Aella spent the first half of the day simply watching. Half a dozen warriors died while she watched; she noted the winners, and how they fought. The festival competitions didn't require a death to win, but Thearans were intense and passionate, and usually the difference between sparring and competition was enough to push the warriors into blood-lust. It was why Aella didn't fight as often as most of the other warriors; she simply didn't feel the same urge to kill. She grew up a Thearan. Was, in fact, pure blooded Thearan; descended from Roxane of Theara, if her mother was correct. But still, there was something about her, and her mother for that matter, that was different to most Thearans. Her mother was always even-tempered. There was something serene about her, even during battle. Aella had inherited her calm, and while she loved the festival, she didn't feel the need to murder dozens of her fellow warriors simply to prove she was better than them. She knew she was better simply by watching them fight; but there was always more to learn by watching combat, even if the warriors were average. So she watched, and learned.

After her midday meal, she joined in the fighting. She only fought a handful of warriors, just enough to show her devotion to Sithares. The fighting was as sacred as the welcoming ceremony, and as important as praying. Sithares required death and destruction to gain power, so combat was not only a natural part of the Thearan lifestyle, but a huge part of Sithares' festival. She beat every warrior she fought against, and though it wasn't surprising, she still felt satisfaction every time she won. She only killed the warriors who didn't give up until death; there were several victories where her opponent was smart or humble enough to concede defeat without giving up their life.

One of the competitions Kerberos encouraged was a battle of pure Fire Magic; no weapons or physical combat was allowed. There were far fewer warriors powerful enough to compete, but the battles were much more intense and interesting to watch. Dakesh was fighting, along with most of Kerberos' fanatics, and Kerberos himself joined in every now and then, although few were stupid enough to challenge him. Aella watched these with great interest. She learned a lot about magic, and about Kerberos.

186

Aella challenged Dakesh to normal combat after he won the match he was fighting. She granted him time to rest, and they stood together watching a fight between Nomiki and a short Shenza man Aella didn't know. They were both quite good, though Nomiki was clearly the superior fighter. She let him believe they were evenly matched for a while, and Aella couldn't help but smile at the familiar ruse. Dakesh was fooled, which shocked Aella.

"It seems an even battle," he said, "care to wager?"

She stared at him, not sure if he was joking. When she realised he wasn't, she laughed and pulled a coin from a pouch on her belt.

"Nomiki will win, a fool could see it!" she laughed, holding the coin so Dakesh could see it. He laughed too, though a little uneasily, and produced a coin to match Aella's.

A few minutes later, after a ruthless kick to the Shenza's throat that sent him hurling to the ground unable to breathe, Dakesh begrudgingly tossed his coin to her. Then they both walked into one of the fighting rings together.

She faced Dakesh. They both stood ready, weapons drawn. He gave her the odd look she remembered from his fight against Andreas, when he first joined their tribe, except now it was mixed with what looked like fear. In that moment, she hoped he wouldn't push her into killing him. She liked Dakesh. He was a good warrior, a good hunter, and a good friend. He took a few breaths, closing his eyes briefly. The sky around him grew darker, like a cloud had formed directly above him. She suddenly felt cold. Was this some kind of Shenza magic? She'd heard about the Shadow Magicians of the Shanaken forests, but surely Dakesh wasn't one of them; he never displayed any magical abilities other than practising Fire Magic. *Then again,* she thought, *I'm hiding my own abilities from the entire tribe*. She remembered how during battle he moved faster than he should have been able to. While hunting and walking, he moved in a way that suggested he was talented, but not very fast. But as soon he drew his sword -

Dakesh launched at her suddenly, and thoughts fled her mind as she settled into combat. He swept his sword in a horizontal arc at her throat. She swayed underneath it and returned the attack, slicing his thigh in a shallow cut. He grunted and rolled away, landing on his knee with his sword in both hands. He rushed at her again, this time leaping at the last second, flipping over her and slashing down. Aella blocked with both her swords crossed, then aimed a kick where she knew he would land. It connected before his feet were completely on the ground, and he fell in a heap. She backed away a few steps, her eyes on him.

He rose, and shadows drew around him again. The cloudless desert sky somehow became harder to see through. She glanced at the gleaming black blade in his hands, and suddenly knew how to rid him of his power.

She rushed at him this time, sprinting the few steps between them and slashing with the sword in her right hand. He took the bait and as he moved to block her first attack, she swept her other sword at his blade, near the hilt. His sword suddenly disappeared. Or rather, it seemed to actually become shadow; she saw it, and her right hand sword was still holding it in place. But her left blade simply passed through it. Off balance and in shock, the momentum of her second attack twirled her too far away from Dakesh. In that instant, too fast for her to comprehend, a sudden sharp pain lanced her side.

She slashed at him in defence, leapt away and rolled back her feet. Her blades were up in a ready stance and she was facing the spot he stood a second ago; but he was gone. She wasted no time wondering; she dived just in time to hear the thump of him landing behind her and the whisper of his blade missing her by less than an inch.

She found her bearings again, and they fought viciously. His blade was everywhere at once. He knew where she would attack before she did, and he moved almost easily around her. She felt rage bubbling up from her core, fighting and scratching and clawing its way to the surface. She didn't try to push it down again. Instead, she embraced it and fed that flame until it roared throughout her entire body. She screamed, and unleashed the fire in her soul.

It was devastating. Dakesh was thrown backwards on a wave of unstoppable fire. It didn't stop there; several rows of watching Thearans were thrown back too, leaving a scorched circle around Aella at least twenty metres in every direction. The only thing still standing within that circle, other than Aella herself, was Kerberos. He stood in a braced position, knees bent, feet wide, forearms crossed at the chest. Once the explosion dissipated, he uncrossed his arms and stood normally, appraising her with a seemingly blank expression.

Dakesh stood unsteadily, shaking his head. His sword had flown out of his hand, and he was searching the ground in a daze when Aella appeared next to him with her swords levelled at his throat. He blinked when they touched his skin, and when he realised what happened his eyes flew wide open. She kicked him to the ground, still holding her blades angled towards his neck.

"Yield," she said calmly. She was still wreathed in flame; her every nerve electric, every muscle bulging with new strength. For a moment, he looked as though he was going to try to keep fighting; but as she predicted, his movements were far slower without his sword in hand. He didn't stand a chance. Still, she remained alert and braced for another battle until he lowered his head and yielded to her.

She sheathed her blades, extinguished her fire and helped Dakesh onto his feet. Several of the Thearans surrounding them started sneering and shouting insults. They wanted to see blood and death. Aella was glad; she would have hated to be forced to kill Dakesh. He dusted himself off, ignoring the shouts, and they started walking to a nearby campfire.

"Aella."

The voice was deep and loud enough to carry without shouting. Aella's spine chilled instantly hearing her name come from that voice. She turned. Kerberos was standing in the fighting ring, his sword already drawn. Trying not to show her fear, she left Dakesh and walked back into the ring.

Atillus

Tarsius was a small Tarsi settlement on the Eastern coast of Omas, north of Omatus. It was right on the coast, and although technically in a different country, the Tarsi still maintained control within its borders. Atillus stayed here for a little while, waiting for the opportunity he knew would come. After a week and a half, it did.

A tribe of Thearan warriors set up camp outside of the settlement and a handful of them entered the gates, meaning to trade and restock essentials for their journey. Thearans were nomadic, and although they were great hunters and made their own clothing and weapons, they liked to trade with the Tarsi. They maintained a respectful peace and could acquire unusual weapons and armour that would be impossible to build in the Omasi deserts. Atillus had read that the Thearans accepted any warrior into their tribe, provided the warrior could prove themselves in battle. He also read they had no structured royalty or noble families, and that their leaders were chosen based on strength, only allowed to ascend if they could defeat the current leader in a fight to the death. The ancient Thearans devoutly worshipped Sithares, although it seemed almost every tribe had forgotten it. They worshipped no gods now.

Atillus left Tarsius and wandered into the camps. There was no hostility, as he expected, merely idle curiosity. There were even a few polite greetings, which he returned. The Thearans were oddly relaxed about a stranger wandering through their camp. He walked and observed until a warrior hailed him.

191

"Stranger!" he called. Atillus glanced in his direction and walked over.

"Greetings, warrior," Atillus said.

"And to you," the warrior returned. "I am Nikolas. You are joining our tribe?"

Atillus nodded. "I am-" he realised he was about to give his full name out of habit. "-Yes, I am joining this tribe."

Nikolas laughed. He had an honest, good natured laugh. "Very well, traveller. I look forward to watching you fight."

The other warriors introduced themselves. None of them pressed him for his name.

Nikolas, the friendly warrior who welcomed Atillus with such enthusiasm, lay dying in the grey sand, Atillus' dagger sunk deep in his heart. There was a wild cheer from the watching Thearans, and Atillus knew he had them. He smiled at the simplicity of these people; your value was your strength and skill in battle. That was it. They were warriors, nothing more and nothing less.

I no longer need to hide who I am, he thought suddenly. *To feign stupidity or play any of those useless political games. These people don't care about overthrowing their leader unless they know they are strong enough. There are no noble families, no petty squabbling.*

Atillus wrenched his blade from the dead man's chest and wiped it on the body. He sheathed it and walked to his new tribe, smiling and letting them embrace him.

Thearans were considered savages by many. They travelled the harshest terrain in Pandeia, attacking villages and cities wherever they found them. They hunted, and ate, some of the most dangerous animals in the world. They had no formal command structure beyond a single leader

192

who was chosen by combat, and even the separate tribes fought each other.

Atillus loved them. He felt a primal connection to these people. And he knew he would be their leader. A few days after the tribe arrived in the Tarsi settlement, they set off again, straight into the desert.

The tribe was small, maybe only a hundred warriors in all, and could travel quite quickly. They made surprisingly good time through the unforgiving landscape. Every warrior carried everything they needed on their person; bedroll, spare food, weapons, water, and to Atillus' surprise, flints to make fire. When he first noticed them, he asked one of the warriors about it.

"Why do you carry these?" he asked, gesturing at the flint.

"To light our campfires, of course!" replied the Thearan, staring at Atillus as though he might be trying to trick him.

"Are you not able to wield fire magic?" Atillus asked, frowning.

"Not for a thousand years or more, warrior," replied the man, "Sithares is dead. All Thearans know this."

Atillus was shocked into silence. When Sithares stopped talking to him, Atillus assumed it was building followers in the deserts of Omas. Thearans were perfectly suited to worship the fire god, even if they believed it was no longer alive. Then he remembered what Sithares said to him: *if you will serve me, you can restore my power.* And the passage from Sithares' book:

Sithares gains strength from destruction; from the burning of objects, buildings and (perhaps most of all) of people. Like all Gods, it also gains strength from the prayers of those who follow it.

He saw what he needed to do in a flash of understanding that felt like a sudden bonfire in his heart.

193

But first, he needed to be the leader of this tribe. He left the warrior and headed straight for the tribe's leader.

The leader heard his approach and turned, nodding a curt greeting. Atillus stopped a metre from the man, standing directly in front of him. He spoke up so his voice would be heard by as many of the Thearans as possible.

"I challenge you for leadership." His hand rested on the hilt of his sword. The leader looked around him, taking in the warriors who were watching. Partway through turning his head a second time, the leader lashed out with his sword. He was fast; but Atillus was faster. He ducked under the blade and drew his own. And the stranger and the leader fought on the grey dunes of the Omasi desert. By the end, the entire tribe was gathered around them, and when their leader was engulfed in magical flame, screaming and clawing at his skin like a madman, they each wore the same awed expression. Not fear, Atillus noted. No fear of fire from these warriors; but awe. And when their old leader stopped screaming and lay as a burning corpse in the sand, they each dropped to their knees and bowed their heads before their leader.

"Sithares has awoken!" He shouted to the small tribe. "You will worship him, as the old Thearans did in the age of heroes!"

The Thearans cheered, still kneeling. They started chanting the name of the fire god.

"We will spread the fire as far as it can go! Burn Shadow from the world! Burn the world, and remain unburned!" He was screaming now, his eyes wide, and his tribe were screaming too. As the final touch, he raised his arms and a cloak of flame rushed over his body, engulfing him completely. He stood that way for a moment, and knew that the tribe of Thearans, though small, was utterly his.

Aella

Dakesh had been inhumanly fast. Kerberos was faster. Aella dodged and blocked desperately, searching his movements for a weakness. She was drained, and not just from the battle with Dakesh. Using that much Fire Magic was taking its toll. Breathing hard, she retreated under Kerberos' relentless attacks. She felt her strength fading. Kerberos, even though he'd already fought several intense battles that day, seemed to possess limitless energy and strength. He stared into her eyes as they fought, and despite the Fire Magic bubbling under the surface between them, his own eyes remained as cold as ice.

They fought for what felt like hours. Kerberos didn't let up, and Aella refused to yield. She blocked everything he threw at her. She was beginning to think she would slip up when he slightly overextended a thrust; she cut his forearm and kicked his hand as hard as she could. His sword flew out of his hand, and as she swept her blade towards his throat, a roaring sound filled her ears. For a single instant, she thought she might be about to kill Kerberos. Her blade passed through his neck, deep enough to kill; but his neck, along with the rest of him, had already been enveloped in flame. He punched her face, hard, swinging his arm down from above. His strength was unbelievable; before she felt the hit, her head thumped into the hard packed dirt of the fighting ring. There was a ringing in her ears and her vision was clouded by pulsing white with streaks of bloody red. She couldn't tell if her weapons were still in her hands.

She blinked, trying to stand, and what felt like a gigantic steel hammer smashed into her stomach. She went tumbling over the dirt, scrabbling to steady herself. Over the screams and cheers of the warriors around her, she heard a painful, chilling cry. Her heart skipped a beat and her eyes flew open. She would recognise that voice anywhere. Her mother was screaming at Kerberos to stop. For a second she forgot where she was, and who she was fighting. She forgot she was the one in danger. That scream pierced her very soul, stabbing right into her core and awakening a beast she didn't know existed. In that second, she somehow thought that Kerberos was attacking her mother. The woman who raised her, taught her to fight, taught her how to take care of herself and how to be safe. The woman who would give anything for her in a heartbeat.

Aella was on her feet instantly. She growled, her voice suddenly unrecognisable. Her fists clenched; her swords were in the dirt between her and Kerberos. She burst into flame, and through her mindless rage she was dimly aware that she had controlled the fire; there was no explosion this time. She launched herself at Kerberos, screaming like an animal. He hadn't bothered picking up his sword. They fought with their hands, knees and feet. Aella couldn't even feel his attacks. She hit him everywhere she could reach, slamming her fist into his throat, her knee into his groin, her foot into his knee. She hit his side, and felt him shrink away a little. She pressed her attack, hitting harder and faster. Her energy was being fed by the fire, and the fire by her rage, and her rage was endless.

He lashed out desperately, connecting with her chest. Instead of falling she jumped with the force of his attack, flipping backwards, landing on her hands and cartwheeling away. She landed low, in a ready stance, and saw her swords laying close by. Kerberos was sprinting towards her. She sprinted and dived, snatching her swords from the ground just as Kerberos reached her. He tried to kick her as she landed. With the swords in her hands, she reached into them and touched her fire to theirs. Kerberos' foot connected with her neck, hard. It had no effect on her. Lost in blood-lust, he lifted his foot and slammed it into her neck even harder. He may as well have stomped on the grey dirt of the plateau. She felt nothing. Nothing but rage. She stood, and though she realised now that she could kill him easily if she wanted to, she didn't.

Kerberos attacked again, unwilling to concede defeat. She moved around him; he looked as if he was moving slowly, like moving was difficult or painful. She dodged easily. He kept attacking, his face growing angrier as she avoided him effortlessly. When she realised he wouldn't give up, her patience ran out. She cut his thighs, shoulders, back and calves in one blindingly fast, twirling manoeuvre. He grunted and fell to his knees.

She placed both of her blades, crossed in an X, against the back of his neck. His fire went out in a rush, leaving him panting in the dirt. She let her own fire go out.

"Yield!" She screamed at him. He remained silent. She regained control of her heart and her breath, and calmed her voice.

"I don't want to kill you, Kerberos. You are the son of Sithares. You are the leader of our great tribe. I wouldn't take that from you. I will not. I swear it, with all of you and Sithares itself as my witness."

She sheathed her blades before he answered. She stepped back, and waited, ready to die. He stood, unsteadily at first, and then with confidence as he realised his wounds were superficial. He turned, regarding her, and the hatred she expected in his eyes was nowhere to be found. Instead he looked at her with what seemed to be new found respect.

"I yield this fight to you, Aella," he said, "but as the Son of Sithares, I could not have lost. If I were in any real danger, Sithares would have granted me the strength to win."

Kerberos' fanatics cheered. Aella knew in that moment she was in no danger. They knew how powerful she was, but they also knew Kerberos didn't see her as a threat to himself.

"But you have shown great power," he continued, "you are the most powerful warrior I have ever seen. From this day forward, I want you to be my second in command."

After that day, the rest of the festival was just like previous years, and Aella joined in the celebrations and competitions as much as possible. She was trying to keep her mind off the fact that she was now going to be fighting, walking and camping much closer to Kerberos and his fanatics. All of the tribe was like a family, but Kerberos and his band of zealots were a family of their own; one that Aella didn't want to be a part of.

Her mother was deeply disturbed by the news. She watched the fight, of course; but when Aella talked to her privately, she seemed to be hearing it for the first time.

"I told you not to reveal your strength, Aella," she said quietly, "now you will always be within reach of Kerberos and his most loyal followers."

"But I have Kerberos' support! Plus they all saw I'm stronger than him; if I can beat him, they pose no threat to me. Surely they wouldn't try anything now." But she knew even as she said the words that she was trying to convince herself just as much as Helene. She would never be safe around them, and they both knew it. She would have to keep her guard up constantly from now on.

Athanasius

Athanasius crouched behind a large boulder. He saw Kerberos summon something from the fire. The thing Kerberos spoke to was unlike anything Athanasius had ever seen. His people, the Thearans, were able to wield fire magic, and could do quite a few amazing things with it; but even so, Athanasius was made uneasy by the sight of the thing Kerberos spoke with. Athanasius was too far away to hear their conversation. The thing stepped back into the flames and Athanasius didn't wanted Kerberos to know he witnessed their meeting, so he ran back to the camp as stealthily as he could.

When he returned to the camp, Athanasius went to one of the small campfires that burned through the night and sat beside it, thinking. Summoning a creature such as the one Kerberos spoke to was unheard of. Fire wights were one thing, and even they were rare; but an intelligent, imposing figure like that gave Athan a feeling of impending dread. Even worse was knowing Kerberos was hiding this magic from him. His past was mostly a mystery, but most people who joined the Thearan tribes after childhood didn't talk much of their past lives. But Kerberos, since becoming something of a mentor for Athan years ago, started to share everything with him. None of that sharing included any mention of a seemingly intelligent fire demon. Kerberos was much more devout in his following of the Fire God Sithares, though, and was an incredibly powerful Fire Mage. Athan realised there were probably many things Kerberos hadn't taught him when it came to fire magic. Besides, Athan knew he wasn't the most talented with magic.

He's probably just waiting until I'm powerful enough to handle more before he shows me that kind of thing, he thought.

Athan decided it wasn't his place to know just yet. He cursed softly and wondered why he followed Kerberos in the first place. He'd ask Kerberos about it soon, but not yet. He wasn't sure of Kerberos' mood, and he could be terrifying and brutal when not in high spirits.

When Athan emerged from his tent, Kerberos was back at camp. Their leader was in his own tent, but Athan knew his mentor well and knew that whenever he was in his tent, he preferred his guards to stand further back from the entrance to show confidence and approachability. The former was mostly unnecessary as the entire tribe was aware of Kerberos' strength and abilities; The latter was pointless because as far as Athan was concerned, nothing could make the muscle-bound, seven foot tall leader of the Thearan army seem approachable. Even Athan was nervous around him, and they'd been training together and taking meals together for years now. The guards were indeed stationed on the other side of the walkway from their master's tent. Athanasius steered clear of his mentor for now, and went to one of the communal fire pits spread around the camp. It was early afternoon and a few hunters were preparing the midday meal. A few birds and lizards were already mostly cooked, being turned on a spit by hungry warriors. Athan sat nearby, waiting until the meat was cooked. He watched the warriors go about their business. He was mostly invisible to the tribe lately, and enjoyed watching them without needing to explain what he was doing.

Athan had never been very social, and didn't fit in with the stereotypical Thearan personality. He had grown up with Aella, his best friend, who was also very quiet. They used to be inseparable, and he'd loved her as though she was his own sister until she fell for a new recruit, an escaped slave from Omatus named Erasmus. The Omati had just barely passed the initiation, and was far more talkative and friendly than Aella or Athan. But when he saw how close Aella and Athan were, he presented Aella with an ultimatum: Athan, or himself. To Athan's shock, she chose Erasmus. Since then, they really hadn't spoken much. That was about ten years ago, and Athan hadn't made new friends. Other than Kerberos.

Kerberos noticed Athanasius after a little while, and approached him.

"You don't talk to the others," he said to Athan. Athan shook his head, eyes downcast.

Kerberos lowered himself to his knees, looking Athan in the eye. "I don't talk to them either. There can be great strength in solitude. But sometimes, we need others. Some things..." Kerberos put his hand on Athan's face. He was surprisingly gentle. "... Can only be done with others."

Athanasius didn't understand what Kerberos was talking about at first. But they started spending time together, and Kerberos started teaching Athan to fight and use Fire Magic. And then Kerberos taught him other things, things they could only do together in the privacy of Kerberos' tent. Athan didn't realise what his feelings for Kerberos meant until the first time they laid together. It hurt for a while, but it was a sweet pain, made all the sweeter for being born of their closeness. Kerberos became Athan's whole world after that. They trained together, broke their fast together, shared Kerberos' bed, and talked of many things. Kerberos treated him well, but he was very secretive and he was a very passionate man, as prone to fits of white-hot rage as he was to moments of intense love. Athanasius still found himself alone every day for some time, while Kerberos dealt with being the leader of their tribe.

So he sat at the fire, and watched; and when the meat was cooked he wandered close enough to cut some off for himself, and then wandered back to sit on his own again.

Two of the warriors sitting at the fire were arguing playfully.

"Can't you see the patterns on its back? It's a Diamondback, look!"

"Haris, you are ignoring other signs again. See the shape of the claws?"

"They look like any other claws, Iliana! What am I supposed to be looking at?"

Iliana laughed and reached over to the cooking lizard. She cut off one of its legs and held it right up to Haris' face.

"See how the curve gets more pronounced on the outside claws, and the diamond pattern is only a thin strip on the back? There's no diamond pattern on the legs or sides. It's clearly a Deathclaw."

Haris deflated a little.

"Yes, yes, you're right. You always are. I don't know why I still argue with you."

"Because you're stubborn and a sore loser!" Iliana threw the lizard's foot at Haris, and hit him square between the eyes. He launched himself at her in retaliation. The two of them laughed and fought for a while, a pretend wrestle turning into a full contact sparring session. There was a noticeable shift in mood, from fun to truly competitive, though the smile never left their faces. Sparring was one of the most common activities among Thearans, and Athan loved watching. He was a decent fighter, but by no means the best. He always learned something from watching the older soldiers spar and was always happy to learn.

He watched Iliana's stance change from an unarmed ready position to a close quarters dagger stance known as *Iro's Fangs*. As most sparring sessions were among friends and were informal, a lot of warriors didn't use weapons. Iliana adapted the stance to use open, straightened hands in place of actual blades. Haris changed stance too, but was still using an unarmed form. Iliana swept her left hand in to Haris' core, aiming for a spot between his ribs. If they'd been fighting to the death, and if she hit her mark, he would have died in moments. But they knew each other well, apparently, and he expected the move.

He deflected the blow with his right hand. Her right hand was already moving, and she stabbed his right shoulder just as he finished blocking her first strike. With a blade, that cut would have disabled his right arm completely. He tried to bat her hand away but she already hit him. He grunted and threw a punch with his left fist towards her face. Iliana swayed underneath it and sliced her left fingers across his belly, and then jabbed her right hand into his ribs, pointing up right at his heart. Haris grunted again, and laughed.

"They say you can only improve by fighting someone better than yourself," he said, rubbing his new bruises, "So why haven't I become any better?"

Iliana laughed too. "You don't learn from your mistakes, Haris." Her smile faltered.

"You need to start paying attention to your weaknesses. It'll get you killed otherwise."

Haris chuckled in response, though his smile had disappeared too.

Finishing the lizard, Athan got up and walked through the camp, looking for someone to spar with. He didn't particularly feel like trying to spar with Kerberos, but wasn't close with anyone else. He saw Aella and Erasmus talking with a third person, a Shenza man he wasn't familiar with, and thought he might try them. Though they didn't speak much, they weren't exactly on bad terms. Athan thought it was worth a shot.

Aella saw him approaching. Her face lit up very briefly, and then she glanced at Erasmus with what looked like a flash of guilt.

So she still wants to be friends, Athan thought. The thought made him feel better about the lack of communication between them. At least he knew now that it wasn't a dead friendship.

The Shenza warrior was the first to greet him, with a friendly nod and a smile. Athan returned to gesture and shook the man's hand.

"My name is Dakesh," he said amiably, "honoured to meet you."

"The honour is mine," Athan replied, "I am Athanasius."

Erasmus turned from their conversation and regarded Athan coldly. "Greetings, warrior," he said. Though technically polite, it was the least friendly greeting Athan had ever heard, but he was used to Erasmus' chilly demeanour towards him despite their rare encounters. Athan didn't see the point in fighting for real, although he knew he could beat Erasmus. A sparring session would be satisfying enough, if Erasmus was stupid enough to agree. He decided to feign amiability instead.

"Hope you're well, Erasmus?" Athan's grin felt odd, but he knew it would remove any possibility of angering Erasmus while at the same time making him uncomfortable.

"Of course. And you?" Athan could see in the look Erasmus gave him that he knew what Athan was doing, and didn't appreciate it.

"Very well. I've been training with Kerberos for a while now. Just wondering if any of you wanted to spar?"

Dakesh looked as if he was about to reply, but a fierce look appeared in Erasmus' eyes. "I'll spar with you, warrior."

Dakesh

The Fire Festival was a wonder to behold. Thearans spent their lives fighting, hunting, killing, and setting fires; Dakesh saw all of these things every day since joining the tribe. But the festival was a new experience entirely; the fights were more brutal, the hunts more dangerous, and the fires many times larger. There was an energy in the air, so intense it was almost a physical presence like the smoke and ash that hung in the air around them.

He spent a lot of time watching and wagering on the battles, and joined in the fighting several times. He won every fight except his last against Aella. When he submitted instead of fighting to the death he was jeered, but he saw relief in Aella's face and it lifted his spirits. Kerberos challenged Aella immediately after their fight. Dakesh couldn't resist watching; he moved to the ring and sat on the sand, sore and tired but watching intently.

The fight was like nothing he'd ever seen. He had felt almost evenly matched against Aella during their battle; but when she fought Kerberos it became obvious he was merely a warm up for a warrior such as her. Even with his *Kaizuun,* he was utterly beneath her. Kerberos and Aella moved like lightning in a storm; twirling around each other, clashing and suddenly changing direction like leaves caught in a hurricane. He was mesmerised.

Then they both unleashed their magic, enveloping themselves in fire, and the battle rose to a whole new level. Dakesh couldn't follow them; they were simply too fast. He sat for a while, watching blurred flames arcing towards each other and away again, not knowing who may be winning but not wanting to look away. Then an idea seized him, and he almost laughed at how obvious it was. He drew his blade, and the second it was in his hand the fight slowed down slightly; they were still moving faster than he could have caught up with, but just slow enough that he understood what was happening. They were both unarmed, and Kerberos seemed to be winning. Aella was on the ground, reaching for her swords.

Just as she swept them off the ground, Kerberos kicked her viciously in the neck. He kicked her again and again, but she didn't even flinch. She stood, her movements so fast now that even with his *Kaizuun* he couldn't follow. He watched Kerberos try to attack her over and over, but she became a flame-filled whirlwind, surrounding him and avoiding him all at the same time. Suddenly, thin sprays of blood flew from Kerberos' legs, shoulders and back all at the same time. He grunted and fell to his knees. The fire covering him disappeared in an instant. Aella's remained as she stood over him and screamed at him to yield. Her rage and power were staggering.

Kerberos yielded to gasps of astonishment from the watching crowd. Dakesh shook his head in amazement; he never would have bet on any warrior winning a fight against Kerberos. The Thearan leader appointed her his second in command right there in the ring where she almost killed him. Aella didn't look proud or pleased, however; instead she wore an intensely troubled expression as she walked out of the ring.

Aella

The festival ended about ten days after Aella was named second in command, and it passed quickly and uneventfully; except for one unexpected development. Aella didn't think anything more could occur during the festival that would shock her. And then Athanasius appeared while Erasmus, Dakesh and her were talking about their possible destination after the festival. She saw him first, and despite their estrangement, the first thing she felt was sudden joy. Then she remembered Erasmus was standing right next to her; She tried to mask her feelings and waited for Athan to greet them. Dakesh was the first to act, however, giving Athan a nod and a smile.

They introduced each other, and Athan and Erasmus even traded cold pleasantries. When Athan asked if someone wanted to spar, Aella's heart throbbed painfully. She missed their sparring, but if she accepted, Erasmus would only grow jealous and petty again. Dakesh looked as though he was about to accept, and she was suddenly very keen to see the two spar; if Athan had improved as much as she suspected, the fight would be very interesting to watch. But before Dakesh could say anything, Erasmus spoke up, the cold tone never leaving his voice.

"I'll spar with you, warrior."

Athanasius

Athanasius and Erasmus stood, facing each other in one of the sparring rings. Athanasius decided to use his spear instead of the short sword he used more often. Kerberos fought at mid range and long range very effectively, and Athan adapted his fighting style with a spear to be able to deal with opponents from a distance. He knew Erasmus would be using a sword, and he wanted to try his long range fighting style against a short range opponent. He also knew he'd easily be able to beat Erasmus, and a part of him was looking forward to the satisfaction of putting him in his place.

Erasmus was holding his sword ready, in a standard combat stance that gave away his mediocre skills at a glance. Kerberos had taught him how to quickly judge an opponent's body language before any battle started.

"You can read skill level, confidence, injuries, habits and speed if you know what you are looking for," he'd instructed Athan, "all before the first strike."

He answered Erasmus' stance with a more confident and advanced opening stance of his own. Right foot forward, standing side on to the opponent, spear in the extended forward hand and pointing down at the opponent's feet. The shaft of the spear ran parallel to his arm, the butt sitting roughly at his shoulder. It wasn't the most practical stance, especially if the opponent started too close, but it showed confidence and Athan knew there was enough time to transition to a more controlled stance by the time Erasmus reached him.

His opponent's stance was melting away as anger took hold. Athan saw his silent, taunting confidence breaking Erasmus' resolve; he fought not to smirk. Erasmus gave in and rushed at Athan. Athan twirled, spinning the spear in graceful loops, bringing it around into a two handed grip as he landed left foot forward and slightly crouched. He was now perfectly balanced on the balls of his feet, his spear secured in a lethal position, blade pointing at the dead centre of Erasmus' chest. As the former Omati slave started swinging his sword, Athan twirled the spearhead around the blade of the sword, adding to its momentum and taking it in an arc out of Erasmus' grip. His opponent built too much momentum of his own, so Athan spun on his left foot, swinging the butt of his spear into Erasmus' back as he ran past. He stumbled and fell, and Athan stood in another confident stance over him, trying desperately not to laugh out loud. Kerberos' training had improved his combat skills drastically; he was still no master, but to the likes of Erasmus, he might as well be Kerberos himself.

Erasmus was falling perfectly for his trap. He dragged himself to his feet, practically spitting with rage. Before he'd even steadied himself into a fighting position, he launched himself again at Athan. He barely needed to try now. He sidestepped and swung his spear into Erasmus' legs as he passed, tripping him up. He was just allowing himself a tiny smile when his feet were suddenly swept from under him, and the ground slammed the air from his lungs before he understood what happened. He rolled, trying to breathe in, and saw Aella standing over him, furious and looking ready for a fight. His heart sank as he realised he'd disappointed her. *Your ego blinded you, you fool,* he chided himself. *Of course Aella would be angry at you for humiliating her love.* He shook his head, dragged a wheezing breath into his lungs and looking up at Aella.

"I'm sorr-" He started to say, but his own spear suddenly appeared, streaking down at his face with incredible speed. He felt the fire-hardened wood smash his forehead. White spots covered his vision. He rolled away from Aella, trying to gain his footing back. The spear came down hard on his back while he was rising. He screamed, dropping back to the ground. She hit him again, and again, and then he distantly heard his spear thud to the ground next to him. He was on his hands and knees, trying weakly to stand, when Aella grabbed him roughly and hauled him to his feet. Though younger than Athan, she was larger than him by a fair amount, and certainly stronger. She was a pure blood Thearan, dark skin and white hair and golden eyes, and she was a true warrior. She was intense with her training and had incredible self discipline. She set him on his feet in front of her, keeping her hands on his shoulders in a vice-like grip. She was breathing heavily, but it seemed to be from rage instead of physical effort. She was not sweating at all, and if he hadn't felt the blows himself he wouldn't have known she just beat someone senseless and picked them up off the ground.

She stared into his eyes for a few unbearable moments, unmasked fury twisting her features. They grew up together, inseparable until she fell for Erasmus, and were like siblings. He still saw her as a little sister, but he was absolutely terrified of her in that moment. Eventually, she let go of his arms and took a graceful step back. She was graceful in everything she did, her movements always perfectly coordinated and smooth. She hadn't taken her eyes off him since she set him on his feet. Her gaze didn't waver as she spoke, her voice quiet but laced with lethal promise.

"I love you like a brother, Athan," she said, "and I always will. But if you hurt Erasmus again, I'll kill you."

Athanasius closed his eyes, his head dropping down. He knew she meant it, and it broke his heart. Erasmus got to his feet. He stood a few metres behind Aella, looking disgruntled and about as furious as she was.

All he could do was nod his head silently. Aella turned and stalked back to camp, Erasmus following behind her. Athan stood for what felt like hours, hating himself for stooping so low as to pick a fight with Aella's love.

Finally he wandered back to the camp. Kerberos was in his tent as Athan passed; he waved and called him in. *At least there's someone in this endless desert who wants to speak with me,* he thought, ducking under the open tent flap. He sat next to Kerberos, and they were silent for a time. Kerberos was a very quiet man, and Athan was used to stretches of comfortable silence in his presence. They sat for a while, until Kerberos turned his gaze directly to Athan and finally spoke:

"You seem tense, Athanasius."

He lowered his gaze, frowning. He didn't know how to discuss the topic of Aella with his mentor. Kerberos was a solitary person, much like Athan. But where Athan's solitude came from his inability to fit in, Kerberos' came from a genuine apathy towards other people; he simply didn't want or need the company of others. Athan did. He envied Kerberos. He hesitated, trying to find words to make him understand how he felt.

"I beat Erasmus today, in a sparring match," he began, "and Aella defended him. She was furious at me. I feel as though I've destroyed the friendship. After all these years of hoping we would still be friends, I ruined everything by giving in to pride."

Kerberos looked at him with a frowning, confused expression, though not unkindly. Athan knew he didn't understand, but he'd always been there when Athan felt lonely, and that was all he could ask for. He seemed to think about it for a while, and they lapsed back into silence.

"Why did you fight Erasmus, if you knew it would upset Aella?" Kerberos finally asked, his intense stare holding Athan's gaze. This was always how conversations with Kerberos went, Athan knew; pure logic, no trace of emotion at all. He hadn't expected any different, but it still exasperated him that Kerberos seemed to have absolutely no understanding of the dynamics of friendship.

"I... wanted to hurt him," he replied, "I tried to treat him well, as Aella would want. But he was so aggressive, and I

211

could tell he wanted to hurt me too." Athan was frowning, thinking about what he'd done and trying to justify it. Explaining things to Kerberos could be therapeutic, if only because it forced him to look at things in the disconnected, impartial way Kerberos looked at everything.

"I... I don't know why I fought him. I wasn't thinking clearly." Admitting it made him so ashamed he couldn't meet Kerberos' eyes. He heard a quiet but exasperated sigh from his mentor.

"Athanasius, you must learn to control your emotions," he said, gently but sternly, "they are powerful, but they are chaotic and can not be trusted. You must remain in control. Think before you act." Athan nodded, head down. He always felt this way whenever Kerberos corrected him; humbled. Stripped down. Inferior. Kerberos suddenly gave a short, sharp chuckle, and Athan almost fell over from shock.

"You fought well, I will grant you that. Until Aella stepped in and beat you easily." *Oh no,* Athan thought to himself. *He was watching the whole time!* He glanced at the massive warrior, terrified, but there seemed to be genuine good humour in those deadly eyes.

"You have obviously paid attention to my lessons when we spar. I am pleased at how much progress you have made." This much praise was almost as shocking as the laugh. Athan stared for a moment, unsure how to respond.

"But that match is the perfect example of why you must remain clear-headed when fighting. You were so blinded by pride and victory, you were unaware of Aella approaching you. She made no effort to hide, and took your weapon and knocked you down without trying."

Athanasius knew what Kerberos wanted to hear. He desperately wanted to please his mentor. He finally met that intimidating gaze.

"I will do better. I will be better." Kerberos only nodded slightly.

They made love that night. Kerberos was distant and cold, but he often was of late, and Athan was accustomed to his moodiness. He didn't say a word while he lay behind Athan, holding his hips and thrusting gently. Athan remembered a time when their lovemaking hurt; now it felt incredible, even when Kerberos wasn't emotionally present.

He moaned and rocked his hips against Kerberos, and smiled as the huge warrior let out a low grunt in response. Pleasing Kerberos wasn't always an easy task. He lived for the moments when the tribe's leader displayed satisfaction in him. It wasn't purely sexual either; Kerberos' approval meant everything to him in battle, hunting, and tactics as well as lovemaking. Praise from Kerberos was incredibly rare, however; he often completely ignored Athan's improvements, focusing instead on his weaknesses and pushing him to rise above them.

When they finished, Kerberos rolled over and went to sleep. Athan lay awake, still thinking about his fight with Erasmus. The only people he'd grown close to in his life possessed such control over their emotions; Aella and Kerberos had that much in common, if nothing else. He wanted to be able to think rationally instead of letting himself be provoked into rash decisions. But Erasmus offered the challenge; they wouldn't have fought in the first place if Dakesh or Aella accepted Athan's invitation instead. He decided it was just as much Erasmus' fault as his own. He knew Aella would never see it that way, and he still hated himself for it. He only hoped she would forgive him; but with their friendship already so thin, it seemed unlikely. He didn't sleep well.

Dakesh

Two weeks later, they left the Heart of Sithares and ventured again into the desert. Dakesh was accustomed to the brutal heat and inhospitable land of Omas by now; memories of the cool green forests of Shanaken and his comfortable old life there were few and far between. Aella was absolutely silent as they travelled, brooding over Erasmus' battle against the warrior who asked them to spar. Dakesh wandered over to a different group of warriors he occasionally practised Fire Magic with. They talked and laughed and threw fireballs at each other as they marched, and Dakesh forgot Shanaken a little more; the desert felt like home to him now.

He was becoming powerful, he felt it. After the festival, journeying through the desert seemed somehow easier. At first he was terrified of the gigantic volcano, but after spending weeks camped on the plateau, he felt magic filling his body like sunlight filling the desert sky. It was as Aella said: their magic was most powerful at Sitharkos. He felt renewed. He marched through the desert with his fellow Thearans, feeling the sun's heat and drawing strength from it.

Though Sithares' voice remained quiet since arriving at the foot of the volcano, he felt a deep connection with the God now. He sparred against a new warrior every day of the journey. Dakesh won every battle. Thearans cheered and embraced him after each victory. Kerberos smiled and nodded a respectful greeting whenever they crossed paths. *If only the* Duulshen *could see me now,* he thought bitterly. *They'd know how powerful I could have been if they'd only recognised my potential. With Sithares on my side, I'll be more powerful than all of them combined.*

The thought, instead of giving him satisfaction, left him feeling empty and furious. Why did they refuse him his *Kaizuun?* They had no right; he was one of their best warriors. He'd proven himself over and over, done everything they demanded. What was he missing? Why wasn't he good enough for them? Growing more frustrated, he left the camp to perform his *Zuunshai* alone. He used it not only to practice, but to meditate. It centred his thoughts and feelings, and he usually found he was at peace after finishing the blade dance.

This time, however, his heart was still racing, his mind still clouded with bitterness. He let his sword fall to the ground carelessly. He clenched his fists and closed his eyes. Instead of trying to remain calm, centred and passive as the *Zuunshai* demanded, he focused on his hate. He pictured the council of *Duulshen*, every wrinkled face, as they stared at him with their judging, condescending eyes. He imagined himself there now with his *Kaizuun* and his Fire Magic, and as their faces continued judging, he used all of his power against them.

As their ancient faces turned to shock and terror, they melted away under a wave of fire. It rose, covering everything, covering his vision. He screamed, feeling his rage burst from within like a volcano erupting. When the fire cleared, the *Duulshen* disappeared and he was staring into the face of a Thearan warrior. His name was Sotiris. Dakesh practised Fire Magic with him occasionally. The warrior looked at him, terrified.

"What happened, Dakesh?" he asked. Dakesh shook his head. "I was trying to meditate, but it didn't work – your guess is as good as mine."

"You exploded, Dakesh. Kerberos thought we were being attacked."

Dakesh sat on the sand, thinking about the *Zuunshai.* The blade dance used to centre him, and made him feel powerful, in control. It had always calmed him down; but not this time. This time, rage made him feel powerful. Fire Magic centred him. The *Kaizuun* was everything he'd ever wanted. Fire Magic gave him more than he ever dreamed he could have.

"I was practising, Sotiris, that's all." He tried to look reassuring. Sotiris clearly didn't believe him, but he left the matter alone nonetheless. They walked back to camp together, and Kerberos approached them as they arrived at Dakesh's tent.

"That was you?" he asked.

"Yes."

"Are you in control of your powers?"

He hesitated for barely a second, but it was enough. He saw doubt in Kerberos' eyes as he replied to the leader.

"Yes, I am in control." Kerberos walked away.

"Keep practising, Shenza," he called over his shoulder, "and never lie to me again."

Losing Kerberos' trust effected Dakesh more than he expected. He tried to come up with ways to repair the broken trust as they marched south. Nothing occurred to him. He felt isolated as he marched, surrounded by thousands of fellow warriors. Kerberos no longer respected him, Aella and Erasmus withdrew from the tribe since Sitharkos, and Sithares' voice was completely silent. All he could do was practice controlling his Fire Magic as he walked.

Sand dunes rose and fell endlessly, soft yet steep and dangerous. The desert moved like an ocean, waves rippling and crashing together. Wind battered the Thearans as they trudged over the dunes, the sand stinging their skin and eyes. Animals disappeared during the day, leaving the dry grey landscape empty and lifeless but for the howling wind. The few trees and clumps of dry red grass in the distance shimmered, completing the illusion of a burning, ash-filled wasteland.

The dunes shrank the longer they marched. The wind calmed, and the ground became harder beneath their feet. When the mountains were in clear view, sand turned to dirt, then to grass. Proper, living grass, not the dry, skeletal grass of the desert. When they reached a river at the mountains' feet, they set up camp. Dakesh saw trees close to the river on their side, and thousands more on the opposite bank. They were nothing like Shanaken, but they lifted his spirits anyway.

Athanasius

During the trip south, Kerberos walked with Athan. He found the powerful man's presence comforting. The dunes of the Omati desert were massive, especially out in the centre, and the tribe never ended up conforming to a single file formation as they meant to. They were always in sight of each other, however, and Athan found that comforting too, even though he didn't particularly enjoy talking to most of them. The journey was brutal, but a thousand generations of travelling through the desert had made the Thearans experts when it came to traversing the impossible terrain.

They sparred each evening after setting up camp, then hunted in the twilight before sunset and at dawn. The rest of the time they walked. Though he was still distant, Kerberos remained by Athan's side for almost the entire journey, and despite the silence Athan felt them growing even closer. After almost a week, Kerberos finally spoke.

"Athan. Do you know where we are heading?" Athan shook his head.

"We are going to the southern mountains, and travelling up the Alpheus. From there we will attack the farmlands along the river until we reach Omatus." Athan was silent for a moment. They'd never attacked farmland before; Thearans usually only engaged in battle with worthy foes, other seasoned armies who could provide a challenge. He trusted Kerberos' judgement, however, and if Kerberos believed this to be their best course of action, he would gladly follow his leader into battle. All he felt at that moment was lucky; lucky to have Kerberos discussing his plans with him, and to have him break the silence of the last week.

"And when we reach Omatus..." Athan knew the answer before Kerberos replied, but he wanted to hear it directly from the war leader.

"We burn everything, and take it for the glory of Sithares." He nodded, and oddly enough, he didn't feel any fear or apprehension about the battles to come. He knew nothing would be able to hurt him while Kerberos remained by his side.

"Why are we attacking farmlands? Would it not please Sithares more to wage war against full armies?"

Kerberos seemed to think for a moment before answering.

"Something has changed, Athan. At the festival, Sithares spoke to me directly."

Of course, he thought, *that was no fire demon, that was Sithares itself!*

"Sithares wants us to burn the fertile lands to the south to punish the Omati for their lack of worship. They have ignored the God of Fire for too long, and have grown fat and lazy. They wage no wars, they burn no sacrifices, and they have even forgotten their God's name. They do not deserve the great city they dwell in. We will burn what can be burned, and build a new city for Sithares. The Omati's time is over."

Kerberos' passion was unnerving. By the time he spoke the last word, his fists were clenched and his teeth bared. Athan had no idea how to respond. Kerberos was given direct orders from the God of Fire, and shared those orders with him. He felt honoured beyond words.

Kerberos watched him intently. He needed to respond; to show his loyalty and his appreciation to his leader for sharing this with him.

"I will do anything I can to serve you and Sithares." It felt stiff and formal, and Athan didn't think it was enough, but Kerberos smiled and put his hand on Athan's shoulder.

"I already have a plan for you."

Aella

Two days after Erasmus and Athan fought, the tribe packed up and headed back down the giant volcano. Aella was so furious with Athanasius that she was still shaking. Even worse, she knew she would have to see him almost every day now she was part of Kerberos' small command group; Athan was never too far from Kerberos these days. He was heeding her warning, at least; he kept his distance from her and Erasmus as much as possible.

The journey down Sitharkos was far easier than the walk to the top. The maddening feeling of impending doom disappeared entirely, as well as the low whispering sound that was almost a voice. As they walked down the volcano's side, Aella became more and more convinced the sounds were merely a temporary lapse in her sanity; perhaps the sheer power of her Fire Blades somehow affected her mind. With that thought, it was pushed from her mind and she quickly forgot about it.

Kerberos led them south from Sitharkos, straight through the middle of the desert. The journey was long and brutal, but otherwise uneventful. Almost directly south of Sitharkos, on the coast, was another large mountain range. From these mountains flowed the beginnings of the Alpheus, the largest river in Omas. They skirted around the mountains, finally meeting the Alpheus at the mountain's feet. They set up camp next to the river. That night, Kerberos spoke to his small group of commanders.

"We are heading towards Omatus," he said, "but first we will attack Mara."

The other commanders nodded at this, as though the plan was obvious. Aella glanced around her, realised nobody else would say anything, and decided to speak.

"With all due respect, Kerberos, why are we attacking such a small city? They are all but defenceless." She was a pure-blooded Thearan, and enjoyed war as much as any of them, but she hated the idea of attacking such a peaceful city. The people of Mara were Omati, not Thearan like most of the settled cities along the west coast and out in the desert. They had an army just like every city in Omas, but it was an army in name only; their entire population was smaller than Kerberos' tribe, and only a fraction of that was dedicated to defence. Several faces turned to her in shock when she spoke. They'd apparently never seen their leader questioned. Kerberos smiled. He looked genuinely amused.

"During the Fire Festival, I spoke with Sithares. We are to be protected in battle from now on, and to serve our God in return, we must spread the fire wherever we can."

Aella suddenly remembered the feeling of dread that had come over her at Sitharkos. What was this protection Sithares offered? What had it cost? Perhaps the feeling should not have been so easily discarded.

"What have you done?" she asked quietly. It was barely even a whisper, and none of the commanders heard her. But Kerberos was still staring intently at her with that amused smile on his face, and saw her speak. His smile vanished, but his eyes remained on her. One of the commanders, a woman Aella did not know, shifted in her seat as if uncomfortable at the sudden silence.

"They'll be easy to kill. It wouldn't even take many of us. I could take a small group and wipe them out myself."

Kerberos slowly turned his gaze from Aella to the warrior who had spoken. His smile returned.

"I like this idea. I will select the warriors. You will leave our camp when we are a day away from the city."

"Yes, my lord."

Aella stared at the ground of the tent in front of her with no idea what to do.

Athanasius

When they reached the Alpheus, they set up camp and Athan gave Kerberos space while he discussed his plans with his commanders. He was relieved; now that Aella was one of the commanders, he didn't want to be present for their meetings anyway. During the rest of the journey to the river, Athan was tasked with discreetly informing all of the commanders of Kerberos' plans for Omatus. Kerberos made a point of excluding Aella from this information, and Athan agreed with the decision wholeheartedly.

With the camp set up, Athan prepared for the battle. He sharpened his sword, sparred with a few warriors, and practised his stealth while hunting. They wouldn't leave for another couple of days yet, and Athan took full advantage of the time.

Finally, just before dawn on the third day, Athan, Kerberos, and eighteen other warriors left the camp. They travelled silently through the dark, and despite the still, dark air, he couldn't help feeling the rush of energy he always felt before a battle. Before long, however, it dissipated, leaving him feeling a little exhausted; Mara was still a day's walk from their camp.

The small group walked in silence, stopping only to eat a cold midday meal; campfires would alert the people of Mara to their presence. There was no hunting or sparring. They carried nothing with them but a small supply of food and their weapons. They stayed within the cover of the trees as much as possible, but on the north side of the river the trees were more spread out, and they found themselves out in the open more often than not.

The day passed in silence. Soft yellow grass masked the sound of their footsteps. Just as the sun started touching the horizon, Mara came into view. It was a sleepy little village, not a city at all. A high wall surrounded it, as with every city in Omas. But Mara's was made of wood. Most of the buildings were also built from wood. For a group of Thearans wielding Fire Magic, it would pose absolutely no challenge. Even twenty warriors was an overestimation for such a task. Athan was sure Kerberos could have killed the entire population and burned Mara to the ground on his own.

In the discussions before they left their camp, Kerberos told his commanders and Athan they needn't fear any counter attack from the people of Mara. He advised the group before him now that they didn't need to bother with stealth once they reached the tiny city and the attack began. His confidence was infectious, quickly spreading through the small group until they were all grinning at his words. Kerberos' faith in Sithares was utterly unshakable. Athan felt invincible; Sithares was going to protect them.

Mara sat right on the north bank of the Alpheus, where there was a small port for trading ships from Dymea, Omatus, and Tarsium. A small cluster of separate huts was spread along the bank close to the tiny city on either side.

They stood out in the open; twenty Thearan warriors, watching the tiny city living its last day. There was no need to hide any more. Now they had reached their target, all that remained was burning it to the ground. Athan glanced at Kerberos. He was looking at Mara, but didn't seem to be seeing it. Athan couldn't read his expression at all. Finally, he turned to the group, gesturing towards Mara.

"Go."

Aella wasn't ordered to join the group attacking Mara, and for that she was grateful. She wasn't sure if Kerberos was being understanding of her objections or if he simply thought the task was beneath her skill level. Either way, she was glad to stay behind as the group left their camp. She knew there was no convincing Kerberos to leave the small city alone, so the best she could hope for was that they died quickly.

Athan was one of the warriors chosen by Kerberos. He looked pleased to be carrying out a personal assignment from their leader. There was no hint of apprehension about killing non-combatants. Aella found herself recognising him less and less; he was almost a completely different person than when they were inseparable.

Twenty warriors were chosen in total. Surprisingly, Kerberos decided to lead the attack himself. Aella was shocked at the group's small size; even considering the fact that Mara posed almost no military threat, twenty fighting against almost a thousand, with protective city walls between them and the Thearans, was not an easy battle to win. She thought about Kerberos' words the night before. *We are to be protected in battle from now on,* he said. What exactly did that protection mean? Did Athan already know? He wasn't present at the commander's meeting; but Aella had no way of knowing what the two spoke about in the privacy of Kerberos' tent.

The small group left their camp before dawn on the third day. Aella sat by her campfire, though the fire was out, and watched them leave. They walked quietly, but Aella heard them perfectly in the silent darkness of the morning.

Athan could die, she though suddenly. There was a little sadness, but not much, and she was shocked at herself. Of course she didn't want him dead; but the pleased smile he wore when Kerberos chose him for the attack slid into her heart like a cold dagger. He was becoming more like Kerberos.

All Thearans were trained from very young to enjoy battle, and even Aella was the same; but to enjoy slaughter? To enjoy killing innocent people who couldn't

225

even fight back? It wasn't the Thearan way of life to revel in pointless slaughter. The only way to enjoy a battle was to be challenged, to be ready to give up your own life if your opponent was skilled enough to take it. These people weren't warriors; they were barely even farmers. Dymea, the largest farmland in all of Omas, was less than a day's march from Mara. The people of Mara barely even grew anything, instead relying on the trade and generosity of Dymea. They had only enough weaponry to defend themselves against the smallest wandering tribes. Against Fire Magic, they didn't stand a chance.

It would take a day's walking for the group to reach Mara, and the tribe had been ordered to wait for them to return. Aella spent the time training and hunting, trying not to think about the small city being burned to the ground.

Halfway through the third day, Kerberos and four warriors returned to camp, dishevelled and exhausted. Athanasius was not among them. Aella's stomach clenched into an iron ball, and her mind went slack and numb. *It happened,* she thought, too slowly; *he's dead.* Erasmus' hand slipped into her own. She barely felt it. The tribe was silent as the five survivors walked to Kerberos' tent.

They stayed in the command tent for over an hour, and the tense, silent tribe could hear the occasional shout. Eventually, Kerberos emerged. The other four warriors stayed inside. Their leader walked to the centre of the camp, and without needing to be told, the tribe gathered around him. He started without ceremony, talking quietly and almost casually.

"We cannot know Sithares' plans, or what role we are to play in the battle between Fire and Shadow. All we know is that we were promised protection. Still, regardless of promises, we are at the mercy of Sithares. If the Fire God wills it, we will die when it is our time."

He looked around the group of warriors. There was a heavy, uncomfortable silence, broken only by the low rushing sound of the Alpheus nearby.

"I admit, I did not expect this. We will stay here for a little while longer, and I will try to commune with Sithares again."

"My lord?" a warrior spoke up. Kerberos turned to her and gestured for her to go on.

"What of Mara? Is it burned?"

Kerberos didn't react for a moment. The entire tribe seemed to be holding their breath. Finally, he spoke.

"Yes. I ordered the group to stay until Mara was reduced to ashes, even after they revealed their full strength. It is why five of us returned, instead of twenty."

There was a sudden stirring at this. She heard anger in the group, and felt it herself; but nobody spoke up directly. Kerberos could have called off the attack before Athanasius died. Before any of them died. She felt sick. She wished she'd been chosen for the attack; she could have protected Athan, or at least pushed for retreat. She stared at Kerberos, funnelling the rage she felt at him into her soul and building an inferno within. She would not act on her rage; not yet. But she could feel her power growing with it, as though somehow rage alone was enough to create Fire Magic. Kerberos was looking around the group, calm and in control. He let the whispering continue. His gaze fell on Aella, and they stared into each other's eyes for a moment which felt like an eternity. She pictured his death, over and over again; tearing his throat out of his body with her bare hands, thrusting her Fire Blades into his heart and stomach, slashing his head off with one clean stroke. The tiniest hint of a smile touched his lips as she relentlessly murdered him in her mind; almost as though he knew what she was thinking.

Try it, that smile seemed to say; *I want you to try it.*

Later that night, Aella sat in a larger tent with several members from her original tribe. Helene was there, her comforting presence giving Aella strength. They were discussing Kerberos. The mood was tense and terrifying; they could be overheard at any time.

"We need to leave this tribe," Aella whispered. Thankfully, she saw more than one warrior nodding in agreement. "Kerberos is putting us all in danger. Who knows what madness we'll be ordered into next! We're heading for Omatus; what if he orders us to attack the greatest city in history?"

Her mother spoke up. "We should go back to Theara," she said, "We can take our tribe, and any other tribe who wishes it, and live the way the ancient Thearans did."

Aella hadn't considered this, but the more she thought about it, the more right it felt. Others were nodding in agreement.

"Spread the word around to our tribe. Be careful; no one loyal to Kerberos can know about this until we are ready."

The next day, Kerberos called a meeting.

"It has come to my attention that some of you-" he shot an unmistakably aggressive glance at Aella – "do not agree with the attack on Mara, or with what you may think will come next." The tribe was silent; no one moved or even breathed.

"I wish to waylay your concerns; so I will tell you my plans. We are waiting for the warriors who were killed in the attack on Mara. I believe they will come back, and when they do, we will move on to Omatus and take the city for ourselves."

Despite their fear of Kerberos, a huge number of the tribe shouted their disagreement. An argument started as those still loyal to Kerberos shouted back. Aella looked around, saw weapons being drawn, and her heart sank.

This is what it would come to. She was prepared for a battle; Thearans always were. But she hoped to avoid it for as long as possible or try to leave their camp before it could happen.

The attack started from Kerberos' side, and spread quickly. Aella noticed Kerberos wasn't attacking. He was searching the crowd, and at first she thought he was looking for her; but he had seen her while he was talking, and was looking elsewhere. She decided to focus her efforts on breaking off the battle as much as possible and getting her tribe away from Kerberos. They couldn't win this fight, even if she unleashed all of her powers. Although her entire tribe was on her side, plus a few dozen more warriors, they were outnumbered. She could give her tribe the chance to get away, however.

She unsheathed her swords and drew as much magic as she could from them. Blocking and dodging, she moved to the centre of the fight, between the two groups. Fire swept over her body, and she focused it into a wave. It rose up between the two warring tribes, and she swept them both away from each other as hard and fast as she could. Kerberos' tribe went flying back towards the Alpheus, and her own were flung north towards the desert. She pushed for as long as she could; she was swept up in the gigantic wave as well, trying to maintain control as she was spun around in the flames. Knowing they could not be harmed by the fire, she pushed harder still, screaming with the effort.

At some point, while the wave was still raging, her energy ran out, and she fell into numb white nothingness.

Dakesh

When Dakesh was told of Aella's coup, he realised how to regain Kerberos' favour. Betraying Aella made him feel sick, but Kerberos was their leader and his approval meant everything to Dakesh. He went straight to Kerberos' tent. The tribe's leader was sitting cross legged on the floor, eyes closed, wearing only a pair of hide pants. He was even more impressive without his weapons and armour, somehow.

"Shenza." Kerberos spoke without opening his eyes. "You have something to tell me?"

"There is a revolt planned. A certain group within our tribe want to leave, and they may be planning an att-"

"Don't protect them by keeping their names silent, Dakesh," Kerberos growled, "I know very well who they are. Aella and her tribe have ever been troublesome. I hoped appointing her as one of my commanders would alleviate her concerns and endear me to her somewhat, but it seems she will never accept my rule."

Dakesh remained standing by the tent's door, uncertain. After a tense few minutes of silence, Kerberos opened his eyes and stared directly into his own.

"You have done well to tell me of their plans. Go back to your tent. I will call a meeting tomorrow, and we will resolve this in front of the whole tribe."

Dakesh didn't sleep well that night. He couldn't escape the thought that he would be responsible for Aella's death.

Atillus

Months of travel brought them to the northern edge of Omas. They stood at the ancient bridge spanning the distance between Omas and Theara. Abandoned thousands of years before, Theara was now only home to lions; or so it was said. There was something in Theara that Atillus needed, however.

During their travel, Atillus' tribe came across a couple of other small tribes. He killed their leaders and displayed his fire magic to them as he had the first time. They were absorbed into his tribe, and he now led almost four hundred warriors. They started calling him *Son of Sithares*. It was a name he didn't discourage.

He taught Sithares' prayer to each of his warriors, and once they all knew it, he led them in a group prayer. They knelt in the sand before him, and just as when he first said the words, the instant they finished they burst into roaring flame. There were some screams of surprise, but Atillus kept them under control, yelling over the sound of fire that they were touched by Sithares and would be more powerful than they ever imagined. When the fire was at its peak, he heard Sithares laughing.

YES!

It said. Its voice was much stronger now.

I knew you would serve me well, Atillus. You will be greatly rewarded for this!

Thank you, my lord. But this is only the beginning. I will bring you more followers, and I will burn everything that can be burned.

Sithares' laughter rang in his head, loud and intense. And burning.

Theara was desolate. Even the sparse trees and plants of the Omasi deserts looked lush in comparison. There was no life. Even the sand had dried up, leaving nothing but scorched, cracked rock. They travelled in silence. They were yet to see any lions, though they remained on alert. The air was still and suffocating, as if it too was unable to survive the barren land. Mountains covered the entire western side of the country, and the main path leading to the city itself was nestled up against their bases. The mountains were so steep and jagged that the warriors were following what felt like a series of cliff walls. To the east, a great flat desert stretched on for miles. On the horizon, a thin strip of darkness wavered, animated by the intense heat waves pouring from miles of cracked grey stone. Atillus knew what it was. The history books referred to it as the dead forest. Thousands upon thousands of dead black trees, so ancient they had turned to stone. It was said that once it was as lush and vibrant as the forests of Shanaken, but Sithares burned the life from it and turned Theara into a barren desert to teach the Thearans the power of fire.

They trudged on through the desert. The heat they could handle; once touched by Sithares, heat and fire held no danger to Thearans. But the silence was brutal. The only sound they heard was their own footsteps stamping on the hard, baked stone. Once or twice a day they would stop and sit on the path, eating their dried charred meat and drinking what little water they carried. After six days, Atillus began to fear they wouldn't make it to Theara before running out of rations. His warriors, who were now fanatically devoted to him, had no such doubts. The absolute, almost wild-eyed certainty on their faces whenever they glanced at him made him a little uneasy. Did they know they were being used like tools to build a larger machine by Sithares' Right Hand? Atillus was certain they didn't. And while he didn't feel any guilt, the idea sat uncomfortably in his mind.

Heading to Theara wasn't the order of Sithares, as Atillus had told the Thearans; it was his own plan. He'd read scores of books on ancient Theara, and was certain he would find what he was looking for. He had to hope the city could provide at least some food and water; if it was as inhospitable as the desert, his tribe wouldn't survive.

On the ninth day, they ran out of food. The day after that, they ran into a much worse problem. One of Atillus' favourite warriors, Nomiki, saw it first.

"Lion!" She screamed, drawing her sword and gesturing at the desert in front of them.

The lion was absolutely massive. On all fours, its head was level with Atillus' chest. Its broad shoulders rippled with pure muscle, and at the end of each of its four legs, four sickeningly long claws protruded from its huge paws. Its head was almost as wide as Atillus' torso, and its black fangs were like something out of a nightmare. Cold, calculating red eyes assessed the warriors, and for a brief moment, locked onto Atillus' gaze. Its lips drew back and it let out a blood-freezing snarl.

The Thearans closest to Nomiki followed her lead, drawing their weapons, and fanned out into a defence formation. Atillus roared over the sudden noise, his deep voice travelling to every ear in the tribe.

"SPEARS, NOW!"

The lion flew into motion, faster than he would have believed possible for an animal that huge. He barely finished the second word when four spears lanced over his head towards the massive beast. Two of them missed. One glanced off the lion's broad back, doing no damage. The

233

fourth thudded into the lion's neck, and the predator roared with fury. It didn't slow down. Atillus gathered some energy and launched the largest fireball he could muster at the lion. It was hit full in the face, and skidded to a halt. There was a cheer from the tribe, but the fire dissipated and they saw the lion was unharmed. It shook its head and blinked in a way that would have been comical were it not for the hiss and flash of fangs that came a second later. The lion leapt forward again, and without waiting for orders, the Thearans threw another volley of spears. One hit home in the animal's back, and the rest clattered uselessly along the stone ground. The lion kept running.

Atillus drew his sword and ran to meet the beast, ignoring his tribe and everything else.

Sithares, he thought as loudly as he could, *if you can help, do it.*

There was no answer.

The lion roared as they clashed, and for a moment of pure terror Atillus was certain he would die. He jumped in close, past the claws and the fangs, and a surge of strength coursed through his entire body. His left arm gripped the animal's neck, and his right hand pumped in and out, stabbing the beast's stomach and groin over and over. He rammed the blade deep into the lion's body, and sawed it back and forth, violently ripping into its innards. He felt the loud crunching sound of the lion's jaws clamping shut just next to his face, then there was an explosion of blunt agony against his side; the air was driven from his lungs and he flew away from the creature, twisting and flipping. He landed on the hot grey stone in a heap, rolling to his knees on instinct.

The lion glared at him, fangs bared. It started moving towards him. Atillus stood, preparing himself for another beating. His tribe were watching now, silent but ready to step in if necessary. He focused totally on the lion. Its steps were slow. As he watched, its eyes drooped closed for a few moments, and it wavered. He started towards the massive predator, feeling the eyes of every Thearan in his

234

tribe follow him. His blade was still lodged in the lion's stomach. He gathered another fireball, pouring energy into it as he walked towards the lion. A low growl started in the weakened animal's throat. It picked up speed. Atillus sped up to meet it.

As it hunched to pounce, he threw the fireball. The second it connected, Atillus dove to the side. His side screamed in pain as he rolled around the lion's pounce. He swept from the roll to his feet, and as the lion landed, dazed from the explosion of fire, he snatched his sword from its belly. It roared and swiped a massive paw at him. It was still blind, otherwise he may have died in that instant. Instead, its paw missed him by a hair and he ducked close to its body, ramming his sword between its ribs and straight into its heart. This time he yanked the blade out and dove away before it could retaliate, and its roar faded into a moan as it fell to the ground.

Atillus walked back to his tribe, exhausted and wounded. A cheer went up from the warriors. Their leader killed a Thearan Lion almost single handedly. They embraced him, then turned to the dead lion. They wouldn't starve after all.

Four days after the lion, they reached the city of Theara.

It was nowhere near as large as Omatus, but it was far bigger than Atillus expected; and the Thearans were awed by its size. They   stood at the main gates, staring at the black stone walls and towers. The gates were open and there were no guards, and thankfully no more lions. Atillus wasted no more time, ordering the tribe into the city. They crossed through the threshold of the main gates almost furtively, as though they expected an ambush. Atillus didn't think this was entirely unreasonable; he'd read that over the thousands of years since its abandonment, many tribes had sought to reclaim Theara as their own. There were no confirmed reports of the city holding any tribes currently, but he thought it likely there may be a tribe or two temporarily living within its walls.

The road leading into the city was narrow, with high walls on either side featuring angled slits that Thearan spears could fit through. Ancient Theara was notoriously impenetrable; and even thousands of years later, dusty and deserted, it held an ominous and intimidating atmosphere.

The walk into the city proper didn't take long. The main road opened out into a circular receiving chamber, large enough to hold the entire tribe comfortably. A heavy stone door was set in the opposite side. It would have been almost invisible against the chamber walls made of identical stone, but it was open. The tribe entered into a short, dark stone corridor which reminded Atillus uncomfortably of the soundless corridor protecting the small magic room where he found and awakened Sithares. There was no dark magic here, however; merely shadows. Soon enough they reached the end of the corridor and entered the city.

Even before they were nomads, Thearans were almost exclusively warriors. The entire city was designed by assassins, warriors, and magicians to be the ultimate battleground for Thearans. The streets were designed as choke points and the homes as fortresses. There were secret passages along every street that could be filled with Thearan spearers at a moment's notice, able to attack through slits or spill out of hidden passages at key tactical points. Atillus couldn't remember being so impressed with a city before. He had no idea why Theara remained abandoned.

He lead the tribe through the desolate city, the sound of their footsteps echoing loudly through empty streets. A harsh cry stabbed the heavy silence. Atillus glanced up, preparing for battle. It was a lone Fire-Hawk, gliding and wheeling low over the city. Although very dangerous, they were small birds and didn't attack people. Atillus relaxed a little and turned his attention back to ground level. There still may be enemies in the city.

A few hours of slowly walking through the city brought them to a central gathering place. Here, the black Thearan stone was complemented by bright white Tarsi marble, shining in the unbroken sunlight. A great white stone fountain, empty of water but otherwise in perfect condition, took up the centre of the square. Atillus could smell the rushing water of the fountain in his mind. The thought of water made his dry mouth ache. He ordered his warriors to search the area. No doubt the city had been ransacked a thousand times since its abandonment, but if anything was left behind, he would find it. They found a great hall that opened onto the city square, easily defensible in true Thearan fashion. The tribe set up a camp inside, and Atillus sat for a long moment while his warriors searched the city. Nomiki approached and sat next to him.

"How long will we stay?" she asked. The lack of pleasantries endeared her to him even more. While his other followers treated him as though he was Sithares itself, Nomiki looked at him as a man. A dangerous man, but a man nonetheless. She was loyal, but she followed him out of respect for his strength and tactical ability rather than out of worship. It was a much more comfortable feeling for Atillus.

He looked into her golden eyes. "Until I have what I came for."

She nodded, as if expecting no further reply. He smiled internally. She asked few questions, and didn't show any interest in meaningless chatter. They sat for a while in silence, and she built a fire. The hall was huge, their tribe filling no more than a quarter of the space. The roof was incredibly high up, and there was no chance of smoking themselves out. A few other fires sprang up around the hall as the sun started setting.

A few hours after Atillus ordered the search, his warriors returned to the hall. He met them outside the door. They found a few sacks of grain which seemed to be edible, a nest of Deathclaws in a small house, and on the other side of the city, what looked like a camp of Thearan warriors. Two of the warriors returned with Deathclaws slung over their shoulders, with the claws and innards removed.

Deathclaws were desert-dwelling lizards, averaging about a metre long with incredibly venomous claws. They moved slowly most of the time, but were capable of huge bursts of speed at close range. Grey skin with black, diamond-shaped scales covered their backs, meaning they were commonly mistaken for their non-venomous cousins, the Diamondback Lizard. If their claws were avoided, the flesh was edible and nutritious, and two large Deathclaws would be enough for quite a few of the warriors to eat well. Atillus sent more warriors out to kill more of the lizards so the whole tribe could eat, then talked to the men who spotted the enemy camp.

"We didn't see much, my lord," one of them said, "just the glow of a campfire through a window."

Atillus nodded. "How large was the building?"

The warriors glanced at each other. "It wouldn't fit more than twenty," the second warrior said, and the first nodded his agreement.

"Were there many buildings close by? Buildings that could be connected by doors or small chambers?" They both nodded. Atillus thought for a moment.

"Very well. Leave them for now, but make sure we have a strong guard during the night. They may have spotted us too." His warriors nodded once again, and rushed off to gather a group of guards for the night. He looked out into the quiet city. Twenty warriors to fight, maybe many more, and the city was his.

Zanela

Time passed. So much time that Zanela began to forget her life in *Kashainuukza*. She spoke to the Zuzuk, who she named

Kaidan. The beast never spoke back of course, but she knew it was listening to everything she said. They passed other Zuzuks on their way up the mountain, but Zanela had lost her fear of them. They watched her lazily as she passed.

The mountain grew steeper as they approached its peak. The last half day was spent climbing a sheer wall of rock. They left the treetops behind as they climbed ever higher. Despite its size, Kaidan climbed effortlessly, making no sounds at all. After a couple of hours, her muscles screamed at her, aching and weak. She paused, breathing hard. Kaidan stopped next to her, watching her intently. Shaking with exhaustion, she closed her eyes and rested her forehead against the stone cliff.

Suddenly, she was yanked off the wall and swept up in a rush of movement. Her eyes flew open and then slammed shut again as she swung face down, catching a glimpse of the forest far below. A scream caught in her throat. Eyes still closed, she reached her arms for something, anything. Even as she flailed for something to grab onto, she knew she didn't have the strength to hold herself up. The pace felt incredible; in her mind she saw a massive, terrifying flying monster carrying her off to its lair to eat.

It took her far too long to realise it was Kaidan carrying her up the sheer cliff wall. By then the terror was mostly

239

replaced by exhilaration; she found she was able to open her eyes briefly and marvel at the distance between them and the treetops on the mountain far below. Even the part of the mountain where they'd left the trees was in the far distance now. Below that were the roiling clouds, and far below that was Pandeia. It now looked like a living map; she could actually see the shape of Shanaken the way it looked on the maps all *Kuulshen* were taught to read as children.

The upwards movement stopped as unexpectedly as it started. One moment, Zanela was staring at the world below her, and the next she lurched backwards and down, intense darkness filling her vision. Kaidan never slowed down, just changed direction. They were heading down now, through some sort of cave inside the mountain, moving even faster than Kaidan had run up the cliff. She saw nothing at all, not even Kaidan's rough fur right in front of her eyes.

Kaidan sprinted further down into whatever abyss had opened from the mountain's peak. Then the beast leapt without breaking stride. For a moment it felt to Zanela like they were flying; they sped through the air for far longer than even a Zuzuk should be able to jump. Finally, they landed lightly, still in darkness, and Kaidan ran again. Something slapped her face and she screamed. It was wet and slimy. Her stomach lurched as she grabbed for it with one hand; her mind conjuring images of terrible giant worms and other disgusting things. She tried desperately to fling it off her hand before she realised it was totally flat and lifeless. It was merely a leaf, pulled off a branch as they sped through the forest – *a forest?* Her thoughts cut off as she finally heard the familiar sounds of the forest all around her.

They surged through trees until they apparently reached their destination; Kaidan finally stopped, lowering her gently onto the thick branch of a tree. They sat together, Kaidan breathing hard and Zanela's muscles aching.

A forest inside *a mountain?* She scarcely believed it. They sat in the dark, resting, listening to the life surrounding them. A river gurgled nearby. Now they were still, she heard everything clearly. Insects and birds chirped, sang and buzzed. Somewhere close another Zuzuk growled. Kaidan moved at the sound, but settled again a moment later.

Eventually, her eyes adjusted to the darkness. She climbed to the top of the tree and stared out into the forest inside the Eternal Mountain. When she saw what lay in the centre, her mouth dropped open and her eyes grew wide.

Dakesh

He awoke surrounded by trees and vibrant yellow grass. Pain blossomed over his entire body, growing as he woke. He groaned and sat up. He saw the Alpheus from where he was, and the battle came back to him. He had stood on Kerberos' side when the fight began. Aella didn't see him, and for that he was immensely thankful. The battle was short, and Dakesh avoided killing anyone before the massive explosion tore their tribe apart, but only barely. The explosion swept him into the air, flipping uncontrollably, and after a terrifying length of time he had hit the ground.

He stood now, peering down at the opposite bank of the river, where the camp-site stood only minutes earlier. Most of the tents survived, albeit battered and flattened. Thearan warriors were everywhere, searching the camp and packing everything that survived the blast. Kerberos stood among them, shouting orders and keeping watch for any members of Aella's tribe.

Dakesh walked down to the river, splashed across it, and joined the tribe. He found his tent and packed it up with the rest of his belongings. Other than a few tears, it was in working condition. It took about an hour for the tribe to pack everything and form up, and when Kerberos gave the order to head east along the river, Dakesh was glad to leave the site of the battle behind.

They marched, keeping a leisurely pace. Kerberos was utterly unconcerned by Aella's tribe.

"She was their most powerful warrior, and that explosion must have cost her most if not all of her magic.

We outnumber them, and they were scattered into the desert. By the time they reach us, *if* they reach us, they will be exhausted and their leader will be unable to match my power. They are welcome to attack, but I believe Aella will wait for us to reach Omatus and engage the city before she attacks. That way she will have us at a disadvantage, caught between two enemies."

"You don't seem worried about that possibility either," Dakesh observed.

"I have reason not to be." He said no more, and Dakesh left him to his thoughts.

The Alpheus was beautiful, and peaceful. Marching alongside it put Dakesh in mind of his old home. Shanaken was teeming with rivers. The sound they made as they snaked their way between the giant trees soothed his mind and soul. The Shenza believed that life had a certain flow to it. They believed without movement, without growth, life would become stagnant and toxic. Water was one of the clearest examples; a flowing river was clean and could be used for bathing or drinking, but a still pool of water would make one sick. Dakesh greatly enjoyed watching the water move ever onward. The land was peaceful here. Not as beautiful, nor as full of life, as Shanaken; but much more peaceful than the desert.

Mara broke the peace like an ambush. Dakesh knew Kerberos' intention was to destroy it, but he hadn't expected the sight that met him now. Mara was nothing but ashes and a few half crumbled stone buildings. A dozen or so large fires were scattered around the ruins, still burning fiercely. There were no bodies. Ashes covered the ground in a thick blanket. Kerberos barked what could have been a laugh.

"Our fellow warriors are saved! We truly are protected!"

243

At first Dakesh didn't understand. But when Kerberos walked to one of the fires and knelt beside it, the shape became obvious to him. He glanced at the other fires, each burning brightly in the otherwise dead city. They were the Thearans who died in the attack, laying unconscious in the ashes of Mara.

The dead warriors woke shortly after. Their fires went out just before they regained consciousness, and when they opened their eyes, none of them remembered a thing. They didn't know who they were or what happened at Mara, and they didn't recognise Kerberos or any of their fellow warriors. Kerberos wasn't bothered by their lack of memory; they followed orders willingly enough, and that was enough for him. Once the dead warriors were awake and Kerberos checked the rest of the city to make sure they hadn't left anyone behind, they marched along the Alpheus again. He paused briefly at one point, scanning the landscape keenly as though he was missing something. He shook his head and muttered to himself, and they moved on.

The idea of resurrection disturbed Dakesh. Life was a circle that flowed endlessly, with one being's death feeding the life of others. It was part of the concept of *Shaiduul,* the philosophy of the Shenza people; the eternal flow of life. Every part of their culture was based on *Shaiduul.* Their moving home, *Kashainuukza,* their flowing Blade Dance, and even their deaths. When a Shenza died, they were laid to rest on the forest floor, out in the open, to complete the circle and do their part for *Shaiduul.* Animals, insects and plants took from their bodies until there was nothing left to take, and the circle flowed ever on.

Returning from the dead broke that circle, and the thought scared Dakesh more than he could have described. He was now like these dead warriors, and when he died he would come back as they did, with no memory and no identity. Why would Kerberos want such an existence for himself and his tribe?

244

To better serve me.

Sithares finally broke its long silence. But instead of relief, Dakesh felt only a deeper disquiet. For the first time, it occurred to him he may have strayed from the path he was meant to take.

Your path is the path to power. I am the only way you will achieve the power you seek. Gain Kerberos' favour once more, and he will guide you. Spread the fire wherever you can, and unlimited power will be yours.

He marched in silence, thinking about Sithares' words. It was true; without Sithares, he would be nowhere near as powerful as he was now. Kailen's *Kaizuun* granted him a great deal of power, but he didn't have the magic of the *Kaizeluun* to control it. Fire Magic, however, was completely under his control. He practised every day, and while he wasn't as powerful as Kerberos or Aella, he was steadily gaining power.

Even more important than power, he was accepted and respected by the Thearans. His own people had rejected him. They thought he wasn't good enough to wield the *Kaizuun.* He hated them for it, and his hate fuelled the Fire Magic within him. He felt it burn in his chest. His muscles bulged as the magic swelled with his rage. The hate, and the power it gave him, felt amazing. Sithares was right. This was his path.

The sun set half a day's march from Mara. Kerberos ordered the tribe to set up camp, and a group went hunting south of the river where the forest was thickest. Dakesh stayed behind and helped build the camp-site. After dark, while the campfires still burned, shouts rang out from the warriors patrolling the camp to the east. Dakesh sat in front of his fire, meditating. He thought about Omatus, though he'd never been there. He planned on distinguishing himself in the battle, showing Kerberos that he was a loyal servant of Sithares. It was a chance to gain even more power. The more Omati he could kill, the more power Sithares would grant him.

The shouts became clashing steel, and Dakesh stood, drawing his *Kaizuun*. He looked towards the edge of the camp-site. Among the bright fiery auras of the Thearans, he saw what looked like an aura made of shadow. There was a purple tinge to it, but other than that it was an odd, glowing darkness. It drew in the light around it, making the auras of the Thearans dimmer. There was something uncomfortable about the shadow, almost familiar. As he watched, the auras of two Thearans flickered out. Seizing the chance to further impress Kerberos, he ran to fight.

The shadow fought against half a dozen Thearans. The magic of the *Kaizuun* made the fight look like bonfires in a hurricane. As he approached, a phantom blade streaked towards his face, and he ducked under it just in time. Two more Thearans fell, and the shadow flew over the remaining warriors, landing in front of Dakesh. His heart stopped as he saw the face beneath the dark aura.

"TRAITOR!" Elana screamed.

Dakesh stared at Elana, awestruck. She was a beautiful woman, and a fierce warrior. She was older than Dakesh by eight years, and he looked up to her; she was the warrior he wanted to be. She stared back at him, smirking, in her sleeveless black tunic. Her face, bare arms and hands were covered in brand new tattoos, ancient Shenza symbols which granted amazing powers to those skilled enough to use them. Angular, aggressive patterns streaked over her skin beside her eyes and over her cheeks. The tattoos flowed down her neck, over her shoulders and covered most of her arms. Each mark held its own spell, and all were under the control of the *Kaizeluun* who wore them. Dakesh had never felt such intense longing in his life; both for the woman and for the power she wielded.

They stood on a wide circular training platform, high above the forest floor. Painted wooden targets surrounded them, hanging from nearby branches and attached to posts on the platform's edge. It was the first time Dakesh had seen her since she took the Shadow Trials. Kailen stood next to him, staring at Elana with the same expression. She leapt over their heads, flipped, and in one lighting fast motion threw three black throwing blades into the centre of three different targets. She landed silently, poised and perfectly balanced. On her wrist, a tattoo of a blade glowed purple briefly before settling back to black.

Dakesh was always smitten by Elana. But in that moment, he fell in love with her. Her grace, her talent, her confidence, her power. She was beautiful. Powerful. Deadly. And she was smiling at him.

"Don't worry, *Kuulshenza*," she said, "One day soon you will forge *Kaizuun* of your own, and we will destroy the Ermoori together once and for all."

Kuulshenza meant "young warriors"; a title usually reserved for the children of the Shenza who hadn't yet passed their tests and become Daishen. Elana used it playfully, but it still stung Dakesh's pride. He wanted her, more than anything except becoming *Kaizeluun* himself, yet she still called him a child.

"I'll be *Kaizeluun* the moment I'm old enough to take the tests!" Dakesh shouted. "You'll see!"

Elana laughed. There was no mocking in the sound; it was the most beautiful laugh Dakesh ever heard. But it broke his heart anyway. She just didn't see him as a warrior. It made him furious. He was younger than her, but that didn't mean he couldn't achieve what she achieved. She was still holding her sword. She frowned at him as his mood darkened.

"Dakesh... walk with me."

Without waiting, she stepped off the platform, down a curved walkway and out of sight. Dakesh ran to keep up. They walked together in silence, Dakesh waiting for her to talk. She led him through the trees until they left the city. She sat on a thick branch and gestured next to her. Dakesh sat down.

It was a beautiful spot; an opening in the trees before them created a valley of sunlight dappled green by the leaves overhead. Clouds of insects floated through the vibrant shafts of light piercing the canopy. Birds darted through the insects, singing to each other. The beauty before him, and that of the woman next to him, calmed his soul. He breathed out, and his fury of a moment ago was released.

"Remember this place," Elana said, "when you feel angry again." She looked at him. He looked at her.

"Do you know why the Shenza live in Shanaken? In the forests?"

Dakesh shook his head.

"This is where all life on Pandeia began. It spread from the Eternal Mountain-" she pointed up at the towering mountain in the centre of the forest – "through all of Pandeia. Amalus lives in a clearing on the peak of the mountain, creating more life every day. It's why this forest is so full of life, and why the further you travel from here, the less life you'll find.

In ancient times, when the trees were young, the first Warrior was put here to protect the mountain until Amalus could make the forest powerful enough to protect itself. The Shenza have stayed here ever since. Though the forest no longer needs our protection, we were created for this place. It is our purpose."

He knew about Amalus, of course; all of the Shenza did. The God of life, born within Pandeia itself. It exhaled life, giving birth to every creature and plant in the world over thousands of years. But he always thought of the stories as myth, simple tales to teach children about the world and how it came to be. He never took them literally, but it seemed Elana did.

"This place is the source of our strength, the source of the *Kaizel*. You are a great warrior, Dakesh, but to use Shadow Magic you must be in control of your emotions. Look closer at the birds."

Dakesh watched them intently for a few moments as they darted among the insects, but he didn't understand what she was talking about. Then one of them went for the same insect as another and they started chirping and pecking at each other in mid air. While the two birds fought, the small swarm of insects flew away. A third bird speared through the swarm as it flew, picking insects out of the air in precise, controlled dives.

As he watched, the two fighting birds tore into each other. Locked in each other's claws and beaks, they plummeted out of the canopy, screeching and bleeding. They fell out of sight. Dakesh heard their screeches stop suddenly. Elana put her hand on his shoulder.

"Strength without aggression. One of the three tenets of the Shenza. Remember it, Dakesh, and you will become a great *Kaizeluun*."

Elana stood before him in the dark, shadow magic coming off her in cold waves. Her bright purple eyes flashed with fury, and her chest rose and fell in short, sharp bursts. Dakesh couldn't remember ever seeing her this furious. She was terrifying. A *Kaizeluun* for over ten years, one of the most talented in the history of the Shenza. And her blade was raised at him. Even with his *Kaizuun* and Fire Magic combined, Dakesh couldn't win this fight.

He remembered the Thearan warriors who came back from the dead. They were still utterly blank, their empty eyes staring at nothing as they mindlessly followed Kerberos' orders. He never feared death as a *Daishen*. But knowing he would come back as an empty shell, unable to grow and learn, stagnant and listless while the world moved on around him; he couldn't handle that. It was unnatural.

Elana disappeared, striking so quickly that his *Kaizuun* offered no warning. Her blade sliced his neck, too shallow to kill but far too close. She struck again. He managed to block, barely, and was smashed off his feet by a foot or a fist; he couldn't tell which. He stared up at her from the dirt. A memory jolted him:

Dakesh is young, still only a Kuulshen. *He, Elana and Kailen are talking about the powers of the* Kaizeluun.

"I heard one of the tests is facing off against a shadow viper," Elana said, excited.

"No way!" Dakesh said, "They're way too fast! No Shenza could hope to win!"

"I could!" she shoved him without warning, and he toppled to the ground. She giggled, and Dakesh jumped to his feet, furious. He shoved her back, but she swayed out of his reach. He tried again, and she avoided all of his attacks with ease.

"See? I am already faster than a shadow viper!"

She stood above him, and he saw murder in her eyes. As he sat in the dirt, knowing he was about to die, there was only one question that came to his mind.

"Did you kill a shadow viper?" he asked her.

Her eyes widened at the unexpected question. But only for the barest second. Then the fury returned, and she stepped closer to him.

"I killed a traitor," she said, and her blade swept towards him, as fast as a shadow. Dakesh screamed a single word.

Atillus

The sun rose on Theara, the morning just as silent as the night.

The enemy camp didn't approach during the night. He gathered fifty of his warriors to attack the enemy camp, and sent another dozen to hunt more lizards and search for anything useful. Atillus himself led the fifty warriors, and they walked silently through the streets. Knowing he was about to attack an enemy force made him uncomfortably aware of the barricades, hidden passages, and spear slits running along every street. There was no way of knowing how long the tribe had been in Theara. He was unsure of how well they might know the city's layout, and how capable they would be of utilising its tactical advantages. He wasn't used to uncertainty; and even less used to battle without a plan. But there was one thing he was certain of: he wielded the power of a God. And, like every tribe he encountered so far, they would follow him the moment they saw fire magic. Especially if it was turned against them.

The building where his two warriors saw the campfire was small; their estimate of twenty warriors was generous. But the building stood empty and silent. Atillus entered and inspected the rooms. The remains of one small campfire sat in a stone basin next to the window on the side they approached from. There was a Deathclaw carcass, and scuff marks in the dust on the floor and stone benches from recent movement, but the area was deserted.

A sudden scream split the silence. Atillus ran out to the street. A spear was buried in the stomach of one of his warriors, coming from one of the slits in the wall next to the building's entrance.

"Ambush!" he shouted, although the Thearans in the street were already reacting. A few of them ran to find a way into the passages behind the street, but most were turning and trying to engage the enemy through the spear slits. Although their instincts were good in open battle in the desert, they were obviously inexperienced in close quarters combat, and definitely against an opponent hidden behind an impenetrable wall. Spears lanced out of almost every slit in the walls, and at least ten of his warriors were horribly wounded.

"Get out of the street!" he ordered, "NOW!" They didn't need to be told again. They ran, but the enemy lined the streets behind their barricades, and spears shot out of the slits as they went, further along the street than he would have believed. Their tribe must have been at least two hundred strong; a very large tribe by modern standards. Wasting no more time, he ran back into the small building, jumped out an adjacent window, and found a side alley. As he expected, it led into the secret passages on the other side of the wall. The enemy warriors were running down the narrow passage away from him, catching up with his own tribe further down the street.

Atillus sprinted down the passage. The first Thearan didn't hear him approach, and was dead before he knew he was in danger. The second and third died the same way, and it wasn't until he reached the fourth that he was finally spotted. The fourth warrior managed a shriek of alarm before he died, and a few of the Thearans ahead of him turned. Atillus snarled at them and hurled a fireball which exploded on contact, utterly destroying one of the warriors and sending the other smashing against the side of the passage, her head caved in and her clothing aflame.

The explosion alerted more of the Thearans, but Atillus had already settled into the hot, electric blood-lust of battle, and he welcomed them with a predatory grin. Fire surged down the secret passageway in an unstoppable wave, and through the screams and smoke Atillus felt his power slowly growing. He ran down the passage, breathing in the smoke, marvelling at how good it felt in his lungs.

The surviving enemy warriors completely abandoned their attack, running from Atillus as fast as they could. He let them go; terrified survivors spread messages of terror and death, and he wanted the remains of this enemy tribe scared to face them again. He found an exit into the street, and came out to see his tribe all the way back in the city square. The street they came from was littered with at least a dozen corpses. The enemy tribe were gone. He started back towards the great hall, wondering how many eyes watched him as he walked.

Atillus doubled the guard that night, but no more attacks came. The next morning, he sent a few scouts to locate the enemy tribe. He spent some time sitting in his tent, recalling information he'd read about ancient Theara. There was almost no information about the layout of the city itself; he would need to search all of Theara himself to find what he was looking for. The more pressing need for now, however, was destroying the hidden enemy tribe. Atillus prayed to Sithares, and waited silently in his tent for an answer.

The day after the ambush, in the late afternoon, Atillus was approached by a group of about thirty Thearan warriors. His own warriors rushed out into the city square, forming battle ranks. He gestured to them to stay put. If this was a battle, they would have brought their entire force. However, weary of their use of sneak attacks, Atillus waved Nomiki over to him and whispered to her.

"Send a watch to guard each side of the great hall. And to the street entrances into the square. We will not be ambushed again." Nomiki nodded and walked briskly back into the hall. A woman strode forward from the group

253

towards Atillus. She was tall, at least six foot tall, broad shouldered and muscular. A longsword swayed in a scabbard against her shoulder blades. Most Thearans wielded short swords or spears, and the sight of the weapon was rare among the tribes. Atillus noted it, and the way the warrior moved, and hoped he wouldn't have to fight her. Her muscles rippled as she moved, and there was a look of determination and steel-like will in her eyes. She came to a stop a metre from Atillus.

"Greetings, warlord," she spoke loudly enough for Atillus' tribe to hear her. It was a term of great respect, but there was a dangerous tone underneath that suggested something else. "My warriors have told me you're touched by Sithares." There was a challenge in her features as she spoke, almost a wry amusement lighting her eyes. It struck Atillus the wrong way, and he was suddenly furious. She was mocking him, and although the survivors of his fire magic would have told her exactly what happened, she obviously didn't believe in Sithares or magic. Distantly, underneath his fury, Atillus was surprised in the total lack of faith that seemed to be present throughout all of the tribes.

Without warning or ceremony, he burst into flame from head to toe. He stoked the fire in his soul with the fury he felt at her, and made it as hot as possible. Her look of shocked disbelief turned quickly to pain, and she took several steps back, shielding her face with her arms as heat radiated from him in waves. He heard gasps and disbelieving shouts from the warriors facing him. He kept pushing the fire, focusing it and intensifying it until nothing else existed. His rage grew, becoming a beast of its own, and it fed the fire even more. He screamed, and just as he thought he'd used all of his magic, a change came over him. Suddenly the rage disappeared. He no longer felt the drain of using magic, but the fire still burned. It held a calm, flickering strength of its own. He could feel it burning through his entire body. He felt a strength and energy he'd never felt before, beyond even the first time he was blessed with fire magic.

This is your true form, my son. You have given me more power than I would have believed for one mortal; I am gifting a fraction of it to you now. While in this form, you cannot be killed. It will run out, but it will take much longer than using fire magic in your mortal body.

Atillus smiled at the tribe leader recoiling from him. She stopped shielding her face and stared at his burning body.

"It *is* true!" She said quietly. The look of fear passed quickly, and was replaced by an almost maniacal conviction. She turned to her tribe. "He wields the power of the God of Fire!" she shouted to them all. There was no response; they were alternating between staring at her, and staring at Atillus.

"Now, behold: the Thearan warrior who killed the Son of Sithares!" She laughed and turned back to Atillus, drawing her longsword as she did.

"You dare challenge the Son of Sithares?" Atillus snarled. She took a step forward and swung her longsword at Atillus' head. Gauging her strength, he judged her swing was easily enough to kill him in one blow. His faith in Sithares was unshakeable, however, and instead of ducking or blocking the attack, he stood perfectly still, calmly watching the blade arc towards him. He realised he was perceiving the attack incredibly quickly; it looked to him as though she was swinging her sword through a pool of thick oil. He raised his hand, watching as it rose. He moved much faster than his enemy's blade. He set it back down at his side, and waited for the sword to strike him.

There was a flash of light and a whooshing sound, and Atillus felt the heavy steel blade pass through his face. He

255

felt the cold of it as it sliced his cheek, through the bone, and briefly tasted metal as it cut into his mouth. He felt it as it exited his face, and felt the brief gap it left behind. But there was no pain. And the flash of light continued, his face burning brightly where he'd been cut. It burned until it fused back together, and while it felt like minutes to Atillus, he knew it was only seconds to the warriors surrounding him.

The warlord of the enemy tribe stared in horror, but the challenge was set. She couldn't back out.

He stepped towards her. She bared her teeth and stood her ground, fighting the wild fear she must have felt, and in that moment Atillus felt a small stab of pity for her. Before this transformation, he would have doubted the outcome of a battle against her, with her strength and speed and mastery of the longsword; but now, her death was all but assured. And she was still ready to fight. Atillus raised his eyes to take in the enemy tribe, wanting to make an example of their leader.

"Those who doubt the power of Sithares will burn with their leader. There is no other choice: Believe, or die."

The woman swung her sword again, screaming in helpless rage, and this time he stepped around it easily. Before she could blink, he grabbed her face with one hand, ignoring his sword, and clamped down onto it with his new found strength. Fire rushed onto her skin, and within seconds she was engulfed. He let go of her head carelessly and she toppled to the ground, her corpse burning as brightly as a bonfire.

The tribe opposite his own dropped their weapons almost simultaneously. They were staring at him as though he were Sithares itself. The fire guttered out suddenly, and the power and strength and speed rushed out of his body just as quickly. He managed to keep his feet, but it was all he could do to avoid stumbling to his knees in front of his new subjects. They barely noticed his weakness, however; they were still utterly awestruck by the deadly display of fire magic. That, coupled with tales from the few survivors of the ambush, would assure their loyalty. In the short term, at least.

He retired back to his tent, letting Nomiki take over the joining of tribes. He put two warriors outside the entrance to his tent and fell asleep almost instantly.

He awoke roughly two hours after nightfall. The warriors were celebrating the merging of two tribes, and were telling each other stories of Atillus' feats of fire magic over the campfires scattered throughout the great hall. He overheard part of a conversation and stayed in his tent as it went on.

"Do you know his name?"

"Nobody does."

"Surely he has told someone. What about Nomiki?"

"You can ask her if you feel brave enough. Even if she knew, she would never tell if He doesn't want her to."

"Why is he so secretive about his own name? His past is on the other side of the desert, just the same as all those who joined Theara by choice instead of birth. He won't be judged or cast out for who he used to be; so why hide it?"

Atillus cursed inwardly. He never meant to go without a name for so long, but he also had no idea what new name to choose. He would need to come up with something, and soon, or there would be too many questions. It was one thing to remain mysterious for a while and build up mystique, but it was quite another to remain nameless as the leader of the largest Thearan tribe in Omas. He thought of what he came to Theara to do, and hoped it would be over soon. He could focus on a name then.

A cheer erupted from the warriors closest to his tent as he pushed past the hide flap, and spread quickly as the tribe saw him. He gestured to them all in greeting, and chose a nearby fire to sit and eat.

Several of the warriors sitting around the fire with him were from the tribe living in Theara. He pointed to one of them.

"Your name, warrior?" He asked.

"Dionysios, my lord," he replied quickly. Atillus recognised his voice as the one who had asked about his name.

"Do you know this city well?"

"Yes, my lord. We have lived here for almost five years." Atillus nodded, but said nothing more. Slowly, conversation started up again among the warriors. Atillus sat for a while, simply listening to them talk. The stories of his own feats had suddenly stopped now that he was present, and they turned their talk to the city of Theara instead. They talked about the caves underneath the stone ground, the clean water which could be found there, and the uncountable secret rooms and passages throughout. They talked about the legends born here, and battles fought here in ancient times. When the Forge of Sithares was mentioned, the ancient forge where Sithares was said to have left a piece of himself so that the fire would burn forever, Atillus snapped to attention.

"Do you know where it is?" He cut off a man who was speaking about Kyriakos, the famous blacksmith who'd been visited by Sithares at the forge, but he was done with legends for now. He was only interested in the forge itself.

"Yes, my lord," the warrior replied, "many of us have been there. It is true, you know. The forge is still burning, as hot as if someone was still down there fanning the flames and throwing fresh wood in every day." Atillus' heart was hammering.

"You will take me there as soon as dawn breaks." The warrior, unnerved by the sudden intense attention, only nodded silently. Atillus grinned, more to himself than to the warriors around the fire, but they returned uneasy smiles and glanced at each other. He knew it wasn't just some legend. He would get what he came for.

Athanasius

Light slowly trickled into existence. Consciousness gradually returned. Despite any real memory remaining elusive, he felt well rested and didn't seem injured. With a soft sigh, he opened his eyes. A blackened wreckage greeted him. He was lying in the middle of the ruins of a small cabin. Everything was horribly burned, the smell of ashes and smoke almost overpowering. He stood, feeling stiff and slow. Once standing, he could see over the half-crumbled walls of the cabin; He was in the burned down remains of a small village on a riverbank. Though the river looked familiar, the name eluded him.

He stretched and assessed his body to check for damage. He was unharmed. He thought that odd, and not just because he seemed to be the only thing in the area which avoided burning; he actually felt *good*. Strong and full of energy.

A sudden flash burned his vision, though it seemed to be occurring in his mind as opposed to in front of his eyes. He groaned and dropped to his knees, and a memory pushed itself into his mind:

There were blades flashing everywhere, the song of steel ringing loudly. Shouting and thudding footsteps, and the roaring of fire. Chaos. Death. A voice, deeper than the others, emerged from the cacophony.

"Rally! Stand firm! No! This is not what was promised!"

It faded, then there was lancing pain in his neck, in his stomach and back, everywhere. He looked down to see swords and spears piercing his body in half a dozen places. He tried to scream and couldn't. His vision turned red then blurred into orange, then there was fire -

He screamed, falling to his knees and looking desperately down at his body where the weapons had torn into him. But he was unhurt. Was the vision a memory? Or just a nightmare? He couldn't possibly be alive if that really happened, let alone completely fine. He looked at the ashes and ruins of the small village again. There was no one else around him. Other than the rushing of the river, there was complete silence. He realised then what happened.

I died, he thought, *that was a memory. I died, and this is the afterlife. That explains why I don't know where I am. Or... or who I am.*

The thought was terrifying. He concentrated as hard as he could, casting his mind back, but there were no memories to draw from. Even his own name had disappeared. He glanced around him again, looking to the horizon in every direction. Nothing helped his memory. But when he turned to the north, he suddenly stopped. In the distance, a gigantic, jagged mountain pierced the sky.

There. That's where I belong. The desert, the mountain. Home.

The shape of it screamed in his mind, and he started walking.

He wandered in the desert for days before he came across the warriors. They recognised him, and all but one looked at him with disgust and hatred burning in their eyes. Only she didn't. The woman who seemed to be their leader. She looked at him with an expression of hope and yearning so vulnerable and naked he almost wept. But he didn't know her. She protected him from the other warriors, some so angry they drew their weapons and made towards him. She took his hand and led him away from the tribe. They sat together and spoke for a while.

She was heartbroken that he didn't recognise her, and she was terrified that he was allied with someone called Kerberos. The name echoed strangely in his mind. He felt a chill run down his spine when she said it. Her name was Aella; his was Athanasius. Kerberos was the leader of the tribe they belonged to before the battle that killed him. The words washed over him, almost familiar, but not connected to anything in his mind. All he remembered was the desert, and the fire he endured while dead. He told her this, and tried to describe what death felt like. When he finished, she simply held him in silence. It was unspeakably comforting, and for a moment he felt a connection with her.

Aella

Aella returned to consciousness suddenly, gasping and wide eyed. She was laying on the grey sand, and although she felt utterly drained, she didn't have any physical damage. Her plan worked. She looked around her. Other than her fellow warriors, there was nothing around them at all. The mountains where the Alpheus began were visible in the distance, but she had flung them much further than she hoped.

The rest of her tribe were either tending to the wounded or taking a brief rest on the sand. She realised they'd left their tents and most of their belongings at the camp-site; the meeting was called in the afternoon, and there was no time to pack anything away. She realised suddenly that the sun was high in the sky; it was around midday.

"How long have I been unconscious?" she asked no one in particular. Natasa turned at her voice and walked over.

"One night," she said softly, "and most of the morning." She was looking at Aella as though she might break at any moment. She frowned at the concern on Natasa's face.

"I'm not hurt, Natasa. I just used far too much magic."

But at that, Natasa's concern seemed to grow even deeper. "Aella..."

Her heart stopped. Something terrible had happened. Natasa knelt down, putting her hand gently on Aella's shoulder. Her mind started racing. She looked around the tribe, thinking she knew what might have happened before Natasa said the words. She couldn't see Erasmus anywhere. She knew he wasn't a particularly strong fighter, and she was so focused on trying to end the battle she hadn't even thought about him.

"Where is he?" she asked frantically. Natasa's eyes dropped from her own, staring at the sand.

"I'm sorry, Aella." her voice was barely a whisper. "... but there's more." Aella could not believe it. What else? How much damage could Kerberos do to them in one afternoon? She was so terrified of the answer she almost didn't ask.

"Who?"

Natasa was silent for what felt like hours. Aella didn't have the strength to ask again. She merely sat in the sand, numb and panicking, until Natasa finally spoke.

"Dakesh is gone, and... I'm so sorry, Aella. Helene is missing too."

The new tribe was perhaps five or six hundred strong, but losing Erasmus, her mother and Dakesh in one blow made her feel completely alone. She had no idea what to do, but she knew she couldn't quite bring herself to push on to Theara just yet. Somehow it felt wrong without her mother. Heading back to the city of their ancestors was Helene's idea, after all.

But there was more. Something told her to wait. She couldn't help but feel like Helene, Erasmus and Dakesh weren't dead; maybe if they just waited a little while longer, the three of them would appear. She knew it was merely wishful thinking, but it was so powerful that she couldn't ignore it.

Something Kerberos said returned to her mind: *We are waiting for the warriors who were killed in the attack on Mara. I believe they will come back...*

She had absolutely no reason to trust him any more, but... what if he was right? What if instead of making them invulnerable, the protection Sithares granted them was bringing them back from the dead? She had to hope it was

263

true; she couldn't face losing the three of them. Almost a dozen more warriors were missing from their tribe. She couldn't bring herself to say out loud what she was hoping, but when she told the tribe to wait a while and set up a camp with what little they had, nobody argued. It was likely the others who were missing loved ones remembered Kerberos' words too.

So they stayed where they were, in the desert, waiting for dead warriors to find them.

Two days went by. The Thearans slept on the sand, under the stars. They had no tents, and not much of anything else. Morale was low and the tribe was starting to argue amongst themselves. Aella became desperate; another split, another battle, would destroy them completely. They needed to stick together. She kept reminding the warriors that although Kerberos was distorting the Thearan way of life, he brought Sithares to them, and the God of Fire would provide for those who worshipped. She made them pray together, and hunt together, and build massive bonfires in the sand. It didn't work at first, but eventually they became more enthusiastic, chanting around the bonfires and sparring. It felt almost like the Fire Festival, and her heart became slightly less heavy.

Two more days later, Athanasius walked into their camp.

Dakesh

"NO!"

The blade sliced his throat so fast he didn't feel it at all, cutting off his scream. Elana walked away, sheathing her *Kaizuun* as she went. She didn't look back. Her movements were almost careless. Rage exploded in his chest. Dakesh burst into flame, his throat healing before so much as a handful of blood was spilled. He stood, still burning, and as Elana turned towards the sudden light, he grabbed the hilt of her *Kaizuun* and kicked her viciously in the chest. The blade came free of its sheath as she flew backwards into the hard grey dirt. Disarmed, she was nowhere near as powerful.

Her eyes were wide. She scrambled backwards, tried to gain her feet. He took a step toward her, and black throwing blades appeared, slicing through the air. He ducked underneath one, but another buried itself in his shoulder. It disappeared a second later in a puff of black smoke. Dakesh snarled and leaped at her, landing with his feet on either side of her torso. As he landed, he used the momentum to bring his fist down into her face. Her head snapped back into the ground, and she lay still. When he was certain she was unconscious, he let the fire go out.

Dakesh bound her hands behind her back and her knees together while she was out. He moved quickly; she didn't remain unconscious long. She woke slowly, dazed. She blinked for a few moments and stared at the warriors watching her. Her eyes fell on Dakesh, and her fury returned.

"You monster!" she screamed. "You took that blade and defiled it. How dare you dishonour Kailen? He was your best friend!"

He defiled the blade first with his unworthy blood. He dishonoured you by forging a blade meant for your hands.

There were tears in her eyes. There were tears in his own. He looked at the *Kaizuun* in its sheath on his belt. If only he could make her understand; he was *meant* to wield this blade! It was his destiny, he knew it. Sithares, the God of Fire itself, told him so. He just needed her to see.

She will never see your perspective. She was sent here to capture or kill you. She has sided with the elders of the Shenza.

"Elana, please," he said desperately, "you don't understand. Join us, join our tribe, and I can show you all that's happened. I can show you why this blade belongs with me."

She will never join us. She will fight until she dies. Her choices are to kill you or die by your hand, and she will not kill you now; her resolve has weakened even as her fury grows. Give her what she wants.

She recoiled as if he'd thrown Kailen's destroyed corpse at her feet.

"*Join* you? You abandoned the Shenza, the forests... You turned your back on the three tenets... You turned your back on *me,* and now you want me to betray my people too?"

Her people will burn regardless of her actions. Their time is almost up. As is hers. Kill her.

266

Dakesh could no longer look her in the eye as she spoke. His gaze dropped to the ground.

"The *Duulshen* were right about you." Her voice turned cold. "You were never good enough for that blade. You never deserved to wield your own, let alone the blade of one who did deserve it."

KILL HER!

Dakesh screamed. The world turned white. All that existed was Dakesh, standing alone in endless white; and Elana, bound and kneeling at his feet. Her face was a pale skull, her violet eyes replaced by bottomless pits of black hatred. She tore free of the bindings holding her down, and stood. Her sword was suddenly in her hand, and a mindless rage twisted her features. She lunged at him, and a wave of fire leaped from his hands to meet her. She screamed but kept coming. Dakesh poured more magic into the fire, screaming even louder as he watched Elana burn. Her black sleeveless tunic disappeared. Her skin melted. Her eyes popped, sizzling in the heat. She dropped to her knees, screaming and somehow still reaching for him. He put one more burst of magic into the flames, and as she died, a part of him broke.

Elana's blackened corpse lay at his feet. She was still bound. Thearan ropes were fire resistant. It all felt so real; Elana standing, pulling free of the ropes, unsheathing her *Kaizuun*, lunging at him. As soon as the illusion dissipated, he knew Sithares had tricked him. He saw her body laying in the dirt, nothing but charred meat and bones. He saw her laughing, young and full of energy. Saw her dancing the *Zuunshai* on narrow branches high above the forest floor. He saw her fighting the Ermoori with her newly forged *Kaizuun*. He saw her sit next to him in the clearing, asking him to take control of his emotions. He saw those birds again, tearing each other apart as they fell to the darkness below.

Dakesh fell to his knees. He felt as though he was waking from a trance. Finally, he saw things clearly. The Fire Magic, the whispers of Sithares, all of it was toxic. He felt sick. He killed the woman he loved; and worse, he killed her while she was unarmed and helpless. He burned her alive while she screamed and reached to him, begging for mercy.

He closed his eyes and tried to make the memory disappear, but it was burned into his mind, repeating on a loop like a waking nightmare. He vomited on the dirt. Some of it landed on Elana's charred, outstretched hand, and he screamed in wordless rage and grief. He forced himself to look at her again. He tried to think. He felt like a stranger, alone and terrified. Kerberos would never understand; he needed to escape, get away from Kerberos. But he couldn't take her body with him, as much as he wanted to. It was too painful, and she would slow him down.

He needed to make things right. Take responsibility for his betrayal, and for Elana. Her sword and belt were undamaged. They would have to do; he could at least honour her by bringing her belongings back to Shanaken. It would mean his death, but that was better than he deserved. He needed to make things right. He snatched her *Kaizuun,* unclipped her belt and sprinted north without looking back.

Fireballs exploded around him as he ran. Shouts and screams followed him. For the second time, he was abandoning his people. His breath burned in his lungs. The hard dirt pounded against his feet. If he unleashed the fire within him, the run would be easier. He knew it, but he wouldn't let himself use Fire Magic again. He'd already insulted the Shenza enough; Elana was right. The *Duulshen* were right. He didn't deserve the *Kaizuun.* He was crying as he ran. He wouldn't abandon the Shenza again. He was coming home. Even though it meant his death; he was coming home.

No one pursued him. After running as long as he could, he collapsed in the soft grey sand. The silence of the desert pushed down on him. The weight of her sword in his hands pulled him deeper into the sand. The weight of her memory made it impossible to keep moving. This place, the place that had gradually become his home, felt ugly and dead. Empty.

Zanela

This is a dream, she thought, *it must be.* She followed Kaidan through the forest, heading towards its centre. Towards... It. She knew what it was, what it *had* to be, but she couldn't accept it. She had trouble accepting the forest within a mountain. All of this was so unreal to her. *I must have died in the forest. I'm being lead to the afterlife by a Zuzuk.* She wondered if that was their purpose now that the forest was old and there were no more Ermoori to defeat.

Kaidan remained silent as they walked. Zanela stayed silent too. She didn't know what to say. For about an hour they walked through the dim canopy. She only just saw the branch she was walking on, and Kaidan was barely a shadow in front of her. The air inside the mountain was different somehow. Her lungs filled with a strange but pleasant cold. Moisture filled the air, cool and still, almost like tiny specks of floating rain.

As they approached the centre of the forest within *Dulkuud*, a soft blue light grew from the leaves above their heads. It spread down, emanating from the thin lines and ridges of the tree bark. Beneath her feet, the light glowed in pulses with each step. She slowed as she drew near the massive clearing she saw earlier, and the thing waiting there. Kaidan slowed down too, until they stopped completely together at the forest's edge.

This is a dream, she thought, *it must be.* What did the stories say about *Dulkuud*? Certainly not this. The clearing formed a perfect circle. Large arched rows of short, soft grass spiralled out from the centre. No bushes or flowers

270

grew within the circle. It was so perfect it looked unnatural to Zanela, as if it had been made instead of grown.

The thing she saw when they first arrived sat on the opposite side of the clearing. She desperately hoped it was a statue, but the heavy feeling of dread tying her stomach into knots was impossible to ignore. A terrifying sense of ancient life filled the place. She stared at the thing even as she struggled to close her eyes to it. She stared even as she feared it would move while she was looking. She tried to will herself to look away, to turn and run back into the peaceful forest. With every second that passed, her terror grew. She was paralysed, helpless before its awful, dead gaze.

It was a gargantuan snake, facing the centre of the clearing. Its head rested at the tree line, its body hidden by the trees on the other side. Dull black scales covered its giant face. Milky, faded eyes stared sightlessly. A long, thick tongue slid out of its mouth – *Oh no, no no no!* - and the pale eyelids slid away to reveal bright blue orbs emanating ancient power. Her heart thudded painfully in her chest. *It's alive! It sees me!* The bright blue eyes pierced her mind, trapping her in her own body. Every inch of her, every fibre of her being, screamed at her to run, *run!* But she couldn't move.

The snake raised its massive, terrible head, drawing itself closer to her. One of its fangs was as tall as she was. The lurching, frozen sickness of complete and utter terror drowned her mind into oblivion. And still it drew closer. The ground moved under her feet, and finally her gaze was pulled from the monster as instinct made her look down. The perfect rows of soft grass were shifting, tightening as the snake moved forwards. Her stomach cramped and her mouth dried instantly; the circular rows weren't made *or* grown. It wasn't grass at all. The snake's body took up the entire clearing. She stumbled backwards and fell, landing on her back even as she kept scrabbling away. She could feel its ancient strength under the palms of her hands as she crawled backwards over its coiled body. Its face

271

loomed above her, filling her entire vision, and her world disappeared into blackness.

Aella

Aella's heart leapt into her throat. *He's alive! That means the others might have survived!*

The whole tribe knew Athan was Kerberos' protégé, and they were far less excited to see him than Aella. But Aella still knew him quite well, and she knew something was wrong. He was not here on Kerberos' behalf; that much she knew for certain just by looking at him. The others obviously were convinced he was, and she was forced to draw her swords to stop a few warriors attacking him on sight. She took his hand and sat down with him in the sand, a little way off from the rest of the tribe.

He looked at her with a blank expression that froze her blood.

"I don't know what I am any more," he said. His voice was flat.

"You mean you're not allied with Kerberos any more?" She couldn't keep the hope from her voice.

"I- who? Do you know me?" Her mouth flew open in shock. She could think of nothing to say.

"What happened?"

Against her will, tears streamed down her face. But when she spoke, her voice was as flat as Athan's.

"Your name is Athanasius, of Theara. You and I grew up together. My name is Aella. You died attacking a small city just over two weeks ago. The leader of our last tribe, a man named Kerberos, took you as his protégé and ordered us to attack Omatus. Myself and my original tribe disagreed, and there was a battle. We have been out here ever since."

Athan's eyes were wide. He was looking out at the horizon. "I remembered the desert," he said quietly, "and fire." Aella put a hand on his arm, and he looked at her.

"That's all there is, in death. Fire. You don't get burned, but you can't see or hear or feel anything else, only the fire." Now there were tears running silently down Athan's cheeks. "I was there for what felt like an eternity. It burned away everything. I don't know what I am any more." Aella moved in close and held him. She had no idea what to say.

Finally, she let him go and sat back.

"I think we need to go back to where Kerberos was." She raised her voice so everyone could hear. "It has been four days and he hasn't come for us. I think he's moving on to Omatus already."

One of the other warriors spoke up. "What do we do once we get there? We can't beat him in battle." There were murmured agreements. Aella had already thought about this.

"Kerberos won't just be fighting us; he will be fighting the Omati army and Royal Guard too. If we get there in time, we will be able to surprise him at his flank while he is busy with his own battle."

The warriors were listening; they seemed a little more convinced. There was at least no more murmuring. She pushed on. Even if they couldn't beat him, fighting him was the right thing to do.

"Kerberos is twisting the Thearan lifestyle into something ugly and wrong. He is using Sithares' name to slaughter innocent people and take Omatus for himself. Thearans revel in combat, but what Kerberos is doing isn't combat, it's murder. We hunt and we kill and we fight, but we don't kill non-combatants. We don't slaughter entire cities. And if we were to stop living as desert nomads, the only place we should settle in is our ancient homeland, the city of our descendants, Theara."

The tribe cheered and she knew there would be no further arguments. Now she just hoped they stood a chance against Kerberos' army.

They marched south again, keeping a fast pace. They were travelling light, and their new found mission drove them harder than Aella would have believed. Athan marched along with them, keeping pace but staring at the ground in front of them blankly. She tried speaking to him while they walked, but nothing seemed to get through to him. Each hour that passed scoured another layer off her already bleeding heart. Her mother, Erasmus and Dakesh all missing, possibly dead, and her old friend miraculously brought back from death but unable to even recognise her. Eventually, after another day of trying to speak to him, her grief turned to anger. They set up camp for that night, and she walked up to him, fuming. She stared at his listless face and her anger grew into rage as she remembered his attack on Erasmus, his befriending Kerberos, and how easily he seemed to have forgotten her friendship after Erasmus joined their tribe.

She punched him in the face, and he went sprawling backwards in the sand. He looked up at her, finally dropping the stupid blank look and adopting one of shock instead. She was beyond guilt; looking down at him now, she felt only satisfaction, and the rage still boiling underneath. He stood, and she drew her swords. He glanced at her weapons, and hesitantly drew his own sword.

Suddenly she remembered something, and her rage blew out like the beginnings of a camp fire in a strong wind. She looked down at her swords, then again at Athan. She smiled, and when Athan saw her broad smile his own mouth seemed to twitch, almost in recognition. She lowered her blades and raised her voice.

"You will be Aniketos!" She shouted it, loud and clear, and then continued, "and I will be Roxane!"

Athan recoiled as if she'd thrown her swords at him, a look of shock on his face that rivalled the one he wore

275

when she punched him off his feet. His sword dropped to the ground. He fell heavily to his knees. His eyes were wider than she'd ever seen them. He suddenly looked as young as he did back when they played this game as children.

After a long time, his eyes focused, found hers, and lit up, emanating joy and grief in equal measure.

"Aella..." he said quietly. She didn't hear it, but she saw her name on his lips and ran to him. She dropped to her knees as she reached him and threw her arms around him. They held each other close, and for the first time in years, the silence between them felt like home.

After Athan recovered a little, they talked. He more than made up for the silence of the last few days; he spoke to her about Kerberos, about the fanatics who followed him, and relayed his perspective on Erasmus' arrival and Aella's relationship with him. It felt so good to connect with Athan this way again. During their talk, Aella almost forgot her grief at losing three of the most important people to her. When it was her turn to talk, she started enthusiastically, telling him everything that happened since they stopped talking. When she reached the attack on Mara, she faltered. Athan remembered now, but he hadn't seen things from her point of view. He didn't live knowing his family and friends were most likely dead. But he supported her, and his comfort helped her talk through everything.

They spoke into the night, and neither of them noticed the morning until Natasa interrupted them to invite them hunting. They both laughed as they realised it was already time to start preparing the morning meal; they kept talking, and Natasa shook her head and left to hunt without them.

Later that day, they reached the scene of the battle between Kerberos' tribe and Aella's. The ground was scorched and dead, the camp-site either blown away by the

276

explosion or looted and packed up by Kerberos' warriors. There were no corpses. They pressed on, towards Omatus. They followed the river, as Kerberos would have done, and soon reached Mara. It was utterly destroyed. Unlike most cities in Omas, Mara was very small and constructed mostly of wood. All that was left of it were the very few buildings and structures made of stone; a small gathering place in the city's centre, the dwelling of the city's leader, and a large storehouse. Everything else was ash. They pressed on again; they couldn't even use the ground to camp on.

Past Mara, about a day's walk, was Dymea. It was a giant farm settlement, larger than the farmland surrounding Omatus. Aella had only seen it a few times before, but she always remembered how vibrantly green it was, how it felt alive and somehow youthful. Living in the desert, it was easy to forget how beautiful the place could be. Now, however, Dymea looked more like the Omasi deserts than the rich green farmland Aella used to try so hard to remember.

It was silent, dead, and empty. Ash carpeted the scorched ground, almost the same colour as the grey desert. What usually looked to her like home now looked like death and danger.

Aella's tribe kept marching. Every burned trace Kerberos left behind steeled their resolve. The desolation of Dymea looked recent to Aella; they were catching up. She urged her tribe on, but they didn't need much motivation. Now that evidence of Kerberos' slaughter was laid before them, they knew he needed to be stopped.

Less than a day's walk past Dymea, they caught sight of Kerberos' army in the distance. Aella couldn't believe they caught up to him before Omatus; perhaps her plan would work after all.

Athanasius

They travelled south again, back toward where he had awoken. His mind was untethered, wandering and lost. There were no memories to think back on, nothing but the endless fires that consumed him in death. Trying to keep his mind off that roaring, mindless chaos was almost impossible with nothing else to think about. Aella tried to talk to him while they walked, but he couldn't focus enough to hear her words. Within the flames overtaking his mind, flashes of random images faded in and out, never becoming clear enough for him to make sense of them.

The most vivid images were battles, but they appeared and disappeared so fast they were meaningless. Aella's face appeared briefly, but much younger. A giant bald man with a terrifying chain weapon appeared, attacking him and shouting that he needed to move faster if he wanted to survive; was this Kerberos? Was it even a memory?

The desert passed them by, and gradually the mountains in the distance grew closer. He still didn't recognise them.

"You will be Aniketos!" She shouted it, loud and clear, and then continued, "and I will be Roxane!"

The desert fell away from his feet, the blue of the sky flashed to white, and suddenly he was flung through an endless ocean of memories. Aella, standing just as she had been; a sword in each hand, confident and vibrant and much younger. Kerberos, huge and deadly and gentle and loving; teaching him and testing him. Hunting, sparring,

278

walking through the desert. The Fire Festival. Chaos and love and fear and fire; it all hit him at once.

After a lifetime, the memories faded, and he saw her again, standing in the desert with her swords drawn. But now she didn't look dangerous; she looked hopeful and beautiful. She looked like his best friend.

"Aella..." he said. She ran to him, and held him, and he'd never felt so relieved in all his life.

Shortly after his memories returned, they reached the camp-site where the tribe waited while Kerberos' small group attacked Mara. His mind still felt fractured, and the ruined remains of the camp confused him more. Aella had told him of the battle, but seeing this much destruction at the last place he'd been with his tribe seemed to push his mind a little further away from his grasp. The images he saw of the battle at Mara started changing, bleeding into the scene before him so that it felt as though he was present at the battle. He saw Kerberos and Aella, and fire everywhere.

He remembered what really happened, but his mind seemed to be forcing new memories to appear; they fought in his head, and flashes of light and sound assaulted him. Sometimes Kerberos was gentle, tender and loving; sometimes he was violent and brutal and terrifying. Aella switched from smiling and giggling and sparring to screaming and killing and burning.

All of his memories changed constantly, and it was all he could do to hold on to the true events. They slipped and moved, never clear and never certain.

Sometime later, they came across vast fields of scorched farmland. He remembered Kerberos' plans; destroy everything along the path to Omatus, and burn the great city to the ground. The horror of it struck him as he stared at the ashes of what used to be the largest section of green, fertile land in all of Omatus. He tried to remember his reaction at the time Kerberos told him; it seemed such a good idea then, and he agreed whole heartedly with his leader.

The silent, dead landscape before him refused to match up with his memories of Kerberos. The tribe's leader was strong, intelligent, caring, and loyal. He took Athan into his arms when he felt most alone, and taught him and nurtured him. Loved him. They talked of many things, sparred and practised together, and made love more times than Athan could count. He would only be doing these things for Sithares, to whom he was utterly devoted. He wasn't evil. He couldn't be.

... Could he?

He didn't come back for you after Mara.

No, but he knew I was killed.

Did he?

Athan couldn't be certain of anything; his mind was a roiling ocean of chaos. Kerberos wasn't evil. Kerberos set out to murder thousands of innocent people. Kerberos loved him. Kerberos left him behind.

He decided to put his hope in the man who'd been there for him all these years, the man who'd taught him so much and loved him so fiercely. Kerberos loved him; he knew it.

Aella

When he saw Kerberos' army ahead of them, Athan seemed to withdraw. He was usually quiet, but Aella could still tell when he was upset.

"Athan, what's the matter?" She asked. He glanced at her. He looked desperate, and he was fighting back tears.

"I still love him. Even after all he's done, I love him. I don't know if I can fight this battle."

Her heart sank. She put her hand on his arm as they walked. "Athan, he's slaughtering thousands of innocent people. If he were waging war against the other desert tribes or the western cities it would be different. But he's destroying farms and murdering people who aren't warriors."

"I know!" Athan yelled suddenly. "Do you think I don't know what he is? I spent every night with him before – before Mara. But you don't know him the way I do. He's not evil. Anything he does is done for our tribe and for Sithares."

Aella shook her head; she didn't know what to say. Athan was in denial.

"I won't make you fight him, Athan," she said, "but please understand that he needs to be stopped."

He appeared to think about what she said, and they walked in silence for a while. Finally, he spoke again.

"Aella, what he was saying about Sithares protecting us... I think there's more to it than that."

She waited for him to continue. He sighed, then went on:

"When we were on Sitharkos, I saw him summon something. I didn't know what it was at first, but all I can think of is that Sithares itself actually spoke directly with Kerberos. He claims to have spoken directly to it before; maybe that's how it happens. When I died... What I experienced was terrifying. It broke me. I refuse to believe that is the afterlife for a devout Thearan."

"What are you saying, Athan?"

"I don't believe Sithares decided to protect us without anything in return. I think Kerberos gave Sithares our souls in exchange for immortality. To fuel its magic. I believe he gave our souls away without us even knowing about it."

Aella was speechless. If Athan suspected that, why was he still refusing to admit Kerberos was evil?

"But you still don't think we should fight him?"

"I know he should be stopped, Aella. After what I went through when I died, I know that what he *did* was evil... But I can't believe that he *is* evil. And I know you will fight him, and I understand that; I'm just not sure I can fight him too."

She nodded slowly, but her heart sunk further.

"We have a connection, Aella. I know he wouldn't fight me either, even if I showed up to challenge him."

Aella wasn't so certain of that, but she thought it would be pointless to argue further. Athanasius was in love with the man they had to kill.

They were catching up. Gradually, Kerberos' army became closer and closer. They had so far not been spotted. Aella ordered her tribe to slow down a little; if they got too close, they would be seen. Their only chance was to wait until the battle started in Omatus, and then enter the city and attack from behind. The city itself was getting closer too; by Aella's reckoning they would be there within a day.

They marched as quietly as they could, keeping their profile low at Aella's instruction. Athan still walked next to her, and for that she was grateful; but how much longer would he be by her side? And what would he do once they reached Omatus? She had no idea, and was deeply troubled by that.

The rest of the journey went fairly quickly and, other than a few tense moments where Aella feared they were spotted, uneventfully. She watched Kerberos' army storm the gates and disappear into the city. She knew her warriors were eager to follow and start the attack, but she urged them to wait.

"He is killing them right now!" One warrior said.

"We need to stop him!"

"We have to attack!"

Aella gestured for silence, and the warriors stopped shouting out. She turned to them.

"I want to attack too, but we need to make sure they're properly distracted by the battle, and hopefully suffer some losses of their own. It's the only way we can win this fight. Kerberos needs to be stopped, but in an even fight he is too strong. We need every advantage we can get." She looked around at all of them.

"Kerberos is evil. He was right when he said we're protected by Sithares, but he didn't tell us the cost of that protection. He gave our souls to Sithares in return for immortality. But when we die, it is pure suffering, enough to drive a person mad. We return from death as an empty shell, with no memory and no purpose. Kerberos did this to all of us. He didn't ask our permission, nor did he think about our suffering. He traded our souls, and he's using them to take Omatus for himself. If we're going to stop him, to bring him to justice, we must wait just a little longer. But I promise you, we will bring him to justice for what he's done to all of us."

Athan was looking at her. His eyes were wide and his lips were pressed into a tight line. She wasn't sure what the look meant, but she couldn't take back what was said. The

283

tribe needed to know what Kerberos was. They needed to know the full extent of his evil. It wasn't just some farms burnt to ashes and some innocents killed; it was the very souls of the tribe who followed him, who called him their leader.

The rest of the tribe reacted the way she expected. They were furious, ready to attack. Some of them looked at Athan with a new sympathy that touched her. She started the march towards Omatus, slowly at first. When they were close enough to hear the battle raging within the city's walls, she drew her swords and broke into a run. Her tribe followed. The gates were still open; no guards were left alive to close them behind Kerberos' army. They ran into the city unimpeded, and saw the death Kerberos had left in his wake.

Omasi stone was naturally black. It made the scorch marks, ashes and blood far less visible. But the bodies were everywhere; the stone couldn't hide them. Aella saw several Thearans laying dead on the city's stone floor. She felt her hopes rising. She glanced at the buildings as they moved. Anything that could be destroyed by fire was reduced to ash. The battle still sounded close. They ran on.

A few turns down wide stone streets later, the flank of Kerberos' army came into view. They ran without war cries, with as little sound as possible, as Aella instructed them to. They were only a dozen or so steps from the enemy warriors when they were heard. Aella unleashed a powerful spear of fire she'd been building during the run. It impaled six warriors and exploded in the midst of the crowd, sending a shock through dozens of warriors and killing at least a half dozen more.

The tribes clashed a bare second after Aella's spear, and for the first few seconds her tribe was bringing destruction and chaos down on the enemy. Then they recovered from the initial surprise. Aella wanted so badly to wreath herself

284

in flame and sweep through the tribe's defences. She could see Kerberos on the far side of his army, pushing towards the royal palace with lethal determination. He was so tall he stood head and shoulders above most of his warriors. But she knew it would do no good. Even if she reached him in time, she would run out of magic shortly after and her attack would be for nothing. She needed to fight through for as long as possible without using too much of her magic.

As Aella and her tribe fought, Kerberos' was backing away swiftly. They almost had to run to keep up; they were making fast progress to the royal palace. Aella didn't care about the royalty of Omatus in the slightest, but if Kerberos made it to the palace he would be in a much more defensible position. She had to kill him before he got there.

"Push!" She screamed, "Kill them! We must reach Kerberos!"

She was staring at Kerberos as she screamed the orders, and at the sound of his name he stared directly into her eyes. He smiled and gestured to the side. Heart beating wildly, her eyes followed his gesture. She saw two of Kerberos' commanders restraining Erasmus, dragging him down a side street. She only caught a glimpse before they disappeared behind cold black stone.

Burning white rage wiped her mind clean. She stopped seeing and hearing and feeling. The world became a stark white field of pure fury, and running through it before her were the two warriors dragging her love away. There was nothing between her and them, just that blank white field, so she stepped to where they were. She found she only needed a single step. She was right behind them in an instant, ready to kill anything in her path, when suddenly a cold jagged pain lanced her stomach and left bicep.

She screamed, suddenly sure this was merely a nightmare; none of what was happening made sense. The white field disappeared, and Aella collapsed to the stone floor. She looked at her stomach and arm, and saw the deep cuts there, bleeding freely. She closed her eyes and recited the healing prayer, focusing her mind on the image of fire as she was taught. The cuts didn't heal. She opened her eyes again. She was in a narrow alley, but one of the walls was somehow obliterated by some powerful explosion. The sounds of battle were now distant and the street she just came from was deserted. She stood, shaking, and suddenly remembered what she was doing. Where was Erasmus?

Mind still curiously blank, she ran down the alley and cast her eyes wildly around the opposite street. She saw stairs leading down to a building which looked like a fortress, and without thinking she ran towards it. At the bottom of the stairs, a low corridor ran straight for what looked like miles, heading in the direction of the royal palace.

She saw them. Three distant blurs, moving constantly. She sprinted as hard as she could. The blurs became people, and the people became familiar faces, and before long she was close enough to stop them. But they turned towards her and shouted, and suddenly the corridor was filling with warriors; dozens of them between her and Erasmus, and dozens more behind her, blocking her escape. She clenched her fists desperately, and realised for the first time that she didn't have her swords.

Dakesh

He stood in front of the elders, the *Duulshen,* as they stared down at him in silence. Twenty raised seats, each containing an ancient Shenza warrior, formed a semicircle around the lowered platform in the centre of the room. The chamber of the *Duulshen* was built within the trunk of an enormous, ancient tree. The only light came from naturally phosphorescent mushrooms which grew along the walls and roof, giving off a faint blue glow. There was a chamber like this in each of the five hubs that made up the *Kashainuukza.* The last time he stood in the chamber, he was refused the right to forge his *Kaizuun.*

Now, he was accused of treason, and breaking the three tenets and his oath as a *Daishen.* The *Duulshen* sat in the dim glow of the chamber, completely silent. But the judgement in their eyes spoke volumes, and Dakesh didn't need them to speak to understand he was doomed. He stood in the centre of the platform, Elana's sword and belt at his feet before them. Kailen's blade was next to Elana's; they had taken it from him the moment he entered Shanaken.

No others were allowed into the chamber. Dakesh was completely alone to face the wrath of the *Duulshen.* He was glad; the Shenza booed and hissed and jeered as he was led here. He couldn't stand their hatred on top of his own. As they stared, he tried to stare back. He needed at least to be brave in his last few days. To take responsibility. But his gaze dropped, falling to the swords of his two best friends.

After an eternity in silent, twilit judgement, one of the *Duulshen* finally spoke.

"Dakesh Zakil. You stole the blade of a *Kaizeluun*. You fled our great forests with it. You joined with the forces of destruction against whom Amalus is sworn to eternal battle. These are some of the greatest crimes a warrior of the forests can commit."

The elder fell again into silence. Dakesh's eyes were still lowered. Tears ran silently down his cheeks. He could only think of Elana and Kailen. He remembered all the times he wanted Kailen to fail so he could succeed instead. The jealousy he felt when Kailen became *Kaizeluun*. And his excitement when Kailen was torn apart by cannon fire and his *Kaizuun* lay at Dakesh's feet. The last memory pierced his heart more painfully than a *Kaizuun* ever could. How much of what he'd done was Sithares working through him? Was he truly a monster; a traitor? He wanted so desperately to believe he was still innocent. Just the tool of an all-powerful God; blameless and helpless to resist. But he knew better.

He remembered Elana too. The way she moved when fighting or walking, her grace never ending. Her wisdom and her beauty. Her strength and her skill. She was the greatest of the Shenza; far greater than these ancient, bitter fools. He wished he could speak with her again, if only to apologise for all the evil he'd done. He would much prefer to face her again in battle rather than endure the judgemental silence of the *Duulshen*.

"You are exiled, Dakesh. You are *Dulzuud*. But there are punishments you must endure before your exile."

Dulzuud. Eternal outsider. Knowing it would be so didn't stop the pain of hearing the word. And he would suffer worse pain before being exiled. He was beyond fighting his fate; he knew he deserved everything the *Duulshen* did to him. He waited for the elders to inflict on him whatever they deemed fitting. It could be no worse than the self-hatred boiling in his veins, searing his heart and tearing into his mind.

"You do not know the power of the *Kaizel,* Outsider. You will be one of the only beings not of the *Duulshen* to witness it. For that you should be grateful. Still, it will serve as punishment for your crimes."

As the last word was spoken, the runes on Elana's *Kaizuun* glowed white and the sword lifted from the ground. Still attached to her belt, it settled in mid-air point down. The belt floated at waist height. Then, slowly, Elana appeared inside it. She was glowing with the same dim light as the mushrooms lining the chamber. Her eyes, such a vibrant, deep purple in life, were now the same faint blue as the rest of her. She looked like an echo; empty and faded.

Dakesh stepped towards her. He couldn't help it. He needed her to understand how sorry he was. She saw him. Her face remained blank. He paused, staring into her eyes. She recognised him, he could see it. But she displayed absolutely no emotion. He stepped back to the centre of the platform again.

"Elana..."

Her dim glow brightened for a fraction of a second. But she remained impassive, staring at him as though he were a mountain in the distance.

"... I'm so sorry," he said.

She stared for a moment longer, and finally stirred. "It's peaceful here, Dakesh," she said quietly. Her voice reached him as though from a great distance. "There is no emotion. I'm free now. *Dulkuud* is beautiful, you would love it here. But you will never see it."

Dulkuud. The Eternal Mountain. So it *was* real. He wondered at the scope of the realisation; He knew Sithares was real, of course, but if one God was real, how could a God from a completely different religion exist also? Were there even more Gods? More than one afterlife? The questions were chased by a disquieting thought: he would never know. Then the last thing Elana said caught up with him: *you will never see it.*

289

Was there an afterlife for him, if not the resting place of the Shenza? She was still staring at him, expressionless. He didn't remember ever being as terrified as he felt in that moment, facing his death without knowing what it would look like. He wasn't ready at all. Elana nodded as though she could hear his thoughts.

"Your time is almost up, outsider," she said. Every time he heard that word, his heart broke again. He would be remembered by the Shenza this way forever; the outsider with the stolen sword. Betrayer of Shanaken and servant of Sithares. He could only imagine what Zanela must think of him. His little sister had adored him, before all of this. He realised he never said goodbye to her.

"Once I leave this room I will never return to the realm of the living. Even the *Duulshen* have limits when it comes to life and death. I don't know what fate awaits you, outsider. But if your love for me was real, knowing that you will never see me again and that I died in fear and hatred of you... that should be punishment enough. May you be a lesson to all Shenza from now on; the three tenets and the oath are binding. Eternal."

She unclipped her belt and lay it at his feet. She faded away as soon as the belt left her hands. Dakesh wept. He no longer cared about dying with his head held high. He didn't deserve to die proud. He fell to his knees. His breath came in gasps, and he sobbed into his hands as the *Duulshen* silently stared.

Two pairs of rough hands seized him without warning and dragged him to his feet. It was happening. He didn't struggle. They led him down a circular tunnel, deeper into the earth. When they reached a chamber which closely resembled the one they'd just left, they pushed him back onto his knees. They held him there as footsteps grew louder in the darkness. The *Duulshen* walked into the chamber and surrounded him, standing this time.

The *Duulshen* chanted, low and deep. They raised their arms, moving into an odd version of the *Zuunshai*. They moved in perfect unison, their motions and voices merging into one. The cold metal floor shifted under his knees. Twisting, pointed branches emerged from the smooth surface around him, forming a cage. There was just enough space for him to stand, though he remained on his knees. The chanting stopped, and one of the *Duulshen* placed Kailen and Elana's sword inside the cage at his knees.

"Your punishment, outsider: The weapons you stole and defiled will lay with your trapped soul forever. You are outside of *Kaduulshai*. Separated for eternity from the circle. Your soul will remain within this cage, forced to dwell for the rest of time on the shame of your failures."

The elder stepped back and the chant started again. The cage grew around him, painfully slow. Darkness overcame him as the metal limbs joined and merged. The chanting of the elders was cut off as soon as the cage was finished. The darkness was as complete as the silence. Then there was only the feeling of the cold metal floor underneath him, and his memories. He screamed, and realised he couldn't hear it. He screamed louder, until his lungs and throat were aching. Silence pressed in, final and merciless. But for the chaos of his thoughts, he might as well have been dead already.

Atillus

The moment the sun rose, Atillus formed a small group to take with him. The man who spoke about the forge, Photios, was the first to report to his tent at dawn. He was pleased, and couldn't help but offer a genuine smile when he saw the warrior waiting for him when he emerged from his tent. Photios smiled back, though he still looked nervous.

They left the great hall shortly after sunrise, and Photios, with a few fellow warriors from his former tribe, led the way easily and without hesitation. They travelled up countless narrow streets, pressed in on either side by impassable walls covered in spear slits. The Thearans who'd lived in the city for years talked comfortably, and Atillus could see the relief on the faces of his warriors. They were unnerved by the heavy silence of the dead city when they first arrived. Atillus couldn't blame them; he grew up in Omatus, and other than the Royal Library and his bedchamber, was constantly surrounded by people. Hearing utter silence in what used to be a massive city was disturbing.

Eventually, they left the streets and entered a massive temple-like building. Photios didn't know what the building's purpose was, or what it was called, but he knew the layout perfectly. They walked through the vast, echoing rooms, and while Photios and his fellows paid no attention to the intricate carvings and paintings that lined the roof and walls, Atillus' own warriors were staring all around them in fascination.

There were hundreds of carvings of flickering flame, so detailed they seemed almost to move. There were faded paintings of ancient Thearan warriors, wearing the full body armour they were famous for wearing before they became nomads. On the roof, an enormous carving of Sithares presided over the room, grinning down at them with malevolent greed as the fires consumed everything below. At Sithares' right hand, a demon made of fire flew, its long, curling tail ending in a black spear-tip. Atillus' heart leapt into his throat as he saw it. The demon's description was written in the fire-bound book, and it was said to be the actual son of Sithares, but its name wasn't written anywhere he could find.

Surrounding the Fire God and its demon son were ten giant birds wreathed in flame. They were at least as tall as a man, and Atillus knew these to be the Phenixes; Royal Guards of Sithares and born from the fires of Sitharkos. The Phenix was an arch-demon, and immortal. Stuck in Pandeia and unable to join Sithares in the fiery kingdom of its domain on the surface of the sun, they were said to be the harbingers of death and destruction in the mortal world. Whenever they were seen in ancient times, Sithares itself had followed soon after. They lived a thousand years, then returned to the volcano from whence they came and threw themselves into the pit. They died and burst into a destructive whirlwind of intense flame, searing the desert for miles in every direction. Another thousand years would pass, after which there would be another massive explosion and they would rise from the fires again to serve Sithares. Unlike the Son of Sithares, who was a full demon, the Phenixes could feel pain and suffering. Every time they died, their piercing screams could be heard for miles. Or so the legends said. No records suggested the sighting of a Phenix or hearing its screams since Theara was abandoned, at least three thousand years ago.

They passed the room and moved into a low but wide corridor. Soon after, they reached a room with many branching corridors and several staircases heading up and down. Without pausing, Photios guided them to the only staircase leading down, and they followed without comment. Anticipation gnawed at Atillus' mind. He felt his heart racing as the warriors of Theara led him deeper underground.

The stairs descended without pause for miles. They followed a long, gradual curve in the same direction, and Atillus was sure if he saw a map of the building, the staircase would be a massive circle; But the curve was so gentle it was impossible to tell how long they would have to walk to travel one entire rotation. Eventually they stopped for a break, sitting on the cold black steps and eating strips of dried meat. They started talking again, cheerful now they were out of Sithares' intense gaze. Atillus remained silent, thinking about the massive image of the Fire God and its minions.

After what he estimated to be eight hours of walking down the same staircase, Atillus finally reached flat ground again. A vast chamber opened from the foot of the stairs; so tall and wide they couldn't see the roof, or the opposite wall. It simply disappeared into shadow. A wide stone bridge without rails led into the abyss, and on an island in the distance stood the Forge of Sithares.

They could see the glow of the fire from where they stood, and Atillus was certain he would feel its heat long before he set foot on that island. He told the warriors to wait where they were and ventured out onto the bridge. He walked for almost an hour. As he predicted, the heat from the forge hit him well before he reached it. The island was larger than he had first thought. It held the forge itself, along with a huge stone tub full of Thearan steel ingots, and on the opposite side to the forge was a small stone cabin. He went inside and found a bench with a bedroll and pillow, a small water basin, and a cupboard.

He returned to the forge, and took note of the other tools and materials neatly stored on hooks and brackets nearby. He stood for a while with his eyes closed, picturing again what he had come to make. It remained nameless in the ancient book that taught how to build it. He read the detailed instructions years ago, and knew he could build it himself. Smiling, he began to work.

Photios

Photios sat, staring into the distant darkness of the gigantic cave, trying to see what their leader was doing. He'd been gone for hours, and the group that accompanied him were growing restless. As well as having to wait for possibly days, they knew another long walk awaited them, back up the endless staircase and through the city once again.

They started arguing amongst themselves. A small group of the warriors, angry and fed up with waiting, wanted to leave the mysterious leader to his business. A much larger group maintained they would wait however long their God-like leader needed them to. Photios finally screamed at them all to be quiet.

"I will go to the forge, and ask the leader myself," he said, "if you want to get up and leave, do it. But I wouldn't be surprised if the Son of Sithares punished those who left without being granted permission."

The argument stopped in its tracks. Photios wasn't sure if they were silenced more by his offer to approach the dangerous warlord, or by the idea that the man at the forge might somehow know who left and who stayed without being present. Either way, the argument was over. Now there was the matter of crossing the bridge and talking to the terrifying Son of Sithares alone, unbidden. He took a few quiet breaths, and stepped onto the bridge.

Aella

The warriors swarmed in on her, holding her in place by her arms and legs. She felt cold sharp blades press against her throat, back and calves. They were taking no chances. They held her as securely as they could; she couldn't move an inch. The two warriors carrying Erasmus dragged him back towards her, until they were barely a metre apart. They were facing each other, and Aella could see the fear and hope in Erasmus' eyes.

One of the warriors holding him down, who Aella recognised as Nomiki, drew a bright white sword and smiled. Aella stopped struggling. She'd never seen a blade like it before. Not even her own Fire Blades looked so filled with magic. Nomiki hefted the sword in one hand, admiring it from different angles. Even in the darkness of the corridor, it shone as if the midday sun was reflecting off its surface. She stared at Aella, a terrifying smile still on her face.

"This is a soul blade," she said softly. Her voice was low and raspy, forcing images of some panther-like predator lurking in the shadows into Aella's mind.

"-Kerberos asked them to be made as part of his deal with Sithares. These are the only weapons that can kill us now. They were forged by Sithares itself, in the fires of the sun."

"Why are you doing this?" Aella screamed at her. She didn't expect an answer; but she needed time to think, time to try to stop this.

"We are taking Omatus for Kerberos and the glory of Sithares." Nomiki spoke as if Aella was a silly child who was asking what colour the Omasi desert sand was.

"But this, I am doing for my own satisfaction." She added her other hand to the sword's grip, and swept the shining blade down into Erasmus' neck. It cut through easily, and Nomiki swung so hard that it buried itself in the smooth black stone floor. Erasmus' blood sprayed Aella's face. She gasped silently, blinking, unable to scream.

Nomiki pulled the bright sword out of the stone. It seemed to slip out with no effort. She admired it again, ignoring Aella's silent shock. There was no blood on the blade. Satisfied, she sheathed the weapon and motioned to the warriors holding Aella without looking. She was already walking away.

"Take her to him. Up the main street, across the bridge. He wants to watch her come."

Aella was completely numb as Kerberos' warriors dragged her back through the corridor. All she could see was Erasmus' eyes at the moment the sword took his life. They changed from wide and terrified to cold and distant in an instant. But after that...

For a split second, she could have sworn she saw endless fires raging and swirling in those dead, tortured eyes. An ocean of flame, roaring and pulsing and destroying everything. Everything but the souls of the Thearan warriors Kerberos had sold. She could see them now, helpless and burning forever. Erasmus, her mother, Dakesh, Athanasius, even herself. An army of tortured souls, conscious without being alive, burning without being burned.

All for Kerberos. All to give him this giant, terrible city. Kerberos' face swam into her nightmare, and she saw his predatory grin, and finally the screams came.

The dark corridor disappeared, and that endless white field replaced it. She could see the warriors who were dragging her, but everything else was gone. She was numb again, but for her fury, there was an intense clarity that came with the rage. The warriors dragging her were terrified, she could see them wanting to let her go but fighting to keep hold. She twisted, twirling out of their grip and landing lightly on her feet.

One of them reached for his sword; she reached up and pulled his throat out in one smooth motion, marvelling at how easy it was. He was still standing as she turned and rammed her fist into another warrior's face. It exploded, but incredibly slowly, and it was only while watching chunks of bone and droplets of blood spreading slowly through the air that she realised how fast she was moving. She watched the pieces of the warrior's head slowly float away, transfixed even through her rage.

A third warrior managed to get her sword out of its sheath and started swinging at Aella's neck. She turned, saw the blade creeping gradually towards her, and simply walked around it. She grabbed the warrior's hand, twisted the sword out of her grip, and swept the blade through the woman's neck while her arm still slowly continued its arc towards where Aella's neck had been.

She started running, and at first each step seemed to take her ten metres down the long corridor. She used the dead warrior's sword to kill and maim every enemy she could reach as she ran. Then her steps became shorter. The enemy warriors started moving faster, and the stark white field faded to grey and then to black. Then suddenly, a few metres from the steps that led up to Omatus, whatever magic she'd been using ran out and she collapsed.

A tidal wave of sound crashed down on her; the clashing of swords, the thump of bodies hitting stone, the echoes and shouts reverberating through the long corridor. Her physical strength was as depleted as her magic, and she couldn't move at first. Her rage disappeared too, leaving her with grief and shock. She lay on the cold stone

299

floor, staring up into the sunlight above the steps, lost and overwhelmed.

The sun shone over the grey Omasi desert. Aella felt its heat on her skin as she leapt lightly over Athan's wooden practice sword. She was ten years old. She didn't have her Fire Blades yet; that was a few months away. The day was clear and clean, and Aella worried about nothing but fighting. She twirled around Athanasius, jumping and twisting and ducking. He was sweating. He grunted in frustration, finally sick of her showing off. He turned and made as if to leave, heading back towards camp. Aella started running after him, and he spun on his heel and smashed his sword into the side of her head.

Everything went white for a moment, and Aella couldn't see anything. She felt dizzy, but she knew she was still standing up and she didn't think she would fall. The world stayed white for a moment, and she waited until it cleared, blinking and trying to breathe evenly. A small sound pierced the silence, almost too quiet to hear. It was jagged and high pitched, and as Aella strained to hear it, it grew until it was suddenly far too loud. The white disappeared and she saw the desert again, saw Athan. He was curled up on the sand, screaming and clutching his stomach. She rushed to him, terrified.

"Are you okay?" she asked. As she reached him, he scrambled away from her in the sand, looking at her like she was a sand panther. She tried to approach him again, confused, and this time he pulled himself to his feet and ran back to camp, leaving his wooden practice sword in the sand.

The sun shone over Omatus. Aella felt its heat on her skin as she lay on the cold stone floor. She felt its energy,

300

and felt the magic born of that energy slowly trickle into her body. There wasn't much of it. She focused on the heat she felt on her skin, and on the burning red circle the sun imprinted on her eyelids. She pictured the sun up close; a whole kingdom of never ending fire, raging and burning for all time. She opened herself up to it, praying for it to enter her and fill her with its brutal magic.

Slowly, slowly, she felt it grow inside her. She could see it in her mind's eye; the place where her soul should have been, replaced with a burning sphere of magic, destroying her and giving her unimaginable strength at the same time. She recited the healing prayer again, and this time she felt some strength return to her body. The cut in her stomach and arm still didn't heal, but she felt strong enough to move.

She stood, slowly at first and shaking. The magic she'd gleaned from the sun was minimal; the small amount of strength and energy she gained depleted it again. She looked down the corridor. The warriors filling it were either dead or far too injured to pursue her. The sword she took from one of them was on the floor near her. Picking it up, she started up the stairs. She had no magic, little strength, and her swords were missing.

She walked into the sunlight, and looked over at the royal palace. The top half was visible from all of Omatus, and at the far end of the throne room was a wide balcony which overlooked the city. The throne itself couldn't be seen from this far, but Aella could see the balcony and the entrance into the throne room. Knowing that Kerberos was within that room, and most likely sitting on the throne, pushed all other thoughts from her mind. She walked towards the palace.

Photios

Atillus was working furiously, sweating and breathing hard, when he heard a shout behind him. He turned to see Photios standing at the edge of the bridge, terrified at having disturbed him. He gestured with his head for the man to join him at the forge, and turned back to his work.

Photios approached slowly and stood a few metres away from him, flinching each time he brought the hammer down onto the thick Thearan steel.

"My lord," he said, only just loud enough to be heard, "a few of the warriors were wondering-"

"They can leave."

Photios was silent for a moment, blinking. His threat to the group earlier was invented, but perhaps this mysterious man *could* actually tell what they were saying from a distance. *Or maybe he can read our minds.* The thought was sudden and terrifying. He stared at the huge man hammering glowing steel, overcome by the feeling he was standing before Sithares itself.

"Will – will they be punished, my lord?" An audible gulp followed the question.

"No. I have work to do. Leave some food in the cabin behind me and tell the group they can head back to the Great Hall. They will wait there until I return."

Photios nodded quickly, eager to please, although the Warleader never so much as glanced at him during the exchange. He scurried away, heading back to the relative safety of the group of Thearans on the other side of the bridge.

Atillus

Atillus was visited once more by Photios, who dropped a sack of dried meat and a large skin of water in the cabin and left without saying a word. After that, he was alone until his task was completed. It took several days of constant work. When he was finally done, he held the weapon up in the glow of the forge and admired it. It looked exactly as it did in the ancient book he read all those years ago.

Suddenly, the image of the Demon at Sithares' right hand leapt into his mind, and he smiled as he realised why seeing the massive carving gave him such a jolt. The weapon he made was a faithful replica of the Fire Demon's tail. It felt good in his hands; it felt *right*. The fact that his tribe had taken to calling him the Son of Sithares felt right also. The voice of Sithares slipped into his mind again. Standing next to an ancient artefact of the God's own creation, and holding a weapon such as the one he made, Atillus felt truly connected to Sithares in a way he never had before.

You truly are the Son of Sithares. The Thearans did not even require the suggestion from me; they could see it in you as I did.

Atillus grinned. "I am honoured, my lord," he said.

You have been searching for a new name. Would you like to know what my Son was called?

"Yes, my lord."

The whispered name brought a shiver up Atillus' spine. It felt *right*.

Photios

Photios sat by a camp fire, sharing stories with a small group while they ate. Almost a week had passed since they left their leader working at the ancient forge and travelled back to the Great Hall. They spent the time leading those new to Theara on tours through the city, showing them every secret passage and every useful building. There was an underground well which still brought up clean, cool water, and an ancient storehouse with a surprising amount of well-preserved grain and dried foods. It couldn't have survived thousands of years; it was likely placed there by temporarily settled tribes like Photios'. There was also a seemingly endless population of Deathclaws, and while hunting them was risky, when caught unaware they were relatively easy to kill. Getting one alone was the difficult part; they tended to nest in knotted, twisting swarms that filled up entire rooms in the abandoned city. They found that waiting on the roof of a nearby building was the best way to catch one. The lizards occasionally left the comfort of their nest to forage for food either alone or in groups of two or three.

They were eating one of the unlucky Deathclaws killed that day and laughing at an ancient joke about a five legged Thearan Lion when their leader walked into the Great Hall. He carried a brutal-looking bladed weapon, attached to a long linked chain wrapped around his body.

He looked different. His skin was dark, his muscles more pronounced, and where before he had the dull brown eyes and beard of an Omati, his eyes shone the brightest gold Photios ever saw, and his beard was an almost blinding white against his dark skin.

The entire hall was silent within seconds. He turned his gaze over every warrior in the vast room, letting each of them feel his intense eyes on them in turn. Then he spoke, and his deep voice carried through the entire camp.

"I know many of you have been wondering about my name. My past is dead to me, and I know Thearans respect this. I have spoken with Sithares, and the God of Fire has granted me a new name."

There were gasps and whispers exchanged at every campfire. Photios stared intently at the Warleader, his heart hammering. He didn't know much about Sithares, and in fact never believed in the God until the Warleader showed them Fire Magic. He didn't know if anyone in history had been renamed by a God, but it sounded like a rare and incredibly important event to him. He felt blessed, sitting at a camp fire in the tribe of someone who could speak directly to Sithares.

The Warleader was standing silently, waiting for the whispers to die down naturally. He didn't rush them. A part of Photios thought maybe he enjoyed the fact that every warrior in the room was talking about him as though he were a legend, like one of the great Thearans from the Age of Heroes. But he tried to silence that thought as quickly as he could in case the Son of Sithares *could* read his mind. He gave no indication of having heard Photios' thoughts, however, and instead kept talking.

"Not many of you have heard the legend of the Son of Sithares, the Demon right hand of the God of Fire. He was immortal, and wielded almost as much power as Sithares itself. His name was lost to time, but Sithares has bestowed it onto me so I may revive the legend and become his true son, reborn."

He looked at them all, and in their silence, and the flickering glow of the nearby camp fires, he seemed to grow even larger.

"I am Kerberos!"

Athanasius

Athan watched as Kerberos' army stormed the gates of Omatus and disappeared behind the great stone walls. He had listened to Aella address their tribe. She'd made Kerberos sound like a despicable, evil being. His heart broke as he saw the hatred in her eyes. He knew what Kerberos was doing was wrong, that it shouldn't happen; but he was only doing it to serve Sithares. Following the orders of God didn't make someone evil, did it? He knew in his heart Kerberos wasn't attacking Omatus for pleasure or personal gain. He just needed to speak to him again, show him he'd survived Mara. If he could speak to Kerberos again, maybe he could make Aella and her tribe see he wasn't evil.

When they caught up to Kerberos' army, Athan felt trapped.

"Push! Kill them! We must reach Kerberos!" Aella screamed. Athan was behind her, separated by a few rows of warriors. He hung back a little, not wanting to fight. He was ashamed, but shame couldn't force him to do what he thought was wrong. So he watched the battle, waiting for the moment he might be able to slip through or around the army and reach Kerberos. He could just see Aella's bright white hair as she turned to the side, distracted.

Without warning, an explosion tore into the clashing tribes, toppling a nearby building and sending every warrior flying. Athan thudded into a wall behind him and smashed to the ground. There were a few moments of silence. For a brief, terrifying second, Athan heard the roaring of fire, and thought he had died again. But when he opened his eyes, Omatus was still there. He recited the healing prayer Kerberos taught him. He wasn't a particularly powerful Fire Mage, but with concentration he could heal basic wounds. It worked, and he stood, his dizziness and bruises gone.

Kerberos and a small group of his army were much further along, but the rest of his army stayed behind to continue the battle. He ran down a side street, hoping he could stop this before too many more Thearans died. Every passing second felt heavy; another second one of his brothers or sisters could be killed while he tried to catch up. He needed to reach Kerberos.

Athan ran as fast as he could. He was catching up, but Kerberos' tribe moved quickly. As he reached the bridge, they were almost halfway across it. He couldn't see Kerberos. He closed the distance as they ran through the Noble District. When he reached the massive doors of the royal palace, they were still open and gently swinging. There was no one to stop him entering. He realised distantly that there were no signs of struggle; no dead bodies.

He ran up flights of stairs, trying to keep his bearings. He heard footsteps ahead of him and was glad; without them he would surely be lost. The royal palace was unbelievably huge. Athan had never seen a building even half the size of it. Eventually, he heard the boom and crash of another massive door opening, followed by shouting. He finally caught up, reaching the doorway that Kerberos and his men just breached. There were about two dozen Omati nobles inside, looking terrified, as well as a large group of the royal guard, and Kerberos' small group of warriors.

Athan slipped into the room quietly, completely unnoticed; one of the nobles was talking loudly. All focus was on him as he addressed Kerberos.

"-savages, all of you," the man shouted, "and though I commend your efforts in getting this far, you don't stand a chance against the royal guard!"

"You mean the royal guard made up of slaves and hired mercenaries... sourced almost exclusively from Thearan tribes?"

Kerberos' voice was low and menacing, but it still carried through the entire throne room. Athan edged his way around the back of the room, keeping his eye on the Thearans near him. So far he remained unnoticed, but he didn't want to take any chances. He needn't have worried; a shuffling sound followed by the drawing of weapons filled the room, and by the time Athan glanced towards Kerberos, he saw the entire royal guard with their weapons drawn... and pointing at the King of Omatus.

The King stared at his guards, shocked and furious, opening and closing his mouth without making a sound. Were it not for the imminent threat of death in the room, the King's reaction would have been humorous. He finally found his voice again, and screamed at the royal guard.

"Traitors! How dare you turn on your King!"

"They have not turned, Alliphis," Kerberos said quietly, "they are loyal to the one true King of Omatus. They serve Atillus Argyris, first born son of Thorinos Argyris, heir to the Omati throne."

The King looked intently at Kerberos, the shock still evident on his face. Mingling with the shock was a look of dawning recognition.

"*Atillus?*"

Athan couldn't see his expression, but he heard the satisfaction in Kerberos' voice as he gave the order to the royal guard.

"Kill them all."

The royal guard made short work of the King and nobles present. The King managed to kill one guard and injure another before being killed; he was the only one of them with a sword. He would have killed more, Athan was sure, if Kerberos hadn't taken it upon himself to throw a fireball at the Omati royalty. Instead of exploding, the fireball simply melted into a sheet of flames, enveloping Alliphis and slowly burning him alive.

Kerberos turned as the rest of the Omati were slaughtered, and Athan caught the satisfied smile on his face before the expression turned to shock as their eyes met.

"Athan!" He shouted, and Athan's fears melted as Kerberos' face broke into a relieved smile. They rushed to each other and embraced. He pulled back from Athan and held his shoulders, looking him up and down.

"I thought you died. I looked for your body before we left for the city, but I could not find you."

Tears sprung to Athan's eyes. He wiped them away quickly. Kerberos *did* care. He knew it. Kerberos put his arm over Athan's shoulder and guided them out to the massive balcony overlooking the commoners side of the city.

"I did die," he said softly, "but I woke a short while later. How long, I don't know, but everyone was gone and Mara was burned to the ground."

"What was it like?" His eyes were wide, lit with a bright intensity that almost resembled madness. "When you died, what was it like?"

Athan blinked, shaking his head. "It was torture. It drove me insane. I was only able to remember who I am because Aella helped-"

"*Aella?*" Kerberos' hand tightened on his shoulder like the jaws of a lion, and Athan winced in pain.

"Athan, do you know what she is?" Athan shook his head, terrified. "She is a traitor. She planned to take half my tribe and disappear. She defied my rule, and tried to overthrow me. She has been made one of the most powerful Fire Mages in Thearan history, and all because of my devotion to Sithares; and what does she do with that power? She goes against me."

Kerberos' grip hadn't let up. Tears were welling up in his eyes from the pain.

"If I am to be King," he continued, "I can not let such defiance go. As much as I want to let her go, she must face the consequences of her actions."

As he spoke, he guided Athan to the railing at the edge of the balcony. He saw the great city before them, and from up here there were no signs of battle. The city looked beautiful.

"Why, Kerberos?"

"Ruling a city is different to ruling a warrior tribe, Athan. Omatus does not tolerate challenges for the crown, and I will not tolerate them either-"

"No." Kerberos stopped talking, shocked. Athan had never interrupted him before.

"Why do you want Omatus? Why have you traded the souls of your army for this black stone? Do our lives mean so little to you? My life?"

Kerberos stared into Athan's eyes, and the sheer, impenetrable cold he found there froze his heart.

"Omatus is mine by birth. I am Atillus Argyris, heir to the throne. I will not let anyone take this from me; not my father, my brother, or Aella. You have no idea how long I have waited for this, Athanasius. How hard I have worked."

"But you had the largest army of Thearans since the Age of Heroes at your command! Why rule some stone city full of weak civilians?"

Kerberos' eyes narrowed. His jaw clenched. He sighed harshly, let go of Athan's shoulder, and looked out over the city.

"I knew you would not understand." He pointed, and Athan's eyes followed his outstretched arm to the bridge. A

311

lone warrior was crossing it towards the palace, an army marching to meet them.

"I want you by my side, Athan, I truly do. But if you can not stand with me after I do what must be done, then you have no place here."

A horrible sinking feeling pulled at Athan's stomach, and he suddenly understood what was about to happen. Already knowing the answer and wishing desperately it wasn't true, he asked anyway.

"Who is that?"

"You know who it is. The traitor." Athan turned to him suddenly.

"Please, Kerberos. Don't do this."

There was a sadness in the giant warrior's voice as he turned to Athan.

"Athan, you need to look at the situation from a higher perspective. You need to understand what I'm doing is the right thing. I want you by my side."

He paused then, and a tear fell from his eye as he stared into Athan's eyes.

"I love you, Athan. I want you to stay with me."

Athan looked down at the tiny, lonely figure of Aella marching to her death. He looked back at Kerberos, or Atillus, or whoever he was.

"Please, just let us go! We'll leave this city, you can have it! Just please, let us live!"

"Us..." he mused. "You have made the wrong choice. I am sorry, Athan."

Athan's heart sank. He watched, numb, as Kerberos drew his blade. It was shining, white and magnificent in the sunlight. He stared into Kerberos' eyes, pleading beyond words. That same implacable cold gaze stared back. The tear he'd shed was dry, and Athan realised far too late that he had never been anything more than a tool for Kerberos to use and discard. He wept, and when the memory of death flashed into his mind, he screamed.

"Please! Not again! I can't go back to those fires! Kerberos, please, no!"

312

But the blade swept forward, and a cold, sharp pain exploded in his chest. The cold spread through his body, and his mind became a blank white field. Cold turned to heat, and the low murmuring of fire began. The murmuring turned to roaring, and flames overtook the endless white, and just before he disappeared into that eternal fire completely, he felt his body rushing through the air as if he was flying. He screamed, and couldn't hear it, and screamed even louder. The rushing of the wind and the sense of flying seemed to increase, building and building until-

Aella

Omatus was a massive city, separated into two sections. Each section fell on either side of the Alpheus, and each was surrounded by a gigantic stone wall. Spanning the river between the two halves of the city was the largest bridge Aella had ever seen. This close to the ocean, the Alpheus was at its widest point. Now, standing at the northern edge of the bridge, the royal palace still didn't look any closer.

She started across the bridge. As she walked, she glanced up at the throne room balcony and saw two figures. One of them was clearly Kerberos; his figure was unmistakable. The other was less clear, but the longer she stared and the closer she walked, the more certain she became. The second figure was Athanasius. They seemed to be talking. She knew Athan would be unable to confront Kerberos; if they were talking alone, he was most likely already loyal to Kerberos again.

As she crossed the bridge, she could see the two figures moving slightly; not a fight, but perhaps an argument. Then Kerberos raised his hand and pointed straight at her.

She was so shocked that she stopped walking. This could only be bad; if he knew she was on her way, at best it meant she couldn't hope to take him by surprise. At worst it meant that he already had a plan to deal with her.

As she stared at the two figures on the balcony, she saw Kerberos draw his sword. It was shining brightly, even from this distance. He plunged it into Athan's chest, and Aella felt an icy dagger of fear, pain and shock rip through her heart as the Soul Blade ripped through Athan's. She screamed, and as her hatred for Kerberos reached new heights, she watched him push Athanasius' body over the balcony railing. She kept screaming as his body plummeted towards the stone floor below. She didn't see him land, and was dimly thankful for the buildings obscuring her view of the bottom half of the palace. She didn't think she could survive witnessing Athan's body hitting the smooth stone floor.

She was still screaming, tears making her vision swim as if she was drowning, when a shout pierced her grief.

"Aella!" It was Nomiki. Aella rubbed the tears out of her eyes. The warrior stood on the bridge less than ten metres from her. Behind Kerberos' favourite fanatic was an army. They covered the entire span of the massive bridge. There were thousands of them. She noticed that the group behind Nomiki was made up of not only Thearan warriors, but members of the Omati Royal Guard as well. How could they already be loyal to the man who invaded their city and slaughtered so many of their people?

Her mind was reeling, her heart broken, and her spirit all but gone. She stood still, almost halfway over the bridge, with an unfamiliar sword in her hand. There was no possible way she could win this fight. She was utterly lost.

Suddenly, from a deep chamber in her mind, an old memory she'd nearly forgotten arose and enveloped her. She was a little girl again, sitting with her mother in their tent:

"There is no shame in being cautious, Aella. And there is no shame in hiding your power from those who would do you harm for it. That doesn't make you a coward. All the bravest Thearan heroes knew that sometimes fighting would achieve nothing. They knew sometimes even they would lose and that it was more important to live to fight another day. They knew that they had to choose their battles."

"- cannot win. We can fight you, or you can surrender to us." Nomiki was talking the entire time Aella relived her memory.

"The choice is yours" she continued, "but either way, you die today." She smiled her horrible, sadistic smile, staring at Aella in satisfaction.

Aella looked down at the dull steel sword in her hand, and up at the army between her and Kerberos. She wanted desperately to fight through them and kill him for everything he'd done to her and her tribe. She thought about her mother, the strong, powerful woman who raised her and gave her strength, courage, and wisdom. She thought about Erasmus, who gave her passion, love, and kindness. And Athan, who gave her friendship, laughter, and humility. She knew she couldn't win. Perhaps, if she had a full magic reserve and all of her energy and strength; but not now. If she tried to fight now, the deaths of those she loved and the thousands of others Kerberos killed would remain unavenged. She had to choose her battles; to live to fight another day.

"Aella!" Nomiki screamed. "Your time is up!" Without turning back to them, she shouted for the army to advance. They moved immediately.

Aella gathered what little strength she had left and hurled the sword at Nomiki. Without waiting to see if her throw hit its target, she sprinted for the side of the bridge. The warriors almost reached her first, but she leapt onto the waist high stone blocks running the length of the bridge, took one step to the very edge, and jumped out into nothing.

316

Zanela

When Zanela came to, she sat on actual grass, in the centre of the clearing. The snake's body still coiled around her, leaving only a small circle for her to sit. She searched for Kaidan, but the beast was gone. Finally, dreading the thought more than she could describe, she looked at the gigantic snake's head once again. It stared at her, head hovering a metre above the patch of grass.

The thick tongue darted out again, straight at her, and disappeared. It was smelling her. Preparing to eat. She felt an odd stab of anger at the snake for waiting until she woke to kill her. Surely it gained nothing from such torture. Still, now her death was certain, she wanted nothing but to have it be done; even if she was to be eaten alive. She briefly contemplated attacking, just to provoke the monster into killing her faster, but her terror kept her seated on the soft, cool grass.

A horrible, grating, growling sound erupted from the gigantic snake's throat. Its mouth opened, revealing shiny black fangs as tall as she was. She almost lost consciousness again; her heart simply couldn't take any more terror. The snake moved back suddenly, moving its head from side to side. The growl grew louder, then changed into a hacking bark. The snake's bright blue eyes closed, and a deep rumbling escaped its mouth.

Finally the sound ceased and the snake stopped flailing its head. The blue eyes opened and found her again, and the snake moved back to where it was when she woke, hovering just above her.

317

"Sorry about that, *Kulnalduul*. It's been a long time since last I spoke."

Zanela blinked. Surely it didn't just -

"Speak? Well, you can't be too surprised; I am a God, after all." It chuckled, more to itself than her. "Though I am beginning to think *you* can't speak, little one. What have you to say to your God, hmm?"

She had no idea what to say, nor even to think. Not only was the giant snake talking to her, it was claiming to be Amalus itself. And to confuse matters further, it was positively *cheerful.* The only voice she could think of friendlier than this was Delan, an elderly Shenza who had spent almost all of his time in the kitchens with Nashan before the cook was sent to fight the Ermoori.

Delan's voice was croaky, scratchy and full of humour. He never had much energy, but all of it was spent talking and laughing. Now she thought about it, Delan's voice was eerily similar to the giant snake's. The monster quietly cleared its throat, moving even closer to her. Without thinking, she moved away from the massive face, crawling backwards until she thumped into its coiled body behind her.

"I do wish you would stop thinking of me as a monster," the snake sighed. "Have I done anything monstrous? Other than give you a bit of a fright of course. Sorry about that by the way." It chuckled again. "It was a little funny though, you have to admit. Still nothing to say? To think I wait all this time for a visitor and when someone finally shows up, she doesn't say a word!"

She sat on the grass, her back pressed against the ancient creature's coiled body, struggling to find something to say. Anything.

"Umm."

The snake's eyes widened, and it leaned in expectantly. If the expression was on the face of anything other than a gargantuan killing machine, it would have been comical.

"Umm," she repeated.

The snake inched closer.

318

"I'm Zanela," she finally managed. The snake raised its head, and actually *smiled*.

"Well, that's a fine way to start! Hello Zanela, I am Amalus, God of the Shadows and creator of life on Pandeia. Now, why are you here?"

Her eyes bulged involuntarily. She barely remembered her own name; how could she answer a question such as that? Amalus laughed, the sound booming and echoing through the massive forest.

"Not to worry, *Kulnalduul*. Nobody knows the answer to that question."

One of its milky, translucent eyelids dipped over its bright eye in an uncomfortably human wink.

"I can't be blamed for having a little fun; I haven't had a visitor in thousands of years! But, since I *do* know the answer to that question, allow me to show you."

Amalus leaned close to her, so close she could have reached out and touched its massive bright blue eye. The vertical pupil dilated, becoming a perfect circle. She saw herself reflected in the shiny black surface. Then she was replaced by a glowing ball of pure white. It exploded into a swirl of colourful stars, flying outward at an unfathomable speed. Eventually it slowed and settled into a gently revolving cluster of multicoloured lights.

They slowly merged, becoming a single blue orb. The surface broke. Cracks spread quickly over it, forming odd but familiar shapes. Some of the shapes rose out of the blue surface of the orb, turning either black or brown. She realised she was looking at Pandeia itself. The orb spun slowly, but she saw a glimpse of green spreading from the centre of one of the shapes – yes, Shanaken, she recognised it – and moving over all the others.

Then, from the other side, bright red flickered to life from the centre of Omas and swept over Pandeia; Fire. Sithares. The red and green clashed, and a crack appeared in the orb at the point where they met. One more shape emerged, shining blue, between the two countries. White light swept in, appearing from nowhere to join the other colours, and a terrifying clash threatened to overwhelm Pandeia. Then the colours receded, and Pandeia returned to a flickering stillness. Zanela stared, but nothing happened. Then she saw cities bloom on Omas and Ermoor and Tarsium, and she realised she was somehow seeing Pandeia as it moved through time, only much, *much* faster. She watched as the world turned. As wars were fought. As disasters came and went.

When she thought Amalus showed her all she could see, the orb suddenly grew in front of her, and Shanaken became life-sized. Amalus' eye was a slightly curved window through which she saw the forest. Her home. Amalus turned to look at the ancient city of Omatus. It looked and Zanela followed, seeing everything the God saw. Underneath a great palace, ancient magicians chanted and gestured around an ornate chest. Fire billowed in a hurricane between them, and was forced into the chest. She felt the heat die down immediately; not from her body, but from the world itself.

Amalus looked again at the chest, but something was different. The room it was in, and the chest itself, felt ancient. A young boy smashed the rusted padlock using a massive book, and the fire was unleashed again. She watched as the eye turned towards the north shore, and her breath caught in her throat.

Dakesh stood on the sand, staring down at Kailen's dead body. Kailen's *Kaizuun* lay on the sand, pure and powerful. Dakesh reached down and snatched it just before his dead friend's blood touched the blade. He turned and ran into the forest. Amalus turned its eye west, to Omas, and Dakesh now sat in a hide tent, praying to Sithares. He opened his hand and an evil red glow appeared in his palm. He gave a wicked grin and closed his hand, plunging Zanela into darkness.

From the Shadows, Zanela saw Amalus curled up in its clearing. She saw its energy dwindling. What was once a mighty God of life became an old, sick animal. She saw it grow older and older, sad and alone, watching as it

320

watched the world start to burn. Ermoor attacked the forest, felling trees and slaughtering animals. Magic grew dim and a horrible lifeless grey spread over Pandeia as Ermoor invaded Tarsium and Omas after Shanaken. Cities fell and people died in the thousands.

Then a burst of power, of life, blossomed from Shanaken, and she watched as a new wave of green spread over the world. At the same time, two new colours exploded into existence. From Ermoor, a pale, crackling yellow flashed in unsteady pulses. From within Shanaken again, this time south of *Dulkuud*, a dark red laced with black bloomed, ominous and destructive.

She didn't understand, but the image disappeared before she could ponder it. Pandeia shrank, pulling away into a sea of absolute darkness. Before long it was a mere speck in the endless black, and then it was gone. Zanela stared into the abyss. Nothing else existed but the Shadow. The sheer weight of it pressed in on her, forcing the air from her lungs and the thoughts from her mind. But the Shadow wasn't empty; there was a deep, quiet... *energy* within it. Everywhere. She felt life growing in the Shadows around her, feeding her and feeding off her simultaneously. Pandeia lay so far beyond her now that it barely mattered. The entire world she'd known just a speck in the endless Shadows.

Out of the darkness, Zanela appeared, sitting on nothing at all, staring back at her. A moment of utter doubt rang through her mind. She stared into her own eyes, floating in nothingness. Wordlessly, she raised her hand and brought it to her face, and the Zanela in the darkness continued sitting still; it wasn't a reflection. Heart hammering in her chest, she reached through the God's eye and lay her hand on Zanela's cheek. She felt the skin of her face, warm and soft. Her own face tingled in the same place. She wasn't sure if it was her imagination. The other Zanela gave her a slow, sad smile, and faded into the Shadows.

Still reaching into the infinite dark, Zanela was pulled in until the clearing behind her disappeared entirely. She floated, alone, for an unknowable time. Seconds and hours and years lost meaning. Floating through the Shadows, she saw a million tiny specks floating with her, too distant to reach. Each speck was as beautiful and fragile and deadly as Pandeia.

She pulled away, wanting to see them all. The further she went, the more specks seemed to appear, until she was looking at an ocean of them, bright and shining every different colour, swirling in whirlwind patterns that brought tears to her eyes. Pulling away yet further, the ocean became a tear drop, and a million tear drops floated around her, each containing its own ocean. Caught in the rush of her discovery, she kept going until the tear drops formed their own swirling pattern, and on and on she went, a new layer beyond every previous layer.

The Universe, she thought suddenly, *that's what this is called. Worlds beyond count.* She pulled back from the Universe itself, and found an ocean of them swirling in an endless cloud. *Universes beyond count. Dear God, where does it end?*

Suddenly she was utterly terrified. *Pandeia is just one speck among countless. Not even that. One tiny, meaningless floating dot within an endless sea.*

It felt as though a thousand years had passed, a thousand lifetimes. She watched worlds that weren't Pandeia, saw the beings living on them, saw the war, death and destruction. New kinds of magic, Gods, and amazing technologies appearing for brief moments before snuffing out in the blink of an eye. The thing that shocked her the most, that stayed with her forever after that, was her discovery that all of the endless worlds she had seen were connected to each other. Some kind of... bridge seemed to span the vast distance between worlds, connecting everything and everywhere. She saw it. She touched it, and it was along this inexplicable bridge halfway between everywhere that she eventually found home again.

322

She searched for Pandeia, and found the speck of light too far to see. She focused on it. The world bloomed before her, growing until she could watch the surface as she did through Amalus' eyes. Only now, she wasn't watching some living map on the surface of a massive eye; this was actually Pandeia. She floated above it, watching over the entire world.

She watched it spin. Watched as a war began, as magic exploded and cities fell. As people killed and destroyed and burned their world. Underneath it all, she felt Fire seething in the minds of men and women. It spread like a sickness. She cast her eyes to the deserts of Omas, to the place where the real Fire burned. And there, she saw it. *Sithares.* Sitting on its twisted, burning throne in the centre of the volcano, staring back at her with a hatred she never knew existed.

Recoiling from Sithares, she looked back towards *Dulkuud,* towards the hidden forest. She found the clearing and it appeared around her, cocooning her in its safe, cool darkness. A sudden feeling of weight and exhaustion filled her, the way she felt when she pulled herself out of a lake after a long swim. She sat in the clearing again. Whatever vision or magic had come over her was done. Amalus lay with its head on the coils of its body in front of her.

"What was that?" she asked the giant snake.

There was no answer. With a grunt of effort, she picked herself up off the grass and walked closer. Not wanting to step on its body, she peered at its face from the edge of the small grass circle it made for her. The God wasn't moving. Its eyes, such a bright, powerful blue before, were now a dull grey. Her mouth opened in shock. Without warning, tears fell in streams down her face. She was alone in the clearing. Amalus was dead.

Epilogue

She woke with a start, gasping and coughing. She rubbed salt and sand out of her eyes as best she could, and glanced around quickly. Her vision was blurry, but there didn't seem to be any immediate danger. She was laying on the beach, facing the ocean. She had no idea where exactly, although the sand was grey, so she was still on Omas. She couldn't remember anything. She didn't know how she got here or why she was waking up on a beach. All she knew was that she felt terrified and furious at the same time. She sat up, trying to focus, but her memories moved like smoke; they were there, but were impossible to grasp.

She stood. Physically, she felt amazing. There were no bruises, no cuts, just a pale scar on her stomach and arm. She felt strong and powerful. Walking inland, she tried to get to higher ground and get her bearings.

The already sparse grass quickly turned dry and dead the further she got from the ocean. There was no higher ground. She saw a gigantic city to the south, and a much larger mountain in the opposite direction. There were mountains on the horizon in almost every direction she looked; but none close to her. She checked her belongings, desperate for any information that might help her. She was carrying a little dried meat, a water skin, some coins, and a handful of arrows in a small quiver. There was no bow, and there were two empty sheaths hanging at her thighs; no weapons.

Something about the desert to the north felt comforting. She kept walking.

www.ingramcontent.com/pod-product-compliance
Lightning Source LLC
Chambersburg PA
CBHW020702110726
47901CB00001B/272